SARGON
THE THIRD

A "Michelle Reagan" Novel
by
SCOTT SHINBERG

SARGON THE THIRD
Michelle Reagan – Book 4
Copyright © 2021 by Scott Shinberg

FIRST EDITION SOFTCOVER
ISBN: 1622536630
ISBN-13: 978-1-62253-663-4

Editor: Becky Stephens
Cover Artist: Briana Hertzog
Interior Designer: Lane Diamond

EVOLVED PUBLISHING™

www.EvolvedPub.com
Evolved Publishing LLC
Butler, Wisconsin, USA

Printed in Book Antiqua font.

BOOKS BY SCOTT SHINBERG

MICHELLE REAGAN
Book 1: *Confessions of Eden*
Book 2: *Directive One*
Book 3: *Fly by Night*
Book 4: *Sargon the Third*
Book 5: *A Shot in the Dark*

SARGON THE THIRD

A Michelle Reagan Novel
Book 4
SCOTT SHINBERG

Chapter 1

The distinctive *crack-crack* of AK-47 rifle fire aimed at the sprinting CIA officer grew louder as the platoon of pursuers raced forward for the kill. The bullets' sharp reports echoed in waves along the narrow canyon's rock walls.

The powerful combination of adrenaline and the human brain's instinctual need to survive powered the American's life-or-death footrace north through the ancient Iranian mountain pass. As each 7.62mm bullet slammed into the dusty rock walls of the old smugglers' passage, shards of superheated lead spewed in all directions. Each fragment searched for soft American flesh to shred.

Shouts from the two-dozen Iranian tribesmen rose in pitch behind the American runner and grew louder with each stride. The barks of their leader motivated his militiamen to catch the thief who dared steal from their sultan's courier.

The narrow pass of timeworn rock formed from compressed volcanic ash weaved through northwestern Iran. It wound its way through the region where historically fluid borders with Turkey, Armenia and Azerbaijan meet in a tangle of map lines whose shapes exist for reasons long-lost to time. The tribesmen pursuing the American knew the trail well. For millennia, they and their ancestors smuggled weapons, drugs, alcohol and slaves through it to eager markets on the other side — in Azerbaijan.

The sprinting thief threw foot after boot-clad foot and pushed a gloved hand off the edge of the narrow pass's fifty-foot-high walls to spin around a sharp turn. A quarter mile ahead, which felt more like a marathon, the border offered the hope of safety. If everything went as planned — never a certainty in this CIA officer's line of work — a ride home waited there, safely inside the far friendlier Nakhchivan Republic of Azerbaijan.

Bullets screamed over the panting thief's head, tearing through the air with the tortured sounds of metal cables *twanged* by unseen hands. The American zigged to the left, dodged a jagged outcropping of rock and grunted in relief at the sight of the bend in the canyon where the narrow path ahead zagged to the right. The runner—dressed in black pants, a mud-brown jacket and black turban concealing both hair and face—skidded to a halt before the bend, kicking up bits of gravel and dust. Ever so carefully, the CIA officer turned the corner, stepped over a barely visible tripwire installed the evening before, and bolted forward, running flat-out for dear life.

A few yards ahead, the winded runner slowed and spun around another curve in the canyon's path. Ten yards further, the rocky ravine ended abruptly and opened into a broad, lush green field across which tall grasses sparkled with dew in the morning sunlight. Without pausing for even a heartbeat, the black-clad figure barreled straight ahead and charged into the flat grassland as fast as the five-foot-five-inch-tall figure's thighs could pump.

Behind the runner, an explosion echoed loudly from the narrow canyon opening. The lead pursuer had caught the tripwire with his shin, detonating four Claymore mines—two in front of the pursuers and two aimed down from above. The canyon's natural shape created a rock-solid coffin. Eight of the pursuers died in the blast as ball bearing-sized shrapnel tore through the men caught in the confined space. Behind them, the militiamen following slowed their pursuit to step over the mangled bodies of their comrades and carefully make their way around the two final turns checking for any more traps laid by the American. The tribesmen worried far more about what their sultan would do to them and their families if they failed to retrieve the stolen items than whatever this lone thief could possibly do to the remaining dozen militiamen once they got to the open field ahead. Once exposed and unprotected by rock walls, the thief would be at their mercy—of which they intended to show absolutely none.

In the verdant field, the CIA officer's heart pounded with each long stride through knee-high grass and crossed the invisible border into Azerbaijan. The runner headed directly toward the open cargo door of a US Marine Corps MV-22 Osprey sitting like a gray monolith in the field fifty yards ahead. A hybrid aircraft, the Osprey has the wings of an airplane on which sit two rotatable engines, each topped by a three-bladed "prop-rotor." When rotated up, the unique design allows the Osprey to take off and land like a helicopter. When the engines point straight ahead, the Osprey flies like an airplane. The prop-rotors of the slate-colored beast in the field that morning spun nearly invisibly above the aircraft's tilted wings, angled up toward the blue sky—and freedom.

Six Iranian militiamen in their traditional tribal dress of white shirts and brown jackets emerged from the canyon and ground to a halt at the unexpected sight of the ungainly aircraft. The men coming up from behind surged into the gaggle in front, and all gasped at the sight of the strangely shaped aircraft in the otherwise empty field of tall grass.

The tallest of the tribesmen looked behind him as the remaining men stepped into the field. After assuring himself that his men were with him, he shifted his gaze to the figure in black only seconds away from reaching the aircraft. More afraid of what awaited him back in his village if he failed than of what the unarmed figure racing away from him might do, he brought his rifle up and aimed. The others followed his lead, confident their sultan would reward them for stopping the thief, regardless of which side of the border it occurred on. After all, one day, if they were successful, borders would disappear once their sultan united all nations under his benevolent rule.

Halfway to the Osprey, the CIA officer glanced back and saw the militiamen spreading out and raising their rifles. Running for your life has a way of focusing one's attention on the task at hand. The thief threw foot after foot, pumped arms like an Olympian and inhaled deeply to benefit from every extra molecule of oxygen the grass field was creating that morning.

Immediately after the runner passed by them in the field, eight camouflaged Kevlar helmets rose in unison from the tall grass. Two four-man fire teams of US Marines rose to their knees, leveled M-4 rifles at the Iranians and opened fire. They unleashed a thunderous refrain of 5.56mm automatic weapons fire, which clashed with the low growl of the aircraft's engines as the pilot powered up for a rapid escape.

Within five seconds, half of the pursuing Iranian militiamen fell to the Marines' deadly fusillade.

The CIA officer never broke stride, barreling past the Marines and directly at the plane and — most importantly — its promise of safety.

The surviving tribesmen returned fire at the Marines, missing everything they shot at.

The Marine Staff Sergeant on the far left of their line fired a 40mm round from the M320 grenade launcher mounted beneath his M-4. Two seconds later, the round exploded against the rock face to the side of the canyon entrance.

Screams of pain rose from three wounded Iranians who fell and rolled in the dirt at the edge of the field — a field becoming soaked with their tribesmen's blood.

The other seven Marines continued firing their M-4s at the Iranians who survived the grenade's merciless detonation.

At the rear of the militia's pack, a teenage Iranian retreated behind the rock canyon's outer wall. His AK-47 clattered in his quivering hands as he tried to control the heavy wood-and-steel rifle against his heaving chest. With a single eye, he snuck a peek around the corner at the slaughter in the field from which he just narrowly escaped. The boy's eyes narrowed into slits at the sight of his fatally wounded uncle, rolling on the ground in agony a dozen feet away. The older man wailed from the combination of grenade shrapnel and chunks of rock impaled into his back.

The boy retreated to safety behind the canyon wall. He howled at the anguish he saw his uncle enduring. Sobbing uncontrollably, the boy extended his rifle beyond the edge of the canyon wall, pulled the trigger and fired blindly into the field until his AK-47's magazine ran dry.

Six feet short of the ramp leading into the Osprey's cargo bay, a lone 7.62mm round from the teenager's rifle tore into the bottom of the CIA officer's right boot. The force of the bullet knifing through the rubber sole threw the black boot forward and spun the American to the ground, ass over tea kettle.

The two Marine fire teams continued firing at the teenager protected by the canyon walls, but their bullets found only rock. Two by two, the leathernecks maneuvered deftly from their firing line, walking backward toward the ramp leading into the Osprey's rectangular cargo bay. The first pair of Marines to reach the CIA officer knelt and lifted their passenger by the first handhold they could grab—straps of the rugged black backpack worn by the grunting figure.

As the last two Marines stepped up the ramp into the Osprey, the MV-22's pilots launched the aircraft from the ground and swung their bird into a violent turn to the west.

The howl of the Osprey's pair of Rolls-Royce engines reverberated throughout the cargo bay as the pilots pressed its two power plants for every ounce of acceleration needed to get the aircraft and its passengers to safety. On the cargo bay's floor, the Marines flipped their passenger faceup and clamped an intercom headset over the CIA officer's ears. A US Navy Corpsman donned his own headset and dropped to his knee to inspect his patient for whatever injury the impact of the Iranian bullet caused.

"Don't worry," the Corpsman said over the intercom, "you're in good hands now. I'm gonna take good care of you, man."

The Navy medic ran his hands down his patient's right leg to feel for anything wet—the telltale sign of blood. He felt nothing out of the ordinary, but his nose wrinkled at the acrid odor hanging in the air—burnt rubber.

The Corpsman inspected his patient's right boot and gasped. The cowardly Iranian's bullet had found its mark, and a semi-circular groove ran the three-inch length of the heel, almost directly down the center.

The patient groaned and reached for the damaged boot and the twisted ankle encased inside.

The medic pulled a hook knife from his belt and easily sliced through the black laces from the top of the boot down to its toe. "Let's see if your ankle is swelling or maybe sprained. Just lay back, man," he said through the intercom. "I got you. You may have twisted your ankle, dude." He slid the damaged boot off, tossed it aside and pulled his patient's sock down.

As the black sock came off, five pink-painted toenails wiggled into view. The medic flinched and dropped his patient's bare foot onto the aircraft's steel deck.

The patient's heel bounced off the cold metal floorplate, and she yelped in surprise. Through the intercom, Michelle Reagan—CIA codename Eden—snarled, "*Oww*! That hurts, *dude*." She unwrapped the turban from her face, sat up and caressed her tender ankle.

"Sorry!" the medic blurted out, and raised his hands in mock surrender. He sat back on his heels, thought for a moment, and added, "Umm, *ma'am*."

Eden slithered the backpack off her shoulders and roughly yanked out its contents. She examined the two Huawei cell phones and a pair of Lenovo laptop PCs, fearing that either the canyon walls she banged against or an irate Iranian's bullet might have caused irreparable damage to the electronics she traveled halfway around the world to appropriate from the terrorist leader's henchmen. Not finding any visible damage, she hugged them to her chest and sighed in relief.

Eden returned the electronics to the padded backpack and zipped it securely closed. Slowly, to avoid falling over as the aircraft banked, she lifted herself onto one of the gray, padded, fold-down seats built into each side of the Osprey's cargo bay and buckled herself in.

The Navy Corpsman pointed to her bare ankle, and asked, "Ma'am, may I? I'll wrap an ice pack on it. You know... to keep the swelling down."

She nodded and leaned back in her seat. As the medic lifted her foot from the aircraft's deck, she keyed the microphone on her intercom. "Have I mentioned how much I hate working inside Iran? I *fucking* hate Iran. Nothing good *ever* happens to me in Iran. Absolutely. Nothing. Good. Ever!"

Eden looked around the Osprey's small cargo bay at the team of eight Marines, one Navy Corpsman, and an aircraft crew chief all blinking rapidly while staring at her. The ten men sat or knelt around her, waiting to see what the woman they just helped escape from an Iranian militia would do next.

She shrugged. "Just sayin'...."

Chapter 2

Back in the Iranian militiamen's village, an eight-year-old sprinted as fast as he could to the far end of town. The boy, dispatched to summon Behrouz Heidari, ran his heart out to the home in which the sultan's man usually stayed when visiting. The boy huffed for breath and slapped his palms on the wooden door of the single-story house until the widow living there pulled it open. She scolded the boy fiercely for the early morning interruption.

Between gulps of air and body-wracking sobs, the boy got his message across. "They killed my father. Tell the sultan's man! My mother sent me to tell you to tell her cousin to come quickly. Now. Right now! *Hurry!*"

The woman's heart fell. Her first thoughts were of the sorrow the boy's mother must be feeling. She became a widow herself five years earlier when her own husband died in Iraq training Shi'a fighters to resist the Great Satan's imperialist army. The pain still hung heavy in her heart every time she looked at her own empty bed—empty except when Behrouz visited. She turned to relay the message to her houseguest but saw his distinctive six-foot-two-inch frame standing in the hallway of the small home she shared with her son and daughter.

"I heard," the lanky man said, and joined her at the front door. He looked at his hostess. "Pack my things. I may not be able to stay as long as I'd hoped."

Heidari knew the way through town perfectly well but followed the boy's lead in the early morning light. He strode purposefully through the ancient village—too small and insignificant to appear on any map—known to the locals as Smugglers Respite.

The front door to his cousin's house stood open, and the gathering crowd parted as he approached. Heidari entered the house he knew so well and stopped short at the grotesque sight. The body of his cousin's husband lay on its back, slumped against a wall with his head cocked at an unnatural angle. Bloodstains dotted the chest of the man's white cotton nightshirt, and pools of red liquid stained the colorful living room rug around him.

Heidari stepped forward and looked around the room. His cousin knelt at her husband's side and wailed high-pitched cries of sorrow and anger. Her four daughters sprawled on the floor of the next room, holding each other tightly and weeping quietly.

Heidari approached his cousin and held his arms out. She stood and embraced the tall man who held her firmly. "What happened?" he whispered in her ear.

It took a minute for the shaking woman to get the words out. "I heard him screaming at the thief. I don't know what happened. I didn't hear any gunshots, but I heard the front door slam and then there was shouting outside. I found him...." She pointed to her husband's corpse and her knees buckled.

Heidari caught his cousin mid-fall and helped her to a chair. There, he left her in the company of three other women from the village. He walked over to the distraught woman's late husband and bent down to examine the body. He lifted the man's nightshirt to look at the wounds. Four bullet holes trailed red and black rivulets of blood. One pair of bullets entered the man's stomach while the others were higher, centered over what Behrouz imagined was his heart. Not being a trained fighter, he did not recognize the expertise of the shooter but concluded correctly that anyone struck by four bullets was unlikely to survive. Heidari specialized in the financial tools his sultan needed to grow their expanding organization, not the military affairs in which much of the rest of the organization excelled.

He stood, looked at his cousin and walked over to her. He knelt beside her chair, and softly asked, "You said your husband was screaming about a *thief*. What did he —"

Behrouz stood and spun around. He rapidly scanned the empty wooden table in the corner that he and the now-dead man had placed next to one of the few electrical outlets in the house. Heidari's face flushed, and he screamed, "*Where* are the computers? My phones!"

His cousin sobbed but didn't answer. She buried her face in her hands while another woman tried to comfort her.

A strained voice from outside the house grew louder. "Move aside. Get out of my way. Let me *in*." A teenager carrying an AK-47 pushed his way through the crowd peering into the house. He inhaled with raspy gasps as he came to an abrupt halt. He leaned against the doorframe while trying to catch his breath. He placed his rifle against the open door, but his hands shook, and the old wood-and-metal rifle clattered to the floor. He took two deep breaths and struggled to get the words out. "They're... all dead." He pushed a hand into his chest as if to keep his lungs from exploding. "The thief... got away." The teenager slumped to the floor and his chest heaved. "I ran... all the way back. My uncle...."

Heidari marched over to the boy and stood above him, growling. Loudly, he asked, "Your uncle was the *thief*?"

The boy shook his head violently. "*No*, sir. My uncle's dead. He gathered the village militia to *chase* the thief. I... went with them. I'm almost a full member now," he said proudly. "We ran as fast... as we could through the old smugglers' pass to catch the thief. Then there was an explosion... up ahead of me, and a lot of men died."

Heidari spoke rapidly, not giving the sixteen-year-old a chance to answer. "What happened to the thief? Did you see what he stole? What was he wearing? Where did he go?"

The boy quivered as he answered. "I don't know what he took. He had a backpack on, but he got away. A *black* backpack." He placed his hand over his racing heart and pressed as if that were the only way to keep it inside his chest. "The soldiers in the field came out of nowhere. They must have already been there, waiting to ambush us. They killed everyone, even my uncle."

"*What* soldiers?"

"I don't know," the teenager said immediately, and used some of his regained strength to stand up straight as he addressed his elder. "Just soldiers. They wore green clothing the color of grass and wore helmets. We thought we'd catch the thief when he ran into the open field, but the soldiers just appeared out of nowhere. The thief didn't stop and just kept running into the helicopter plane. The soldiers killed everyone in the militia. They shot at me but missed every time. The soldiers had grenades and machine guns. We shot at them, too, and then there was *another* explosion. The thief in the black turban and brown jacket just kept running and running, right up the ramp and into the helicopter plane."

Heidari eyed the boy who'd finally managed to catch his breath, and slowly asked, "'Helicopter plane?' What do you mean? Was it one or the other?"

The boy straightened his posture and addressed his elder more formally, "Sir, I shot the thief. I'm *sure* I got him because he *fell*, but the soldiers picked him up. They carried him inside and flew away."

"Boy, *answer* me! What is a helicopter plane?"

"I've never seen anything like it before. It was big!" The boy struggled to describe the MV-22 Osprey. "It had two propellers on top like a helicopter but two wings like an airplane. It was *both*. The thief and soldiers ran right into its big open back. It took off straight up like a helicopter and then flew away forward like an airplane. I'm telling you the truth, sir. It was both."

Heidari shook his head in disbelief. With no military training, he didn't understand the boy's ramblings. How could something like he described possibly exist?

"So," Heidari asked, "if the soldiers killed everyone else in the militia, how did you survive?"

The boy's shoulders rolled forward. "I... I kept shooting and shooting at them. I must have hit the thief because he fell down. I... knelt down to pick up two magazines of ammunition from the man near me and just kept shooting until the thief flew away. I shot at the helicopter plane until I ran out of bullets. Then I ran home as fast as I could to tell you what happened. I was sure you'd want to know everything."

Heidari knew he wasn't getting the full story from the young man and chewed his bottom lip while debating what to do next. He looked at his cousin's dead husband and shook his head. The sultan would be beside himself at the loss of the computers—computers the dead man who worked for Heidari was responsible for. But, ultimately, it was his own responsibility, and his alone. He felt the smallest satisfaction knowing the financial transactions on the two computers were encrypted on the hard drives, so the information would be useless to whomever stole it—or at least that's what he'd tell the sultan.

Heidari looked again at the body slumped against the wall. He frowned at the thought that he'd now have to find another multi-lingual courier experienced in the subtle arts of concealments and smuggling. Someone who wouldn't draw attention while carrying financial orders to Malta in place of his cousin's dead husband. The murdered man whose centuries-old family business of running contraband across a half-dozen borders had made him a natural for the job and would be hard to replace. Hard, yes, but, eventually, everyone's replaceable.

Heidari looked at the teenager and decided it would be better to bring a scapegoat to the sultan to explain the loss of the computers and cell phones rather than face Sargon alone. "You will come with me," he said to the boy. "I don't understand what a helicopter plane is, so you'll have to explain it to the sultan's men yourself."

"No, sir, I can't leave. I have... I have to tend to my uncle's flock. Now that he's dead, we have to have the funeral and—"

Heidari stepped close to the teenager, looked down at him, and slowly said, "The other men of the village will attend to that. So, go. Pack a bag. You'll be gone for one week." *And,* he thought, *probably won't live past that, anyway.*

Chapter 3

Michelle Reagan sat on the sofa in the safe house with her right foot propped up on an ottoman. She lowered the temperature of the heating pad wrapped around her ankle and watched her team lead, Michael, as he rose from the chair to her left.

"They're late," he grumbled, which accentuated his fading West Texas drawl. The athletic man with white hair glowered at his watch and turned to the window beyond which the streets of Yerevan, Armenia's capital, stretched in a tree-lined grid. He pulled the curtain aside a few inches to peer outside. He scanned from the driveway to the front lawn and into the distance where a snow-capped Mount Ararat loomed on the horizon southwest of the city. The almost seventeen-thousand-foot-high peak on the Turkish side of the border — believed by some to be the final resting place of Noah's Ark — soared above the Ararat Plain which extended across the borders of Turkey, Armenia and Iran.

"They'll be here," Michelle assured him. "Don't worry. Alex knows what he's doing."

Her boss nodded in agreement at Michelle's confidence in Alex Ramirez, her partner on their covert action team from CIA's Special Activities Center — the SAC. He let the curtain fall back into place. "It should only be a forty-five-minute drive from the airport."

"Sure" — she turned the heating pad off, letting it fall away from her foot — "*if* you're not running a full surveillance-detection route. I planned the SDR with him. It'll be *fine*. It's a three-hour route, and he has the experience to do it perfectly well."

Michael nodded at his protégé and looked at his watch again. "Yes, but it's already been four hours." He looked over at Michelle. "Do you want me to make you an omelet, or something?"

"Michael, stop mothering me, will you? I'm *fine*." Michelle pulled her sock on and folded the top down to match the one on her left foot. "My ankle didn't swell much to begin with, and it's almost all gone now. I can't even feel it, what with all the ibuprofen I've been taking."

The revving of a car pulling into the driveway brought a smile to the face of the CIA team lead. He nudged the curtain aside again, and, with measurable relief, said, "That's them." He turned to look at Michelle whose right hand now rested on the handgrip of the Sig Sauer pistol resting on the end table. He let the curtain drop. "I'll open the garage door."

Michelle nodded. She placed the pistol on the sofa next to her and covered it with a throw pillow.

Michael, Alex Ramirez and a third man Michelle did not know entered the house from the garage. The newcomer carried a briefcase and pulled a well-traveled black roll-aboard suitcase behind him.

Alex made the introductions. "Mike, this is John from the Directorate of Science and Technology. John, Mike. And on the couch over there is Eden. Watch your wallet around her. She's a terror at the poker tables."

Michael shook hands with the newcomer. "Welcome to Yerevan. How was the drive?"

"Fine, thanks. We ran into a couple of friends along the way, but Alex took care of them." John looked around the room. "May I set up on the dining room table, or should I work upstairs?"

Alex hefted his guest's suitcase onto the wood veneer of the dining room table.

Michael gestured to the table. "Use whatever space you need. You're our guest of honor."

Michelle withdrew her pistol from under the pillow. She depressed the Sig's decocking lever with her thumb, and the hammer clicked twice softly as it dropped into its safe position.

At the sound of the metallic clicks, John snapped his neck to look at Eden as she placed the pistol, topped with a five-inch suppressor, back onto the side table.

She covered it with the pillow and smiled at the newcomer. "Never know who's going to walk through the door, do you, John from DS&T?"

The pudgy redhead in his late twenties gulped. "No, I guess you don't."

Alex clapped John between his shoulder blades. "And you also shouldn't make any bets with her on the firing range, either. Trust me," the former Navy SEAL advised his guest. "I learned *that* the hard way."

John opened his two bags and began setting up his equipment on the dining room table.

Michael asked Alex, "So, you ran into a few *friends* on the way here, did you? What was that all about?"

"Oh," the athletic man with a scruffy black beard said to his boss, "it's nothing I couldn't handle. Three cars followed us once we left the airport. I ran the SDR just like Eden and I planned it. I lost them in a parking garage when we made the vehicle switch about an hour later. After that, I used two of the contingency routes she and I scoped out, so it took us longer to get here than I hoped. But it worked."

Michael's head nodded almost imperceptibly. He would have preferred Eden had picked up their guest after his flight from Germany but had chosen to let her rest her ankle. "Well," the white-haired CIA executive said, "the Armenians are either going to continue watching that car or, by now, they've already installed an electronic tracker on it. Forget about that one, Alex. I'll tell the undercover travel coordinator where it is, and they can let the rental agency know where to pick it up."

A few feet away, John booted up two laptop computers. He attached a power adapter with two round European-style plugs onto a power strip and watched his electronics come to life. He looked at Michael. "Where's the equipment you want me to examine?"

"Under there," Eden said, and pointed to the cabinet below the television. "Two cell phones and two laptops."

"Okay," John said. "I won't ask where they came from."

Eden shrugged as the technical services officer retrieved the equipment she'd liberated from Iran.

He looked over the equipment, photographed the outsides and began his forensic examination.

Alex soon bored of the technical work and plopped down next to Eden on the sofa. "How's the ankle?"

"If one more person asks, I'm going to scream."

Alex grinned at his boss. "Sounds to me like she's back to her old self."

The team lead grinned and nodded. "Come on, Eden. You want that omelet, now?"

Eden rose. "It's lunch time. I think I'll make a salad." She gestured to Alex and John. "You guys want anything?"

Eagerly, John said, "I'll have both, if there's enough. But no nuts in the salad, please. Allergies."

"Alex?" Eden asked.

"Both sounds good. With extra nuts."

"You *are* nuts," she answered, and turned toward the kitchen.

***

The foursome ate at the kitchen table while John updated them on the progress of his work.

"I cracked the two Huawei cell phones already and am downloading the contents now. When that's done, I'll upload it all to Langley," he said.

"That was quick," Eden remarked.

"They're Android devices, not iPhones, and they're running operating systems about three generations out of date. So, the security is pretty much non-existent. Google used to use food names for each version, like 'Gingerbread' or 'Jellybean.' In our office, we just call it 'Swiss Cheese.'"

The three members of the SAC's Ground Branch kept eating.

"That's a joke," John confessed.

Alex shrugged.

Eden forked a tomato into her mouth.

Michael took a sip of water.

"Anyway," the technical services officer said, "once I upload the data to our servers for analysis, then your analyst—what's his name again?"

"Wilson Henry," Michael answered.

"Yeah, he can access it online using the case number you gave me. The data should be available to him first thing in the morning, Washington time."

"Excellent," Michael said, and laid his fork across his empty plate. "What about the laptops?"

"*That's* a different story. Those are encrypted, and I can't break that level of security in the field."

"*Aww*, crap," Alex said.

"So, after the phones are done, I'll upload full images of the hard drives to our cloud server. The supercomputers back home will have to do their thing. It'll take a while. There's always a wait for time on the big iron."

"Let me know when they're in the queue," Michael offered, "and I'll make a call. I can get the priority raised."

"Impressive," John said. "This must be an important case."

"You could say that," Michael answered. "We're trying to prevent the next ISIS from forming and want to keep the next wanna-be Osama bin Laden from getting the funding he needs to build his organization. Those phones and laptops belong to the financial side of his operation."

"Sounds important to me. Maybe someone should just drop a bomb on his head and call it a day."

Michael smiled, lifted his water glass and took a sip. "Unfortunately, he's also doing favors for someone high up in the Turkish government by helping them against the Kurds in Iraq, Syria and eastern Turkey. So, as the State Department likes to say, it's complicated."

"Helping them *against* the Kurds?" John asked. "That whole situation seems more like persecution *of* the Kurds, if you ask me."

Eden pushed her empty plate forward a couple of inches. "You're unusually well informed. For a techie, I mean."

"Hey," John remarked, and scrunched up his lips. "We read newspapers in DS&T, too, you know. So, what's this guy's name?"

"No one knows, but he goes by the pseudonym 'Sargon the Third,'" Michael said. "His followers call him 'the sultan,' and seem to think of him as royalty."

"Bin Laden liked to be called the sheikh, and this guy's the sultan. What *is* it with these guys' supersized egos, anyway?" John asked.

Michelle smirked. "Must be the Middle Eastern version of having a Napoleon Complex."

"And why," John asked, "is this guy 'the *third*?' Have we already killed the first two?"

"Not us, no," Michael answered. "Four thousand years ago, the first Sargon ruled much of the Middle East from eastern Turkey, down through Iraq, and over to modern-day Kuwait. Two thousand years later, Sargon the Second extended his kingdom to include Egypt, as well. Apparently, Sargon the Third seems to have similar goals. Wilson Henry told me that the name Sargon means 'the king is legitimate' in whatever ancient language he spoke. I happen to disagree with that sentiment, though, and we intend to end his reign as soon as we find him."

A beeping from the dining room table got everyone's attention.

Chapter 4

John glanced over to his equipment in the next room. "Cool. The cell phone data finished uploading." He looked at Michael. "What'll happen now is that the phone's contact list and call records will be automatically compared to both our database as well as NSA's. The network analysis of first-, second- and third-degree separations should only take an hour or so. It'll take longer for the facial recognition algorithms to finish running against all the photos on the phones. That may take a day or two, and the results are always iffy. Consider them leads to follow, not absolute conclusions. It's not the Gospel According to John, as I like to say."

"Good to know, John. Thank you," Michael said. "I'll send a message to Wilson later and let him know to watch for the results. In the meantime, can we take a look at the photos on the phones just to see what's on them?"

"Sure thing," John said in an upbeat tone. "I'll get 'em." He brought the phones to the kitchen and launched the Photos apps on each.

Michael and Eden thumbed through the pictures.

Eden finished first and placed the phone on the table. She grunted. "Only three on this one. Nothing interesting."

Michael turned his around so the others could see the photograph of an employee identification badge.

Eden leaned forward and read the text along the bottom of the ID. "Dario Turchi works for Banc Rilatus in Valletta."

"Valletta?" Alex asked. "As in the capital of Malta? That really nice little island in the middle of the Mediterranean? Warm breezes... good food... sandy beaches...."

Michelle looked at him and tilted her head. "Hmm. Did a certain former sailor meet a certain little lady in a certain little pub on a certain sunny little Mediterranean island? Maybe one called Malta?"

Alex shrugged. "That's all on a need-to-know basis, I'm afraid." He looked at his boss. "So, is it Malta?"

"I don't know," Michael answered. "It doesn't say, but we can figure that out easily enough by looking into Banc Rilatus. I'll have

Wilson do the digging and identify Mr. Turchi. If it takes him more than fifteen minutes, I'd probably better get us a new analyst."

Michelle looked at her watch and did some quick mental math. "It's only 4 a.m. back home. He won't get to the office in Virginia for another three hours or so. Why do you think they took a picture of an ID? To know which guy the courier—Sargon's man who owned the phones I stole—was sent to meet?"

"Or," Alex added, "maybe to create a fake ID?"

John interjected. "To create a fake badge—or a convincing fake of any document, really—you'd want to have the original in hand, if at all possible. Otherwise, you're going to get the look of the plastic and shades of the colors all wrong. I'm not a document specialist, but *that* much I know for sure."

Alex nodded. "Yeah, sure, that'd be best, but maybe they just couldn't get their hands on it."

"Maybe," John agreed, more to end the speculation than anything.

"I like Eden's idea," Michael said. "Terrorists do a lot of in-person meetings because they know how much communications intelligence we gather from their phone calls. That's why bin Laden didn't allow telephones of any kind into his house in Abbottabad, Pakistan. This could be the way for one of Sargon's couriers to know who he was supposed to meet."

"*Um-hum*, meeting a banker," Michelle said. "That's definitely in character for a group moving money. Every terrorist needs a dirty banker in his back pocket to launder money from charities and front groups back to the home office of Evil Incorporated."

Michael nodded. "Wilson will be able to find out what we need to know about that bank and many of the less-than-savory clientele they cater to. Next up for us, though, is to find out what *this* particular banker is doing for Sargon, and how. Right now, we need Wilson to tell us where the money's coming from and where it's going."

Chapter 5

Wilson Henry arrived in the team's covert office in Tysons Corner, Virginia, after weaving through scattered detritus clogging up the already over-congested Route 7. The previous night's torrential wind and rain had drenched the nation's capital with a vengeance. Downed tree branches and power lines made morning traffic even worse than usual.

At his computer, he checked his email and read the one from Mike first. After that, he clicked menu options on a half-dozen web pages to get to the DS&T analysis results for the Sargon case. He scrolled down the page and made a few notes on the results from the first cell phone, but it showed little more than a few calls to one phone number attributed by NSA to a Turkish organized crime family. *Mmm,* he thought, *we already knew about that.*

The second cell phone yielded more. The call history listed a dozen long calls between the Iranian area code in which Eden had recovered the electronics and Valletta, Malta.

Sunshine in the Med, Wilson thought, *sounds so much better than rain in DC or snow back home in Boston! Let's see... the calls to Valletta were to... a bank. That fits with Michael's email about the ID and are not at all surprising for a terrorist group raising or laundering money. Like the famous man once said, 'Follow the money.'*

Wilson navigated his browser to see what CIA's facial recognition application found in the photos from the courier's cell phones. He scrolled down the page and read that only the employee ID resulted in a match: Dario Turchi. The analysis report showed that, according to his LinkedIn profile, Turchi works for Banc Rilatus in Valletta.

Well, that's not exactly news, now is it?

Wilson ran a free-text search, and the computer spat back only three results that included both Turchi's name and any connection to Malta. The first was for a mid-level Italian Mafioso involved in weapons trafficking to African migrants crossing illegally into Europe. *You're too old and in the wrong country. Not our banker.*

The second and third listings were reports from DEA. Both peripherally referenced Turchi's involvement in money laundering that they'd identified more than a decade earlier during Operation Cassandra. Back then, a DEA source reported that Turchi was a junior banker moving dirty money for the Lebanese terrorist organization Hezbollah that trafficked cocaine throughout Africa and the Middle East. *Drugs and money laundering sound more like it. Anything for a dollar, euro or franc, eh, Dario?*

When Wilson finished reading the reports, he typed up a short message and sent it to Michael's cell phone via the team's encrypted voice and text message app. His message read: *Good news: Turchi is a solid lead. Bad news: We've got nothing significant on him beyond DEA's old history of him laundering drug money. Still waiting on the laptop images to be decrypted. They tell me it may take a while.*

***

At dinner time in the team's safe house in Armenia, Michael read the message on his phone and grunted. He told Eden and Alex what Wilson reported.

"So, what do we do now?" Alex asked.

Michael pushed a wayward lock of white hair back over top of his head. "I'm going to have Wilson submit a collection request to Malta Station for them to find out more about both the bank's clientele and Mr. Turchi's background. That'll get a local case officer to start digging up dirt on Dario. Meanwhile, I'll get Logistics to move our gear there so if we need it, at least it's on the right island. As for us, we'll all head there later this week as well." He looked at their DS&T guest, John. "Not much else for you to do here. You can go home tomorrow."

"I'm glad I was able to help," John said. He reached into the basket in the middle of the table for seconds of *plov*, a local favorite dish of saffron-flavored rice, lamb and onions.

Michael looked at Eden. "Besides, a few days off your feet will let your ankle heal completely."

Eden tilted her head, and said as defensively as she felt, "How many times do I have to tell you? I'm *fi-ine.*"

Chapter 6

The hundred-mile drive over poorly paved roads from Smugglers Respite, Iran, to eastern Turkey took Behrouz Heidari a full day. Since Tamerlan, the teen soldier, did not have a passport, Behrouz borrowed the boy's late uncle's truck for the journey. The young man fit easily into the hidden compartment between the truck's cab and the flatbed most often used to transport herd animals to markets in neighboring towns. For the two hours he had to lie in the smuggler's compartment, Tamerlan couldn't wait to get away from the odor of the contraband cigarettes his uncle routinely snuck across Iran's borders.

The line of vehicles queued up for inspection by border troops of both Iran and Turkey seemed to Behrouz to not move at all for an hour. He exhaled loudly when he finally made it to the checkpoint at Gürbulak. Border guards on both sides checked his Turkish passport and Iranian visa thoroughly, but neither paid any attention to the visibly empty vehicle.

Two hours later, Behrouz pulled the truck through the gate of Sargon's walled compound on the shore of Lake Van in eastern Turkey. Behrouz sent the teenager to eat dinner in the guest house, while he reported the events of the previous evening to the sultan in his mansion.

In the office next to his sultan's throne room, Behrouz related the story of the masked thief's escape and floundered as he retold the boy's description of what he called the 'helicopter plane.'

The sultan sent for one of his military counselors and told Behrouz to summon the boy.

Once Tamerlan arrived, Behrouz ushered the lad into the throne room. The teenager hesitantly approached the bearded man sitting in the low-backed golden throne covered with silver roses. The seated man, wearing a light blue suit and black wingtip shoes, gestured for the boy to approach the throne.

Behrouz made the formal introduction. "Young man, today you have the honor of being granted an audience before His Majesty Sargon the Third, King of Akkad, Assyria and Sumeria, and Wielder of the Sword of the Faithful."

The teenager stared wide-eyed at the middle-aged monarch his elders taught him to revere. Tamerlan addressed him with a shaky voice. "Good... um, good *evening*, Your Majesty."

"You have had quite an eventful week, Tamerlan," Sargon said effusively, "for someone so young. But I can see that you are *right there* on the cusp of manhood. There is such strength in your face and a clear yearning in your inquisitive eyes — eyes which I'm certain are destined to see more of the world than just your small village. We have only just met, but already I can tell that you are very much like me. You and I are men who were born to spread the joy of Allah's word across his bountiful Earth throughout all the days of our lives. Tell me what happened back in your village and what you saw. Spare me no detail, however small. I'm excited to hear of these events told by someone who was there himself. Please, Tamerlan, tell me what you saw and did."

Tamerlan spoke with difficulty at first but gained confidence as he related his story. He finished with a description of the helicopter plane taking off from the grassy field and his sprint back to the village.

Sargon gestured with two fingers to his counselor. Rifaat — a short, rotund man with gray streaks spreading like veins through his stark-black beard — lifted an iPad from a nearby table and approached Tamerlan. He tapped the tablet's screen twice and proceeded to show the teen a series of pictures of eight large American and Russian helicopters.

The boy looked closely at the American twin-rotor Chinook cargo helicopter but lifted his head, and said, "*Tsk.* No, the helicopter plane had its propellers on the sides — on its wings — not in the front and back like that one."

The counselor swiped through several more images and stopped on a medium-size, two-engine Russian cargo plane, the Antonov An-26.

The boy looked closely at the tablet, and again said no.

Rifaat swiped the iPad once more, and Tamerlan reacted immediately.

"*Umum*," he said, and dropped his chin in the region's typical gesture of agreement. "*That's* it!"

"You're sure?" the sultan asked.

"That's it, yes. I'm *certain* of it, Your Majesty."

The counselor swiped through several similar images and asked Tamerlan to recall any markings or letters on the aircraft. Not familiar with English, the boy couldn't recall specifics.

Sargon dismissed Tamerlan and instructed him to talk to his housekeeper next door. She would show him one of the five bedrooms in the other house within the fenced compound, and he would be Sargon's honored guest for the night.

The boy stood up straight and puffed his chest out proudly. "Thank you, sir! It's an honor to help Your Majesty."

The three adults looked closely at the iPad and waited until the boy left.

Once the door shut securely behind Tamerlan, Rifaat addressed Sargon. "The aircraft is an American V-22 model. They call it a *balikkartali* – an Osprey." He loaded the Wikipedia page on his iPad and scrolled down. "They have a lot of them at military bases across Europe and the United States. In America, they're located at multiple bases all over Southern California and North Carolina. Those places are far apart." He tapped on the iPad a half-dozen times and read the screen. "According to the map, they're as far apart as it would be for us to drive from here to London, England."

Sargon slowly paced about the room and pressed his lips together firmly as he thought. Each time he passed his low-backed golden-hued throne, he let his index finger brush gently across one of the inlaid silver roses on the arm of the ornate chair.

After a half-minute of silent planning, he raised his hands above his head to stretch and turned to his counselor. "Rifaat, are our two soldiers in America ready for their first assignment?"

"Yes. Their training here went well, and their English is excellent. They can drive from where they live in New York to North Carolina in just a day or two. Driving their equipment to California might take a week and would be riskier. But if you give the word, it shall be done, Your Majesty."

"You did fine work getting them ready," Sargon said. "Tell them they will have the privilege of carrying out our first attack on American soil. They are to go to North Carolina and visit upon the Americans casualties like the heathens inflicted upon my subjects in Iran."

"I will send that message immediately," Rifaat answered. "And tomorrow, recall, you and I have that *other* matter to attend to for the public face of our organization."

"Yes, yes," Sargon said, his eyes brightening. He looked at Behrouz Heidari who had been quiet for some time. "Has the money been transferred for that event or did the thief complicate things?"

"It's ready, Your Majesty. There's no problem at all. You're all set for tomorrow, and the team in America got their funding some time ago. There's nothing standing in your way. It seems that I will now have to meet with the banker in Malta again myself before I'm able to get a replacement courier identified and trained." He shrugged. "It's no problem—just a minor delay and more work for me. I am keeping your money flowing smoothly to our loyal soldiers in Turkey, Iran, France and America. And, of course, to our government contacts in Ankara and Istanbul to buy their information and cooperation."

Sargon smiled. "Good, Behrouz, very good. Make sure *that* money continues to flow without interruption—until I tell you differently. They are our agents for only as long as they get what they want from me. All my plans depend on those greedy sons of whores staying out of our way until we are strong enough to kick them out of office. I will cut off their money at the same time I cut off their corrupt heads." He looked at his counselor. "Rifaat, as for our soldiers in America," he said, pounding his fist into his open palm, "tell them to make the heathens bleed!"

Chapter 7

The midday sun shone brightly over the weathered stone buildings of Valletta, Malta's capital city. Located sixty miles south of Sicily, Italy, the island's half-million citizens enjoy the soft blue skies and consistently warm breezes that waft through its ancient streets from the nearby Mediterranean Sea.

Eden adjusted her sunglasses as she walked. She focused on the man a half-block ahead of her as he strode along the narrow sidewalk. At the end of the block, she stopped on the curb and watched the subject of her team's surveillance—the *rabbit* in the vernacular of the intelligence profession—make his way across the street in front of the Church of St. Catherine of Alexandria.

"He's heading your way," she said quietly into the small, low-powered surveillance radio's microphone concealed beneath her blouse.

"I've got him," Alex Ramirez replied from the end of the next block. "I have the eye."

Eden crossed to the opposite corner and walked briskly down a parallel street. She passed the Royal Opera House and waited for the light to change.

"I see you guys," she radioed to Alex. She watched the pair take a right turn, and she crossed when the light turned green.

"He's crossing in the middle of the street, but I'm going to continue straight," Alex said.

"Copy." She watched their subject, Dario Turchi, jaywalk across the street and enter an Italian restaurant. "He's landed for lunch. Let's meet up in the park on the next block."

"Okay," Alex replied.

When Eden arrived in the park, Alex handed her a bottle of water he'd just purchased from a street vendor. They sat on an empty bench under a stand of Carob trees, and Alex took a long draw from his bottle of spring water.

Eden twisted the plastic cap off hers. "Our guy really likes Italian restaurants, doesn't he?"

"Second one this week. I guess when you're dining on your bank's expense account, you can live it up. Then again, I do too, sometimes, when we travel."

"Yeah," Eden agreed, "it's one of the few perks of this job. In another ten minutes I'll go walk through the restaurant, see who he's dining with and use the ladies' room."

"Kinda boring work for us here this week, you know?"

Eden shrugged. "Gotta get to know your targets."

"Yeah," Alex said, screwing the cap back onto his water bottle, "but do you think Mike will even make him a real target for us? So far this week, it's just been spot surveillances around his house, the bank, a couple of lunches and that one doctor's appointment he took his wife to. Not exactly earth-shattering activity for a terrorist financier."

"Bankers are boring, predictable and easy to find. So, let's just enjoy the sunshine while we can."

Alex sat back and looked up at a jumbo jet climbing into the sky for destinations unknown.

Eden sipped from her bottle of water, and they sat in silence for a few minutes. When she finished her drink, she glanced at the hands of her wristwatch. "All right, I'm heading back to the restaurant. After that, let's burn off and go back to the safe house."

Alex nodded as Eden stood, and then watched her walk out of the park.

**

Two hours later, Michael greeted Alex and Eden from the comfort of the safe house's living room sofa. "How'd it go?"

Alex looked at the other man in the room and remained silent.

Michael took the cue and made introductions. "Alex and Eden, this is Carl Sapienti. Carl is the Malta Station case officer who's been looking into Dario Turchi for us."

The newcomers took turns shaking Carl's hand.

"Turchi's a rather boring guy, if you ask me," Carl said. "You know, other than laundering money for drug dealers, that is. He's fifty-nine years old, third-generation Maltese of Italian descent and has worked for Banc Rilatus for almost his entire career. Some time back, he was on our radar for suspicion of money laundering. In his personal life, except for his wife's ongoing battle with bone cancer, he doesn't seem to have anything going on. We don't see any obvious bad habits or red flags in his financials, but we haven't been digging into him for long enough to find out much more than that."

Eden leaned forward. "We followed Turchi and his wife yesterday afternoon to her doctor's office in Valletta."

"We pulled what records on him we could in the last week. Since you guys said you don't want us contacting the locals about him, I'll admit we don't yet have complete information on either of the Turchis. His wife sees a local doctor for pain management but flies to Rome once a month for chemotherapy. She has family in Italy. I've asked Rome Station to find out what they can from their end. My ex-wife's the deputy chief of station there and, since this seemed like a high priority for you guys in the Special Activities Center, I asked her to bump it up their priority list."

"*Ex*-wife?" Alex asked. "Is it going to end up on the top of her station's list or the bottom?"

Carl smiled and nodded knowingly. "She's only my ex because she cared more about her career than her personal life. She'll do you a solid on this one. Don't worry about Helen. But money laundering can't be why the SAC is leading this case instead of our Station. What's your interest in a boring banker with a sick wife? This is an unusual way to run a case."

Eden and Alex sat silently.

"You're right," Michael said. "There *is* more to it, and we certainly appreciate Malta Station's help. Turchi is laundering money for an up-and-coming terrorist group we're trying to stop. Unfortunately for us, this group is paying off high-level officials in the Turkish government for protection. We don't know exactly who, but it's clearly working out well for all involved. Over the past few years, Ankara has been playing Moscow and Washington against each other, so headquarters is experiencing some institutional paralysis on this particular topic. Between this issue and what's going on with the Kurds and the never-ending shit show in Syria, Headquarters Station wants to keep this operation out of Ankara Station as much as possible. That way, it won't affect NATO or local intelligence and law enforcement relationships. As someone famous once said, 'It's complicated.'"

"Yeah, sounds it," Carl agreed. "Well, what else can I do for you?"

Michael pushed a lock of his white hair back over the top of his head and thought. After a moment, he said, "I think for now, Carl, we're just about done here." He tapped the two-inch-thick file the case officer had given him earlier. "I need to do some more reading, but I have the basis of a plan in mind. It seems to me that there's a trip to Rome in our future. Please keep digging into Turchi and send what you come up with to my point of contact, Wilson Henry, back at Langley. If there's anything else we need from you while we're in town, I'll let you know." He tapped the file again. "Thanks again for this, Carl. It's going to make a real difference, especially the report on how the bank's electronic systems work."

Carl thanked Michael, shook hands with all three SAC officers and left the safe house.

"So," Eden said, "he seems nice. What's next?"

Alex scratched his chin, and asked his boss, "Are you going to give us the green light on Dario Turchi?"

Michael drummed his fingers on the file. "No, not yet."

"Then what?" Alex asked.

"Turchi is just a link in the middle of a chain which starts with money coming into Malta from around the Middle East and Africa. Then, it goes somewhere before it gets to Turkey and Iran where it funds Sargon's expansion and terrorist activities. Right now, we need to find out where that middle piece is — the next link in the chain. If we cut Turchi out too soon, we'll lose our visibility both up and down the chain. Sargon would just replace Turchi, and we won't have gotten any closer to identifying and stopping him."

"So," Alex asked, "how do we work our way up the chain?"

"We follow the money to the next link. Eventually, it'll lead us to the big dog — Sargon himself. Carl Sapienti will continue digging into Dario Turchi's activities on the ground here in Malta while Wilson does the same back home with a lot of help from NSA. The courier's cell phones that Eden liberated in Iran led us here to Turchi, and now we need to see who Turchi leads us to. If we follow the money trail, it'll eventually lead us to the right people."

Eden shifted on the sofa and tucked her legs underneath her. "Follow it how? Isn't that more like something NSA would do, tapping everyone's phones, email and data feeds, then analyzing the calls and financial transactions?"

"Yes," Michael replied, "but *which* accounts would they analyze? It'll take them forever to analyze every linkage to every account Banc Rilatus has. I'm sure they'd come across a lot of dirty money, but we're only interested in a small fraction of that. To narrow it down for them, we need to first give them something specific to go on. It's up to *us* to find out which account numbers Turchi manages for Sargon. After that, we can ask NSA for help doing the detailed data analysis and number crunching. So, as for our next steps, I have an idea about how to get that information from Mr. Turchi."

"What are we going to do?" Alex asked. "Ask him nicely?"

Michael grinned from ear to ear. "Precisely."

Alex leaned back. "Cool. I'm enjoying the fresh air here in Malta."

"Don't get used to it," Michael retorted. "You and I are going to Rome."

"What about me?" Eden asked. "Not Rome? Somewhere better, I hope."

"Better," Michael said with a grin. "Much better. You, young lady, are first going to talk to Wilson Henry back home about research I've asked him to do to find us just the right kind of person we need to crack Dario Turchi wide open. After you're done in Virginia, you're off to recruit an agent in a real garden spot. Or at least the Garden State. You're going to New Jersey."

Chapter 8

Sargon and his counselor, Rifaat, squinted in the bright morning sun as they stood on the makeshift dais. They only half-listened to their host's speech as the man droned on, talking to the crowd assembled before them in the grass field ringed with trucks, buses and tents that served as temporary homes to this growing throng of Syrian refuges. The self-proclaimed king of a wide swath of the Middle East and the counselor he planned to one day name as his prime minister waited patiently while the audience listened with great anticipation for the big announcement promised by the event's host.

Rifaat leaned toward Sargon's ear, and whispered, "This guy must think you're paying him by the word."

The corners of Sargon's lips turned up, and he gave a curt nod. He enjoyed the accolades and effusive expression of appreciation afforded to him by the people he would one day rule. He already thought of them as *his* people. While he had to keep the two parts of his organization separate for the time being—the smiling face concealing the sharp teeth—he longed for that not-too-distant day in the future on which he would finally unite the organization and his followers under the flag of his caliphate. First, however, he had to expand his concealed army and solidify his political power over the diverse factions which have been pulling the Middle East apart for thousands of years. He alone, Sargon the Third, as he had dubbed himself at his private coronation three years earlier, would unite the warring factions of the region into a powerful nation that even the Ottoman Empire would have feared.

In front of him, the speaker at the podium concluded his remarks and introduced Sargon by his public name. "It is my distinct pleasure to introduce to you the man who is making our new hospital a reality through the generous charitable donations he made from his family's successful trucking company. *Very* generous contributions, I might add. I am happy to present to you our patron and benefactor, Ziya Önder."

The audience applauded enthusiastically, and Önder stepped up to the microphone at the podium.

Sargon waved to the gathered crowed. "Thank you very much. Thank you. I know the medical equipment we are bringing to you today is long overdue, but it is *finally* here. You have all come from nations and cities and towns and villages affected by the horrible wars in our neighboring countries, and we are glad that you have found peace here in Turkey. The civil war in neighboring Syria has driven millions of families out of their homes, and what has happened in Iraq over the past several decades is practically unmentionable. We in Turkey have the moral responsibility to be generous hosts to our brothers, our sisters, our neighbors and our fellow believers. I cringe at the knowledge that the Crusaders' repeated invasions of Iraq and their unending occupation have left millions more of the faithful wounded, hungry and desperate to return home. I know you all feel the same."

The crowd erupted in applause. Önder paused and waved to the crowed, letting them cheer for him.

"My new hospital brings to you advanced equipment like X-ray machines the doctors need, medicines which will help heal your wounds and crutches and prosthetic legs to enable the severely wounded among you to carry on a more normal and productive life."

The crowd applauded briefly, and Önder smiled in appreciation. He continued his remarks and laid his future plans bare.

"We and our generous donors give you these things for free. We do not ask anything in return because you are our guests. We owe you this not as charity but as fellow human beings—as brothers and sisters. I know you hope to return to your homes in the coming weeks or months or maybe years. I cannot predict the future or tell you when these wars of foreign aggression will end, but I can tell you *this*: I hope you will remember us and think well of us while you are here in Turkey. I hope when you return home or are safely resettled elsewhere, you will someday be generous in return and donate what you can, when you can, so we may continue to bring hospitals and food and clean water and job training to other needy brothers and sisters around the world. My compatriots and I will not stop until the Prophet's word is revered by every man, woman and child. I know that I can count on each and every one of you to support my charitable and outreach organizations in the future when you return to your own countries or settle in the West, whether it's in Europe, Canada or America. We are proving that *you* can count on us here today, and I know that *I* will be able to count on each and every one of you in the future when I need your help." Önder turned to his host and traced a large circle in the air with his arm. "Let's get the equipment set up so we can declare this hospital open!"

Sargon stepped back and raised his hands over his head as the crowd erupted in cheers and applause. The hospital equipment his multi-national transportation company started delivering that morning would be operational in less than a week, he knew, and the doctors would be assisted by trained men his caliphate had planted in the organization with an eye toward identifying among the refugees sympathetic ears for his true message. He silently thanked his late grandfather who had, as the Second World War drew to a close, established the trucking company which now gave Sargon the financial means to spread his fundamentalist message and the logistical reach to make his caliphate's expansion across the region a reality.

He smiled broadly and waved enthusiastically to the crowd. He saw the path to victory in front of him and beamed at the knowledge that his plans progressed unhindered. His organization would heal the sick, recruit the grateful and attack his enemies with ferocity. The minor skirmish he ordered against America would be just a simple test run of their global reach. His army of refugees, once recruited, trained and resettled in the West—right beneath his enemy's nose—would stalk the heathens with the stealth of a tiger, infiltrate their institutions from within their own borders and strike at their evil hearts with the speed and lethality of the poisonous asps so prevalent throughout the Middle East.

Chapter 9

At one of the ubiquitous strip malls off State Route 46 in Denville, New Jersey, Michelle Reagan listened to the surveillance radio chatter through the plastic earpiece hidden beneath her wig of shoulder-length jet-black hair. As she heard the report from her team of surveillance contractors, she glanced toward the street.

"The prostitute's turning into the parking lot's first entrance," the surveillance team lead reported over the encrypted radio.

Michelle responded to his radio transmission, softly saying, "I'm in place at Starbucks, and I've told you before, don't call her that. Once she parks her car, set up for the take-away to follow her when she leaves."

"Ten-four," the disembodied voice acknowledged.

It seemed to Michelle that, just like back home, every strip mall in New Jersey also had a coffee shop on the corner most visible from the main street. Michelle shifted slightly in her wrought-iron chair as the subject's car entered the lot and parked nearby.

An athletic blonde woman in a white tank top and form-fitting purple stretch pants stepped out of her Toyota Camry and walked toward the coffee shop where Michelle waited at one of two sidewalk tables.

As the woman neared, Michelle raised her sunglasses onto the top of her head and waved. "Hi, Cynthia. I got you a Chai tea with lemon."

Michelle pointed to the cup sitting in front of the only other chair at her table. "I'd like to talk for a minute, if that's all right with you."

Cynthia Robinson squinted at Michelle in the morning sunlight. "Do I know you?"

"No," the CIA officer replied, "we haven't met yet. Please, sit with me. Your tea is getting cold." Michelle's stomach churned at the newness of recruiting a potential agent—something she never trained for, but Michael insisted she attempt.

Her boss had reassured her that this would be more like offering someone a job than making a real CIA recruitment of a clandestine source behind enemy lines. In this instance, Michelle hoped with every fiber of her being that the money would indeed do the talking for her.

Cynthia looked at the tall cup with her name written on the side. "This is sort of creepy. I mean—"

"You know," Michelle said, interrupting, "it's a sunny Thursday morning, and we're in a public place. So, what's the harm? I don't bite, although I hear that you will, if the price is right."

Cynthia spun toward the coffee shop's front door and away from Michelle.

Michelle's mouth went dry, and she scrambled for what to say next. *Did I come all this way just to screw it up? Dammit. Was buying the Chai tea for her going a step too far?* Quietly, she offered, "I'll pay double your usual rate."

Cynthia stopped. Her hand rested gently on the door handle, but she couldn't bring herself to pull it open just yet. She turned her head and looked at Michelle but didn't speak.

Could this actually work? Michelle thought. She wasn't sure she could talk without stammering, so she silently gestured to the chair across the table.

"I'm sure this is a bad idea," Cynthia said, and pulled the chair out from under the table. "I'll give you thirty seconds before I get up and buy my own damned cup of tea. How do you even know what I usually drink? Are you stalking me?"

"I always do my homework before I offer someone a job."

"I don't need a job. I'm a full-time student."

"Yes, getting your second master's degree, I hear. Very studious of you, and not a bad cover for your weekend, um, *extracurricular* activities in New York City."

"You're down to twenty seconds."

"Studious *and* as strict as a schoolmarm, I see. Okay, then, we'll do it your way. I have a job I need done for a client and, as I said, I'll pay double your usual rate for two hours of work this Saturday afternoon. In fact, it's really for future jobs that I'll pay double. Because this is a short-notice arrangement and we don't know each other yet, we need to establish a degree of trust between us. For my part in building that bridge, I'm willing to pay you *four* times your usual rate for this first job. So, what do you say? Can I trust you?"

Cynthia sat silently and considered the offer. After a moment, she asked, "Are you a cop?"

"No, and if I were, offering you so much money would be considered entrapment, so nothing would happen to you anyway."

"My usual rate is fifteen an hour."

- 34 -

"Nice try. Your usual rate is one thousand an hour, but for Saturday's job, I'll pay you eight grand because it's short notice."

Cynthia looked closely at Michelle and studied her intently. Her straw-blonde eyebrows narrowed slightly. "Your homework, as you call it, is pretty damned good. Who are you?"

"I'm a woman who accomplishes things for my clients that they can't get done through more traditional means. I provide or arrange for special services. *Very* special services, and your particular talents are just a small piece of the big picture."

"Then why don't you do this job yourself on Saturday and pocket the cash?"

"That's a valid question, and there are two answers. The first is that the man you'll be meeting knows me, but in a completely different context. I can't... shall we say... *interact* with him the way you'll need to. The second answer is that I have one specific future job coming up which would require me to be in two places at once. That, unfortunately, is a skill I have not yet mastered. I'm good, but not *that* good. If you do well at this first job, then maybe you're the right woman for the second one, too. What do you say?"

Michelle had no intention of telling Cynthia that the real reason she wouldn't do the job herself was simply that the CIA officer had no intention of ever having sex with anyone on a mission. The thought of letting her guard down so completely and becoming utterly vulnerable turned her stomach. Michelle enjoyed working undercover but would never work under *the* covers.

Cynthia considered the offer while she rubbed at the rough tip of one of her fingernails. "If I agree to do this, what do I have to do?"

"Saturday afternoon, I'll pick you up in a limo so we can speak privately during the drive into the city. You'll meet the client in his hotel room and, for two hours, you rock his world and make him forget the rest of the planet even exists. After that, I'll pick you up at the hotel, pay you in cash, and then it's a quiet ride home in a stretch limousine. Oh... and I always provide or pay for all transportation, too."

"*Gee*, that's nice of you," Cynthia said with a sarcastic edge to her voice.

"It's more than me just being gracious," Michelle said. "I need to make absolutely certain that you show up exactly where I need you and at exactly the right time. I make precise plans and leave nothing to chance—that's *my* job. Your job is being a goddess with as many parts of your body as he can fumble over during the course of those two hours. So, are you interested in making good money?"

Cynthia thought about the job and the obscene amount of money the woman in front of her was willing to pay for just two hours of rolling around in a bed with thousand-thread-count sheets. She smiled. "Sure, why not? What time do you want to pick me up?"

***

Early Saturday afternoon, Cynthia Robinson slid into the back of the six-passenger limousine wearing a navy blue miniskirt, white sleeveless button-down blouse, and black three-inch pumps. As the chauffer closed the door behind the blonde, Michelle Reagan greeted the new arrival and raised the privacy barrier to prevent the CIA officer driving them into the city from listening.

"You look lovely," Michelle said. She admired the smooth contours of Cynthia's face and jealously admired the luster of her new recruit's rosy cheeks.

"Thank you. I try to dress the part, but on Thursday you didn't tell me anything about this particular client."

"I'll get to that. We have time. It's an hour ride into New York. Why don't you tell me a bit about yourself? I know you're getting a second master's degree. That seems like overkill, doesn't it?"

"Maybe, but it's really just an excuse to look productive. You know, so I can tell people why I don't have a job. Since I'm in school, I can say I'm living on scholarships, grants and tuition loans. That way I can spend my cash freely and no one bats an eyelash."

"Smart," Michelle agreed, nodding. She started to relax slightly, hoping that her boss's crazy idea for the future job he planned for Cynthia in Rome might just work.

The ladies chatted throughout the drive into Manhattan. As the limousine exited the Holland Tunnel, Cynthia looked at Michelle and furrowed her brow.

"You know, this is crazy, but I just realized you never told me your name."

"Michelle McMasters," Michelle replied.

"Well, nice to meet you, Michelle. We must be getting close. Which hotel are we going to, and who's the client?"

"This job's pretty simple," Michelle replied. "Your client's name is Joe. You'll be meeting him in his suite at the Andaz Wall Street at 2 p.m. He works in international finance and is based out of Chicago but travels extensively. He's in town for a few key meetings and managed to get in a round of golf yesterday with my client."

Cynthia chortled. "Is there anyone who works in finance who *doesn't* play golf?"

Michelle smirked. "I doubt it."

The driver steered the limo off FDR Drive and wound his way up Water Street.

Two blocks from the hotel, Michelle withdrew a plastic hotel keycard from her purse. "Golf, actually, is why you're here. Yesterday, my client intentionally lost the round he played with Joe, and *you're* the prize. They bet such that the loser pays for the winner to spend two hours with a beautiful woman. That's you and, here, you'll need to use this key in the elevator to get upstairs. Floor 28, room 2831."

Cynthia took the keycard and put it into her purse. "I've always considered myself to be a real prize, but never thought about selling 'Cindy gift cards' before." She chuckled at the thought. "Speaking of payment...."

Michelle withdrew a thick envelope from her purse and opened it. She fanned eighty one-hundred-dollar bills for Cynthia to see.

Michelle said, "I'll have this for you here when we pick you up — if you complete the job."

"Oh, *trust* me," Cynthia said as she pushed a strand of blonde hair back behind her right ear, "Joe will be dreaming about me for a month."

"I have no doubt you'll be giving him the ride of a lifetime. But that's only part of the job."

The limo driver turned off Wall Street and onto Pearl. He steered the limo toward the curb and up to the hotel's entrance.

"What do you mean?" Cynthia exclaimed. "I thought — "

Michelle reached into her purse again and pulled out a small white plug, about one-inch square. "Joe's golf clubs are against the window in his hotel room near the wet bar. In the outer pocket of the bag is an iPhone. When he's not looking, insert this plug into the phone where the power cord goes. You *do* know your way around an iPhone, don't you?"

"Sure, but that's — "

"Good. I'm paying you a shitload of money for this, so make sure you do it right. Plug it in, count to five, and pull it out. It's that simple."

"What *is* that thing? What if he *sees* me?"

"He has to go to the toilet sometime during the two hours you're there. Or tell him to go wipe himself off with a washcloth between innings. I don't care. Get creative, if you have to."

The driver opened the curb-side door to allow Cynthia an easy exit.

Michelle put the white plastic plug firmly into the center of her new agent's hand and curled the woman's fist closed.

Cynthia frowned and recoiled slightly.

Michelle squeezed Cynthia's shoulder and, ever-so-gently, nudged her toward the open door. "Room 2831. Rock his world and make me proud."

Cynthia Robinson exited the car and turned to look back at the woman she thought she had gotten to know on their ride into the city. The well-paid escort realized with a start that, in truth, she knew nothing at all about the woman inside the limo holding an envelope of cash which no longer sounded like easy money.

The driver closed the door behind Cynthia, returned to the driver's seat, and pulled the limo away from the curb.

Cynthia looked at the doorman standing outside the hotel's entrance, then ran her eyes up the side of the tall building. "Oh, what the hell," she mumbled under her breath. "2831."

Chapter 10

Two hours later, Michelle smiled as Cynthia buckled her seat belt in the back of the limousine. The CIA officer looked intently at her new agent. "So? How'd it go?"

The blonde smiled and put her purse on the seat beside her. "It was easier than I thought it would be. Or, easier than I *feared* it would be after you pulled that last-minute stunt with the plug. His golf bag sat right where you said, against the window near the wet bar. He didn't let me out of his sight for the first hour—"

"Can you blame him? Look at you."

Cynthia grinned slyly and shrugged. "And, you know, I wasn't sure how I'd finagle getting him out of the room. But you were right, he was drinking enough beer that eventually nature called. As I was counting to five, I thought I was screwed. I heard the bathroom door open and, well... I hope I left it in there long enough. How do you tell? It didn't beep or anything."

"No, it doesn't. I'll find out later if it worked or not. It's too late now, so don't worry about it."

"What does it do?" Cynthia asked with honest curiosity.

"That's not your concern," Michelle replied, and pulled a white envelope from her purse. "What I'm sure *is* of concern to you, however, is this."

Cynthia took the envelope and rifled through the stack of Benjamins. "Thank you," she said, and looked at Michelle. Shyly she asked, "You mentioned another job. Is it the same kind as this? With a phone?"

Michelle shook her head. "No, every job is different."

"Well, if I do more work for you, I'd want to know everything about it *up front*, you know? No last-minute surprises, okay? You're the one who mentioned *trust*, right? So, I want to know in advance exactly what I'm getting myself into. I mean, what if Joe *caught* me? I'm taking extra risks here, so I deserve to be well-compensated. More than just two grand an hour."

Michelle didn't answer directly. She paused for a moment. "Now that I know you can handle being creative, we'll talk more about the next job *if* and *when* it materializes."

The driver turned off FDR Drive onto East 34th Street.

Cynthia looked at the street signs for the first time since getting back into the limo. A tinge of concern intruded upon her voice as she said, "This isn't the way back to the tunnel. Where are we going?" She turned her head to get her bearings in an unfamiliar part of America's most populous city.

"Macy's," Michelle answered.

"We're going shopping? I'm sure you can do better than *Macy's*."

"Not *we*, just *me*. I'll be getting out there to go meet my client and tell him the job is done. The driver will take you home or drop you off wherever you want."

"Home's fine."

"Good. Before I get out, give me your cell phone number so I can call you about future jobs."

Cynthia pursed her lips. "With all the 'homework' you said you did on me—even finding my home address—are you saying you didn't manage to get my digits?"

Michelle kept a straight face and replied calmly. "Let's assume for the sake of argument that I'm being polite and asking you for your phone number because that's the way normal people do this sort of thing. So, let's just pretend for a few minutes that we're both normal people."

Cynthia grinned. "I should be mad at you for what you sprung on me with that plug—*oh!*" She reached into her purse, pulled out a wadded-up tissue and offered it to Michelle.

"Here's the plug-thing back. You might want to wash it, though...."

Michelle's eyes opened wide, and she gave Cynthia a quizzical look. The CIA officer made no move to accept what the natural blonde held in her outstretched hand.

Cynthia continued. "As I was saying, Joe came out of the bathroom as I was putting his iPhone back into the golf bag. He walked over to me, and I had to hide the plug somewhere. I was naked so, you know, I didn't have a pocket. He came over to the bar to get another beer, and I had the thing in my fist, but didn't want him to see it. So, to distract him, I got down on my knees in front of him, and, well... you're a woman. I'm sure you get the picture. I had to hide the plug somewhere so, as you said, I got *creative*. You'll probably want to wash it off the first chance you get."

With just her thumb and index finger, Michelle gingerly picked up the balled tissue and dropped it into the outside pocket of her purse. She considered throwing her purse away once she got home and filing an expense report to make Michael pay for a replacement. Maybe stopping off at Macy's wasn't going to be just for catching a taxi after all. "Thanks," she said sheepishly.

As the limo pulled up to the curb outside Macy's flagship store, Michelle held out her hand. "I need the keycard back, as well."

"*Oh*, yeah." Cynthia fumbled through her purse and produced the hotel key for Michelle. "Here you go." Cynthia waved the white envelope full of cash in the air as the limo driver opened the door for Michelle to exit. "Thanks for this. I hope you *do* call me about the next job, but I really want to understand it completely before I say yes. Okay?"

Michelle stepped out of the limo, looked back at her first-and-only agent, and put on her best 'you can trust me face.' "Sure thing," she said, and walked off to catch a taxi back to the Andaz.

***

Michelle knocked on the door to room 2831 and shifted on her feet impatiently.

Josue "Joe" Reyes answered and warmly invited his guest in. He asked, "Why'd you knock, Michelle? Did you let Cindy keep the key?" He looked at the ceiling, put his hands together as if praying, and said, "Please tell me you did."

"No way, Josue. I simply wanted to be sure you were dressed."

Reyes looked at Michelle and put his hand over his heart. "I think I'm in love." He looked up and feigned falling backward into oblivion. "Or at least deeply in lust."

"She was that convincing?"

"Oh. My. *God*! Where do I even begin? She has the most incredible—" The technical services officer from the CIA's Directorate of Science and Technology—the DS&T—looked at the covert action officer and stopped. He straightened up. "I mean, the way she...."

Joe wiped a drop of spittle from his lower lip, and added, "Oh, *hell*, Michelle, this isn't fair. I can't talk about this stuff with a woman. Where did you find her, anyway? And more importantly, where can *I* find someone like that *mamacita rica*?"

"You can't and don't try. Besides, you can't afford her on a government salary."

"Well, she was worth every penny of whatever you paid her. When you called me up out of the blue on Wednesday and asked me if I wanted to get laid, I thought you were kidding. I mean, talk about workplace sexual harassment, right? Now that I think about it, if you *don't* set me up with Cindy again, I think I *will* report you."

Michelle laughed. "Oh sure, you're going to report to HR that you spent eight thousand dollars of the taxpayer's money to have sex with a high-priced escort? *That* would be a rather career-limiting move on your part, don't you think?"

Joe shrugged and considered the situation. "Eight grand? I didn't realize it costs that much to get a woman to sleep with me nowadays. I mean dinner, a couple of drinks and maybe a pair of decent tickets to watch the Washington Nationals play usually does it back home. I'm not even losing my hair yet. How can it have come to this *already*?"

Michelle smirked and walked to the nightstand next to the king-sized bed. She picked up the alarm clock. "Did you get the video of her at the golf bag from the concealed cameras?"

"Did I? Come *on*. You and I have been lab partners in three or four technical training classes now, right? Have I *ever* let you down? Anyway, we can see it from either angle — from the camera hidden in the clock or the one in the golf bag itself. Want to check it out?"

Michelle nodded. The tech officer pointed to an electronic tablet sitting on the table on the other side of the suite. He walked over to it and queued up the footage for his guest.

Michelle adjusted her chair in front of the table. "I hope you aimed the two cameras at the right spot, so we can see her using her plug on your iPhone."

"*Oh*, yeah! Tab A definitely went into Slot B this afternoon. Several times, in fact." Joe grinned wickedly.

Michelle shook her head and covered her eyes in embarrassment.

The clandestine audio-video recording specialist had no intention of telling Michelle about the third camera that he concealed in the ceiling-mounted smoke detector and aimed at the bed. That footage would forever stay in his private collection.

"Here," Josue said, and slid his finger across the screen. He pushed the triangular play button on the screen. "This is where she snuck out of bed while I went to take a leak. I turned the sound off so you... we, *um*... don't have to listen."

"I'm thankful for the small things in life," Michelle said, and turned her attention to the tablet's screen. The video showed Cynthia bending over in front of the golf bag. The naked woman found the iPhone in the exterior pocket and inserted the white plastic plug just as Michelle had instructed.

Michelle counted until Cynthia removed the plug. "How long was that? About four seconds?"

"Using the time marks on the video, it came to four point six."

"That's damned good."

"Yup, if this had been a real phone hacking implant operation, she would have been successful. She gets high marks in my book."

"I'll bet she does. By the way, here's the plug back." Michelle pulled the wadded tissue from the outside pocket of her purse and dropped it on the table.

Joe looked at the white blob. "When I walked over to the bar, I knew what she was up to, but only because I set the whole room up for this exercise just like you and I planned. Otherwise, it all seemed perfectly natural to me. Keeping the beer on top of the bar gave me a natural reason to approach her, and she was right there opening another beer for me like any good woman should."

"*Watch* it, now," Michelle said, and squinted at Josue.

"Oh, come on. I'm just egging you on. Anyway, Cindy's operational act was very discrete—completely clandestine. She gets top marks for an amateur. I never saw her holding the plug, either. It must have been in her left hand, but once she handed me the beer with her right, well, she, *um*, distracted me, so I had something else on my mind entirely."

"Yeah, I know exactly how you had some*one* else on your some*thing* else. She told me how she distracted you."

"She *did*? That's not fair. Can't I have a *few* private memories of just her and me? So, anyway"—Joe pointed to the tissue—"was it in her hand?"

"Yeah, it was in her hand at first. Then it was... well, somewhere else. She said you probably want to wash it before touching it or using it again."

"Oh, that's gross. No thank you. You can just throw it away."

"Why *me*? And don't you need it back? It's government property. Doesn't it have some kind of super-secret Agency spy tech inside?"

"First of all, she's *your* agent, right? So, she's *your* responsibility. And second, no, there's nothing special about that plug. It's just a power adapter left over from when Apple converted its iPhones from the old, wide, thirty-pin plugs to the new, small Lightning plugs. We bought those adapters in bulk back then but rarely need them anymore. Consider it a covert operations training placebo. Just chuck it."

Michelle walked to the bar and brought back a napkin and small trash can. She used the serviette to push the tissue wad off the table and into the small black wire basket. "Thanks, Joe," she said. "I appreciate your taking one for the team this week."

"No problem, Michelle. If there's ever a need for Cindy to have, maybe, you know... an annual refresher or something, I'm definitely your man. You can count on me."

Michelle smiled, patted the DS&T officer on the shoulder and headed for the door. She needed to report her success with Cynthia and see how Michael anticipated the CIA bringing her particular set of skills to bear on the operation he and Alex were planning with Rome Station.

From a booth in the hotel bar downstairs, Michelle texted Michael via the team's encrypted app. *Success in New York! What's next, boss?*

Michael replied: *We're on track in Rome. She did what you needed?*

Like a champ. Got high marks from my friend.

Can you have her in Rome in 10 days?

Michelle typed her answer: *I'm sure. Will confirm it with her tomorrow.*

Give her a day or two to spend the money.

$ ☺ $

You kids and your emojis. See you when you get here.

Michelle smiled and ordered a glass of Chardonnay.

Chapter 11

The bright-green sign on Highway 24 outside Jacksonville, North Carolina, read, "Marine Corps Air Station New River, McCutcheon Field." A large, white reflective arrow pointed to the right, but Zeki Aga kept the steering wheel straight. He drove past the exit and continued onto Route 17. His instructions from Sargon were clear: exact revenge on the Americans who killed his courier. Whether this particular Marine Corps unit was the one that conducted the specific attack on his people in Iran or not, Zeki didn't care. Sargon had given him and his partner their orders and, like loyal soldiers the world over, they faithfully planned their attack to achieve their king's goal.

Zeki followed the directions he'd memorized to take himself and his partner to Jacksonville Mall. There, he parked the car in the largely empty lot. At one end of the mall, the entrance to a former chain department store that had been a mainstay of American commerce sat shuttered. Streaks of swirled whitewash covered its doors and wide plate glass windows. At the other end of the mall, an appliance store saw little traffic on this early weekday afternoon.

Zeki's partner, Onur Tabak, grunted in relief as he twisted his portly frame out of the car, finally able to stretch his legs. The overnight drive from New York City left him tired and sore. Both men stretched their arms and backs as they walked toward the mall's entrance. Inside, they studied the directory and map to consider their options for lunch. They read the list of a half-dozen restaurants available and looked at a burger stand closely. Not seeing a sign advertising halal meat, they settled for slices of veggie pizza at Tony's.

Onur finished his lunch first and wiped a napkin across his lips. "I miss my beard, but the pizza's not bad."

Zeki looked around the empty corridor and nodded. "You'll regrow it when we get back home. For now, remember we're living undercover. And, for the record, I think the pizza in New York is better. This is too doughy."

Onur shrugged and watched his commander finish his last slice. "Let's check out the parking lot on this side of the mall and look for those stickers. Then, we'll look around the other side on our way back to the car."

The men stuffed their empty plates into the trashcan at the exit and walked into the mid-day sun. Two dozen cars sat parked almost randomly spread across the lot.

"Let's go buy coffees at the Starbucks across the parking lot," Zeki said. "It'll give us an excuse to be walking around the cars."

The men walked a row to their left on their way across the lot. On their return trip, they walked slowly down another lane.

"There," Onur said, dipping his head slightly in the direction of a car to their right. "The sticker on the back of the pickup truck."

"I see it," Zeki said. "That's the Osprey aircraft. Follow me."

He led Onur between the parked cars and into the next row. On the narrow, horizontal rear window of the pickup truck he saw what he expected to find.

"You see the circular black-and-red sticker?" Zeki asked.

Onur sipped his coffee and made a face. "This stuff is so weak. At least New York has passable Turkish coffee. And, yes, I see the Marine Corps sticker with the globe and anchor."

The men walked back to the sidewalk outside the mall and took the long way around to their car.

"Good, at least some of the pilots or their wives shop here," Zeki said. "We must be close to where some of them live. We'll look for that tonight. Right now, let's check into the hotel and see where we can buy the rest of what we need."

The men retraced their drive for a half hour and checked into a Residence Inn by Marriott not far off the highway. The two-room suite afforded them the space they needed for a temporary workshop and a kitchen for cooking both food and, Onur's personal specialty, homemade explosives.

Zeki plotted the locations of a dozen apartment and housing communities on a map while Onur identified the hardware and grocery stores most likely to carry the common household goods needed to create the means of their revenge against the Americans.

After dinner, the pair returned to Jacksonville and drove through apartment parking lot after parking lot, methodically looking for the right kind of car with both an Osprey sticker and military decals.

After almost two hours of driving, Onur pointed to an orange Jeep Wrangler. "There! It has the Osprey sticker on the cover of the spare tire mounted on the back. It's perfect."

Zeki slowed to a stop ten feet past the Jeep and ordered his partner out of their car. "Hurry. Check for other stickers on the car. Run!"

Onur lumbered through the parking lot of the East Fork Apartments and stole a glance at the sides and rear of the vehicle. He hurried back to the car, and Zeki started forward before the door had latched closed.

"It's there," Onur said, huffing. "A black-and-red Marine Corps sticker on the right-side window. I memorized the make and size of the tire as well."

Zeki looked around to see if they'd been spotted during their twenty-second stop. Confident they had not, he congratulated his solider, sped up and took the first exit out of the apartment complex's parking lot. "That's exactly what we came for. Now, we need to go shopping. According to Google Maps, there's a Lowe's hardware store just off Highway 24. They'll have almost everything we still need. We can buy the remaining ingredients like chlorine bleach and hydrogen peroxide at any supermarket."

He slapped the steering wheel with his open palm and smiled at his companion. "We will have our revenge before the week is out!"

Chapter 12

Cynthia Robinson sat in her hotel room across the small table from Michelle Reagan and turned toward the window to yawn. The two women admired the view of Rome's ancient domed, sand-toned buildings juxtaposed next to colorful and more angular examples of modern architecture.

"How was your flight?" the CIA officer asked her agent.

"Great. I know you said you paid for all travel, but I didn't expect you to pay for *business* class to Europe."

"I hope you get over your jet lag tonight. I need you well rested for what I've planned for tomorrow evening."

"That's when the client I'm supposed to pick up at the bar will be there?"

"Yup. You *can* pick up a middle-aged man who hasn't been laid in a while, can't you?"

"Like I told you on the phone last week, if I'm so out of practice on that front and it turns out I *can't*, then I not only won't take your twenty grand, but I'll give you twenty grand of my own. Unless the guy's gay, *I'm* your woman." Cynthia smiled. "And at the risk of being called egotistical, even if he is, I think I still have half a chance to make him at least bi-curious for one night."

Michelle grinned. "You certainly *are* a charmer, so my money's on you or I wouldn't have had you come all this way."

"Now that you bring that point up... I mean I'm already here and wouldn't be talking myself out of a lot of money, but why *didn't* you just hire a local girl? You know, instead of flying me halfway around the world?"

"That's a fair question. The reality is that Italy's quite a-ways outside my usual network. I need someone I can trust, and you also proved in New York that you can be creative when you need to be. Those qualities, combined with your boldness and natural charm, make me confident that you're a shoe-in. And that's what I need, someone who can indeed pick up a married man when you two just happen to meet in a seemingly random bar on a seemingly random weekday evening. Especially *this* guy, who has been faithful to his wife for decades. Of course, if it *were* as easy as New York, then I *would* simply hire some local girl and just send her to his room. That's most definitely not the case this time!"

"Well, thank you for the pat on the back, but why does your client want this particular guy to get lucky tomorrow night?"

"My client needs the gentleman in question to get his emotional shit together and agree to a very specific business deal. My client wants to get this guy into the right emotional state of mind to make that happen. Your client's name is Dario, and the problem is that, unfortunately, his wife has been battling a rather painful type of bone cancer for the past two years. Needless to say, that has been very stressful for both of them. They have the financial resources to travel as often as they need from Malta—where they live—to here in Rome and pay for the cancer treatments. That's not a problem. The issue—or at least *one* issue for Dario—is that the bone cancer eating his wife away from the inside is *sooo* painful that she hasn't been able to physically tolerate being intimate with him for a very—"

Cynthia waved her hand and nodded. "Okay, I get it. I don't need the unpleasant details. What's Dario's last name?"

Michelle rotated the glass of water on the table in front of her and tapped it gently on the paper coaster printed with a stenciled drawing of the hotel's façade. "This is where we need to talk about how you plan to get him interested in you. It's not that I don't want you to know his last name, but since you don't already know him, you wouldn't have any way of knowing it tomorrow when you just happen to sit next to him in the bar downstairs. It'd be too strange and would probably scare him off if you slipped it into the conversation accidentally. I also don't want you to react oddly if he lies to you and tells you his last name is Smith or Jones or something he makes up on the spot. Does that make sense?"

"Sure. Got it," Cynthia said. "No problem. I never asked Joe his last name in New York, so, you're right. It doesn't matter."

"Good. If he tells you his name, then fine. If not, then in reality, you shouldn't care this time, either. Now, as for you two hooking up, the easiest way for me to put you in the same room with him is for you to be already sitting at the same end of the bar he always sits at. He comes here regularly after his wife has a medical treatment. The drugs take the wind out of her sails, and he leaves her to nap upstairs while he enjoys a few drinks before dinner."

"They stay in *this* hotel?"

"Yes, usually upstairs on the club level."

"So, I might run into him afterward?"

"You *do* think ahead! I like that. We're going to get along really well. No, I've thought of that, too, and got you a hotel room at the airport. So, you'll meet him downstairs in the bar tomorrow, bring him up to this room and make his day. Once you're done, I'll get you a ride to the other hotel. I will have already checked into that room for you and have the room key in my purse. If all goes well, you can fly home the following morning."

Cynthia looked out the window and watched a half-dozen birds land on the roof of the centuries-old bleached stone building across the street. "What if he doesn't show up to the bar? Or he has to stay at the hospital with his wife or... you know, has to take a business call or something?"

"If he doesn't show, and we have to try again the next night, then we'll do that. If he never shows up, and it's a complete bust, as I said on the phone, I'll still pay you half of the agreed upon amount for your time."

"I'm confident I can get him into bed," Cynthia said, and shook her chest. "I have a winning smile." She grinned wickedly and tapped a fingernail on the small table between the women.

Michelle smiled. "Good, now that *that's* settled, tell me why a beautiful woman like you is sitting here in a bar all alone in this gorgeous city."

"What do you mean? You paid for—"

"No," Michelle said, and grinned slyly. "At some point in the conversation with Dario, he's going to ask you the stereotypical bar question of what's a beautiful woman like you doing in a place like this. You need a story so believable that's it not simply going to *allow* him to accept your eventual offer of sex, but rather it'll make him feel like you *need* it more than he does. Like you *deserve* it. That it's his *duty* as a man to satisfy your unfulfilled needs as a woman. And you have to do it without either of you ever mentioning his wife, which would almost certainly scare him away in a heartbeat. You're going to have to convince him that sex with you is not cheating on his never-to-be-mentioned wife, but, instead, you two are simply a pair of deserving but neglected human beings who so desperately need each other to fill the emotional abyss into which you both stare each and every day. It *has to* feel to him like mutual therapy and not a torrid one-night stand. So... what's your plan?"

"Oh, jeez. I hadn't given it that much thought. I figured I'd charm him with the usual bar talk and—"

Michelle crossed her arms for effect. "For this to work, you need a solid back story and a damned good reason to be drowning your own sorrows at *that* particular bar in *that* particular city at *that* particular time. If you're simply there for a roll in the hay, it'll never work."

Cynthia inhaled deeply and held her breath until it hurt. She exhaled slowly and studied a dozen black birds in the distance circling whatever they were hoping would be their next meal. The woman half-way through her second master's degree looked at Michelle and tilted her head. "In the limo in New York, you told me you always made detailed plans and leave nothing to chance. So, I'm guessing you already have the answer you want to hear in mind. You've already thought this through, planned for this and are simply going to tell me how this is going to go down. It doesn't even matter what I might think of, myself, does it?"

Michelle smiled broadly. "Brava, Cynthia. Beauty *and* brains." She reached into her purse and placed a diamond ring on the circular table between them.

With a hot-pink fingernail, Cynthia nudged the four-carat rock set into a platinum wedding band and whistled softly. "Shouldn't you be on one knee for this?"

Michelle chuckled. "It turns out that your fictitious husband is down the street attending the medical convention underway there this week. He's a cardiac surgeon in Philadelphia where you two live. He's been spending fifteen hours a day at the convention for the last few days instead of showing you the sights of this gorgeous and historic city like he promised. You realized too late that he just wanted you here as arm candy to show you off to his European colleagues. He's hoping your winning smile earns him an invitation to speak at another medical convention planned for Geneva later this year. It's been like that between you two for the past few years—ever since you told him you wanted to start a family. He has barely touched you since then, at least while he's sober. And when he's drunk, well... you do everything you can to stay away from him on those nights. Tomorrow, while you're at the bar downstairs telling your sob story to Dario, your never-there and horribly neglectful husband will be playing golf with a few other doctors at the Tiber Golf Club a few miles outside the city."

Cynthia recoiled in mock horror. "That *bastard*!"

Michelle chuckled. "You probably should have seen it coming after you heard about the way he treated his first wife."

Cynthia shook her head, leaned back in her chair and smiled. "You're a class act, Michelle. You really do plan for *almost* everything, don't you?" She swept her right arm around the room, and said, "But you forgot—"

"And just for show," Michelle said, interrupting, "I have a suitcase to bring up from my room which has your philandering husband's clothing and toiletries in it."

"Oh, so the *bastard* is cheating on me, too? I should have known." Cynthia laughed and raised her hands in surrender. "Okay, I get it. You're good."

Michelle raised her hands face up and shrugged. "What can I say, I'm detail-oriented by nature. By the way, since your husband doesn't want to have kids, there are even a couple of condoms with the toiletries, so there's no need for you and Dario to make a pit stop in the hotel store on your way upstairs."

Cynthia shook her head slightly. "How in the world does someone get a job like yours? Even if you started out as an escort—and you could do *very* well at it, Michelle, I should know—the jobs you get are so... I don't know, so utterly *foreign*. I mean, you obviously have corporate clientele with deep pockets, but *who*? The trading desks of investment banks or hedge funds or something?"

Michelle pursed her lips as she considered her response. "Nobody puts out help-wanted ads for the work I do. I just fell into this line of work by happenstance when someone offered me an opportunity out of the blue. It started out with small jobs and, over the years, things have grown well beyond anything I could have imagined back then. What about you? How did you get started?"

"Well, that's pretty much how it went for me, too. I was a broke college sophomore hanging out at a bar at the South Street Seaport in Manhattan just hoping to get a couple of free drinks on a Friday night. I think I was more bored than looking to meet guys. In the ladies' room, I ran into one of the Resident Assistants from my dorm the year before. She said I looked sad, and maybe I was. Out of the blue, she asked me if I wanted to make four hundred bucks that night. She'd been in the business for three years and had a client who unexpectedly showed up with a buddy of his. She didn't want to entertain both guys that night, so she asked me if I'd be interested."

Cynthia watched out the window as a green-winged bird dove out of sight behind a blue-striped building. Four other birds sitting on a nearby ledge dropped off and followed it down. "After that night, one date led to another. I gradually built up my client list and landed a few regulars. I even worked through an agency for a while, but I didn't like that arrangement. The owner took too large a percentage of each date."

Michelle didn't mention that it was Cynthia's association with the woman running the so-called agency that led Wilson Henry to her in the first place. After the FBI arrested the madame, the G-men uploaded the woman's contact list into their database. Although Cynthia had never been arrested, Wilson found her particulars in that list and traced her address by geo-locating her burner cell phone. The fact that Cynthia successfully flew below law enforcement's radar for so long made her a prime candidate for Michelle to recruit for the CIA's occasional needs.

"Eventually," Cynthia said, "I landed a partner at one of New York City's Financial District law firms as a regular." She stabbed her finger in the air at Michelle. "*That's* where the real money is."

"Lawyers?" Michelle asked.

"Not so much the lawyers themselves, but their clients. Lawyers are boring homebodies for the most part, but their *clients* are all the wannabe bad boys who like to party far, *far* too much. That's gold, I'm telling you. When the *lawyers'* clients become *your* clients, that's when the real money rolls in. They're the ones who deal in cash and have plenty of it to burn. More than a few of them want to party like it's going out of style, and so they'll have something to remember while they're serving a five-to-ten-year sentence for fraud or tax evasion or whatever. So, now I'm on cruise control until I decide to retire and hang up my stilettos for good."

Michelle stood up. "Before you do that, I hope to have a few more jobs for you, but as always, it'll be up to you. Anyway, I'll go bring your absentee husband's suitcase up, and you can unpack his clothes while you think through how you're going to tell your sob story. I'm sure it'll be convincing and full of real emotion. After lunch tomorrow, I'll show you Dario's picture, and we'll get you all set." She pointed to the ring on the table, and said, "Also, you should try to get used to wearing that, so it feels natural."

The CIA officer left the room and returned ten minutes later with a black garment bag. She said goodnight to Cynthia and urged her to sleep off her jetlag.

After leaving her agent's room, Michelle walked down the hall until she felt confident Cynthia could neither still see her through the door's peephole nor was likely to open the door to call out to her. Once safe, she doubled back down the hallway and gently knocked on the door to the hotel room two down from Cynthia's. A man in his mid-thirties pulled the door open wide, and Michelle entered.

"You're smooth, Michelle," Johnny Riordan said. "We watched it all on CCTV. Are you sure you're not a trained case officer?"

She smiled at the youngest of the impromptu Task Force's three CIA case officers—someone whose full-time job is manipulating foreigners to betray their countries and work for the United States. "No, John, I'm just a simple country girl—an Okie from Muskogee."

Johnny snickered at the kind of self-deprecating phrase so often uttered by case officers as they softened up would-be assets and tried to appear more like straight-forward, down-home folk than devious international spy masters. He led Michelle from the bedroom into the expansive suite's central room. Johnny had rented the two-bedroom ensemble for the CIA's use in Cynthia Robinson's part of the group's operation. The bedrooms at opposite ends of the central living room were individually accessible from the hallway and, when the connecting-room doors were closed and locked, appeared no different than any of the other five-hundred guest rooms in the hotel.

Michelle hadn't told Cynthia that her room was one of the suite's two bedrooms. The escort had no idea that the CIA had an entire monitoring team working in the large living room between the bedrooms. The Agency's technical team had watched and listened to everything the two women said in Cynthia's room.

Three CIA technical services officers from DS&T would stay holed-up in the suite for the duration of the operation. They'd watch, listen to and record everything said and done in Cynthia's room via the bevy of concealed cameras and microphones they'd installed before Michelle's new agent arrived.

As Michelle entered the living room, she waved hello to another Rome Station case officer, George Mattson, and the three-man DS&T monitoring team. The tech officers gave her silent "golf claps" for her performance next door. She had watched them spend the past two days preparing the suite for Cynthia's arrival and recovering from their own jet lag, having crossed the Atlantic Ocean only a few days before Michelle's new agent had.

George rose to shake Michelle's hand. "The deputy chief of station walked in just about the time you started talking with Cindy next door. I thought you did a great job, but I'm not sure she did. While she watched you and Cindy, she was sweating and looked like she feared you were going to flub the recruitment and agent tasking. Don't tell her I said this, but she acted way too much like an instructor at the Farm who was just *dying* to criticize a student in the middle of an exercise." He squeezed Michelle's shoulder, and added, "But *I* think you did great. Hard to believe it's your first one."

Michelle thanked George for the professional compliment. "I spend so much time undercover and spinning tales of my own that, after more than a decade of this, it comes naturally. Maybe *too* naturally sometimes."

The bathroom door behind the suite's wet bar opened, and a soft voice Michelle had never heard before joined the conversation. "So, *you're* the Agency's madame, are you? Or this is just what you SAC fucks do for fun in your spare time when you're not getting us involved in some pissant war in the Middle East or Africa?"

Oh, hell, Michelle thought. *Who peed in her Rice Krispies this morning?*

"You must be Helen," Michelle responded, and turned around. Michelle did a doubletake when she saw that the five-foot-nothing figure standing in front of her with hands firmly planted on her hips did not match the mental first impression she'd formed upon hearing the new voice.

"Michelle, is it? I didn't get your last name," Helen Sapienti said. "You call *that* a recruitment? I think we'll be lucky if Cindy doesn't bolt for the door before dinner."

"It's good to meet you, too," Michelle said.

"You're putting this whole operation at risk," the woman with jet-black hair said as she waved her arms about, "and you don't even realize it. What I just watched was amateur hour. You may be in the Directorate of Operations, but you need to leave the real spy work to us. That's what *we* do for a living. What is it exactly that you do?"

Keep up this attitude, lady, and I may be tempted to show you. "Well," Michelle said, "it's complicated."

"Recruiting and running agents is *complicated*," Helen retorted. "You're out of your league and need to go home. I've already put the request into Headquarters Station to have you removed from this case and for *my* station to run the show."

Oh, hell, is she going to ruin everything? She must have sent that request to Langley before coming to the hotel to see how things played out. This is our only link from Dario to Sargon. She better not.... Michelle couldn't be sure Helen didn't have the political pull to get the change approved but decided to bluff. "I'm sure your request will be given all the consideration it warrants," Michelle said, "and I'm equally sure it will be summarily denied. Would you care to place a wager on that?"

Helen scowled at Michelle, and hissed, "You've got some set of balls coming into *my* city and telling *me* how to run operations here."

George Mattson stepped up to the women. "Do you two want to keep your voices down to a low roar, please? Cindy's still right next door."

Helen Sapienti looked at Mattson and furrowed her pencil-thin eyebrows. "What's the status of the tech installation?"

George pointed to the tech team at the table. "The tech services guys have all the cameras and mics up and running and everything checked out perfectly. They have the two concealable cameras and radios for Johnny and me to wear tomorrow night in the bar when Cindy meets Dario. They'll charge the batteries overnight, and we'll be good to go."

"*Good*," Helen said. She looked at Michelle and growled under her breath. "Just make sure you understand that *I'm* running this operation and we need to get a few things straight right from the start. *I* give the orders, and *you* follow them. *Capiche*? I need to know I can trust you to do your job and not interfere in my case officers' work."

Out of the corner of her eye, Michelle saw one of the DS&T technical services officers grimace at Helen's putting her DO officers in the preeminent position on the team and diminishing the role the technical experts would play. As often as they hear comments like those, the TSOs never get used to them. To Helen, Michelle said, "It's a mystery why you and Carl got divorced. I just *can't* figure it out." Michelle's lips stretched into a wry smile.

Helen poked her finger into Michelle's stomach. "Just do your work and don't get in my team's way."

Michelle ignored her and walked over to the conference table on which the DS&T techs had set up their computers and video monitors. Three high-definition screens showed Cynthia Robinson unpacking her mythical husband's suitcase. One of the DS&T techs handed Michelle a set of padded-leather earphones so she could hear Cynthia's rustling with luggage and clothing in the adjacent room.

Michelle watched Cynthia inspect the contents of her "husband's" Dopp kit before arranging the never-to-be-used toiletries around the bathroom sink. She removed two Brooks Brothers suits from the garment bag and hung the thousand-dollar threads in the closet. She pulled a dresser drawer open and started to load it with men's briefs.

"*Eew!*" Cynthia screamed and dropped a pair of underwear on the floor. Under her breath, she said, "She never said the underwear would be dirty."

Cynthia shook her head and went to the bathroom where she selected a washcloth from the pile of towels neatly stacked on a wooden shelf under the sink. She returned to the dresser and used the small towel to pick up the worn briefs and deposit them into the dresser drawer.

Cynthia quietly pushed the drawer shut and threw the washcloth into the corner of the room. "Details are one thing, lady, but *that's* just gross. Your money's green, but I don't think I can take any more surprises."

The DS&T tech removed his earphones, and softly said to Michelle, "She is *not* going to be happy with you tomorrow."

Michelle handed her headphones back to the tech, and thought, *I'm not sure I'm going to be happy with me tomorrow, either.*

Chapter 13

Late the following afternoon, Cynthia Robinson entered the hotel bar at a quarter after six, precisely as instructed. She wore a knee-length floral pattern skirt and white Cashmere sweater over a pink sleeveless blouse. Her choice of attire highlighted her size-three figure and small C-cup chest spectacularly. The diamond wedding ring on her left hand glittered in the soft glow of the lights hanging from high above the cherry-wood bar. As Michelle had coached her, Cynthia sat in the third seat from the wall and ordered a glass of Chardonnay from Italy's Marchesi di Barolo winery.

In the suite upstairs, Michelle sat at the conference table between Eric Connors, the task force's third case officer, and the three DS&T techs. She and the TSOs watched silent video transmitted by cameras concealed in George Mattson's tie clip and Johnny Riordan's lapel pin. Unbeknownst to Cynthia, the pair of undercover CIA officers sat across the room from her sipping their own drinks and pretending not to watch the gorgeous woman at the bar reading the news on her cell phone.

Michelle frowned. "Too bad we can't listen to what she and Dario say. I'm *dying* to hear how she's going to make this happen."

One of the DS&T techs shrugged. "How hard can it be for a gorgeous woman to pick up a guy at a bar? But anyway, Helen decided it wasn't worth us bugging the bar itself, and from where they're sitting, we wouldn't get a clear ear on the targets from most body-worn microphones. It'd require a shotgun mic in a briefcase and probably some post-processing amplification and noise reduction, so—"

Michelle held up a hand. "Thanks, but forget I asked."

The tech sat back, and his shoulders slumped.

Michelle felt bad she had shut him down so directly and, sensitive to what she knew was coming, didn't want to leave yet another upset man in the suite.

"I'm sorry," she said. "I'm not technical. But I get it, though— they're too far away, and it'd be too hard to hear without a lot of other sophisticated electronics."

The tech's eyes brightened slightly, and he pointed to the screen. "No problem, and there's our guy."

A tall, lanky man in his late fifties settled into the seat against the wall at the end of the bar, leaving the seat between him and Cynthia empty. Dario Turchi raised his hand to get the bartender's attention and gave a nod, signaling he wanted his usual.

Michelle watched the two figures on the screen sit in silence. While they were within arm's reach, they had not yet crossed the invisible barrier of the empty chair between them.

Turchi stirred his drink and took a sip. Cynthia appeared disinterested and shifted from reading something on her cell phone to looking at the bartender off to her right.

Michelle leaned forward and unbuckled the straps of her high heels. She tossed the pair onto the end of the sofa behind her and leaned back in her chair to watch her pick-up artist work her magic.

Turchi stirred his drink and an ice cube popped out with a splatter. It skittered a half-dozen feet down the polished cherry wood and stopped in the middle of the bar. He looked down, groaned and brushed a drop of liquid from his tie.

Cynthia extended her left hand to the napkin holder next to the plastic swizzle straws in the bar-top container and waited.

Turchi remained engrossed in drying his tie and didn't realize until too late that his hand was not the only one reaching for a napkin.

The two figures on the video monitors recoiled from their "unexpected" contact, and Dario Turchi apologized to Cynthia profusely.

Michelle could imagine hearing his effusive expression of contriteness, followed by Cynthia countering with a "no, it was my fault" riposte. Her "woe is me" act wouldn't start until later.

The DS&T tech farthest from Michelle spoke first. "We have con-*tact*."

The tech in the middle nodded. "That was clever of her. Do you really think she'll be able to pull this off, so we can get at the USB drive in his necklace?"

"I have every confidence in her," Michelle said, "but if it turns out he *is* gay, we'll send *you* in to take her place."

The tech's face turned bright red, and he sat back silently.

The two figures on the screens continued to talk and, before long, began to smile at each other.

At one point, Cynthia motioned to the bartender and pointed to her empty wine glass. Turchi pointed to his own glass and then to himself.

"He's buying another round of drinks for them. This seems to be going well," one of the techs said.

The tech closest to Michelle leaned closer to her. "Two drinks is just lubrication. But four drinks... well, now, that's fornication."

The other techs chuckled.

Michelle leaned back and crossed her arms. "I wonder how many drinks it's going to take for him to realize she's a sure thing?"

The tech closest to her shook his head. "He's a married man not looking to get laid. Is he thinking about it? Hell, yeah, just take one look at Cindy and half the Vatican would be thinking about it. But she has her work cut out for her tonight. My money says he resists her charms and stays faithful to his wife."

"I hope you're wrong," Michelle muttered, and the four of them watched the scene play out in high definition. "I really do."

One of the monitors seemed to shake as Johnny Riordan's face flashed across the screen. The video feed from George Mattson's tie-clip camera bounced unevenly as he stood up, walked out of the bar and continued down the hallway. Riordan's lapel-pin camera remained steadily aimed at Dario and Cynthia while George's seemed to float down the hallway. A disembodied hand pushed open the men's room door, and an array of brown marble sinks and white porcelain urinals came into view on the screen.

The feed seemed to zoom in on a chrome handle as George bellied up to a urinal.

"Okay," Michelle said to the tech next to her, "we don't have to watch this, do we?"

"Sorry!" the middle tech exclaimed. He reached for the monitor and pushed the power button to turn it off. "I'll give him a few minutes to get back to the bar. The system records everything, but I don't think we'll need to review that part later."

"I certainly hope not. I have a really good idea where Cynthia's going to end up later, and it ain't in there."

On the other monitor, they watched the blonde closely as Cynthia appeared to be telling Dario a story. She waved her hands in circles to emphasize whatever point she was making.

Michelle inhaled deeply and raised her bottle of water in a salute to her agent. "She's good, but here's to hoping that tonight she's great."

Dario's and Cynthia's conversation continued into their third drink of the evening and that's when the scene changed. The smiles disappeared, and Cynthia's rose-red lips pouted. She leaned closer to

Turchi, spoke softly and gestured defensively. Her earlier grandiose arm movements evolved into delicate finger motions up and down his forearm.

Turchi nodded and nursed his drink as Cynthia spun her yarn. The conversation continued until Dario Turchi stood up.

"Uh oh," Michelle said under her breath.

"What the hell's going on?" the tech next to her asked rhetorically.

The tech in the middle made a comment about it being too bad no one had taken his bet.

Turchi pushed his chair back up to the bar, reached his hand out and squeezed Cynthia's shoulder.

"Is that a good thing or a bad thing?" a tech asked.

"Cynthia's not moving. This can't be good," Michelle replied, barely above a whisper. *Oh shit, what's going on? Is it over?*

The video from George's tie-clip camera showed Turchi exit the bar and Johnny Riordan standing up to follow the subject. George stayed seated as Johnny followed Turchi.

On the third monitor, Riordan's video feed followed the rabbit down the hall and disappear into one of the side doors. The view from Riordan's camera closed in on the sign to the men's room, and the CIA officer pushed it open.

Turchi stood at the urinal farthest from the entrance. Riordan approached the first tall, white porcelain urinal. Its chrome handle and plumbing valve filled the TV screen in front of Michelle. One of the techs reached forward to turn the monitor off.

"No," Michelle insisted. She leaned forward and wrung her hands. "I need to see what Dario does. This is important."

Riordan finished first in the bathroom and walked out the door.

"At least he washed his hands," Michelle said to break the tension.

Riordan's video feed showed him exiting the men's room and walking away from the bar. He sat down in a large leather chair facing back up the hallway toward the men's room and the bar. He picked up a magazine from the adjacent table and opened it onto his lap.

Michelle and the three DS&T techs watched Dario Turchi exit the men's room and stop in the hallway. She stared intently at the target of her operation as he took a long look at the bar where the object of his desire sat nursing her third glass of wine. Then, his eyes shot to the bank of hotel elevators that offered him an easy means of escape.

On the other video screen, George's camera showed Cynthia sitting at the bar, touching up her lipstick.

Dario Turchi stood undecided in the hallway outside the bar as he pondered his next move.

"Will he or won't he?" the tech next to Michelle asked the universe.

Michelle held her breath and silently urged Dario to think of his own urges.

She didn't have to wait long for an answer to the tech's question. Turchi turned toward the bar and took the seat next to Cynthia.

Michelle smiled at the screen and gave a single clap. "*That's* thinking with your head, Dario."

On screen, Cynthia smiled, too. She resumed her conversation with Turchi, and they both drew their chairs closer together.

Turchi ordered another drink for himself and offered one to Cynthia. She waved off his suggestion, but when he persisted, she accepted his advance.

"Playing hard to get," the tech in the center said.

Michelle bobbed her head slightly. "Yeah, and now she's going to let him chase her until she catches him."

The tech next to her squinted as he replayed Michelle's statement in his head. Once he caught on, he smiled and nodded. "You really know how to be devious and screw with men's heads, don't you?"

"*That* particular genetic trait is on the X chromosome," Michelle offered. "I have a double dose."

On the screen, Cynthia returned to telling her tearjerker of a story. Turchi caressed Cynthia's shoulder through her thin sweater.

"I should have taken your bet," Michelle said to the middle tech.

"It's not over yet," he said.

"Oh, *yes*, it is," she said, and leaned back. "Hook, line and got-you-now, you stinker."

Cynthia returned Dario's affections. She held his hand in both of hers and leaned into him. She rubbed the back of his hand with a light touch as she closed in and made her maudlin plea.

Dario Turchi signaled the bartender for the check. He charged the tab to his credit card and held Cynthia's chair for her as she stood up.

Michelle clapped her hands twice, and announced, "Drop the mic."

The DS&T tech at the far end of the table turned to the third computer monitor and cycled it through multiple views of Cynthia's room next door. All six cameras worked perfectly.

"We're good to go," he reported as Cynthia and Dario disappeared from the other two screens. "The happy couple will be out of our view until they get to the room next door." He looked at Michelle. "Helen didn't think it was worth the risk of us tapping into the hotel's closed-circuit TV system, so we're blind until they get up here."

Michelle nodded and frowned at the small chip in the nail polish of her left index finger.

"Don't worry," Helen Sapienti said from across the room. "I think your girl will get us everything we need tonight."

Michelle spun around. "You've been so quiet back there. I almost forgot you were here."

Helen shrugged. "I'll admit, I had my doubts, but it's been fun listening to the four of you act like NFL commentators on the game going on downstairs in the bar. As soon as our two lovebirds get up here, I'll text George and Johnny to let them know they can come back up safely and watch the fat lady sing from our box seats in here. Then, we'll all get ready for the third act of this play."

"I would say break a leg," Michelle added, "but you might take me literally."

Helen smirked. "I only took one theater class at Yale, and that was because my roommate talked me into it as an elective. Interestingly, that class was taught by the same professor who consults for the CIA. A few years later, I almost had a heart attack when he walked into our classroom at the Farm to teach our operations class the kind of acting skills we'd need for undercover work. Kind of funny running into him again in such a different context. Where did you go to college?"

"*Me*?" Michelle asked. The high school graduate who never spent a day on a college campus — if you don't count two nights at frat parties — answered, "I've got a Ph.D. in screwing people over from the school of hard knocks."

Helen jutted her chin at the video monitor showing Dario and Cynthia entering the adjacent room.

One of the DS&T techs glanced at Michelle. "From the looks of it, you graduated Cum Laude."

"*Eew*," Michelle responded. "Why do you men always have to make everything into a sex joke?"

The tech to his right shrugged. "We're guys. If we didn't, there'd be nothing else for us to talk about."

"Quiet, everyone," the lead tech whispered, and pointed to the monitors. He handed headphones to Michelle and Helen to listen to the sounds of puckers and smooches starting in earnest in Cynthia's room as clothing flew over chairs and onto the hotel room's dresser.

In the central suite, the exterior door opened, and George Mattson and John Riordan walked in, eager to see how the rest of the operation would play out. The men crossed the room and joined the small crowd that had its eyes glued to the trio of video monitors on the table.

"And now for our feature presentation," Johnny said quietly. He looked appreciatively from screen to screen at the peep show playing from three angles.

Michelle took her cue and walked over to the sofa to pick up her shoes. She took them into the suite's empty bedroom, placed them on the dresser and retrieved one of the plush white bathrobes hanging in the closet. Then, she rejoined the crowd around the large table in the suite's living room.

The three video screens displayed different views from cameras concealed in Cynthia's room. One focused on Dario Turchi's face as he lay naked on the bed and enjoyed Cynthia's rhythmic movements on top of him. A second camera showed a wide-angle view from behind Cynthia. Her pale, bare back arched, and she swung her blonde hair in sync with her pelvic gyrations.

Helen narrated the action on the screen. "Ride 'em, cowgirl."

Michelle gave her a pained look.

"*What*?" the deputy chief of station complained without taking her eyes off the third screen.

Michelle asked, "Carl never really got to know the real you, did he?"

Helen shrugged and continued watching Cynthia.

The central monitor showed the view from the camera concealed in the ceiling-mounted smoke detector above Cynthia's bed. Dario's enthusiastic expression was fully visible, as were Cynthia's bouncing breasts. The combination of her flinging her long hair from side to side and her erect nipples thrusting forward kept Helen's eyes glued to the screen.

The DS&T tech on the end clicked his computer mouse to freeze the on-screen action. With another few clicks, he backed the video up a half-dozen frames. He selected the specific view he wanted and printed a full-color, eight-by-ten snapshot of the couple *in flagrante delicto*.

Helen Sapienti twirled her index finger in the air and mouthed the words "line up" to two of her case officers. She walked to the front of the line and took her position at the intra-suite door to Cynthia's room. Johnny Riordan and George Mattson lined up behind her holding the printed photo. A barefoot Michelle Reagan pulled up the rear, robe in hand.

One of the DS&T techs gave a thumb's up signal to Helen. She twisted the deadbolt lock to the adjacent room and pushed the door open. The line of undercover CIA officers burst into the room.

Helen asked loudly, "What the hell's going on in here?"

Cynthia screamed and rolled off Dario. She tried, only half successfully, to pull the bed's top sheet over herself.

Dario Turchi's face froze in fear of having been caught in the act with another woman. His face registered the range of questions he peppered himself with: Was one of the men her *husband*? What the *fuck* is going on? Is this a *robbery*? Who the *hell* are all these people?

Michelle rushed to Cynthia's side and held the robe up to her shoulders. Earnestly, she insisted, "Here, put this on and come with me!"

Cynthia's face flushed. "What the *hell*?"

Michelle didn't let her finish and wrapped the robe around her asset's assets. "Come with me right now," she repeated, half-prodding, half-pulling Cynthia through the intra-suite door and into the living room that, seconds earlier, Cynthia hadn't even known existed.

The two barefoot women surged through the suite as three DS&T techs stared at the stunned woman. Cynthia's eyes opened wide as she tried to make sense of the sudden intrusion, the table full of laptop computers and three large video monitors all sitting only twenty feet from where she had just been having sex. As Michelle pushed her forward, Cynthia craned her neck to get a better look at the three men staring at her from the suite's long, wooden dining table.

Michelle forced Cynthia through the far door and into the second bedroom. She shut it behind them and wrapped the robe around Cynthia. She half-spun Cynthia to get a better angle on the robe so she could pull it closed in front of her agent.

Cynthia shoved Michelle's hands away and recoiled onto the corner of the queen-sized bed. She tried, mostly unsuccessfully, to draw the robe closed across her mid-section. The highly paid escort shook uncontrollably and fumbled with the robe's belt until she got it tied well enough to stay closed.

Michelle sat on the bed next to Cynthia and reached her arm around the shaken woman, but Cynthia pushed her away. The CIA officer moved to the opposite edge of the bed and quietly sat an arm's length from the woman she'd paid to fly across the Atlantic Ocean just two days earlier.

Tears streamed down Cynthia's face, and she cried silently. Michelle walked to the bathroom to get a box of tissues and offered them to Cynthia. The sobbing woman reluctantly accepted two, and her sniffles grew steadily louder.

Michelle sat silently while Cynthia recovered enough from the shock of the evening's events to be able to talk.

She looked at Michelle with red-streaked eyes. "Who... who are all those men?"

Michelle answered simply, "They're with me."

The tears started again and flowed in steady streams across Cynthia's flush cheeks. What began as soft moans grew louder and Cynthia convulsed a few times as she wept.

Michelle handed Cynthia several more tissues and waited patiently until she was ready to continue talking.

After a minute and a half, Cynthia asked, "You... you *planned* this whole thing? That's your job, isn't it, Michelle?"

Michelle nodded.

"It's not about the sex, is it?"

Michelle shook her head.

Cynthia loosened the robe's belt, slid her arms into the sleeves, and pulled it around her firmly. She retied the belt, crossed her smooth legs and dried her cheeks with the robe's left sleeve.

"In New York," Cynthia asked, "it was all about the cell phone, right? And here, it... it...." She took a deep breath and looked down at her hands in her lap. "That picture. The one the man who barged in on us was waving.... It was a photograph of me and Dario in bed, right?" She wiped a tissue across the bottom of her nose and looked up at Michelle.

Michelle paused momentarily, then nodded.

Cynthia tilted her head at Michelle. "Are you going to say something or just sit there?"

Michelle locked eyes with Cynthia. "Thank you for doing your part so well. You are truly an amazing woman."

"Seriously! *That's* all you have to say to me after having a bunch of strangers barge in on me with a client?"

Michelle kept her eyes locked with Cynthia's for emphasis. "Cynthia, there's an important point you have to realize here, and that is that *I'm* your client, not Joe and not Dario. Do you understand? *I'm* the one who pays you, and that's all that matters."

"I... you...." Cynthia broke from Michelle's focused gaze and stared down at her own bare toes. "So...." She buried her face in a tissue and wept.

Michelle slid a foot closer to Cynthia but made sure to not touch the confused and upset woman. Michelle gently tugged the bottom of her own blouse and smoothed out the top of her cream-colored skirt. She picked a piece of white fuzz from the hem, flicked it onto the floor, and tried to recall why she'd chosen to wear that outfit instead of her black capri pants. She decided she'd wear the capris the next day.

Cynthia dropped her hands to her lap. Her voice trembled as she asked, "What's going to happen to Dario? Are you going to tell his wife? That's *not* what I agreed to."

Michelle answered quickly. "I understand that you're confused and want to know more about what's going on, but from this point forward, he's not your concern. You'll fly home tomorrow afternoon and never see him again. You've earned your money, and I'll pay you every penny of the twenty thousand dollars I promised."

Cynthia's jaw quivered. She met Michelle's gaze and held it for a moment. "I *knew* something didn't feel right when you offered me so much more money than I normally make to do your jobs. But it's a *lot* of money, so I said 'yes.' I feel like an idiot now. The sex is just some kind of excuse to get close to people, isn't it? First the iPhone and now this. When we first met, you said you provide your clients with 'special services. *Very* special services,' or something like that."

Michelle nodded. "Yes."

"This is one of those services, isn't it?"

Michelle nodded again.

"What's going on in the other room, now?"

"My friends are talking to Dario. That's all. He's not going to be harmed."

"Talking to him about what?"

"The business deal I mentioned yesterday, but the details don't matter. You did your job flawlessly, and I'll pay you every penny I promised."

"But what's with that picture of him and me?"

"I understand that you want closure, but in truth, it doesn't matter. Your part's done, and you did it remarkably well. I'm impressed. You're a rare talent."

Cynthia realized she wasn't going to get an explanation from Michelle, so she probed. "You're blackmailing him with that photo, aren't you? You told me he's married, so—"

"It's best for us to just leave that part of the conversation there, I think."

Cynthia frowned and gestured to the wall behind which three CIA case officers were threatening to show the picture of her and Dario to his wife if he didn't cooperate. "So, you were watching on those TVs everything that happened in that bedroom, right?

Michelle nodded.

"And recording it?"

More nodding.

"So, in the bedroom, I was the one getting *screwed*, but now Dario's the one getting *fucked*?"

Michelle smiled inwardly but didn't respond directly. Instead, she changed the subject. "When you get home, I'll arrange for either the limo driver to hand you an envelope of cash or, if you'd prefer, I can FedEx you a check made out to look like it's a scholarship payment. It's your choice. Just let me know which you'd prefer."

Cynthia cocked her head to the side. "You can do that?"

"I can do a lot of things."

Cynthia looked down and picked at the cuticle of her pinky. "Apparently so."

Cynthia jumped at the sound of a knock at the door.

Michelle stood and gently laid her hand on Cynthia's shoulder. "Don't worry. It's just your clothes."

The CIA officer answered the door to the suite's living room, took the neatly folded clothes and pair of shoes Johnny Riordan held out for her, and closed the door without saying a word. Michelle laid the small pile on the bathroom vanity and sat back down next to Cynthia.

"What happens now?" Cynthia asked.

"Now," Michelle answered, "you get dressed. Then I'll have that nice man drive you to the Airport Hilton. You'll order room service for dinner and charge it to the room. I'll pack up your suitcase from next door and bring it over to you in about two hours." Michelle pointed to the now-closed door. "That man's name is John. He has the key to your new hotel room. I checked into the Hilton for you earlier this afternoon, so you can head straight upstairs."

Cynthia reflected on Michelle's plan. "Yesterday, you mentioned the hotel by the airport. You knew what was going to happen and that I wouldn't be able to stay in this hotel anymore, so, you planned *that* in advance, too. Everything you said would happen *did* end up happening, just not at all like I expected. Damn, girl, you're thorough. And *devious*."

"I also ordered a bottle of white wine and some chocolate-dipped strawberries for you at the Hilton. That way, you'll have something special waiting for you in the room when you arrive."

"You did that for *me*?" Cynthia asked, incredulously.

"Of course. You did a great job here, Cynthia, and I want you to know how much I appreciate it. I'm a very good friend to those people I can count on."

A tear slipped from Cynthia's left eye, and she choked as she spoke. "Thank you. By all rights, I should hate you, but... thank you for that, anyway." She scrunched her upper lip. "And the money? I *do* get that, too, right?"

"Yes, absolutely." Michelle put her left arm around Cynthia and squeezed. The robe-clad woman shook twice and laid her head on Michelle's shoulder.

Michelle squeezed her firmly and offered a friendly warning. "With all the alcohol you've had tonight, I don't want to give you a sleeping pill, but the extra wine in your room should help. I already set the alarm in your new hotel room for 10 a.m.—just in case. Tomorrow, you can sleep the whole flight home."

Cynthia lifted her head from Michelle's shoulder and looked at her. "Damn. What have you *not* thought of?"

Michelle grinned. "It's my job to be thorough."

The CIA officer stood up and padded barefoot to the door. "You get dressed while I check on your ride to the Hilton, okay?"

Without waiting for an answer, she slipped into the suite's living room leaving Cynthia to freshen up in the bathroom and get dressed.

In the suite's central room, Helen Sapienti and the three DS&T techs peered over a video monitor. Lines of computer code streamed up the screen.

Michelle looked at the screen, and her eyes glazed over. "So, did it work?"

Helen grinned from ear to ear. "Oh, yeah. My plan worked like a charm."

What the hell? Her *plan!* Michelle thought, struggling to keep a neutral expression on her face. *What a bitch!* The back of Michelle's neck turned red.

Helen continued, "I told Dario that, as we like to say here—*tenere qualcuno per le palle*—we had him by the balls. He took one long look at the photograph I shoved in his face, and he folded like a cheap accordion. He was so petrified that we'd out him to his sick-as-hell wife and her rich-as-fuck family that he gave me everything I asked for. He gave up the necklace he keeps the USB drive with the banking information hidden in and told us how to access everything: his client list, their bank account numbers, PIN numbers, his fingerprint for the bank's biometric security system and, very conveniently, the passwords."

"Wow," Michelle said, choosing to stroke Helen's ego, "you guys must have been very convincing." Helen's team got everything Michelle and her boss wanted. Picking a fight with Rome Station's deputy chief served no purpose other than possibly to alienate her ex-husband in Malta, whom Michelle might need in the future.

Helen cracked her knuckles, grinned broadly and boasted, "No one does it better than Rome Station."

Michelle pursed her lips, and agreed. "Impressive."

Helen pointed to the video monitor which showed a naked Turchi being questioned by George Mattson. "George is debriefing him on as much operational tradecraft as we can learn about how Dario moves the terrorists' money throughout Europe and the Middle East to avoid anyone tracing it. It's good stuff, and we're recording it all on the DVR. We're keeping him naked because —"

"Thanks for mansplaining Interrogation 101, Helen. It's not my first time, you know."

Helen looked closely at her guest. "Michelle, do you know what the two most powerful human emotions are?"

"Love and hate, I suppose."

Helen shook her head emphatically. "No, but that's the most common misconception. The two emotions which will drive someone past his or her breaking point and their ability to act rationally are, one, the desire to be accepted and, two, the fear of being rejected. Tonight, we used both against Dario. First, he found it impossible to push himself away from Cindy's sob story, feminine wiles and tits to die for. Ultimately, he couldn't save himself from getting her to demonstrate her ultimate acceptance of him by dropping all her defenses and letting him take her to bed. Then, after we barged in on them, we shoved indisputable photographic evidence of his being unfaithful to his wife right under his hang-dog face. He had no way to deny the obvious, defend himself or escape from the situation we steered him into. One second, he was in ecstasy with Cindy and the next, we rocketed his brain out of a cannon all the way to the opposite end of the emotional spectrum when we threatened to show his wife that photo. His fear of rejection by the woman he loves and who depends on him in her time of need cracked him wide open. He gave up his clients in a heartbeat, knowing it was the only way he could avoid crushing his sick wife. As ill as she is, the news of his infidelity might very well kill her and piss off her family, who would certainly ensure he got none of her money once she died."

"Wow, you're quite the professional anti-Cupid, aren't you, Helen?"

"I do what I can to ensure America comes out on top in our ongoing games of international tug-of-war. It's not my job to help the Turchis stay married."

"No, marriage is not your strong suit," Michelle said, and pointed to the series of emails streaming up the central computer monitor. "But if you want to be helpful, you can explain the tech stuff."

"I'll let the TSOs do the honors, but I did want to mention that although we ran this op here in Rome, we need to have a case officer from Malta Station be Turchi's handler for future contacts. I'll hand him off to Carl. As inadequate as he is in some areas, running agents is something he's actually pretty good at. He'll do well for you, should you need more information from Turchi later." Helen clapped one of the DS&T techs on the shoulder. "You can do the honors and explain the geeky stuff to her. I'm going to light up a cigarette on the balcony."

"Sure thing," the TSO said, pleased to be able to talk to Michelle more. "Turchi kept his email decryption key in a USB drive on his necklace, concealed inside his crucifix. He never took it off, so, uh, anyway, I know it was really *you* who figured out how to get it from him, no matter what Helen says. We uploaded everything we got to the Center for Cyber Intelligence, CCI, back at Langley. They'll use that crypto key plus the password he gave us to decrypt his emails. The analysts back home can start sorting through them in a few minutes."

"Cool," Michelle said.

"The analysts back in Virginia are going to have a field day with all the emails between Dario and whoever he's been chatting with. There's a *lot* to go on. The crypto key on the USB drive unlocked an archive of all their instructions for illicit payments and the accounts' PIN numbers. From what we've seen so far, the emails include names, dates and amounts of the payments and transfers he's made on their behalf. With what we've got, plus the high-resolution copy of his fingerprint George took a few minutes ago, the CCI can now track all his wire transfers, both incoming and outgoing. We're in like Flynn."

Michelle patted the tech on the shoulder. "Great job, guys. Keep up the good work." She knew her team's analyst, Wilson Henry, would be going through Turchi's email archive and account records within the hour.

Michelle brushed her hands together as if cleaning them off. "Looks like I'm done here, so I'm going to get Cynthia on her way to the Hilton." She looked over at Riordan. "Johnny, you ready to go?"

He gave her a mock salute. "Born ready."

"Good," Michelle said. "I need to make a phone call."

Chapter 14

In the kitchen of their Residence Inn suite in North Carolina, Sargon's solider Zeki Aga watched as his explosives specialist Onur Tabak carefully drained the homemade concoction from a Pyrex pan. He watched intently as the last of the final batch slowly dripped into the spare tire they'd purchased to replace the one mounted on the rear of the Jeep they'd identified the previous day.

Once he scraped the final drips of gray, creamy plastic explosive from the pan, Onur handed it and a stained spatula to Zeki, who placed them into the sink.

Tired, Onur removed his work gloves and tossed them onto the coffee table. He grabbed a chair from the dining room table and positioned it in the suite's living room under the air conditioning vent. He dropped his large frame into the chair roughly and grunted. He fanned himself and enjoyed the cool breeze falling upon him from above.

Zeki sat on the sofa a few feet away and put his feet up on the coffee table. He groaned. "That took longer than expected. I don't remember the last time I worked in a kitchen all night. Probably never, but at least it's done. Next time, we'll need more men for this kind of thing. I underestimated the amount of work it takes for even the small volume of plastique we need for this attack."

Onur bobbed his head up and down lazily. "Yeah, but it wasn't so much a large volume of explosives, as much as too small a workshop to do it in. If—or when, really—we cook more in the future, we'll need more time, more men *and* more space." His stomach growled. "And more food!"

Zeki was too tired to laugh but grunted approvingly.

"In a minute, I'll place the remote detonator inside, but I need to sit here for another minute or two. This process is always easier when I'm teaching it to the recruits back home. Doing it oneself is a real chore."

Zeki chuckled. "Yeah, you don't get to pop out for as many smoke breaks when you have to do the work yourself. Well... no one ever said that serving the sultan and our cause would be easy, eh?"

"No," Onur agreed, "but it will be worth it in the long run."

Zeki stood and twisted his back until it let out a pair of cracks. "Indeed, but in the meantime, I need a glass of water."

Onur raised his hand. "Me too, if you please. After that, it's time for the last layer of ball bearings and the detonator. Then, we'll wait until it all dries before putting the tire onto the rim. But first things first. If water is all you have, then water will have to do."

***

In her hotel room in Rome, Michelle pulled her shoes off, sat down on the edge of the bed and rubbed her feet. "Oooh," she said with relief, and slowly thumbed through her cell phone's list of apps. She tapped on the icon for the team's encrypted voice and texting app and pressed the contact at the top of the list to call her team lead.

Michael answered on the third ring. "How did everything go in Rome?"

"Oh, man," she replied. "We got everything we needed, and I'm glad it's over. Just between you and me, Carl Sapienti gets this year's award for the man best able to tolerate a complete bitch. *Now* I understand why they got divorced."

"I'll take your word for it. I've never had the pleasure of meeting Helen, but I do want to congratulate *you* on a job well done. *Very* well done, in fact. You successfully recruited and ran your first agent, Michelle! I'm impressed. That's not something we non-case officers ever get to do. It's a specialty we're not trained for, but maybe you're a natural. You should be very proud of yourself. I am. And now we're going to do more of the work you and I *are* trained for."

"Really? What's on tap?"

"I'll explain when Alex and I see you in France."

"*Ooh la la*! Where in France?"

"Nice."

"I'm beginning to like these assignments around the Mediterranean. A girl could get used to the warm breezes and having wine at lunch every day."

Michael snorted. "I'm glad you're enjoying it because we're going to be here for a little while longer. Wilson got quite a lot of data back from DS&T once they decrypted the two laptops you liberated in Iran. Plus, we now have the information from Dario Turchi on the bank accounts he manages. The analysis is still ongoing, but Wilson has already traced the money to a boutique commodities trading firm in Nice. We're going to figure out how to disrupt the flow of money to Sargon. I'm still working on the plan. When you join us in Nice, you, Alex and I will figure out how to get the information we need from the commodities brokers here in France. We need to figure out how the money gets from these brokers to Sargon. Then we can take the fight to the man himself."

"Well," Michelle said, "I'm sure in Nice I can find a bottle of white wine from a Bordeaux winery I haven't tried yet. Sounds like fun. Text me the hotel's address, and I'll see you there tomorrow afternoon. Cynthia's pretty shaken up. I want to make sure she gets to the airport on time tomorrow for her flight home."

Chapter 15

Late that night in North Carolina, Zeki Aga and Onur Tabak rolled the tire out of their hotel suite and looked around the dimly lit parking lot.

"It's clear," Onur said softly. "No one's out this late at night."

"We can't be too careful," Zeki replied. He pushed the tire down the sidewalk and rolled it over to the waiting car.

Both men grunted as they hefted it into the trunk.

"Oh, man," Onur complained as he settled into the passenger's seat. "That was heavy. And I thought carrying all those bags of ball-bearings out of Lowe's was going to break my back. At least there we had shopping carts."

"Yeah, they're heavier than the machine screws and bolts, but packing all layers of ball bearings into the tire with the explosives is what we need to do the trick for this mission."

"I know. I'm just venting. Sorry. I'm more used to cooking the explosives than lugging the finished product about," Onur said, and stretched out his shoulders. He picked up a four-way lug nut wrench from the car's floorboard. He twisted the X-shaped tool in his hands while Zeki drove out of the parking lot and onto the highway.

A half-hour later, they arrived at the East Fork Apartments. In the parking lot, Zeki turned off the car's headlights and slowed to a stop just past the orange Jeep. He left the car running in case they needed to make a quick get-away and glanced at his watch. The pair of glowing mechanical hands showed the time as just after 3 a.m. He jabbed his finger at the trunk-release button, and whispered, "Okay, Onur, let's be quick *and* quiet."

Onur exited the car first and looked around for early risers heading to work, residents out walking dogs or anyone returning home from a swing shift. Satisfied the coast was clear, he lifted the trunk's lid and helped Zeki remove the explosives-laden tire.

The two Turks, who had worked for Sargon's trucking company for the better part of the last decade, made quick work replacing the original spare tire on the Jeep with their own. Once done, they capped off their creation by replacing the cover over the new tire, ensuring the sticker of the V-22 Osprey sat upright—the same orientation as it did before their switcheroo.

Back in their car, Zeki drove to a shopping center a half-mile down the main road. He parked the car in a lot across from the apartment complex's entrance and within walking distance of a twenty-four-hour Dunkin' Donuts at which he bought coffee and muffins to last them through the morning.

Onur announced his distaste for the weak American coffee, and the men settled in to wait and watch for the Jeep to leave for the morning.

Not long after 6 a.m., Onur's heart froze as he heard sirens blare from the road to their right. As the wail got louder, his hand instinctively contracted, crushing the remaining half of a blueberry muffin.

The men didn't realize they were both holding their breaths as they watched two white-over-blue North Carolina State Police SUVs speed past them on the main road.

After the second disappeared around a bend, Onur rubbed his chin and exhaled in a high-pitched wheeze. He asked, "Do you think they're looking for us?"

Zeki jutted his jaw forward and slowly shook his head. "No. I can't see why they would be. They passed both us and the apartment complex without slowing down. I think we're in the clear."

Onur looked at him sideways, slightly reassured but still not happy. He brushed muffin crumbs from his pants onto the floormat and looked around nervously.

After a minute, he said to Zeki, "I need to use the bathroom." He pointed behind him. "I'll go to the Starbucks over there. Want anything?"

Zeki looked to where his partner was pointing. "No, I'll go after you come back. I'll wait here in case the Jeep shows up. When I go later, if you have to follow the Jeep while I'm in the bathroom, you *do* know how to use the remote detonator, right?"

"Yes, Zeki," Onur said with mild irritation, and reached for the door handle. "I *can* push a simple button."

One after the other, the men returned from the coffee shop with large cups of what they still considered a weak blend. They waited another half-hour in the car until Onur pointed across the intersection.

"There!"

Zeki nodded and drew his lips back in a half-smile. "Finally," he muttered. He started the car and followed the day-glow orange Jeep from a distance.

The Jeep headed West along Route 24 and turned south toward the Marine Corps Air Station. After it turned right at the traffic light leading to McCutcheon Field, Zeki turned left into the parking lot of a strip mall replete with a grocery store and a half-dozen fast-food restaurants. He parked next to three other cars in front of a dry cleaner and left the engine running.

From the passenger seat, Onur watched the brightly colored Jeep inch forward in rush-hour traffic toward the gate at the Marine Corps base. One by one, cars and small trucks approached the large guard shack and vehicle inspection station protecting the base and its combat-ready aircraft and crews.

Zeki shifted in the driver's seat and, to himself, said, "*Allll-most* there." He peered intently through the rearview mirror and mumbled, "A few more seconds...." Slowly, he eased his car out of the parking spot and toward the strip mall's rear exit. To Onur, he said, "Count down from five and then press the button."

Onur silently mouthed the countdown in Turkish: *beş... dört... üç... iki... bir.* He jammed his thumb onto the black button in the middle of the repurposed garage door opener and instinctively closed his eyes.

The force of the blast shot two hundred superheated ball bearings that Zeki and Onur had packed around their improvised explosives through the Jeep's rear window and to every side. The superheated grapeshot shredded the female Marine who had just checked the Jeep owner's military ID and motioned him forward. Two Marines inside the guard shack died instantly from the blast wave's overpressure. The colonel driving the car behind the Jeep was beheaded by the explosion, two weeks to the day before he was due to retire.

Black smoke rose from the remnants of the orange Jeep which came to rest on its side. Fuel tanks of three other cars waiting to enter the base erupted in sympathetic secondary detonations from the heat of the spare tire's blast.

Zeki slapped Onur on the thigh, made a right turn at the traffic light, and pulled the car onto the main road to merge into traffic. "Well *done,* brother! Well done. These stupid Americans will spend months or maybe years and many millions of dollars reinforcing their military base entrances against another such attack—an attack we will not repeat. These people always prepare for the previous battle, not the next one. This is just the beginning for us. Be proud of your achievement here today. Let's go back to New York and report our success to His Majesty. We are going to be *celebrated!*"

Chapter 16

Tamerlan awoke to a rapid knocking on the bedroom door. He rolled over and rubbed his face as the unfamiliar surroundings came into focus. Slowly the memories returned, and he recognized the bedroom in Sargon's guest house.

"Come in," he said hoarsely, and squinted toward the door.

One of the young housekeepers opened the door halfway. Tamerlan remembered the teenage girl from the day before, when he arrived from Iran. She smiled at him. "I'm not allowed inside the rooms when a guest is inside, but His Majesty sent word that you are to go to his house after breakfast. I will put your breakfast on the dining room table while you're dressing. We have eggs, cheese, vegetables and *sucuk*—Turkish sausage. Do you like spicy foods?"

Tamerlan swung his feet over the edge of the bed and sat up. The blanket fell away revealing his bare torso.

The house girl stepped further back into the hallway and shifted her gaze to look down the hall and not at Sargon's guest.

Tamerlan looked at the girl who recoiled from him back into the safety of the hallway. He thought, *A year or two younger than me, maybe? She's pretty, even in that drab work dress.* "Yes," he said, "I *love* spicy food." He stood up and stretched his arms toward the ceiling, partly to wake his muscles from a good night's sleep and partly to show off to the pretty girl.

"Good," she said. "I'll have it ready for you very soon." Slowly she pulled the door closed, but not too slowly to get a good look at the sultan's guest standing in nothing more than his shorts.

Tamerlan looked toward the girl, and thought to himself, *Did she just smile at me?* As the door latched shut with a solid metallic click, he concluded, *I think she did!*

***

In the two-story foyer to Sargon's house, Tamerlan gawked at the brightly colored art adorning the walls. In one corner, small, elegant paintings hung almost from floor to ceiling. Opposite them, two tall Persian rugs hung from the walls to each side of the receiving room—or perhaps it was what rich people called a *parlor*, he thought, but wasn't sure. No one in his village had a home even a quarter the size of His Majesty's.

Tamerlan looked closely at a pair of stone vases on display and leaned in closely to inspect the human figures painted on each. He craned his neck around the side to try to follow the action and figure out what the line of eight people were supposed to be doing.

A man's voice startled Tamerlan. "Those vases were liberated from the basement of an Iraqi museum," he said. "When the Crusaders invaded, untold thousands of pieces of our people's history were looted by thieves. Those two were recovered by the faithful and given to Sargon to protect. He displays them proudly here for all to see. They belong to all of us. They are an integral part of our culture."

"You are Iraqi, then?" Tamerlan asked the tall, thin man.

"No more than you. We are all brothers. Arbitrary lines on a map mean nothing. The countries created by the Crusaders when the British colonizers left this area a century ago mean nothing to me. You and I, however, *we* are joined by our faith, dedication to the caliphate and unwavering loyalty to His Majesty Sargon the Third. The sultan told me of your battle with the Americans and how bravely you fought against them."

Tamerlan stood up straighter. "I shot one of the soldiers before he could escape, but the others pulled him into their helicopter plane before they flew away, so...."

"You're a brave young man. I look forward to working with you. My name is Bayram."

"*Working* together?" Tamerlan asked, surprised.

"Yes. You'll be my new assistant driver. You know that Sargon owns a trucking company, right?"

"Yes, my uncle was a driver. He used to do work for His Majesty from time to time in Iran, but *I* don't know how to drive. I was learning to be a shepherd."

"That's a wonderful profession, but with what happened in your village, Sargon told me he wants his bravest men to work directly for him. I'm to teach you how to load and drive trucks. We'll start here over the next couple of days, and then you'll accompany me to make a special delivery in France. Sargon's counselor, Rifaat, is working on getting you an identification card, but you won't need a passport to travel throughout the European Union. A smart young man like you — I can tell you're going to do well here. Yes indeed. Very well. We'll have a lot of fun, too, you and I. It'll be a blast. That much I can promise you. Would you like to learn how to drive a truck?"

Tamerlan's face brightened, and he smiled broadly. "That sounds *great*! My family never had enough money to buy a car or truck, but I really want to learn how to drive. By the way, Bayram... Do you happen to know the name of the servant girl in the guesthouse? The one with the white rose embroidered onto her black dress?"

Bayram chuckled and smiled. He put his arm around Tamerlan's shoulders and guided the horny teenager toward the front door.

***

Sargon slid his finger slowly up the iPad's screen as he read the short news article about the explosion at an American Marine Corps base in North Carolina. He grinned as he handed the tablet back to his counselor and clapped the man on the back. "Wonderful, Rifaat! That's terrific news. Well done. Express my appreciation to Zeki and his team."

"Yes, I certainly will. They put their training to good use. Very creative and effective."

"It was a good first attack." Sargon looked over at the tall man and pointed at him with an extended index finger. "You see what's possible when you don't try to micromanage good men from this far away? We let them use their own judgment and creativity, and they did not disappoint."

"It worked out very well," Rifaat agreed, "and is a model for our future attacks. But not for Paris."

"No," Sargon said, and lowered himself into a chair against the wall of his office adjacent to his throne room. "*That* will require more coordination. Is the boy ready?"

"No, certainly not yet. Bayram is out now teaching Tamerlan how to use the truck's liftgate to load and unload cargo. Then he'll go over the basics of driving the particular two-ton truck our mechanics altered for the trip to Paris. In a few days, the boy will be ready to start working as an assistant, and that's all we'll need him to do. Bayram will do the driving. Right now, he's talking up the boy's courage under fire from the incident in Iran. That, and some driving lessons, will be all the motivation needed to get the boy to be *eager* to go to Paris."

"Good. That fucking little coward let a thief escape from Smugglers Respite with laptops containing extremely valuable financial information—*my* financial information. I do *not* tolerate failure."

"Of course not. He will serve your purpose in Paris, just as you ordered."

Sargon nodded and stood up. "Make sure of it, Rifaat. Meanwhile, come. You and I have other work to plan. It's time for us to send out the two teams that just completed their advanced training. I've decided to send one to London and the other to join our recently successful brothers in America for their next attack—in Los Angeles. We will take our successes to the next level and bring the Crusaders to their knees in their own countries."

Chapter 17

Low, gray clouds obscured the sun over southern France as Michelle Reagan entered the Hotel Villa Eden on Nice's famed Promenade des Anglais. She walked up the stairs of the budget hotel and knocked on the door to Michael's second-floor room.

He opened it and, without a word, stepped aside for her to enter.

"What a dump," Michelle said. "Why'd you pick this place? I'll bet it was because of the name, right? *Thanks*, boss. I appreciate the thought, but just so you know, I appreciate room service more."

Alex finished sweeping the room for listening devices and removed the antenna from the scanner. He shook his head to his partner. "Room's clean. No bugs." He returned the equipment to its nylon case and sealed the Velcro enclosure.

Michael gestured to Michelle. "Help yourself to a bottle of water, if you'd like. But no, I didn't pick it because of the name. This small hotel's out of the way, not conspicuous and is not the kind of place our rich targets are going to have any friends or informants in. No one's going to pay any attention to people staying at a place like this. The French *Gendarmerie*, *Deuxième* intelligence service and all the opposition intelligence agencies will spend their limited resources watching the pricier hotels where Comrade Oligarch and Sheik Oil Cartel like to rent out entire floors for their entourages. We'll be much safer here for what we have to do."

"And what would *that* be?" Michelle asked, and sat down in the chair at the small desk at the far end of the room.

"Oh, you're going to like this one," Michael said, and grinned.

Michelle squinted at her team lead and crossed her arms. After a few moments of staring at him, she asked, "Why do I get the feeling that I'm really *not*?"

Michael smiled broadly. "Surveillance galore."

"That's the way *every* mission starts," Michelle said with a grunt. "What's so special about this one?"

"Three of them," he answered, "and three of us."

- 83 -

"Not possible," Alex interjected. "Even a Girl Scout could spot us."

Michelle pointed to her partner. "I may share my ammunition with you on occasion, but do *not* get between me and a box of Thin Mints."

"Actually," their team lead cut in, "you're right, Alex. We'll need some help on this one. And just for reference, Eden's right, too. Don't risk life or limb just for a cookie."

"*Just* a cookie?" Michelle exclaimed. "Those are not *just* cookies."

"Important survival tip," Alex said to his boss, and grinned at his partner. "I'll remember to buy my own. So, who's going to be helping us? You bringin' in a team of surveillance specialists to do the heavy lifting?"

"Not exactly, but wait until you see the toys I've ordered up from headquarters. You two got to train with the electronic gear last year at the Farm."

Alex perked up. "Are you talking about the remote con—"

Michael nodded and interrupted, saying, "Yep, but Logistics won't have it here for a few days. First, boys and girls," he said, and pointed to a flat package on the hotel room's desk, "take the maps out of the folders in there. We have some low-tech planning to do. I need to figure out whether we're going to go hunting first, or fishing."

Chapter 18

The next morning, the sun rising over Nice shone brightly through a patchwork of high, wispy white clouds.

"Holy Mother of Mansions," Alex said over the team's encrypted radio. "Look at that place."

"Apparently, crime really *does* pay," his team lead responded. "I'm sure his guest suite is larger than my entire house."

"While you two debate which realtor you want to call for a showing," Eden said, "I'm set up for a north-bound takeaway. Let me know when you see the boss man leave for work."

"I'm in place to the south. I have the eye," Alex advised.

"I'm entering the hotel parking lot now," Michael reported. "And while the other two commodities brokers have nice condos closer to the city, this guy's certainly not shy about flaunting his ill-gotten gains, is he?" Michael asked rhetorically. He parked his car in the parking lot of an upscale tourist hotel on the exclusive peninsula of Saint-Jean-Cap-Ferrat just east of Nice. Formerly home to kings and princes, Cap-Ferrat's exclusivity and year-round good weather attracts a modern jet-setting crowd which considers being a multi-millionaire as barely middle class.

While he awaited Alex's radio transmission that the senior commodities broker they were surveilling that morning had left his gated estate, Michael watched cars pass on the main street in front of him. A Mercedes S800 with dark tinted windows slowed along Boulevard General de Gaulle and turned into a small country club. *Time for your tennis lesson, is it?* he thought.

Alex's voice over the radio intruded on Michael's thoughts. "The gate's opening now. Wait one."

Michael adjusted the vent to blow cool air in his direction. After the overnight rain, the strong sun heated up his rented Peugeot, straining the underpowered air conditioner.

"Yeah," Alex continued, "that's his car. White 8-Series BMW convertible." Alex narrated the car's departure until Eden confirmed she saw it.

"Heading north on the M125," she reported. "I have the eye."

She followed her target north off the peninsula and onto the scenic Boulevard Napoleon III coastal highway, toward Nice. On their half-hour drive into the city, she and Alex traded off the eye several times. As the rabbit's BMW exited the highway in downtown Nice, Michael took the exit three cars behind the subject's car and reported to his team that he now had the eye.

He followed the BMW through several turns and onto Boulevard Gambetta, a main north-south street in the heart of the ancient French city. He continued behind the target's car at a safe distance and watched it enter the gated garage in the commodity trading firm's building. At the next intersection, he turned north to rejoin his team at their hotel.

Eden was already halfway through a bottle of water when Michael arrived.

With his cell phone pressed to his ear, the team lead entered the room. "Okay, Wilson, thanks. Let me know if you hear anything more specific."

"News from the home front?" Eden asked.

Michael nodded as he ended the call and plugged his cell phone into the wall to recharge. "Wilson's been on the phone with NSA non-stop, but they haven't found any links between our three traders and Sargon's group."

Eden sat down in one of two underpadded chairs against the window, twisted the cap off her bottle of water and let out a dejected, "Hmmphf."

Michael took a bottle of water for himself and sat in the chair opposite Eden.

"These guys will be easy targets," she said in a more upbeat tone. "What now? We've gotten a good sense of their usual movements—home, work, country club, a few overly expensive bars and high-end restaurants. Nothing we've seen over the last week of surveillances has gotten us closer to figuring out who their contact is."

"Well," Alex offered sarcastically, "if all else fails, we can just ask, 'Pretty please, with a cherry on top.'" He pulled a chair out from the desk and straddled it to sit facing his team lead and partner.

Michael looked at him and furrowed his brow. After a moment, he said, "You know, Alex. That's a very good idea."

Alex looked down the bridge of his nose at Michael. "I was kidding, boss. Although maybe if we softened one of them up with a few knuckle sandwiches, he might be more agreeable. None of these guys would know the first thing about resisting an interrogation."

"Properly used, aggressive techniques like that may eventually get us what we're after, but I'm not sure that's our best play here. I do have an idea, though, but even *I* don't have the authority I need to use the resource I'm thinking of. Let me make a few calls up the chain back home and see if there's a vacancy at the inn."

Eden's head tilted slightly. "What *inn*?"

"Well, it's more like a specialized bed and breakfast. *Very* specialized. The Special Activities Center euphemistically calls it the Roach Motel. I should get a quick 'yes' or 'no' answer from up above with just a phone call or two. Either they'll let us use it, or they won't. I should hear back within the hour. Even if I do get permission, though, we're going to need some help from Carl Sapienti and Dario Turchi to pull this off."

***

Just after noon, Carl Sapienti stepped onto the sidewalk of St. Ursula Street in Valletta, Malta, and sped up until he was abreast of Dario Turchi.

The banker looked over at the CIA officer and grumbled. "I'm late for a meeting with a client." He hoped the case officer would turn away and leave, but he also hoped his wife's cancer would go into remission. Neither seemed likely to happen on its own.

"Good to see you, too, Dario. I need you to make a phone call to your friends in Nice."

"Haven't you people done enough to me already?"

"This'll be easy for you. Just a phone call to introduce your friends to a new client who's looking for professionals to clean his money from some less-than-ethical business dealings in Africa and send it all into a new, clean bank account in Bucharest or Berlin or Brussels, or wherever."

"Just a phone call?" Turchi asked, looking sideways at Carl.

"Yup, just a simple phone call."

"And who's the new client."

Carl Sapienti smiled. "Me."

Chapter 19

"But, Michael," Eden groused, "she already doesn't like me. I don't think she'll go for it again. Not after what I did to her in Rome. She doesn't trust me."

Michael shrugged. "That's what running an agent is all about, Eden—gaining and manipulating their trust. Make the call to Cynthia and extend the offer. You'll never know until you try. After all, if you never ask, the answer is always 'no.' Besides, it's good money for her, and she seems to really enjoy the kind of work she does."

Eden glanced at the clock on the hotel room's nightstand and did the time-zone math in her head. It was just after 9 a.m. in New Jersey. Cynthia Robinson would most likely be awake and still at home. Eden twisted her cell phone in her hand and lazily thumbed through her contact list while trying to think of what to say to a woman most likely to simply hang up as soon as she heard Eden's voice.

She tapped the number and waited for the international connection to complete. Cynthia answered and, as soon as she heard Eden's voice, she yelled, "*You* did this to me!"

"Cynthia, I know you didn't like how the last job ended, but that's over. You have to put it behind you. You did get my check, right?"

"Yeah, and now that bastard wants half of it. *You* sicced him on me, didn't you? Everything was going fine until I did your two jobs. It's all *your* fault!"

"Wait, Cynthia, what are you talking about? Who sicced who on who?" Eden asked, confused. She pulled the phone away from her ear as Cynthia screamed out her frustrations at the woman she blamed for ruining her life.

Eden listened intently to her agent for two minutes and looked at the carpet as she paced around Michael's hotel room.

"I don't know anything about what you're talking about, Cynthia. You did a great job in Rome, and now I have another job for you back here in Europe. You—"

The high-paid escort continued her verbal assault on the CIA officer. Eden let the upset woman vent and explain the situation in more detail.

When the other end of the telephone conversation went quiet, Eden said, "I see. Well, I'll have to get back to you about that. I'll give you a call back as soon as I can, Cynthia, I promise."

She pressed the red button on the screen of her phone ending the call and looked at her boss. She took a deep breath. "Michael, we have a problem. How far are you willing to let me go to get Cynthia on board with your new plan?"

Her team lead glanced over to Alex and then back at her. To Eden, he asked, "Why do I get the feeling I'm *not* going to like this? What's the problem?"

Chapter 20

Three days later, Michelle Reagan led Josue Reyes up to Cynthia Robinson's apartment door in Denville, New Jersey, and pulled the key out of the pocket of her coveralls. Josue nervously adjusted his dark blue baseball cap embroidered with the logo of a fictional plumbing company. The same logo adorned a large, drab magnetic sign on the side of the van Michelle had parked at the curb.

Inside the apartment, Michelle removed her hat and jammed it into a pocket. "Okay, Joe, this is the place I told you about. I need full audio and video coverage of the living room, kitchen and master bedroom. I don't know who's going to be standing where, so I need to be able to see everything remotely on my tablet. Now that you can see the place in person, I need to know if there's going to be any problem doing that."

Joe wheeled his tall, hard-sided equipment case to the side and out of the way. He quickly surveyed the apartment, then walked back to Michelle. Softly, he said, "No problem. This is junior varsity work."

Michelle tightened her ponytail with a tug. "There's no need to whisper. I got the homeowner's permission for this. Who do you think gave me the key to the front door?"

Joe shrugged. "All right, let's get started. Audio won't be a problem in such a small area as this, so I just need to scope out the best sightlines for video." He led Michelle around the apartment and studied the electrical outlets, smoke detectors, sprinkler heads and arrangement of furniture.

He installed four wireless cameras in the living room and two audio bugs at opposite ends of the apartment to be sure they had overlapping coverage ranges throughout most of the twelve-hundred-square-foot space.

Joe carefully withdrew two table lamps from his large case and handed one to Michelle to carry. She followed him into the bedroom where he replaced both existing table lamps on the nightstands and tried to put the originals into his case. Only one fit, so he set the other aside to carry it back to the van separately.

"What's in the lamps?" Michelle asked.

"These have both audio and video capture capability, but I'm only going to use the video. The audio from the two bugs I installed in the electrical outlets earlier is wa-*ay* better. I don't use these lamps too often—they're kinda old school—but they fit right in for a simple hotel room or bedroom setup like this. I just need to make sure the sightlines for the video will be all right even if doors are open or someone's standing right in front of one of the lamps."

Joe surveyed the room again as he walked around the bed. He opened and closed doors to the bathroom and walk-in closet while evaluating video coverage and quality on his tablet. He lifted the slanted, hinged top of the bureau and glanced inside before letting the top down gently. His eyes darted to Michelle and back to the bureau. He lifted the top again and looked at two framed pictures inside. One showed two smiling women in ski jackets lifting their poles in apparent celebration. Another showed a blonde woman in a black mortar-board cap and graduation gown holding a diploma, flanked by her pleased parents.

He lifted the graduation picture from its shelf and held it up for Michelle to see.

She flinched, and blurted out, "Dammit! I told her to get rid of all the pictures. Josue, you have to put it back and forget you ever saw it."

"You never told me this was *Cindy's* apartment. You—"

"No, *you* need to put it back and finish the install so we can get this show on the road."

"Why are you spying on Cindy? Did she do something wrong?" Joe's stomach tightened.

"*No*, no, it's nothing like that."

"I know you don't have a FISA warrant to be doing this kind of surveillance on a US citizen. If you did, the FBI would be doing the install, not me." He looked around the apartment and paused for a moment. "You said I should trust you, but I'm sorry, I'm taking everything out—"

"No, Joe, *don't*. Okay, I'll tell you the rest."

Josue Reyes glared at her. "This better be good."

Michelle clenched her jaw. "Well, it's not really good for anyone. It's just what needs to be done. I told you the truth when I said I had the homeowner's permission for this, and Cynthia really did give me the key. It's not *her* I'm spying on. In fact, I'm *protecting* her. She's in on the plan."

"What's the plan?"

"Really, Joe, you just have to trust me on this."

"I wish I could, but if I'm taking the risk of going to jail, I think I should know that what I'm doing is worth it."

"You're *not* going to jail, Joe."

"Then tell me!"

Michelle hesitated, then relented. "Okay. You know that Cynthia's a professional, right?"

Joe nodded. As much as he wanted to think they had something special during their afternoon in Manhattan, he knew that, for Cindy, it was just an act. A *very* convincing act.

"Well, she got caught. Sort of."

"By the police?"

Michelle wagged her head from side to side. "Well, sort of. By *a* cop, not *the* cops."

"Huh? I don't understand."

"One of her regular clients got busted for fraud at work. As part of his plea deal, he ratted on Cynthia. On the plus side, the police don't pursue prosecutions against individual sex workers. They look at the girls as victims and just try to bust the pimps or madams. So, Detective Shithead took it upon himself to shake Cynthia down, saying she needs to fork over half of her income to him or he'll arrest her. She's beside herself worrying that if all this becomes public, she'd be ruined, both personally and professionally. So, I'm doing this—*we're* doing this—to help her out."

"How," Joe asked, "is bugging her own apartment going to help her?"

"I'm going to turn the tables on the detective. That's all you need to know. Oh, and make sure you disconnect *your* own tablet from the audio and video streams. *Seriously.* I need it only going to the two tablets you give to me. *No* other copies, understand?"

"You're right. I *don't* want to know. But if you're sure this will help Cindy, well...."

"It *will*, I promise. I need her to help me with an operation overseas, but she won't do it unless I first help her by getting this detective off her back. And you have to admit, she has a *really* pretty back."

"Don't remind me," he said, and thought for a moment. Grudgingly, he agreed. "All right, I'll finish up. We can be out of here in ten minutes. Normally, I do these kinds of installs overseas in the dark at 3 a.m. It's a real luxury having free reign of the place during broad daylight."

Michelle wandered about the apartment while Josue completed his install and cleanup. She looked around the bedroom from a few angles and walked into the bathroom. She sat down on the edge of the tub and admired Cynthia's assortment of cosmetics lining the vanity. *Tools of her trade. Almost as many bottles as I have in any one of my disguise kits, but hers ensure she gets noticed by men while mine makes sure I don't.*

Josue appeared at the open doorway and handed Michelle two tablets. "Here you go. There won't be any other recordings. If there's a cop involved, we don't want to create any evidence that can be used against us." He extended the electronics to her. "So, it's just these two."

She took the tablets and replied appreciatively. "Thank you, Joe. You know how much I appreciate this, right? I promise, it *will* help both me and Cynthia out a lot."

He shook his head gently and grumbled. "Just don't make me regret this. I wouldn't look good in an orange jumpsuit."

Chapter 21

The next afternoon, Michelle sat on the closed lid of the toilet in Cynthia's apartment, listening through her earpiece to the NYPD detective in the living room threatening her agent. The CIA officer scratched around the edge of one of the silicone rubber disguise pieces she'd affixed to her cheeks, then stopped herself before she mussed it up. She particularly disliked the brown wart—complete with a long, black hair—she'd glued to the left side of the tip of her nose. She thought it comical, but the intent of her disguise was not to look like someone else, but rather to ensure the detective fixated on facial features so striking he would not remember any other part of her. So disconcerting were the facial prosthetics she chose to wear that, even after a face-to-face conversation, the crooked cop would not be able to remember so much as the color of her eyes.

Michelle could hear most of the conversation through the closed bathroom door and looked at her tablet for the hundredth time to make sure it continued recording everything. She cycled through several views of the detective from among the cameras Joe installed the day before.

Nice guy, Alex texted to Michelle through the surveillance app. *I've learned a few new choice curses from New York's finest. Being a former sailor myself, I didn't think that was even possible.*

A bit of friendly advice, Michelle responded, *don't ever use any of those to describe a woman.*

Yeah, I'd like to keep my nuts attached for a while longer.

Michelle grinned. *Anyone outside?*

Nope. Coast is clear. Got enough incriminating video yet?

No. We'll wait 'til she gives him the money.

Michelle could hear Cynthia through the bathroom door as she led the detective into the apartment's only bedroom. Cynthia's voice quaked as she told him she kept her cash in the safe on the floor of her bedroom closet.

"Hurry up, bitch," the gravelly voice urged from the other side of the bathroom door.

- 94 -

With her left hand, Michelle lifted her silenced Sig Sauer pistol off the vanity. The white towel on which she'd laid it prevented it from scraping on the Formica countertop. She held the surveillance tablet in her right hand and watched the crystal-clear video of the detective in the next room looking over Cynthia's shoulder as the shaking woman pulled two stacks of cash from her safe.

"This... this...," Cynthia stammered, "is all I have. Sixty-five thousand. Please don't take it all."

Michelle clenched her jaw as the detective smacked the back of his hand against the side of Cynthia's face. The stereo effect of hearing the *smack* both through the earpiece and the door in front of her made Michelle shiver.

"Don't tell me what I can or can't do. I'll take what I want. I *own* you now." He shoved four bundles of rubber-banded bills into his jacket pocket and threw two bundles at the woman kneeling in the closet.

Now, Michelle texted to Alex, and carefully laid the tablet down on the towel.

Detective Shithead's voice got louder as his threats mounted. He growled, "You'll be making payments on a schedule from here on out. You'll have ten grand for me every month like clockwork or I'm gonna work your face over like you never —"

Michelle yanked the bathroom door open, raised her pistol to the level of the detective's chest, and asked, "You'll work it over like *what* exactly? I didn't catch that last part."

The detective's head spun toward Michelle, and his right hand instinctively moved to draw his service pistol from its holster on his right hip.

"*Don't* do it," Michelle cautioned the wide-eyed man. "You're not nearly fast enough to draw your weapon before I can pull this trigger." She kept her silenced pistol leveled at his chest and waited for him to make his life-or-death decision.

The detective's hand froze in mid-air, and he retreated two steps before coming to a halt. His eyes darted to Cynthia and back to Michelle. His head telegraphed his next move, dropping slightly as he rushed away from Michelle and out of her field of view, trying to get out the apartment door.

Michelle stood her ground and waited. She motioned for Cynthia to stay where she knelt, just inside the closet.

Cynthia nodded.

Slowly, the detective reemerged into Michelle's line of sight, walking backward. He stopped next to the queen-sized bed with his hands raised over his head.

"What?" Michelle asked him. "Did you think I'd come without backup?"

The detective shook his head. "You's guys are making a *big* mistake here. A big *fuckin'* mistake."

"Maybe," Michelle said, "or maybe not. But I'll tell you this much for free: I get a real charge out of this kind of thing."

Alex's voice drifted from around the corner. "She does. Trust me on that. She lives for this shit. Not too sure you're going to, though."

Cynthia's eyes shot sideways as if looking at Alex through the closet wall, then fixed on Michelle, pleading. Softly, she asked, "You're *not* going to kill him, are you? That's not what I wanted. That's *not* what I meant when I asked you to help."

"You's guys should listen to her," the detective said. He looked from Michelle to Alex and back again as he assessed the tactical situation for his opportunity to make a break for the door or draw his weapon.

Michelle glanced at Cynthia and shrugged her shoulders. "Eh, well, I guess you're right." With her Sig Sauer in her left hand pointed steadily at the detective, Michelle raised her right arm forward.

The detective recognized the blunt green cap on the front of the Taser stun gun. The green cap symbolized the twenty-five-foot length of the electric leads contained inside the stun gun's cartridge. Below the cartridge, a red aiming laser flashed and came to rest on the detective's chest. He locked eyes with Michelle, although his threat barely made it past his lips. "*Don't—*"

Michelle ignored him and pulled the Taser's trigger. The compressed gas in the stun gun's cartridge shot two steel probes a dozen feet and into the detective's belly. Wires connected to the probes trailed from his abdomen back to the Taser and vibrated as they flooded fifty-thousand volts of electricity through his body.

Cynthia watched in stunned silence as the portly man who'd smacked her across the face earlier convulsed uncontrollably and fell to the floor of her bedroom in a tangled mass of flailing limbs. Later, she'd recall being surprised at how quietly it happened, except for the clicking of the Taser that seemed to go on for a long time.

Michelle admired the Taser's neuromuscular incapacitation effect as the pudgy cop convulsed on the ground, having lost all control of his muscles.

Alex immediately holstered his pistol and lunged for the man twisting uncontrollably on the carpet. The former Navy SEAL dropped to the floor and yanked the detective's left arm behind his back and into a hammerlock, hyperextending the lawman's shoulder painfully. "Don't fight it," he advised the shaken detective fighting to regain his breath.

As the electric shock abated and he regained control of his muscles, the detective groaned and tried to roll in the opposite direction to find relief from the searing pain Alex was inflicting on his left shoulder.

Michelle approached the detective, removed his handcuffs from the leather case on his belt, and handed the metal restraints to her partner.

Alex relaxed the detective's shoulder slightly, slapped one of the metal cuffs on the detective's left wrist and adjusted his grip using the length of the handcuffs to create a larger lever effect to continue inflicting the highly effective incentive of pain on the restrained man's shoulder. Alex tugged slightly. "Give me your right hand behind your back."

"Fuck you," the NYPD detective answered.

Alex pulled harder on the handcuff, lifting the detective's arm away from his back a few inches. A searing flame ran across the restrained man's shoulder as Alex twisted the joint into to an unnatural angle.

"Aiiiiiiihhh!"

"Your right hand," Alex repeated.

"Fu—"

Alex lifted the handcuff farther and pulled it toward the man's head.

"*Aiiiiiiii*! Ah ri—"

Alex eased up on the detective's shoulder and secured the officer's other hand behind his back.

Michelle patted the detective down. She removed his service pistol and key ring, then added his NYPD credentials and badge to her collection. From his rear pocket, she withdrew a leather wallet and then retrieved Cynthia's cash from the outer pockets of his jacket.

Alex rolled the restrained man up and searched him for other weapons. Finding none, he pushed him back against the side of the bed. He stepped behind Michelle, drew his own pistol and stood guard while his partner spoke to the corrupt cop.

"First things first," Michelle said, and handed Cynthia the money taken from the detective's pockets. The CIA officer removed two one-hundred-dollar bills from one stack, handed the rest to Cynthia, and said, "Put everything else back in your safe and lock it."

Cynthia did as Michelle instructed, locked the safe and stood up.

Michelle handed her the two C-notes. "Take these and go out to dinner and a movie. You don't need to see what happens next."

"Please, you're not going to—"

"Go to dinner, Cynthia, and I promise you this fat pig will never bother you again."

"I didn't—"

Michelle held up her hand, and Cynthia stopped speaking. Calmly, Michelle replied, "No, I'm not going to kill him, and do you know why?"

Cynthia shook her head.

"Because then I'd have to replace the carpet. You can't bleach out *that* much blood."

"I—"

"*Go*," Michelle said, and pointed toward the door. "Take two Benjamins and call me in the morning."

Cynthia walked away without another word to gather her purse and car keys from the kitchen counter.

Michelle waited until she heard the front door close behind her agent, then opened the detective's wallet. She read over his NYPD ID card, and said, "And now to you, Detective... Brendan Sean Cleary." She typed the man's name, NYPD badge number, driver's license number and home address into her tablet and transmitted the data to Wilson Henry in Virginia.

The detective sat silently as Michelle tapped on her tablet and slid her finger across the bottom of the screen. She removed the earplug cable, turned the tablet to face the man on the floor, and pressed play by tapping the triangular button at the bottom of the screen. The tablet blinked to life with a view from one of Josue's hidden cameras. The detective watched and listened to himself threaten Cynthia, strike her across the face and fill his pockets with the cash from her safe.

Michelle turned the tablet back toward herself and tapped a few buttons to read Wilson Henry's reply. His quick information gathering from CIA analysts on the New York City Joint Terrorism Task Force watch center floor provided Michelle with the detective's life story— enough of it for her purposes, anyway. "Well, Brendan, I'm sure you thought this would be easy money. You know, threatening a defenseless woman. I guess you figured she'd decide it's easier to just pay you off rather than try to find an honest cop and have to admit how she makes a living. Well, unfortunately for you, Cynthia has friends like me."

"You'll never get away with this," Detective Cleary said.

"*Get away* with what?" Michelle asked. "*Get away* with giving this video of you to the FBI for a Public Corruption investigation? *Get away* with emailing it to your wife, Helen? Or *get away* with giving a copy to all your co-workers in NYPD's Criminal Enterprise Investigative Section? The guys there might appreciate your choice of a beautiful woman like Cynthia but, *mmmm*, your wife? *Ehhh*, probably not so much. Or could I *get away* with sending it to Internal Affairs? What do you think *they* would say?"

Cleary sat quietly against the bed and stewed as his neck flushed and warmed uncomfortably. He chaffed at the handcuffs biting into his wrists and bit his lower lip.

Michelle enjoyed the look of surprise on the detective's face as he tried to figure out how she could possibly know so much about him. He'd never even told Cynthia his real name.

Michelle looked over at Alex, who still aimed his pistol at the detective wriggling his wrists inside the handcuffs. "So, Brendan, do you want to know what's going to happen now?"

The middle-aged man looked at her blankly. "What?"

Michelle leaned back against the wall behind her. "Nothing."

His eyes narrowed and he looked intently at Michelle. "Nothin'?"

"That's right, *nothing*. You're not going to bother Cynthia or any of the other women you've been blackmailing any more. You're done with them, for good. *Capisce?*"

The detective did not respond.

"If you behave yourself," Michelle said, and waved her tablet in the air, "this video will never see the light of day. But if your face so much as shows up in Cynthia's rearview mirror even by accident, well, then I'm going to make you an overnight Internet sensation. You'll need a new gig like that because your days as a cop will be over. No pension for you and likely no wife or house, either. And if you ever lay a hand on Cynthia or *any* of the women again, I'll make damned sure that *my* face with this ugly-ass wart on the tip of my nose is the *last* thing you ever see."

"You wouldn't dare kill a cop," the detective said, hopefully.

Alex shook his head and poked the cop in the thigh with the tip of his work boot. "You really don't know who you're talking to, buddy. *Really*. You *don't*."

Cleary looked from Michelle to Alex and back again.

With a straight face, Michelle said, "You wouldn't be the first. Not sure about the last, though. That remains to be seen. What I *am* sure about is that if, after you wake up this afternoon, you ever go within a million miles of Cynthia, it'll be the *last* mistake you ever make in your short, uneventful life."

Cleary's brow furrowed and he inhaled sharply. "When I wake up?"

Michelle pulled a silver packet labeled "Product Strength 4" from the back pocket of her jeans and pulled open the resealable pouch. She removed a moist pad from inside and climbed onto the bed behind the detective.

Alex steadied the seated detective by putting his foot against the man's chest and pushed his back into the side of the mattress. Michelle threw her legs over Cleary's head, steadied it between her knees and cupped the moist pad over his mouth.

The detective struggled, tried to roll to his right to escape, but had no leverage against the two CIA officers. His struggles slowed and soon stopped completely as the CIA's potent chloroform took effect.

Michelle and Alex relaxed and let the unconscious man tumble slowly onto the floor. Michelle double-checked that the handcuffs were secure and then emptied his pockets of a Parker pen and the rest of the odds and ends he carried.

"Okay," she said to Alex, and took a satisfied look down at the unconscious detective. "Bring in the shipping trunk and handcart. Then, back the van up to the apartment door."

"On it," he replied, and left the apartment for a few minutes.

While he was out, Michelle called Josue Reyes from her cell phone. "Joe, it's done. Time for you to remove all your equipment, and I mean *all*. Don't think of leaving anything in place. Besides, Cynthia's moving into a different apartment complex this weekend to get away from the memories of the threats this cop's been making. Give me fifteen minutes to finish what I'm doing in here, and then you have ninety minutes to remove your electronics. Is that enough time?"

"Yeah, no problem, Michelle, and I'm insulted you think I'd leave a camera or two behind."

"Yeah, you be insulted. I just want to make sure you understand me clearly." She hung up before the technical services officer could respond.

Alex returned wheeling a large black storage trunk on a hand cart into the bedroom.

They tilted the case onto its side, rolled and shoved the unconscious detective inside and put the trunk back on the handcart. Alex rolled it out the front door and up the ramp of his waiting van. He pointed to the detective's car and Michelle tossed the keys up and down in her hands. She took a pair of gloves from the back of the van and walked to the unmarked NYPD sedan.

Alex led the two-vehicle procession east along two-dozen miles of back roads to a site deep in the Great Piece Meadow Preserve that Michelle had scouted the day before. She followed him into the seven-thousand-acre wildlife reserve and parked the detective's car at the secluded end of a dirt road. Once he regained consciousness, the detective would have no trouble finding his way home on nearby Interstate 80. The Manhattan skyline was easily visible twenty miles to the east.

The CIA operators unloaded the detective from the trunk in the back of the van and manhandled him into the driver's seat of his car. Michelle left his keys on the dashboard but kept the contents of his wallet. After wiping down his pistol, badge, credentials and empty wallet to remove any fingerprints, she placed each item on the seat next to him.

She knew he'd easily replace his "lost" driver's license, and his knowing Michelle had his original would be an effective reminder that he would never be completely out of the woods. That—and the video, Michelle hoped—would keep him out of Cynthia's long, blonde hair for at least as long as the CIA officer still needed her agent's services.

Before leaving, Michelle removed the handcuffs from the detective, wiped any fingerprints off the stainless-steel bracelets, and tossed them onto the dashboard.

On the ride home, Michelle called Cynthia from the van's passenger seat. "How was the movie?"

"I don't know. I wasn't paying attention. Brad Pitt's easy on the eyes, so... you know, I just sat there. Are you done?"

"Almost. You can go home in an hour, but not before that. Are you all set to move to the new apartment?"

"Yeah, I pick up the keys the day after tomorrow."

"Good. Once you have all your stuff moved in, I have one last job for you."

"I *really* want to be done with this, Michelle," Cindy said. "I just want to start my life over again."

"I helped you out of a huge jam, and in return, I need you to do this one last job for me... at a discount."

Cynthia thought for a moment. "Okay, I know I owe you, but I don't know if I can take another one of your surprises. Can you tell me what that is in advance?"

"Okay, I'll do it just this once. You'll be hanging out with me on a yacht in the south of France for up to a week. Maybe less, but I don't know the exact schedule right now."

"That doesn't sound like your usual kind of surprise. Sounds kind of wonderful, actually, if you ask me."

"No," Michelle said, "the surprise is that *this* time, I need you to bring a friend."

Chapter 22

Zeki Aga slung his overnight bag over his right shoulder and scanned the faces of the crowd waiting to greet family and friends arriving at Los Angeles International Airport. He walked past two-dozen hired drivers holding signs for arriving passengers. Further back, a woman in a teal hajib held the sign he was looking for: "*Tanidik.*" To most people it looked like someone's last name, but to him and other Turkic speakers, the real meaning was clear: *acquaintance* or *contact*.

He approached the woman, and in Turkish, said, "I'm Zeki."

The short woman looked up at Sargon's soldier. "My name is Asli. Welcome to Los Angeles. Have you been here before?"

Zeki looked around the crowded terminal and shook his head. "No, but while it's a lot smaller than Istanbul...." He wrinkled his nose. "Somehow it still smells worse."

"The traffic will remind you of home, too," Asli said, and waved her hand for him to follow her. She led him outside and across four lanes of traffic in the bustling arrivals driveway. "You have to watch out for the taxis here, too. The drivers in LA are even worse than back home, if you can believe that."

Zeki chuckled. "I live in New York City right now, so you and I may have to compare horror stories about taxis. Some days, I'm not sure whether His Majesty should have sent *us* to America, or just flooded it with more African taxi drivers. Some days, it's hard to decide which plan would be better for extracting our revenge against these people."

Asli snickered. She'd expected the sultan's soldier to be all business, not a man who would show his personality right away. She knew that her part in the mission to come was going to be easy. Not so for him, though. She silently reaffirmed her commitment to her sultan and their cause to make Zeki's tasks easier while he was her guest — and a handsome one at that.

Zeki stowed his luggage in the trunk of her Subaru and got comfortable in the passenger seat. Asli eased her car out of the parking garage and accelerated up the on-ramp to head north on the 405

Freeway. Once in the Westwood section of Los Angeles, she navigated along several side streets, turned down a narrow alley, and stopped in front of a wide, dark-green wooden door in the side of a three-story apartment building. The newly painted door would not have looked out of place on the carriage house of an old French country estate. Asli got out of the car, unlocked the large door and pushed it open. It swung inward easily on well-oiled hinges.

She pulled the car into the courtyard of the small, upscale apartment building and locked the large door behind her. Bright tarps with vertical red-and-blue stripes completely covered the building's façade.

"This is one of the apartment buildings I manage. When I got word from His Majesty about what you needed, I gave all the tenants advance notice that they'd have to stay out of their apartments for a full week while we had the place tented and fumigated for Drywood Termites. That's actually a very common thing here in Southern California. You see it all the time. So, other than the usual gripes about having to live in hotels for a week, the residents didn't complain much. They don't like the thought of termites, even fictitious ones, eating away at their furniture. No one will bother you and your team here for the next five days. The tenants park in a garage next door. We use the alley we came in through and this courtyard mostly for deliveries and maintenance access. It's completely private."

Zeki inspected the small courtyard and nodded his approval. "Excellent. This space will be large enough for us to hide four vans and load them up. You have those already?"

"No, but I know where we can steal them from. That won't be a problem. I just need more people to drive them. When your men arrive, I'll take you there. Also, there are three empty apartments in this building for your men to sleep and work in while you're here. I delayed a few new tenant move-in dates until after the termite fumigation to make things easier for you. No one will suspect a thing."

"Good. We only need two apartments. Onur Tabak is scheduled to arrive tomorrow. It's a long drive from New York, but we need the equipment he's trucking in before we can start setting up. Once he gets here, I'll begin work on that part of the plan so you and he can pick the other men up from the airport when their flights arrive from Europe."

"Good. Come upstairs," Asli said, and headed for a door in the vine-covered wall of the courtyard. "You must be hungry after your long flight from the east coast. I'll get lunch ready."

***

The following day, Zeki hauled equipment from Onur's van into one of the empty apartments while Onur and Asli met the arriving travelers at LAX. Zeki stored the empty boxes and disassembled shipping crates in the master bedroom while he started assembling the key components in the kitchen. He left the more specialized equipment untouched until Onur returned with the others.

Once enough of his soldiers arrived from the airport and Asli fed them a respectable Turkish meal, Zeki put them to work setting up the equipment they'd trained on in Turkey. He dispatched Onur and another man to nearby hardware and grocery stores Asli had scouted out. There, they purchased supplies they needed to cook large quantities of plastic explosives. Meanwhile, he and two others installed a plastic ventilation hood over the stove and fed black-and-yellow ducts out the window to vent the noxious gasses from the cooking explosives into the courtyard. They struggled to extend one particularly troublesome duct through a tight seam in the tarps encasing the building, which cost them an hour of time and one near-fall from the second-story apartment.

After finishing the assembly, Zeki took a few steps backward and surveyed the scene. He liked the larger scale of the setup, compared to what he and Onur had to use in North Carolina. With only two men, that mission had to be smaller in scale. This time, the team he and Onur had trained in Turkey was finally together again and already proving its worth.

Zeki committed himself to putting every ounce of his energy into making his sultan proud. Again.

***

Michael walked slowly along the beach outside his hotel in Nice, France, and listened on his phone to Carl Sapienti of CIA's Malta Station relate his conversation with Dario Turchi.

"I had Turchi make the call for you, Mike. He played voicemail tag with his clients in France for an hour or so, but once he got ahold of them, it went smoothly. Normally, I'd have recorded the call, but since you told me not to...."

"No, that's fine, Carl. Thank you. That's perfect. Will the commodities brokers take the meeting with you posing as a prospective client?"

"Yup. To those guys, cash talks, and they're all ears. Dario introduced me as the new client, and I'm ready to go whenever you give the word. I signed out a new undercover cell phone already, and it's a short hop over the Med to wherever you want the meeting to take place."

"Good. I've arranged to use one of the Company's larger covert yachts for the week. It'll be here the day after tomorrow. And by 'here,' I mean Monte Carlo."

"Great. I'm excited," Carl said. "Sometimes it's hard to call this *work*, you know?"

Michael smiled. "Yes, it certainly is."

"Who else will be there?"

"You've already met Eden and Alex. In addition to them, Eden is bringing a couple of her girlfriends along. I think you'll be suitably impressed by the company she keeps."

Chapter 23

Tamerlan's driving lessons started out well, and he impressed Bayram by learning quickly. He found it easy enough to control the truck at low speeds but needed more experience to learn how to shift the manual transmission quickly enough to drive on the highways. As he and Bayram made their way across Turkey's wide expanse, Bayram let the teenager drive occasionally when they were on secondary roads to gain experience, as the boy's new Turkish ID would not allow him to operate the truck once they crossed the border into Bulgaria.

An experienced driver, Bayram enjoyed teaching Tamerlan how to pump gas, use credit cards for expenses and about the things border guards looked for on shipping manifests. The truck's cargo of figs, dates and olive oil matched the manifest perfectly. Even the hidden compartment was empty—for this part of the trip. They took no chances of being caught on their almost three-thousand-mile drive to Paris.

As Bayram drove through the heart of Istanbul along the Anatolian Motorway, Tamerlan's eyes remained riveted on the exotic scenes rolling past his window. From one end of the bustling city of fifteen million people to the other, colorful houses, rectangular office buildings and wiry antenna towers stretched up one hillside and down another in an unending stream of humanity. The teenager had never seen so many people, buildings and vehicles in one place.

After crossing the 15 July Martyrs Bridge over the Bosporus strait which separates two continents, Bayram welcomed Tamerlan to Europe. Tamerlan craned his neck to look back to the Asian side of the city. "Europe looks exactly the same."

"Here it does," Bayram agreed, "but you'll see the differences become more pronounced the further we go into the lands of the Crusader."

"In my village, I thought I knew a lot. I was even in the village militia! But here...." He looked over to his new mentor. "Thank you for this opportunity and for teaching me." He stared out the window again, and softly said, "I could never have imagined...."

No, Bayram thought, *you certainly cannot imagine what awaits you in Paris.*

The long days of driving from Turkey to Paris wore on Tamerlan. He tried to get a taste for the kind of coffee Bayram drank, but only twice during the trip could he bring himself to finish a full cup. To Tamerlan, Bayram seemed to have a bottomless stomach for the strong, black drink. To pass the time, the young man enjoyed gazing out the window trying to pick out the key differences between each of the countries they drove through. As they entered France, he commented that the scenery had gone from tans and browns in Turkey to drab grays and browns in between, but Germany and France were more verdant and greener than the lushest harvest he had ever seen back home. Bayram complimented him on being so observant, which made the teenager feel valued.

Outside of Paris, Bayram pulled the truck into a garage in Clichy-La-Garenne. The large immigrant population in that northwest suburb of Paris provided an eager market for Turkish produce—a market Sargon's transportation company made excellent money supplying. Several local businesses owned by five of Sargon's trusted cadre provided other valuable, albeit far less visible, benefits for their sultan. Combined, they created for the caliphate a well-positioned base of operations for its true, and entirely non-commercial, activities.

Bayram let the workers in the garage offload the cargo while he and Tamerlan stretched their legs on the street outside.

Tamerlan pointed across the street to the narrow front of a small neighborhood restaurant. "Halal kabobs. That sounds *sooo* good right now. Are you sure we don't have to help unload the truck?"

Bayram gently clapped Tamerlan on the back. "Yes, I'm sure. We just drive the trucks. The customers will unload the cargo today and then load up crates of machine parts for factories and some machines for hospitals that we'll take back with us when we drive home to Van, Turkey. You and I have the rest of today off to stretch our legs. It's Saturday, so the workers will finish loading everything by tonight. We'll leave tomorrow just before lunchtime so we can get through Germany before stopping for the night."

"Going home so soon..." Tamerlan mumbled. "Well, the kabobs sound good, but since we're not staying here that long, can we find something French to eat?"

"Why not? Let's walk down the street a block or two. I think there's a café just off the park."

***

The next morning, Bayram encouraged Tamerlan to eat a full breakfast so they wouldn't have to stop until they crossed the German border near Saarbrucken. The teenager enjoyed thirds of buttered croissants, a new and flaky favorite unlike anything he could get in his village in Iran. Tamerlan wrinkled his nose at most of the French cheeses on the breakfast plate in the middle of the table, but he helped himself to a heaping serving of the feta.

When they were ready to leave, the teenager settled into the truck's passenger seat and watched the city streets pass. After fifteen minutes, he asked Bayram, "This isn't the way we came in, is it?"

"You're catching on quickly. You'll be a great driver one day. It's important to have a nose for navigation. No, it's Sunday morning, so there'd be too much church traffic going the other way. We'll head down toward the south part of Paris and pick up the highway there."

Ten minutes later, Bayram turned right on a city street and pumped the clutch. He tugged at the gear shift and brought the truck to a halt on a residential street. To their right, worshipers streamed out of the Coptic Church of Saint Mary and walked across the street to a neighborhood park lined with lilacs and horse-chestnut trees. A large sign invited the congregants to gather under a line of white tents and celebrate the church's 70th anniversary.

Bayram fiddled with the clutch and gear shift, then grabbed a pair of gloves from the pocket on the door. "I'll go check the transmission and see what's wrong. Slide into the driver's seat, and, if I yell for you to step on the clutch, then hold it all the way down, all right?"

"Okay," Tamerlan said. "Just say when."

Bayram stepped down from the truck, closed the door firmly and walked to the rear of the vehicle. Out of sight of Tamerlan, he continued along the sidewalk to the end of the block.

In the truck's cab, Tamerlan searched the side mirror for a glimpse of his mentor. When he couldn't find him, he asked loudly, "Should I push it in?"

Not getting a response, he twisted the window handle on the door and jumped as it popped off in his hand. Tamerlan pulled the door handle to get out and find Bayram, but the door wouldn't budge. He pawed at the lock to pull it up, but the mechanism refused to move. His eyes grew wide as he glanced from side mirror to windshield to the other side mirror trying to find any sign of the man who'd driven him across two continents.

At the end of the block, Bayram hurried around the corner as he removed a remote control from inside one of the gloves he took from the truck. He donned the gloves and peeled away the clear plastic protective cover jury-rigged onto the top of the remote. With his index finger, he pressed the gold, rectangular button in the center of the modified garage door opener.

From around the corner behind him, a deafening blast erupted as the explosives loaded into the truck the night before by the staff at the shop detonated. Bayram sped along the adjacent street to stay ahead of the rapidly expanding dust cloud and debris flying from what remained of the church and its members in the park. In an instant, what had started as a celebration turned into a conflagration incinerating eighty churchgoers and one teenage Iranian.

Bayram dropped the remote detonator into a nearby trashcan and, with a smile, softly said, *"Allahu Akbar."* He removed his gloves, shoved the pair into his back pocket and made his way to *Gare du Nord* for the long train ride home.

Chapter 24

In Los Angles, Zeki Aga sat in the front seat of Asli's car while Onur Tabak and two soldiers sat uncomfortably cramped in the backseat. The early morning quiet in the industrial neighborhood just north of LAX would become far busier in an hour once the first employees started to arrive for their 5 a.m. shift. Zeki expected his team to be long gone by that time.

Asli guided her Subaru along the access road between the fenced-off parking lot and the 405 Freeway. "Remember," she said in Turkish, "to drive back on the route I showed you on the map. Don't use the highway. There's less chance of you getting stopped by the police on the side streets — or what people here call 'surface streets.'"

Zeki tossed the small ring of three keys up and down in his hand. As they landed in his right hand, he clenched his fist around them and looked at Asli. He thought of her as a plain woman, but one who some would find attractive — especially since she cooked well. Most importantly, he reasoned, she had access to what he needed for this mission. "Your uncle won't be suspected if we used these keys, will he? Will the theft lead back to him? Or you?" *Or*, he thought, *to us. Or to Sargon!*

"No," she said, and shook her head. "He made copies a few weeks ago and put the originals back in the lock box in the office. Lots of people at the delivery business have access to that box. There'd be no reason for anyone to suspect him, specifically."

"Okay, good," Zeki said. He twirled the keys around his index finger and tapped it gently against the plastic mask lying in his lap.

Asli guided her car around the side of the parking lot and pulled up to the corner. "Here's where you get out. I'll wait here until I see you all get through the fence."

Zeki stepped out of the car and walked up to the chain-link fence. He peered through the colored privacy slats and listened in the dark for any signs of guards or dogs. Traffic whooshed above him on the freeway but there were no sounds coming from the business behind the barbed wire-topped fenced. He listened intently and studied the parking lot on the other side of the fence but saw no signs of life.

He glanced back at his three companions, all of whom had donned their masks. He pulled his semi-transparent mask over his head, secured the elastic strap over his hair and adjusted it to give him an unobscured view.

The three men followed Zeki to the gate where he made quick work of unlocking the padlock. They entered the parking lot quietly and hurried to the front door of the small office building. There, Zeki used another key to open it, and the four men entered with ease.

Zeki led them down the main hall, as Asli instructed, and to the third door on the right. Inside the dispatcher's office, a metal box hung from the wall. He opened it with the third key — the smallest on the ring. Inside, he selected four sets of keys to delivery vans parked in the lot outside.

Underneath his mask, Zeki smiled. With the information from Asli's uncle, a maintenance laborer at this business, the vans were easy to poach. The hard part would come once the other men who were cooking the explosives back at the apartment shaped their creations and inserted the detonators. That, though, wouldn't happen until the following night.

All four vans started without incident, and Zeki led the procession through the gate. He relocked the gate behind the last one and led his team back to Asli's apartment complex along the streets she'd scouted in advance.

After parking in the apartment's courtyard, he stepped out of his van and exhaled audibly. *That went smoothly*, he thought. *She's a smart woman and, with her creativity and attention to detail, might have a bright future serving Sargon. But I'll have to see how things go at the end of this mission.*

***

Michelle Reagan gave a half-wave to Cynthia Robinson and Denise Jarrett from the railing of the 182-foot superyacht's main deck. On shore, Cindy paid the taxi driver, and the two newcomers flashed bright toothy smiles as they eagerly wheeled their suitcases up the yacht's gangway.

"Oh my God!" Cindy exclaimed as she reached Michelle at the top. "If I'd known you had a yacht like this at your beck and call, I would have gotten to know you *much* better and *much* sooner!"

Michelle smirked. "Well, it's a charter, so don't get too used to it." She extended her hand to the other woman. "You must be Denise. I'm Michelle." She shook hands with the smiling brunette and introduced the new arrivals to the man standing next to her. "Ladies, this is Stefano. He's one of the two cabin stewards aboard and will show you to the stateroom you'll be sharing. The other stew is named Maria, who's around here somewhere. They'll both take excellent care of you."

Stefano, an undercover CIA officer—as were all of the crewmembers—smiled. "Welcome aboard *Positive Latitude*. If there's anything I or any member of the crew can do to ensure you have a wonderful week, just let us know."

Denise smiled at Stefano and marveled at the yacht's superstructure. "Wow, you've even got a helicopter. Color me impressed." She went on to ask him several questions about the ship as he led the group slowly toward the interior.

Cindy hung back, and said to Michelle, "We had the connecting flight from hell. We got to Paris, no problem, but Air France couldn't seem to find whatever part broke on the smaller jet to Nice, so we couldn't even board for what seemed like forever."

"Is that why the flight was delayed so much? I followed your progress online, but their website doesn't give any details. Sucks when that happens, but you're here now, and it's a good thing, because our schedule got moved up by a day."

"Is that bad? What are we going to be doing, anyway? I'm afraid to ask what kind of fast one you're going to pull on me *this* time."

Michelle looked up at the blonde woman two inches taller than she. "Look, I know I've been a huge headache for you on the past two jobs, and this one's no different. But don't worry, no one's going to barge in on you this time. It's just a pure entertainment job for you both. I *promise* that's all you have to do—just keep your man happy. I *know* you can do that."

"That's all? Seems too easy."

"Well, you *are* only getting half of the usual payment because I solved your little cop problem, so it averages out."

"I guess so. And thanks again for that. I guess a good discount for this job makes us even."

Michelle held the yacht's outside door open for Cindy and told her the rest of the plan for the day. "There'll be three men and three women: you, me and Denise. So, you two just keep your guys happy, and we can all enjoy the beautiful weather, some fine champagne and more food than you can throw a stick at. It's not all fattening, either. I made sure they'd have a great selection of fruit aboard."

"I'm glad to hear that. So, *you're* going to work this job with us? That's new."

"Yes, and the complication—" Michelle said softly.

"I *knew* there had to be something else going on," Cindy muttered. "Nothing with you is ever what it seems."

"—is that our timetable has been moved up. We start this afternoon. Sorry, no rest for the weary. I have a few Five Hour Energy drinks if you need, and you'll get plenty of sleep later. First things first. In a few minutes, you'll meet my client, Carl. He's bringing two prospective clients of his—more financial types I'm afraid—aboard late this afternoon. We three women will keep all the guests happy, and Carl will do what he needs to do to make the sale and close his business deal. So, I need you and Denise to be ready this afternoon. Is that a problem? I hope you're not too jetlagged."

"No," Cindy said, "if that's all it is, we just need to change clothes and maybe down one of those energy drinks or something, especially if we'll be having champagne. And, hey, this *is* France! So, you just say when, and we'll be there."

"Good. Follow Stefano down below and get settled in. Then, you and Denise grab some lunch. He'll show you where the main dining room is. I'll join you two later and let you know what the exact schedule is going to be. Throw a beach coverup on over a sexy bikini so you'll be ready to go as soon as I give the word."

Michelle watched Stefano lead the two newcomers down the carpeted staircase and out of sight to the deck below on which most of the staterooms were located. After they disappeared from view, Michelle headed aft to the rear sun deck to ask Carl if he'd reached the commodities brokers by phone and knew what time they'd arrive.

On the yacht's bridge, the captain leaned back in his oversized padded chair and listened intently to Michael.

The CIA team lead from the Special Activities Center's Ground Branch addressed the yacht's undercover skipper—a member of the SAC's Maritime Branch—as a professional colleague.

"How long will it take us to get to international waters once we leave?" Michael asked.

"Not long. Figure one hour to get harbor clearance and go three miles offshore once your final guests arrive. Another hour to get us out to the twelve-mile limit, which is almost universally recognized as

International Waters nowadays. What's your team's plan now that the schedule has been moved up?"

"When our guests arrive, Carl and the women will entertain them. Carl's the case officer, so he'll drive the conversation as he sees fit. They'll all enjoy some snacks, champagne and what I'm sure will be a beautiful sunset on the back deck."

The captain grinned. "Yeah, sunsets are just one of the great perks of this job. Beats sailing a desk back home."

Michael smiled and nodded. "I'm sure with a little practice I could get used to it. After dinner, we'll play it all by ear. I'm sure there'll be a lot of alcohol flowing. If we need to, can your helicopter pilot fly at night?"

"Well, he can certainly take off at night, but I don't like conducting nighttime landings unless it's absolutely necessary. We have the required lighting aboard, of course, but it's never as safe as a daylight landing. Besides, this is supposed to be a pleasure vessel, so nighttime landings are generally reserved for medical emergencies."

"Okay, no problem," Michael said. "Just curious. Shouldn't be any need for that."

They talked through several contingency plans until Michelle joined them. She told them that Carl confirmed the two commodity brokers planned to arrive a little after 3 p.m.

The captain looked at his black G-Shock watch. "Okay, Mike. I'll make sure we're ready for a three-thirty departure."

"Excellent," Michael said. "Okay, Michelle, let's go down to the kitchen and make sure Alex is ready to play his part."

"Do you think he can pull this off?"

Michael shrugged. "I should hope so, but it's not like our team ever trains for this scenario."

"True," Michelle replied. As she followed her boss down the stairs, she said, "I'll keep my fingers crossed."

Chapter 25

Shortly before 3 p.m., a black BMW 7-Series hired sedan let its two passengers out at the quay in front of *Positive Lattitude*. Carl Sapienti greeted the pair of commodities brokers as they boarded 'his' yacht. He introduced them to the two cabin stewards who took their luggage to their staterooms below while Carl impressed his soon-to-be financial team with a quick tour of the luxurious amenities on the main deck.

Afterward, they settled into plush seats on the aft sun deck where Stefano served cocktails and a cheese plate. Over the course of two hours, Carl skillfully led the conversation through the necessary phases of rapport building, identifying common interests and laying the groundwork for establishing trust. After reaching a level of comfort well-known to the CIA case officer, he outlined for the money launderers his need to creatively transfer his funds from his business interests in Africa to the banks of more stable and investor-friendly nations, such as Switzerland and the Cayman Islands.

One of the brokers asked Carl if he'd ever considered setting up a Cook Islands Offshore Trust.

Below deck, Michelle knocked on Cynthia and Denise's stateroom door.

Denise opened the door and invited her hostess inside. "Love your T-shirt!" she exclaimed.

"Thanks," Michelle said, and spread the front out so Cindy could read it more easily. The T-shirt she wore over her black bikini read "No good story every started with the words 'Here, hold my salad.'"

"Too true," Cindy added. "So, what's the plan?"

"My client, Carl, is finishing up his initial discussions with his two guests. Their names are François and Louis. You can easily tell them apart. François has more hair, and Louis has more belly."

Denise curled her upper lip. "Well, you're the boss, so I guess you get your choice."

Michelle sat on the edge of one of the two beds in the stateroom. "Carl's mine, girls. It'll be fun to watch the men fight over the two of you, though. Since François is the more senior of the two guests, I'm sure Louis will defer to him." She looked at Denise who wore a pink string bikini. "But, damn, there's no wrong choice here, I'll tell you that."

Denise grinned in appreciation. Michelle explained to both escorts her plans for dinner, and how she expected the rest of the evening to go—or at least the parts she wanted the women to know about. As always, she kept the most important details to herself.

***

When it was time for the women to go up on deck, Michelle met Cindy and Denise at their stateroom. Denise finished brushing out her shoulder-length brown hair and leaned forward to check her makeup in the mirror. She looked at herself for a moment, hummed and then selected a pale pink lipstick from the vanity.

Cindy stood next to her bed and pulled a sheer white beach cover up with a plunging V-neck over her bright red bikini.

Michelle looked at Cindy. "That's beautiful, but lose the heels. You never wear hard shoes onboard a yacht, and since we've been sailing south for a couple of hours now, we're well into the Med and it can get choppy occasionally. Besides, hard shoes can scuff the decks, which is a yachting protocol no-no." She pointed to her own feet on which she wore turquoise flip-flops below a knee-length sarong. "You might as well just stay barefoot. I'm going to take these off when we get up on deck, anyway."

Cindy reached down and pulled off her shoes one at a time. "Good, I was wondering about how steady the boat would be. It seems okay so far, but I haven't spent much time on yachts. Anyway, we'll be more comfortable barefoot. I guess you need to invite me to spend more time on fancy boats with you and less time in big-city hotels."

Denise dropped her lipstick tube into her makeup kit, zipped it and agreed. "You and me, both. I could get used to this."

Yeah, you say that, now, but just wait.... "Okay, ladies, let's go show 'em what we've got," Michelle said, and led her two companions out of the stateroom on their way to the yacht's aft deck. "A day or two of you two giving these guys the full Girlfriend Experience, and they'll be spoiled forever."

As the women stepped through the sliding glass door and into the fresh Mediterranean air, Carl Sapienti spread his arms wide and greeted them. "Ahh, *there* you are. Right on time. Ladies, say hello to my new best friends."

Michelle stepped toward Carl and gently slid her arm under his. Denise made a beeline to the senior commodities broker, François Arsenault, and Cindy snuggled up to Louis Marchand.

Michelle made a show of stepping to the side and pulling her sarong and T-shirt over her head. She tossed them playfully onto a nearby chair and shifted her stance to accentuate her figure.

Cindy looked at Michelle across the large, circular table between them to follow her lead and tilted her head in surprise. Scars in the form of a jagged number four stood out above the bowtie of Michelle's bikini bottom. Cindy stared noticeably.

Denise followed Michelle's lead by removing her own coverup and, after a moment, Cindy put her game face on and caught up. Their guests watched every seductive move the women made as if — for those few moments — the rest of the world had ceased to exist.

Michelle noticed Cindy's staring and sat down next to Carl on the well-padded bench seat. She reached an arm around the back of Carl's neck and made a show of extending her athletic legs across his lap. She leaned against her fellow CIA officer and twisted her hips slightly to hide her scars among the cushions of the yacht's large semi-circular bench.

Carl continued his discussion with his guests about timing the first transfer of his mythical dirty money from Africa to accounts that Dario Turchi and the French brokers could access. As he talked, he ran his cupped hand along Michelle's smooth shin and circled his index finger around her kneecap.

Michelle smiled and focused her attention on the two brokers across the table.

As François and Carl talked, the Frenchman pulled Denise close. She snuggled in against his arm and laid her head on his shoulder. He slid his hand along her tanned leg, not stopping at her knee.

"Excellent," Carl said, and drew his lips back into a toothy smile. "The fee we agreed upon earlier is acceptable to me for the kind of bespoke services you gentlemen provide. I think I'd like to start on the fifth of next month. Will that work for you? I can have my bank in Lagos wire the first tranche of funds to your shell company's account in Bucharest. I'm going to be very interested to see how your operation works. What do you say, do we have a deal?"

"*Absolument!*" François exclaimed. "How we do what we do is —

how do you say — proprietary? But you will be very pleased with the results, *mon ami*."

"I'm sure I will," Carl said.

Michelle sat up straighter. "I don't know what you gentlemen were talking about, but it sounds to me like this calls for a toast. *Champagne*, anyone?" She reached behind the bench and pressed a recessed button.

Moments later, Alex Ramirez emerged from the yacht's interior. Michelle suppressed a chuckle at seeing him dressed in the yacht crew's uniform — white shorts with a vertical red stripe on the side and a pale-yellow polo shirt with *Positive Latitude* embroidered on the left breast. He pressed his hands together in front of himself. "Is there something I can get for you?"

Cindy recognized Alex from when he helped Michelle deal with the crooked cop in her apartment but played along. She wiggled in Louis's lap and ran her hand along the dark brown hair on his forearm.

Michelle answered her partner. "Yes, we'll have a plate of cheese, an assortment of crackers and six glasses of champagne. Make sure it's real French champagne. I wouldn't want to insult our guests."

"Yes, ma'am. Of course. Anything else?"

"No," Michelle answered, "just those. Everything's good here."

"Very well, ma'am. I'll send Stefano out with the cheese plate and see to the champagne myself," he answered, giving his partner the verbal confirmation that he understood her code phrase that it's time to move to the end game of their time on the yacht.

Five minutes later, Stefano laid out platters of crackers and cheeses on the table in the center of the curved bench and retreated back into the yacht.

A minute later, Alex appeared carrying a tray of six long-stemmed champagne flutes, half-filled with bubbly. "This is a Louis Roederer Cristal Brut. I'm sure you'll enjoy it." He served Michelle first, lowering the tray so she could easily reach the glasses. She lifted the two closest to her partner's thumb from the tray and handed one to Carl.

Carl gave a toast, and the group enjoyed the glasses of Brut. He steered the conversation away from business and asked Louis about a prominent French soccer star who recently married the ex-wife of a German national team player.

Louis laughed and launched into a diatribe about the love lives of a few of his favorite players. When he and François finished their drinks, Alex poured seconds for the Frenchmen.

The conversation continued at a lively pace for a quarter of an hour. As the high-finance discussion and stories from François' days running trading desks on the Paris Bourse got technical, Denise struggled to keep her eyes open. The escort laid her head on François' shoulder and gently ran her hand across his chest.

Slowly at first, François' accent grew more pronounced, and he began slurring his words. Soon, he was fighting to keep his eyelids from drooping as he spoke to Carl. Twice, he lost his place in the animated story he was telling and backtracked, unsure of what he'd just said. Almost mid-sentence, his arms dropped to his sides. His head rolled to his right and bobbed violently before his chin came to rest on his chest.

Denise lay unmoving against François, and to Michelle, the pair looked comfortable with each other.

I wonder if they'll even remember this? Michelle asked herself.

"Are you all right?" Carl asked François, clearly concerned.

Michelle looked over at Cindy as the blonde slid off Louis's lap. Michelle frowned as the escort slid onto the deck and recoiled as her asset's head *thunked* against the table between them.

"*Qu'est-ce qu'il se pas—*" Louis muttered as he tried to stand up. He teetered to his left and plopped back down on the bench at an uncomfortable angle. He tried to stand again by pushing on the seat cushion, but his rubbery arms gave way. His eyes rolled back into his head, and he careened over in slow motion. He came to rest face-down on the plush cushion of the curved bench.

Carl tried to stand, but Michelle sat firmly on his lap and pulled down on the back of his shirt collar to keep him in his seat.

"Stay here, Carl, and don't move," she instructed quietly. "Just sit back and let it happen."

"What's going on?" he practically screamed. "This is going to sour the deal! What did you do?" He looked at his empty champagne flute on the table in front of him and turned to Michelle. His eyes shot daggers as he said, "Did you *poison* them? Did you poison *me*?" Carl ran his hand over his face and throat.

"*Relax*, Carl," Michelle said, "it's *not* poison. It's just a strong sedative. They're fine, although they won't be too happy with me when they wake up later."

The sliding glass doors to the yacht's interior opened with a whoosh and Alex appeared pushing a pair of large, hard-sided storage trunks on a wheeled dolly.

Carl snorted, shoved Michelle's legs off his lap and stood up. "What the *hell*? Why did you put sedatives in the champagne? How did you only get it into *their* glasses? What about—"

"Man," Michelle said, and shook her head, "you sure ask a lot of questions. First, I took the two champagne flutes closest to Alex's thumb for us because those weren't dosed."

Carl glared at Alex, and asked accusingly, "*You're* in on this, too?"

Alex shrugged. "Welcome to the dark side, Carl. We have cookies. And apparently champagne, now, too. We've definitely stepped up our game in the beverages department. I hope you enjoyed it. That bottle cost the American taxpayer over four hundred bucks."

Michelle snickered at the thought that the bottle of champagne may end up being the least costly part of the entire operation. "And second, Carl, since you're wide awake, you also get to help Alex carry the women downstairs to their stateroom."

Carl looked at the four unconscious people across the circular table and stood fast, unsure what to do next. He'd expected to spend the next couple of days negotiating the many remaining details of a faux-business agreement and possibly recruiting one or both as an asset. He'd spent a week planning how to solicit the details of François' illicit money laundering operation from him while Michelle and her team lead listened to the microphones concealed around the ship—and in the staterooms—for anything the brokers might say of interest when they thought they were speaking privately. Seeing the subject of his expected week of sun, fun and scheming now snoring softly on the cushioned bench across from him did not fit into his pre-conceived plans for the week at all.

Alex shifted Denise's feet to get a better grip and looked up at Carl. "So, *Car-rl*, are you going to help me or not? Pick her up under her armpits."

Carl looked at Michelle first and then back to Alex. He ran his hand through his hair and chewed on his bottom lip. After a few seconds, he threw his hands up in resignation and edged his way around the circular table toward Denise's head.

On the count of three, the men picked Denise up. They took an uncoordinated lurch forward as they tried to walk together without dropping the alluring brunette. She bounced in Carl's arms as he jostled her. While re-securing his grip under her armpits, Denise's string bikini top slid up and off her right breast.

Chapter 26

Carl Sapienti mumbled, "*Uhhh....*" He looked from Michelle to Denise and back again.

Michelle curled her lip, caught Carl's gaze and shook her head. She glowered at him, and said, "Don't even think about it." She waved her hand to have Carl and Alex Ramirez walk out from between the curved bench and table onto the open deck. Once they shuffled into a more open area, Michelle adjusted Denise's bathing suit top and checked to see that it was secure—or at least as secure as the small triangle of pink fabric could be, under the circumstances.

Veins popped out on the side of Carl's neck. "I wasn't thinking about that. I mean, I would never—"

Michelle dismissed them with a curt flick of her wrist and walked over to the shipping trunks stacked on the wheeled dolly. She lowered one of the trunks to the deck, unlatched its hard-plastic lid and lifted it open. Inside, short empty leather belt-like straps hung from the top and bottom of the reinforced trunk. The straps at the top would hold the French commodities broker's hands securely while the larger pair at the bottom bound his ankles.

"I'll help you with those," a man's voice said.

Michelle turned to see her team lead maneuvering the second trunk. Michael lowered it to its side. "The captain sent the rest of his crew down belowdecks earlier. I told him to keep his eyes on the ocean ahead of us while we finish up back here. He mentioned to me this morning that he'd participated in a few extraordinary renditions of terrorists a few years back, so I'm confident he'll play ball. When Carl comes back, I'll tell him to remain downstairs once he and Alex finish moving Cindy."

After Alex and Carl finished moving both unconscious women safely to their stateroom, Alex returned to help Michelle and their boss load the two Frenchmen into the trunks. After the three CIA officers lifted the two shipping trunks onto the dolly, Michael stood fully erect and stretched his back.

"Careful, boss," Michelle said, with concern in her voice. "Don't overdo it. We can get the crew to help if we need."

"I'm fine," he said, and rubbed the small of his back.

"I thought that's supposed to be *my* line," Michelle quipped.

Michael smiled as he walked off to fetch the yacht's helicopter pilot.

While the pilot made his pre-flight checks, Alex and Michelle used the yacht's elevator to take the trunks up to the flight deck.

With the pilot's help, the team loaded the trunks into the chopper's cargo compartment behind the four passenger seats. Once the pilot satisfied himself that the cargo was secure, Michael loaded his suitcase, climbed in next to the pilot and turned to Michelle. "I may not see you at the Roach Motel tomorrow, but you know what to do when you get there, right?"

"Yes, I memorized the instructions you gave me. Doesn't sound too hard."

"Maybe not," Michael said, and pulled a headset on, "but it can be unnerving."

Michelle shrugged. "When I see you back in Nice, I'll let you know all about it."

She closed the helicopter's door and slapped it twice to tell the pilot they were cleared to leave. She stepped back a safe distance and stood with Alex to watch the helo lift off. Once the noise of the departing helicopter faded enough to talk without yelling, he looked at Michelle, and said, "I'm going to go take the champagne flutes from the table on deck to the galley and rinse them out. I need to pour the rest of the bottle down the sink, too."

"That's a pity," she said wistfully, and watched the helicopter bank and accelerate away from the yacht. "I rather enjoyed it. I know the girls didn't though, and I'm going to get an earful in a few hours. All right, then... well...." She looked at the ship's clock hanging on the wall behind her and did some mental math. "I need to make flight reservations for the girls for tomorrow. After that, I'll have plenty of time before they wake up, so I might as well lay out on deck and get some sun. Then I'll shower and change so I'm ready for when they unload both barrels at me."

Alex whistled softly. "Better you than me. I wouldn't want to be on the receiving end of the names they're going to call *you*."

Michelle drew her lips back and shifted on her feet. "Yeah," she said softly, "I'd rather not be there, myself, but it's not like I have much of a choice, now, do I?"

Chapter 27

Michelle straddled the high-backed chair and looked over the seatback at Cindy and Denise. The two escorts lay in their beds, rubbing their eyes in the dim cabin light. Denise groaned and rolled over. Cindy pulled a pillow over her face to block out the glare from the stateroom's single desk lamp Michelle had turned on to spare them the pain of the brighter overhead lights.

Cindy's muffled voice rose through the pillow as she asked, "What the hell happened?"

Michelle took a deep breath, and calmly stated, "I spiked the champagne. Your headaches are the only real aftereffects. You'll be fine in the morning."

Denise peeked at the alarm clock but couldn't focus her vision. "What time is it?"

"After eight."

Denise thought for a moment and lifted her head off the pillow to look at the clock again. She gave up, and asked Michelle, "Eight a.m. or p.m.?"

"It's evening. You only slept for a few hours, not through the night," the CIA officer replied softly. "You slept through dinner, but the kitchen staff will make you whatever you want when you feel up to eating. Use the stateroom phone to call downstairs later, and Maria will bring up whatever you ask for."

Cindy lifted the pillow a few inches over her head. "Why?"

"So you can have something to eat. I don't want you to go hungry."

"No," Cindy said, and replaced the pillow over her eyes. "I mean *why* did you roofie us?" She lifted the pillow slightly and glowered at Michelle through narrow slits. "You *do* know what the phrase 'sure thing' means, right?"

Michelle ignored the verbal jab. "Well, it wasn't Rohypnol, just a fast-acting sedative. I needed something from the men that they weren't going to give up voluntarily."

"You mean like Dario?" Cynthia asked.

Denise looked confused. "Who's Dario?"

"No one," Michelle said. "It's not helpful to talk about that. What *will* be helpful, though, are the Extra Strength Tylenol and water I put on your nightstands." She pointed to the bedside tables between the pair of twin beds on which the women lay.

The women looked over at the two plastic cups and four caplets sitting in front of the stateroom's telephone and alarm clock on the glass-topped tables.

Cindy slid the pillow back over her face. "Who knows what's in those pills. Why should I trust you? *You're* the one who gave me this splitting headache in the first place. And speaking of that, now that I think about it, right when we came aboard earlier today, you specifically said that you had been a huge headache for me in the past. You *planned* this. You *knew* right from the start exactly what was going to happen this afternoon, didn't you?"

"Yes," Michelle said simply. "I've told you before that I can't leave anything to chance. I have backup plans for my backup plans."

"Bitch," Cindy replied softly.

"Maybe I deserve that," Michelle said, "but then again, I did you a huge favor in New Jersey, so you owed me one. Now we're even."

"What favor?" Denise asked.

"Never mind," Cindy said. "Forget I mentioned it." She looked at Michelle. "I'm sorry. I feel like shit. You're right, you helped me out when I needed you and had no one else to turn to. I didn't mean anything by it, really. I'm just not feeling myself right now. I apologize."

Calmly, Michelle said, "And since you asked, I'll tell you *exactly* what's in those pills on the nightstands. Five hundred milligrams of acetaminophen. Each. So, don't take more than two at a time."

"Acetaminophen." Cindy repeated softly.

"That's Tylenol," Denise said.

"I *know* what it is," she retorted. "I'm a *natural* blonde, not a *dumb* blonde."

"Sor-*ry*. That's not how I meant it," Denise mumbled. "And rub it in while you're at it, why don't you?" She rolled onto her side to face Cindy. "Well, I don't know about you, but *I* want them." She pushed herself up slowly, reached for the pain relievers and stopped halfway. She looked down at her bikini top and wiggled it firmly back into place. She looked at Michelle, paused briefly, and asked, "Did we have sex?"

Michelle started to answer, but Denise cut her off. "I don't mean *you* and *me*, 'we.' I mean François and me, 'we'—if that makes any sense." She squeezed her eyes tightly, thought for a moment and reached her hands under the sheets to feel her bathing suit bottom.

"No," Michelle answered. "Nobody had sex with anyone."

"But wasn't that why you hired us?" Denise asked, and reached for the Tylenol. She washed the pills down in a single gulp.

"Yes, but plans changed. Things got sped up far more than I'd expected."

A look of concern crossed Denise's face. "Do we still get paid? We came all this way —"

Cindy's voice boomed from the other bed. "Damned straight we get paid!" She immediately jammed the pillow tightly over her head. In a soft voice barely audible from underneath, she said, "*Sorry*. Too loud. My bad, but it's still all your fault."

"Yes," Michelle said softly, and ignored the barb. "You both get paid in full. You did everything I asked you to do. So, you'll get every cent I promised when you arrive home late tomorrow."

"*Tomorrow*?" the women asked simultaneously.

"Yes. Tomorrow morning, we'll dock in Genoa, Italy. I've made flight reservations for you to fly back to New York through Schiphol airport in Amsterdam."

"What about Louis and François?" Cindy asked.

"They left hours ago."

"Are you going to fly back with us?" Denise asked.

"No," Michelle said. "*You're* going home tomorrow. I, on the other hand, have to go for a cruise on an entirely different kind of ship."

Chapter 28

A thin strip of orange on the eastern horizon intruded into the inky darkness of the early morning sky over Los Angeles. Zeki Aga looked up through the van's windshield, and said to the driver, Asli, "Pretty sunrise. Almost as pretty as you."

She smiled and stole a glance at the distant sky's changing colors. "Thank you.... Unless that's actually smog out there. Hard to tell sometimes."

Zeki peered lazily at the sunrise in the distance until Asli turned the steering wheel of her stolen van to the left. As the van turned, concrete stanchions supporting the freeway's on-ramp blocked his view.

Asli led the other three stolen vans up the on-ramp and south on the 405 Freeway.

"You're too self-effacing, Asli," Zeki said. "You're exceptionally talented. I saw that the moment you showed me the tented apartment complex. You've arranged everything perfectly. I see why His Majesty trusted you and your uncle to be the vanguard of our logistics operations here in the midst of the enemy."

Asli smiled. "I can't do what you and your soldiers have done. I don't know how to cook explosives. I'm a good organizer, so I'm just glad I could help by doing my part. I'll get you to and from the hotel, but what goes on there... well, that's *your* specialty, Zeki."

"We make a good team."

"Might you stay a bit longer? The suitcases in the back would suggest otherwise, but maybe you could...." Asli smiled at Zeki. "You know, stay for a couple of days to reconnoiter another site or something?"

Zeki briefly considered her invitation and watched silently as she turned the van east onto the 10 Freeway toward downtown Los Angeles. "No, we all have to leave. Onur is driving his truck back to New York as we speak, and my team and I have to fly back to Turkey as soon as we're done here. I need to report our success to Sargon and see what he has planned for our next attacks. Unfortunately, I don't know when I'll be able to return to Los Angeles."

Asli made a show of frowning at Zeki. To her left, the three other vans accelerated and passed her. She slowed slightly and checked the freeway signs as she drove to make sure she did not miss her exit. As the minutes ticked by, she checked and rechecked the dashboard clock to ensure she and Zeki did not arrive too early.

***

The shining glass windows of the Westin Bonaventure hotel in downtown Los Angeles gleamed brightly in the morning sunlight. The iconic hotel's five cylindrical towers made the landmark a favorite aerial view in movies since it was completed in 1976.

Behind the hotel's expansive conference center, Zeki's soldiers backed their three vans into open loading dock bays. The men tugged the bills of their Los Angeles Dodgers caps lower to hide their faces and wheeled catering carts from the vans into the main reception hall. One by one, they placed the locked aluminum carts along the walls, positioned perfectly for waiters to empty later if there had actually been food inside.

On his final trip out of the large hall, one of Zeki's men swiped a pamphlet from a plate sitting atop one of the two hundred round tables at which well-dressed men and women started to gather. He scanned his eyes over the title of the pamphlet, "Annual Los Angeles Interfaith Prayer Breakfast," and dropped it into the back of his van before locking the door.

The men walked up the inclined alley to street level, met Asli's van at the corner and hopped into the rear. She pulled away from the curb slowly and retraced her path back onto the 10 Freeway West, toward LAX. Morning rush-hour traffic slowed them, but not enough to make a difference. Five minutes before arriving at the Tom Bradley International Terminal, the radio station's news anchor interrupted the weather broadcast for a special report on a series of explosions at the Westin Bonaventure in downtown Los Angeles.

In a live cut-in for Los Angeles' two million commuters to hear, reporters covering the prayer breakfast described the carnage. The combination of multiple explosions, the resulting fire and inevitable stampede of panicked attendees reigned chaos throughout the hotel's cavernous event center. One reporter speculated it would be days before fire crews could clear the rubble to determine how many dozens — or likely hundreds — of guests died that morning.

Zeki's men listened intently to the broadcast, and Asli translated portions for them. When she finished, the men erupted in cheers and congratulated themselves on a job well done. In unison, they chanted, "*Allahu Akbar*!"

Chapter 29

The day after her two hired escorts disembarked the CIA's yacht in Genoa, Italy, Michelle Reagan stepped down out of the yacht's helicopter onto the most dangerous four-and-a-half acres in the world — the active flight deck of a US Navy aircraft carrier.

USS Ulysses S. Grant patrolled the Mediterranean Sea surrounded by its carrier battle group of fierce-looking surface combatants bristling with antennas while a pair of hunter-killer submarines patrolled silently beneath the surface.

A sailor in a white, long-sleeved shirt and helmet with matching color-coded panels in front and back held out his hand to Michelle. With his assistance, she steadied herself on the carrier's gray deck and slung the strap of her black travel duffel over her shoulder. The sailor alternatingly rushed her forward and held her back, depending on who or what needed to cross in front of them on the rough, non-skid surface of the carrier's flight deck. At one point, she yelped when he yanked her arm hard to let two sailors in green shirts pull a steel cable across the deck.

No worse for the wear, they arrived at a metal doorway where a man in civilian clothes stood just inside the ship and gave her a welcoming wave. He thanked the "white shirt," who turned without a word and ran back to the helicopter.

The man with the scruffy, sandy-colored beard that matched his hair introduced himself. "I'm Dan. Dan Green. You must be Eden."

"Guilty as charged. Good to meet you."

"You too," he said, and he led her through the metal jungle to a stairway. "We can't take the elevators onboard unless we're moving heavy gear, so we'll get our exercise going up and down the ladders." He looked at Michelle and pointed to the metal stairs with chain-link handrails. "That's what the Navy calls stairs."

"Yeah," she replied, "I've deployed off carriers a few times. I've almost gotten used to calling the bathroom a *head*. Almost."

"I'm retired Navy, so the lingo is second nature to me. It goes with the territory."

"You don't look old enough to have retired."

"Thanks, I guess," he said, and glanced back over his shoulder. "I retired after twenty years, one month, and two days as an interrogator. I joined the Company after that. Same work, same food, better pay." He threw a grin back at Michelle. "We can talk more when we get into our suite."

Dan led Michelle along one tile-lined corridor after another until they came to a metal door with no handle. He removed a proximity card from his jeans pocket and waved it at the black, rectangular badge reader on the wall. The mechanism clicked and the door popped open an inch. He pushed it open and held it for Eden.

Once inside, she dropped her bag on the floor and stretched her arms over her head. "That helicopter gets smaller and smaller after an hour inside." She twisted her torso to loosen up her muscles. "Thanks for meeting me upstairs, Dan. I'm sure it'll take me a few days to get my bearings onboard."

"Yeah, at least—"

The walls and floor vibrated, and the scream of the ship's steam catapult roared overhead.

When it quieted down, Dan said, "They just launched a jet. They do that about eighty times a day. And *night*, unfortunately."

Michelle smiled. "I've learned to always travel with a good pair of earplugs."

Dan's face lit up. "Ah, the voice of experience. Well, welcome to the Roach Motel. I'm glad you're here, because we have a problem."

Michelle sighed. "Why is nothing ever easy? What's the problem? And is Michael still here?"

"No, he left yesterday, and there's nothing he'd be able to do, anyway. I doubt there's anything you can do, either, but hey, this is *your* interrogation. What happened is that one of the subjects got sick, and the doctor is working overtime on him. Let's drop your duffel off in your quarters, and then you can meet Doc Jim."

Michelle picked up her bag. "Lead the way."

Dan led her through another prox-card-protected door and into a corridor lined with posters of US naval vessels hanging from the walls. "We don't actually call this place the Roach Motel onboard. We just call it 'the suite.' The Navy provided this space to the Agency for intelligence analysis and coordination work. I'm told that we tried to create a small forward-deployed task force here, but it just didn't work out as well as the suits back home hoped. So, the analysts went back to doing it all on land. Now, we use this as the blackest of black interrogation sites. No rubber hoses or waterboarding here. No videos ever leave our onboard computers, so there's no evidence to show how we get the intel we collect. You know what an absolute cluster *that* turned out to be last time the Agency used black interrogation sites. So, anyway, we *do* record the interviews on DVRs so we can review it onboard as often as we like, but after that, we delete it all, and I wipe the hard drives after every job. And do you know about the drugs?"

"Michael only told me that they exist and are experimental. I'm here to guide your questioning of the prisoners and then take out the trash when you're done."

"We call them subjects, not prisoners. It makes it easier on the doctor to think of them that way, but he's cool with it all. He just won't do the... you know... the end. Have you been on Mike's team long? He came here the first two times a couple of months ago, but never mentioned you until yesterday."

"Yeah, I've worked for him for quite a while," Michelle said. "Years. So, yeah, long enough. Interesting that he never told me about you either until recently."

"Need to know and all that." He led her through another door as he continued the tour. He waved his hand in a circle, explaining the layout. "Our suite is configured as three concentric rings, although there're actually rectangular, not circular. But... whatever. The outer ring is where we sleep and eat. There's also a very small gym at the end of this hall. One thing you need to know is that when we have subjects here, we absolutely always have to have at least one person in the suite. There are *no* exceptions to *that* rule unless the ship is on fire or sinking. Let's hope it never comes to that. The middle ring that we're entering now is for medical and observation. The inner ring, well, that's where we get down to business."

Chapter 30

Dan Green pushed open an interior door on which hung an engraved sign with the medical caduceus symbol of two snakes intertwined around a winged staff. "Doc, meet our new —"

Dan and Michelle entered the medical office and were met by two empty gurneys, a rack of medical equipment and four large cases in one corner, but no doctor. Michelle recognized two of the cases as the shipping trunks into which she helped pack Louis Arsenault and François Marchand on the yacht for transport here.

Dan put his hands on his hips. "Hmm. Well, I doubt he went out for lunch, so let's try over here."

He led Michelle down the hall and opened an unlabeled door. As he did, the gray metal ceiling vibrated, and the roar of a jet being flung aloft by the carrier's steam catapult drowned out the *whoosh-whoosh* of a stationary bike being ridden energetically.

An elderly Black man with a full head of white hair rode the bike like he was trying to punish it for some unknown past affront. Upon seeing his visitors, the tall man slowed his pedaling to a halt and removed a pair of earbuds. He pulled a towel from the handlebars and wiped his face vigorously.

Once the sound of the aircraft launching above them quieted to a dull roar, Dan made the introductions. "Doc, meet Eden. Eden, this is Doctor James McFadden. Doc Jim is our rep from the Office of Medical Services. OMS as a whole has no idea what we do here, but we need a qualified physician on hand to observe the subjects both during the interrogations as well as in between sessions to record how they react to the drug. We ran into some unexpected problems early on, but we don't have to go into that now."

Jim waved to Eden. "I don't mean to be impolite, but maybe we'll shake hands later. I think that'd be better."

Michelle waved in return. "I'm with you on that. Good to meet you, Doc."

"Jim, why don't you finish your workout. In the meantime, I'll take Eden to get some chow. I'll bring back lunch for you and both subjects. Okay?"

"Works for me. I'll take my usual Caesar salad, but with a grilled chicken breast this time, if you please."

Dan threw the doctor a mock salute and led Eden to the mess hall.

When they returned, they found Jim in the interrogation observation room. Dan Green set three boxes of food on a table and plopped himself down in one of four brown, padded leather chairs against the long wall of the rectangular room. He sorted through the trio of boxes to find Jim's salad and set it aside for him.

Michelle looked around the observation room and extended her hand to Jim McFadden. "You clean up well, doctor."

Jim chuckled, turned away from the array of large, flat-panel TVs on which he was observing the subjects in the interrogation suite and turned to the new arrival. "I don't get out of the suite much and, at my age, I need the exercise."

"Me too," Michelle said as they shook hands, "even at my age. It's good to meet you. Again."

"You too, young lady," he said. The septuagenarian took the lunch container Dan pointed to and sat down to eat in the chair next to him.

Michelle examined the wall-to-wall and floor-to-ceiling array of televisions on the bulkhead opposite the leather chairs in which Dan and Jim relaxed. Except for the thin black bezels at the edge of each screen which made a grid-like outline of the scene they projected, the views from the dozen hidden cameras on the far side of the wall gave the effect of seeing right through the solid steel wall.

Dan glanced at his watch and did a few mental calculations. To Michelle, he said, "It's almost time for me to feed Louis. We only give the subjects one meal a day. The lack of food on top of the stress of being captive here ensures they're hungry enough to eat their sandwiches and thirsty enough to drink the Kool-Aid. Literally. We've found through trial and error—mostly error, really—that the drug has a pretty sour taste to it. The too-sweet taste of cherry Kool-Aid masks it quite effectively. So, if you and Doc want to get acquainted in the meantime, that'll give the drug enough time to take effect. You can watch the interrogation from here."

Michelle answered immediately. "That'd be great. Michael told me that you have quite the voyeuristic setup here. This is, at the same time, both impressive and more than a little creepy."

Dan chuckled. "Well, it's not quite virtual reality, but someone spent a whole bunch of money on large-screen TVs, so you might as well watch them all at once, right? Okay, I'll see you both after lunch."

***

In front of the chair in which Doc McFadden sat, the array of large screens showed Dan Green sitting at a small dining room table. The almost lifelike effect of the televisions nearly tricked the viewer into thinking they could be looking through a glass wall or two-way mirror into the secure interrogation suite on the other side of the bulkhead.

On the screens, Michelle watched the two men in the center room of the three-room interrogation suite. Dan sat at the table next to Louis Marchand who held half of his *jambon-beurre* sandwich in one hand and gulped cherry Kool-Aid from the plastic cup in his other. The French commodities broker wolfed down half of the ham and butter sandwich and then looked at the empty cup longingly.

Jim McFadden started a stopwatch and laid it atop a clipboard on the small table to his right.

Michelle glanced to her left where the televisions showed another room in the inner ring of the Roach Motel—the subject's quarters. The connecting door between the center room and Louis's empty bedroom stood half-open. The spartan bedroom contained a wood-frame bed with white sheets and a navy blue blanket. Michelle marveled at the fact that Louis had made his bed earlier that day. She wondered why he bothered. To her right, and unseen by either man in the central room but clearly visible to Michelle and Jim in the observation room, François Arsenault rolled over on his cot and scratched the top of his right ear.

At the table with Louis, Dan pulled a water bottle from the messenger bag hanging from the back of his chair and filled Louis's plastic cup.

Louis looked surprised. "You should leave a couple of those in my room. I get very thirsty."

"I only have this one," Dan said, while Louis took another bite of his sandwich, "but I'll try to find another."

"Or," Louis said through a mouthful of ham-and-butter sandwich, "you could just refill that one and leave it with me, no?"

Having no intention of acceding to the man's request, Dan ignored the obvious suggestion and made small talk while the Frenchman finished his one meal of the day.

In the observation room, McFadden gestured for Michelle to sit in the chair next to him. He offered, "Dan's not going to give him anything else to eat or drink today. That way, the subject will be far more likely to consume everything he's given tomorrow for his third and final interrogation."

Michelle sat down in the chair Jim offered. "Nice chairs," she said, and stretched her legs forward quickly getting comfortable.

Jim grinned. "Interrogation sessions can get long, so we furnished the room appropriately."

Michelle almost felt guilty that, on the opposite side of the wall in front of her, Dan and Louis sat on unpadded wooden chairs while she and Jim relaxed in comfort.

"So," Michelle asked, "the drug is in the Kool-Aid?"

Jim nodded and picked up the clipboard and a pen from the table between them. "Yeah. Early subjects told us that when we gave them the drug in a bottle of water, it tasted sour. The excessive sweetness of the cherry punch masks it. Only giving the subject one glass of juice and one bottle of water a day ensures they're thirsty enough the next day to drink it all again." He motioned to the stopwatch. "I'm timing the lapse between the ingestion of the Russian drug and its first visible effect on the subject."

"*Russian* drug? You get these drugs from Russia?"

McFadden looked at her for a few seconds. "You didn't know about that?"

Michelle shook her head. "I didn't know anything about this place until a week ago. I just assumed that the truth serum was a CIA drug. You know, something DS&T concocted."

"Nope, and there's no such thing as a 'truth serum,' anyway. You guys didn't create the drugs. You stole it."

"From the Russians?"

"No. One of your agents in China pilfered part of the shipment that the Russian SVRR shared with the MSS in Beijing to aid in Chinese interrogations. Your mole in the MSS gave it to his CIA handler. We've been through six subjects so far, not counting Louis or François. After these two, we'll only have enough left for two more subjects."

"What happens then? You have to close up shop?"

"Maybe," Jim said. "DS&T and a couple of their contract labs are trying to reverse engineer it so they can synthesize more. Last I heard, they've not been successful. These subjects must be pretty important to warrant this treatment."

"I guess so," Michelle said. "I don't make those decisions, but the people these guys are working for are pretty bad *hombres*. This new group of terrorists must have learned a lot from al-Qaeda. We've not been able to identify the boss yet because he's not using cell phones, email or any electronics we can trace. It's all hand-to-hand and face-to-face communications done by trusted couriers. If you ask me, they've learned their lessons *too* well. NSA can't do squat to track them, so it makes us have to work much harder to figure out who they are."

"And when you *do* find them?"

Michelle shrugged and left the answer open-ended, saying, "More frequent flyer miles for me, I guess."

The doctor listened as Dan talked to Louis and jotted a few notes down on the clipboard. "Sorry," Doc Jim said to Michelle. "You'll have to excuse me when I jump in and out of a conversation to take notes. I want to be able to give Dan feedback during a session if I can. We record everything on those servers over there." He pointed to a rack of computers housed in a six-foot-tall black cabinet standing in the far corner of the room. "But I'd rather catch as much as I can in real-time to support his questioning. He'll come out mid-way through for a brief tag-up."

"Makes sense," Michelle said.

"Oh, and if Dan didn't already tell you, the red button next to the computers over there—the big one under the clear plastic cover—will destroy everything on the hard drives. You know, just in case."

"In case we're discovered, you mean? To destroy all evidence to protect the guilty?"

McFadden shrugged. "I guess we're all guilty of something, but, still... I'd rather not spend my remaining days in jail. We've all crossed a line or two in our own way, I suppose."

"Well," Michelle said, "I certainly can't argue with that."

"We all have our own ways of coping with the work we know needs doing."

"So, why do *you* do this?" Michelle asked. "I mean, I know why *I'm* here. I guess I would have expected someone with just, you know, paramedic training to be the permanent party here, but not a physician."

McFadden sat quietly for a moment and studied the screen. Louis was starting to slur his words as he talked to Dan.

The doctor checked the stopwatch, wrote down a few lines of text and tapped his pen on the clipboard. "I retired from treating patients almost ten years ago. I work for the Agency and the Office of Medical Services on contract. While I still maintain my license, I don't really have the need to protect it like a practicing physician does. So, about two years ago, I got asked to help out on 'a special project' that no one else in OMS was briefed into. It turned out to be this. I do my part to monitor the subjects' health and response to the drug, but at the end of the interrogations, I won't...." He looked at Michelle, then averted his eyes.

"No, no, I get it. That's why I'm here. I understand, but from what Michael told me," Michelle said, "the drugs are fatal, anyway. So, why, umm... why not just wait?"

"We did, at first," the doctor said, "and that's how we found out about the side effects. But it turns out to be quite a painful and drawn-out end for the subjects. I'm not in favor of assisted suicide, but, well, in rare cases euthanasia can be an act of mercy, I suppose. Even for these people."

"*Mmmm*," Michelle mumbled, not sure what else to say. She sat for a moment, and then asked, "I understand the licensing thing, but that's not really the issue for you, is it? I can tell *that's* not really why you're here."

He met Michelle's gaze, then looked down at his shoes. He sat silently for a while, and answered, "No, not really." He took a deep breath, held it for a few seconds and continued. "Some time back when I lived in New York City, I practiced medicine in Manhattan. My son lived in Silicon Valley but was planning to have his wedding at a very nice banquet hall at the north end of Staten Island. The venue overlooks the Hudson River and has a wonderful view of the Statue of Liberty — if you strained your eyes a little bit, anyway. My son's fiancée was visiting us to apply for the marriage license, listen to a few bands they were considering and then she signed some of the other contracts. You know, for the photographer, flowers, centerpieces and such."

Michelle nodded and waited patiently for him to continue.

"My wife and James Junior's fiancée flew back to California together." He looked at Michelle and paused. "They flew out on United Airlines Flight 93. That was on September 11th, 2001. Needless to say, there was never a wedding."

Michelle reached toward Jim McFadden and placed her hand gently on his forearm. Softly she said, "The flight that crashed in Pennsylvania. I remember. Oh, Jim, I'm *so* sorry." There was nothing else for her to say, nor did Jim need to say anything else for her to fully understand the widower's motives. She picked at the cuticle on her left index finger, and thought, *Even a doctor can feel the need for revenge against the terrorists who killed his wife, even if he can't bring himself to admit it out loud.*

McFadden lifted the pen from the clipboard and made a few more notes.

On the screen, Michelle watched Louis bury his head in his hands. The Frenchman folded his arms on the table in front of him and laid his head down. "I'm tired. I don't feel well."

Dan gently pushed him back to an upright position. "That's okay, Louis, you can go to sleep in a few minutes, but not just yet. I'm really impressed with what you told me earlier about the way you move the money from the banks in Athens to the agricultural auction houses in Moldova. Whose name did you say is on those accounts?"

Louis raised his head and appeared to look directly into Michelle's eyes. He convulsed and a stream of vomit spewed at the television screen so fast that Michelle flinched. The remains of Louis's lunch coated the concealed camera in the interrogation suite, darkening that TV screen completely.

Dan's yelp from the other room erupted through the speakers, surprising Michelle. "Oh, shit!" he yelled. "Help, guys! I need *help* in here."

Doc McFadden pushed himself out of his chair and beat Michelle to the door. They raced into the interrogation suite's entrance, and the doctor stopped before the inner door. He looked at Michelle and pointed to a wooden nightstick hanging by its leather lanyard from a hook on the wall. "We don't allow firearms in the interrogation suite, so that's all we have in case the subjects try to escape. Even if they get by us, they'd get stopped by the doors between each ring which require a prox card to pass through, but I trust you know how to use a baton?"

"Old school," Michelle said, and picked up the wooden trowel. "Don't worry," she said confidently. "I've got your back."

McFadden punched the combination into the door's lock and led the way into the interrogation suite. Dan knelt on the floor over an unmoving Louis Marchand and scooped vomit from the prone man's obstructed airway.

The doctor knelt beside his patient, and Michelle stood watch from in front of the closed suite door, a dozen feet away. McFadden lifted Louis's arm and placed two fingers across the still man's wrist. "No pulse," the doctor said.

McFadden looked at Dan and told the retired sailor to begin administering CPR.

As Dan Green shifted around to Louis's side, the doctor turned to Michelle and spoke rapidly. "In the infirmary, there's an Automatic External Defibrillator. It's inside a white metal box hanging on the wall—"

"Yup, I'll find it! I had the training a couple of years ago. I'll be right back." Michelle tapped the lock code into the suite door and sprinted to the medical bay.

When she returned with the briefcase-sized box, Dan stopped applying compressions to Louis's chest. He and Doc McFadden scooted to the side so Michelle could join them.

Dan raised Louis's polo shirt up to the man's armpits while Michelle unfolded the AED's electrode pad. Doc Jim took the pad from her and nudged Michelle out of the way. She backed up on her knees and turned the AED's display panel to face the doctor.

McFadden placed the pad's large red 'plus sign' over his patient's heart and secured it on Louis's bare chest with two adhesive strips.

The doctor pressed two buttons on the AED's control panel and rocked back on his knees.

A calm electronic voice emanated from the plastic grill on the yellow-and-gray AED box. "Analyzing heart rhythm. Do not touch the patient." After a moment, the AED announced, "Shock advised. Charging for automatic shock."

The machine buzzed softly, and Louis shook for a moment. Michelle looked at him, perplexed. She had expected him to convulse wildly. The small movement seemed too muted.

In its almost annoyingly calm voice, the AED continued, "Shock delivered. If needed, begin CPR. Warning, battery at twenty-five percent."

Michelle sked Jim McFadden, "Is there anything I can do? Should I call for the ship's doctor?"

McFadden shook his head and waited for the AED to analyze Louis's cardiac activity again and compute the recommended treatment. The machine administered two additional shocks, but Louis's heart refused to restart.

McFadden turned the AED off. He stood slowly and rubbed his knees. He shuffled to a chair against the wall and sat down roughly. "No, we'd never call the ship's staff for help. Besides, it's too late." He sighed and rubbed his temples. "After Louis arrived onboard, it took him a very long time to regain consciousness. François woke up relatively quickly, but not Louis. He must have suffered brain damage during transport."

"*Brain* damage?" Michelle asked. "What happened? And what about François?"

"François is fine, don't worry. We gave him the first dose yesterday, and he reacted as expected. This was Louis's second dose, and I thought it'd be all right. He reacted well enough to the first one yesterday."

Michelle asked urgently, "But *what* happened?"

The doctor screwed his lips together and looked at the concern spread so clearly on Michelle's suntanned face. "There was most likely a problem with his airflow while he was sedated for the flight. He must have either been lying at an odd angle in the shipping trunk or maybe his tongue kept slipping too far back into his throat. Either way, he went too long without getting enough oxygen. He regained consciousness and was ambulatory—you saw that—so it seemed like he'd recovered. All in all, though, it must have been too much for his heart, so he ended up in cardiac arrest here today. There's nothing else we could have done for him, either yesterday or today." He pointed to Louis's corpse. "Honestly, there's nothing the ship's medical staff could have done, either. Best case, they might have stabilized the body with a ventilator to get him to a hospital onshore, but—"

"Yeah," Dan cut in, "but there's no way in *hell* we could let that happen. It would expose the program."

"No," Michelle said, and took a deep breath. "I understand. I'm with you on that."

The doctor stood and headed for the door. "Let's get him to my infirmary. Eden, would you come help me wheel a gurney in here?"

***

Later, in the infirmary, Michelle lifted a white sheet from the head of the corpse and took one last look at the pudgy Frenchman. "Well, good, at least it was Louis."

"*Good?*" Dr. McFadden asked.

"Well, *no*," Michelle said, "of course not 'good' in *that* sense. I just meant that François is the leader of his group, so he's more likely to have the information we need. We can still get that from him, right?" She whipped her head around, looked at Dan, and asked urgently, "Right?"

"Yes, right," Dan said, defensively. "He's fine."

Jim McFadden walked to the far side of the room and moved three cardboard boxes from the top of two silver, rectangular cases. The end of the case Michelle could see had a red-and-white sticker labeled *Head*.

Dan tapped Michelle on the shoulder. "Well, it looks like we'll get to use the ship's elevators, after all. Would you come help me wheel a couple of our carts and coolers to the ship's galley? We'll need about a hundred pounds of ice a day to keep the body from—"

Michelle held up her hand. "Yeah, I get the picture. I've seen mortuary transfer cases before. I've just never put anyone inside one before."

With an edge to his voice, Doctor McFadden asked her, "But isn't that why you're here? Because *I* won't do it?"

"Yes, well," Michelle added, "I just meant... I mean I've never actually *placed* someone inside one before. Physically. I mean of course I've...." She paused, looked at Dan and scratched the back of her neck. "*Umm*, Dan, you mentioned ice? Why don't we go get that now?"

Dan Green turned quickly to conceal the thin smirk on his lips. He gave Michelle a "come this way" wave, and she followed him through the infirmary's door without so much as a glance back at the doctor.

By the time they returned pushing a pair of carts topped with large ice-filled Igloo chests, Jim McFadden had already prepared one of the aluminum transfer cases. He had placed its two-inch-thick base on a gurney and wheeled it next to the one on which Louis's remains laid.

Each coffin-sized case weighed over one hundred twenty-five pounds empty. Loaded with the late commodities broker's remains and the ice, it tipped the scales at over four hundred.

It took fifteen minutes for the team of three to pack Louis's corpse and ice into the transfer case and seal it closed.

When they finished, Michelle rocked back on her heels, crossed her arms over her chest, and looked at Dan. She said, "Not that we need to treat François with kid gloves, but right now, he's the *only* link we have left in the money chain from the bankers to the terrorists. I sure as hell hope we have better luck with him."

***

Zeki Aga's flight from Los Angeles landed in Turkey a half-hour early. He stretched his shoulders as he walked to his rental car in the Premier aisle. There, he selected a Nissan with what he hoped were comfortable seats.

He drove straight from the airport to Sargon's compound and parked outside the main house. Sargon's counselor, Rifaat, met Zeki in the reception room adjacent to the two-story foyer and led the soldier directly to the throne room.

Against the far wall, Sargon sat on a low-backed, gold-plated throne perched on a narrow dais. Silver roses embedded in the throne's arms glinted in the light of electric candelabras lining the walls. His counselor announced the visitor immediately. "Your Majesty, Sargon the Third, King of Akkad, Assyria, and Sumeria, and Wielder of the Sword of the Faithful, I present to you Zeki Aga, triumphant in his attack on the heathens in America."

"Your Majesty," Zeki said proudly, "I bring great news from Los Angeles." He recounted his team's success in California, and then backtracked to describe their earlier success attacking the Marine Air Station in North Carolina.

"You have done well, Zeki. You have my praise and heartfelt thanks. This is a *great* day for all of us as we rebuild our kingdom. I have great faith in you and your loyalty to our struggle, and it is because of skilled and dedicated men like you that we will be victorious. Are you ready for your next assignment?"

"I am, Your Majesty. How can my team and I be of service?"

"The Americans continue to spread the evils of their hedonistic way of life into Turkey, and I will not allow it. Your next target is closer to home. The American embassy in Ankara is sponsoring a so-called cultural exchange in Istanbul with their half-naked dancers, sacrilegious paintings and movies filled with violence and drugs. It is *harem*—forbidden! Go find Bayram in the guest house. He returned not long ago from a successful attack in Paris and will tell you more about how I plan to teach the Americans a lesson they will never forget. Your expertise will be important to our future successes in battle, both at home and abroad. I *know* I can count on you, Zeki."

"Yes, Your Majesty. You certainly can," Zeki said, and walked tall as he left the room.

When they were alone, Rifaat advised His Highness, "By all accounts, he and his team did well in California."

"Yes indeed," Sargon agreed, and cracked his knuckles. "It worked out well. Every successful military campaign needs its distraction to keep the enemy looking in the wrong direction. The attacks in America are nothing more than a way for us to split their forces. The more of their treasure we make them spend on the defense of their homeland, the less they can spend in Iraq or Syria or corrupting our people here in Turkey. The Crusaders won't see us coming in Istanbul, and we can continue purging them from Turkish soil. After that, our soldiers who are now infiltrating Western Europe along with throngs of refugees will be our vanguard to spearhead our next attacks which will enable our rise to power across the continent. We need to make sure their funding arrives unimpeded."

"I have a meeting about that early this evening. I will make sure that goes as well as the attacks in America went."

Sargon slapped his counselor on the shoulder. "Yes, Rifaat. They went very well indeed."

Chapter 31

The next morning, Michelle awakened with a start as a Navy fighter jet screamed off the carrier's flight deck — propelled either by the world's most advanced nuclear-powered steam catapult or an irate Banshee, she wasn't sure.

The CIA officer strained to read the red digits of the alarm clock on the nightstand next to her bed and groaned. *Six. Ugh.* She rolled back and wrapped the foam pillow around her head as the catapult launched another jet into the clear morning sky over the Mediterranean Sea.

Michelle took the hint that she was destined to start her day. Reluctantly, she stood up slowly and stretched. She looked around the empty room, illuminated by a single overhead fluorescent safety light. She rubbed her face, changed into workout clothes and made her way to the small gym in the Roach Motel's middle ring.

After a long session of stretching and folding into a half-dozen yoga poses, she rode the stationary bike for a half an hour and then showered. Refreshed, she made her way to the ship's General Mess for breakfast, glad for a chance to eat a leisurely meal. Afterward, she returned to the suite and checked her work email on the CIA's secure network.

She read the message from her team lead first. Michael's short note from the team's covert off-site office in Tysons Corner, Virginia, simply said she should call him each day after they finished with "the boys," as he referred to Louis and François. "Crap," she cursed under her breath, realizing she'd not updated her boss on Louis's premature demise. She didn't want to put the details in an email — even a classified one — which would be archived by the CIA to comply with Federal records retention laws, so she simply typed: *Ran into a real problem but hope to make progress soon. Will call you sometime after lunch today, Virginia time.*

She knew he would not be happy and resigned herself to dealing with that confrontation later. Maybe when she told him about Louis's death, she'd be able to soften the blow with actionable intelligence she and Dan pried from François that afternoon. She hoped so, anyway.

An email from Wilson Henry, the team's intelligence analyst, updated her on his latest findings. He continued to receive data from NSA's intercepts of financial transactions made by François' team and other brokers in their firm. Unfortunately, none of the records stood out as viable leads he could use to identify the terrorist network or unmask Sargon's true identity.

Michelle double-clicked on an article Wilson attached from CIA's Directorate of Analysis' daily newsfeed, the "eWire." The article detailed an attack on a US Marine base in North Carolina which the FBI was investigating as an act of international terrorism. Michelle grimaced at the mention of four deaths and six gravely wounded civilians and Marines who were caught in the blast at the gate of the airfield at McCutcheon Field in North Carolina, home of a US Marine MV-22 Osprey squadron. A knot grew in Michelle's stomach at the sight of the stock aircraft photo embedded in the article. Her mind rewound to her headlong sprint into the back of a similar aircraft just weeks earlier. Her thoughts turned inward. *Can't be a coincidence, can it? Am I responsible for this attack? Is this revenge for my work in Iran?*

She stared at the screen for a minute and let the feeling subside. The best she could do now to prevent future attacks was to get the identity of Sargon's financial cut-out from François. That was her only path forward to finding Sargon and ending his rise to power.

She replied cryptically to Wilson that she and the team on the carrier would be "having additional conversations" that afternoon, and she'd pass along anything they learned.

After finishing up with her work emails, she sent a short note to her boyfriend to let him know she missed him. She looked at the computer's clock and figured that even if Steve Krauss got to work early, as he often did when she was out of town, he still wouldn't get the message for another three or four hours.

As she logged out, Jim McFadden pushed the door open. "Oh, hi, Eden. I was just going to order more supplies for next week's milk run, as the Navy calls it. But if you need the computer —"

"Nope. Just finished up, Doc. It's all yours. Is Dan up yet?"

"Yes," he said, and took the seat Michelle just vacated. "He's in his office planning the questions he'll ask François."

"Great," she said, and headed for the door. "That's exactly what I wanted to talk to him about."

***

That afternoon, Michelle sat next to the doctor in the interrogation observation room. On the screens in front of them, François Arsenault chewed the last bit of the sandwich Dan Green had brought him earlier and lay back down on his bed.

Jim McFadden looked at his stopwatch. "Should take about twenty minutes or so for the 'Kool Aid' to take effect. We have some time, if you want to take a break."

"No, I'm good. Thanks," Michelle replied. "I *really* need this to work. François is our last link to this group."

"Dan's an expert," the doctor assured her. "That's why he's in charge of this little off-the-map postage stamp of a CIA station. If anyone can do it, he can. In fact, *you* don't even need to be here, if you'd rather not."

Michelle shook her head. "I've already worked out today and don't have anywhere else I need to be. I'd rather be here in case I hear something that sounds familiar so I can quarterback the interrogation."

"'Quarterback,' eh? You know the lingo. You've done this before?"

"Nothing quite like this, no. I've gotten information out of some people, but not with drugs."

"Maybe thumbscrews and rubber hoses are more your style?"

Michelle chuckled. "No, nothing like that." She thought back to one particular mission in Cuba. "One time, there was this one woman I interrogated late one night. It was a very calm and quiet situation, actually. No drugs. No violence. Not even any shouting. In the end, she told me everything I wanted to know."

"And how did that one end?" Jim asked.

Michelle looked at the screens showing François lying on the narrow bed in his cell. Softly, she said, "Same as this one will, pretty much." She looked at the doctor, paused for a moment and then asked, "Why do *you* do it? I mean, I understand the 9/11 connection, and I'm very sorry for your loss, but you know... medical ethics and all that. I mean, I'm grateful for your help here, but... I don't know. I was just wondering about that while I worked out this morning."

Jim McFadden lifted a ballpoint pen from the clipboard, held it between his thumb and index finger and tapped it against his knee. "The Hippocratic Oath, you mean?"

"Right. Do no harm and things like that."

"*Harm* is a relative thing, Eden."

"Really? How so?"

"In medicine, especially with regards to ethics, the end justifies the means. Many physicians would claim to disagree, but you can tell it's true by their actions."

Michelle tilted her head slightly. "I've heard plenty of other people say that, but not doctors."

"Well...." McFadden thought for a moment, then gestured with his hand. "Consider this example. If I took a scalpel and cut you with it right here and now, would you agree with me that such an act would be doing you harm?"

"Yes, clearly."

"Of course, it would. Now, tell me, have you ever had surgery?"

"Yes, a few times."

"I don't need the details, but can you give me an example?"

"Sure. I was shot in the left thigh. A surgeon went in to remove the bullet and patch me up."

"First, I'm glad to see you've fully recovered. Second, did the surgeon use a scalpel on you?"

Michelle nodded at the doctor, and the corners of her lips turned up into the start of a grin. "Although I was sedated at the time, I'll assume the answer is 'yes.' I think I see where this is going."

"I never said it would be a complex example, just a clear and compelling one," the doctor said, and continued to tap his pen. "So then, do *you* consider that particular surgeon's actions to have done you harm, or were they part of helping you?"

"I'd say he was very helpful," Michelle said, and didn't notice that she rubbed her fingertips across the bottom of her left thigh.

"I'm glad to hear it. So, there you have it. The same act—cutting someone with a scalpel—can be a bad thing in one instance but a good thing in another. It's all situationally dependent. No particular action— the *means*—is good or bad in and of itself. It's the intended outcome— the *end* or *ends*—are all that matter in any discussion of good or bad. So, with that stem-winding introduction, is what we're doing here in the Roach Motel good or bad? Are we doing these things to these men out of retaliation for past acts? Are we exacting revenge?"

Michelle briefly considered telling the doctor about the terrorist attack in North Carolina but decided against it. She feared doing so would expose her actions in Iran, which the doctor simply did not have the need to know about. "No," Michelle said energetically, "definitely not. We're trying to stop *future* terrorist attacks."

"Exactly," Doctor McFadden agreed. "We want to stop future attacks. So, in my mind, if we're successful in preventing mass murder, the net effect will be positive for everyone involved."

On the screen, Dan Green led François Arsenault into the interrogation suite's main chamber.

"Well," McFadden said, "*almost* everyone."

***

Doctor McFadden jotted down the time the interrogation ended on his clipboard, and said, "Well, that was rather unhelpful I'm afraid."

Michelle stood and arched her back to dispel stiffness from having sat still far longer than she'd have liked while watching the unfruitful interrogation. She looked up at the gray, steel ceiling and groaned. "Why was François able to avoid answering Dan's questions? I could see him straining, but... I guess I need to talk to Dan."

"Maybe the third time will be the charm?"

Michelle exploded. "If not, *then* what?"

Jim McFadden recoiled visibly but managed to respond calmly. "I don't know, Eden. The Russian drug is usually more effective than this. Maybe Dan will have some ideas. Best to discuss the interrogation strategy with him."

The door to the observation room opened, and Dan Green stepped in. He took a deep breath, tossed the empty water bottle he'd given François with lunch into the room's rectangular trash can and expressed exactly what Michelle was feeling. "Well, *that* was a complete waste of time."

"Dan," Michelle said with urgency, "drugs or not, this is getting serious. We have only *one* shot left with him. We need a new plan."

Chapter 32

The following day, Michelle stared intently at the TV screens in the observation room as Dan Green quizzed François Arsenault. Doc McFadden sat silently in his padded chair, alternatingly checking his stopwatch and scribbling notes on his clipboard.

Michelle found herself leaning toward the screens as Dan put his face close to François' and repeated his questions with increasing urgency.

"Are *you* the one who authorizes payment, François? I mean, you're the boss, right? You're the broker who the other account managers work for, right? *You* have to approve the transfers yourself, François, don't you? Tell me where the money goes."

Sweat trickled down the left side of François' face. The Frenchman groaned and rubbed his lower back with both hands. Over the past three days, the Russian drugs had ravaged his kidneys. Now, he alternated between rubbing his aching back and wiping sweat from his face. His head bobbed as the drug's effect made him appear drunk.

"*Oui*," François admitted. He propped his chin on his hands, leaned forward onto the table and angled his eyes up to Dan. "I approve all transfers in and out. What of it? It's a charity, why do you care? They collect money to resettle refugees."

"Yes," Dan agreed, to keep the money launderer talking, "that *is* a noble cause. But why do you have to play so many games to get it from Africa into Europe and then on to wherever it goes?"

François wiped his brow with his sleeve. The drug's destructive effect on his kidneys forced his body to expel its fluids in other ways, namely sweat. "Dario Turchi sends the money from rich donors in Africa. He said they sell used cars for big profits and want to help the less fortunate."

Sure, Dan thought, *they sell used cars. And drugs. And weapons to warlords. And women into slavery.* "Cars, huh? Interesting. That sounds like a good business with noble goals. They must send you a lot of money. What do you do with it, then? You know, to get it to the *refugees*."

A knot formed in Michelle's stomach as she watched François' face contort. He lurched forward as if leading with his chin. The Frenchman opened his mouth and paused as if unsure what to say. Instead of speaking, he shuddered and vomited onto the table between him and Dan.

The CIA interrogator recoiled. He slid his chair back and jumped to his feet.

Doctor McFadden jumped to his feet, and muttered, "Shit!" He looked at the clipboard in his hands and flipped a few pages. "Why is this happening to *both* of them?" He glanced at his stopwatch, then back at the TV screens.

For a moment, nobody moved until François coughed and gripped his stomach.

Michelle leaned farther forward. "Are you going in there?"

The doctor stood still and watched François intently. The Frenchman coughed twice more and wiped his mouth with his sleeve.

Dan slowly moved across the room but kept his eyes glued to François. The interrogator took a towel off the countertop near the entrance door and picked up the plastic trashcan nearby.

"No," Doc McFadden said, studying the interrogation subject closely. "He seems all right, now. I *really* want to know why both men vomited. That's only happened once before, and I thought it was just a fluke back then. Now, I'm convinced there's more to it than that, but I don't know what. I wonder if it has something to do with their diets. I wish we could have autopsies performed, but that's out of the question. Remind me to take blood samples from both bodies later after you...."

He glanced at Michelle and then focused on the TV screens on which Dan Green was cleaning the table in the interrogation suite. The doctor sat down without another word and watched François' reactions carefully.

Michelle let the doctor's sentence remain unfinished. They both knew what awaited François later that day.

In the interrogation suite, Dan waited until François recovered his composure and asked him to continue.

François coughed once, then took a deep breath. As he exhaled, he seemed to physically deflate and sink into his chair. His head slowly tilted to the left, and he muttered, "*Mmmm...* The money... We use their money to buy commodities on the Intercontinental Exchange. I always tell my guys... stick with lumber or cocoa. Maybe use soybeans sometimes, you know? Those prices are not as volatile as natural gas or copper. You can lose your shirt overnight on those. Have you ever placed a trade—"

Dan clapped François on his back. "Yeah, man. You're right. I know what you mean. Then you just turn around and sell the lumber or whatever into a different account? Is that it?"

"*Non, non, non*," François mumbled in French, and proceeded to explain the roundabout way of routing sales of untraceable physical commodities through European commodities exchanges in Sofia, Bulgaria, and Bucharest, Romania. "The money ends up in the Liechtenstein Trust Bank. The LTB bankers can be trusted to keep their noses out of their clients' business. Money gets wired from Sofia and Bucharest to Liechtenstein. When I tell them to, LTB puts the cash into one of my two safe deposit boxes. Then either Louis or Pascal flies to Liechtenstein. He stacks the euros inside a briefcase and places it in the other safe deposit box." Still resting his chin on his hands and looking bored, François angled his eyes up at Dan. The Frenchman grinned. "I buy a counterfeit attaché case for thirty euros and charge my client *five hundred* for it as if it were a real Coach or Floto Milano case!" He laughed at his own ingenuity.

Dan patted François on the shoulder in mock appreciation. "You are one *shrewd* businessman, François. I'm impressed. After that, how does your client know to pick up the money?"

A thin line of spittle dripped from the corner of François's mouth as he spelled out for Dan the email address and code phrase that told Sargon's courier the money was ready for pickup. Dan asked about the safe deposit boxes, and François recited the numbers without hesitating.

Dan had him repeat all the critical information he'd just provided, and Michelle wrote it down verbatim. She confirmed it the second time through, certain she'd written it down properly but knew this was their last chance to pump François for information. His kidneys were already failing.

"Don't worry," Jim told her, and pointed to the rack of computer equipment in the corner of the room. "You can replay it from the DVR as many times as you want to ensure you got everything you need."

She looked at the equipment in the far corner, double-checked her notes and nodded.

"And *then*," François announced proudly, "we do it all again the next quarter. It's *good* business. I'm really fortunate Dario introduced me to them. And he gets his fair share, too, you know? I'm good about that. It's good business to treat your friends well. Who knows who else he may introduce me to next time, eh?" His head swiveled and fell off his hands. He caught himself before he lost his balance and tried his best to straighten up. He shook his head gently. "Can I have more water, Daniel? I'm dry. Do you have Perrier?"

Dan smirked. "Let me see what I can find for you. I'll be right back. Relax for a minute."

Dan left François at the table and joined Michelle and Doc McFadden in the observation room.

"So," Dan asked Michelle, "what do you think?"

Michelle looked at her notes and scratched the side of her face. "He gave us the name of the bank, the account numbers, safe deposit box numbers, email address to send the message to Sargon's guy and the code phrase. With the account numbers, the analysts back in DC can tell us how much money has been transferred and where. If Sargon's people are simply moving it as cash in a briefcase, it's probably just a few million at a time in five-hundred-euro notes. Cash also makes it easier for them to pay off Turkish officials for protection from on high."

"A few million euros here," Dan said, "a few million there... and pretty soon we're talking about real money."

Michelle thought about the bombing at the McCutcheon Field Marine Corp Base and wondered briefly how much it had cost Sargon to murder four innocent Americans at the gate. Much less than a million, she was sure.

"Well," Michelle said, "I think that's about it. What about you?"

Dan shrugged. "He's *your* guy, so it's up to you. I'm just here to be a good host and ask the questions you need answered. We're done when *you* say we're done."

Jim placed his pen down on the clipboard and kneaded his hands. He looked around the room. "I think I'll busy myself in the medical suite, if you don't mind." He stood and picked up his clipboard. "I have to type up my notes anyway. Might as well start that now."

Michelle watched the doctor as he left the room.

After he was out of earshot, Dan said, "I have the locked case that Logistics sent ahead for you. I'll go get it."

He left the room, and Michelle turned to watch François. The Frenchman paced around the interrogation suite, to his bedroom and back again as he waited for Dan to return — with water, he hoped.

A few minutes later, Dan returned to the observation room carrying a small, red, hard-sided Pelican case. He handed the case to Michelle by the handle, and she placed it onto a table with other items she'd prepared earlier in the day.

She unscrewed the small plastic cap from a bottle of Evian on the table and poured half of the mineral spring water into a clear sports-drink bottle which had a silkscreened image of Switzerland's Mont Blanc—the tallest of the Alps—on the side. She turned the locked case toward her and dialed a six-digit code into the combination lock. From inside the case, she removed the three-inch-diameter screw cap with a matching Mont Blanc image on it. She twisted it onto the top of the sports bottle and flicked the integrated straw up with her thumb.

Michelle lifted the bottle for Dan to see. "Ready as I'll ever be. If I need help, I'll use the word 'popcorn.' But before I go in...." Michelle looked at the rack of computer equipment in the corner. "Please turn off the recording."

Dan walked over to the DVR system and tapped a few buttons on the touchscreen. He turned back to Michelle. "Done. The cameras and TVs have to stay on, or I won't be able to see or hear you, but it won't record anything."

She nodded and walked into the interrogation suite.

François did a double take, as he was expecting Dan to return.

"Hi," Michelle said, and showed François the bottle of water. "Dan said you were thirsty, so I came with the water you asked him for. He said your hands were shaking, so I thought you might like it if I put the Evian in this bottle with a built-in straw." She flicked up the rubbery straw with her thumb and placed the bottle on the table in front of the commodities broker. Then, she sat down and watched.

François stood in his bedroom doorway. He rubbed the small of his back and stared at Michelle for a few moments. "Do I know you?"

"I don't *think* so."

Above them, the screech of a jet launching from the carrier's flight deck interrupted their conversation but passed in seconds.

"What *is* that?" François asked.

"A train," Michelle answered.

"A train? *Ce n'est pas un train.* It's not a train. Is it?" he mumbled and looked at the ceiling. "Are we underground? Is that why there are no windows? I thought we were on a yacht. I could swear I felt it turn. I don't remember ever leaving the yacht with... What was his name?" He thought for a moment, and asked himself, "Carlson maybe? Or Carl? I can't think straight right now. My head hurts. My back hurts. My throat hurts...."

Michelle looked carefully at his half-shut eyes wondering if the Russian drug were wearing off already. She pushed the bottle toward him an inch. "Dan mentioned that you haven't been feeling well and asked for Perrier. I couldn't find any, so I brought you Evian instead." She tapped the side of the sports bottle. "And he said your hands were shaking, so you might appreciate this straw. I hope it helps."

She pushed the bottle another two inches across the table toward François and sat back.

"You said that already," François said, and rolled his head left and right.

"Well," Michelle said, and pulled the bottle back toward herself. "If you don't want it, I'll just—"

"No," François said emphatically. "I do." He shuffled to the table and put his hand on the back of the chair opposite Michelle. He looked at her, cocked one eyebrow and tilted his head slightly. "I *do* know you. You were on the yacht, no? You sat with Carl—across from me. So, that's it! We're still on the yacht."

Michelle ignored François' rambling. She leaned forward and gripped the water bottle with her fingers. She tapped her red-painted nails against the Mont Blanc logo and then slowly drew the bottle across the tabletop away from François. "If you don't want it...."

Instinctively, the Frenchman stepped forward as if connected to the bottle by an invisible string.

Michelle pulled the bottle close to her and made a show of standing up. "I'll tell Dan you weren't thirsty. We don't have any wine, but maybe you'll have this with dinner later?"

François stepped to the side of the table and reached his hand for the bottle. Almost begging, he asked, "*S'il vous plaît?*"

"Of course," Michelle answered, and handed the Frenchman the styrene bottle. She sat back down, extended her leg under the table and pushed the other chair back a few inches. "Have a seat, François. If you'd like, we can talk while you drink."

François sat down and took a sip of spring water through the straw.

Michelle gestured to the bottle. "I don't know about you, but I prefer flat water. I don't care for Perrier. You like it, though?"

François nodded as he sipped. He drank deeply and paused for breath. "*Oui*, I prefer French mineral water. 'With gas,' as you Americans say."

"What makes you say I'm American?" Michelle asked.

François seemed taken aback. "Your accent. What else could you be?"

In Spanish, Michelle asked if he had ever visited Mexico.

François responded in English. "I speak very little Spanish. But... you don't look Mexican."

Michelle feigned indignation, asking, "And just *what* are Mexicans supposed to look like?"

"*Non! Je m'excuse!* I meant only—" François thought for a second and did not see a way out of that conversation. To escape, he lifted the bottle to his lips and sucked heavily at the straw. After a half-dozen long sips, the bottle dropped to the table and he grabbed his throat with both hands.

Michelle sat up straight and looked intently at François' face. His eyes bulged as he struggled to breathe. The poison CIA's Directorate of Science and Technology had embedded in the straw constricted the man's throat, making breathing impossible.

François lunged across the table at Michelle. She slid her chair back a foot and out of his reach. She rose from her chair and walked around the table toward François. He tried to stand but fell to his knees, clawing at his throat. Michelle moved his chair out of the way, placed her hand on the back of his neck and extended her arm fully to keep him away from her.

François grasped for the tabletop, but missed, then gripped his throat tightly. He toppled to the floor, and Michelle turned him face up. She took two steps backward and watched him until he stopped moving.

She ticked off five minutes on her watch, then knelt at his side and felt for a pulse. Unable to find one, she looked at one of the concealed cameras and shook her head. François was dead.

A minute later, Dan opened the door to the interrogation suite and propped it open. He walked to where Michelle stood over François' lifeless body and double-checked for a pulse. Satisfied that François' heart had stopped, he stood. "For a minute there I wasn't sure he was going to drink it. When your boss, Mike, was here last time, the subject was so dehydrated he practically jumped at the poisoned bottle you guys use. I was afraid François was going to insist on Perrier or throw a wrench in the works like that. What would you have done then?"

"*Ehh*, there's always a way," Michelle said, and tapped her wristwatch. "If it came down to it, I have a needle with fast-acting poison concealed under the crown of my watch."

"Technically," Doc McFadden said from the doorway, "if it's injected, then it's a venom. Poisons are swallowed."

Michelle shrugged. "I *do* think DS&T mentioned that factoid way, way back, and I'm equally sure I told them I didn't really care as long as it did the job."

"Fair enough," the doctor said, and stepped into the room. He pointed to the gurney in the hallway he'd wheeled over from the medical suite.

"And on *that* happy note," Dan added, and pointed to the corpse on the floor, "let's get this over with, shall we?"

They took François' body to the medical suite where Doc McFadden had already opened the two shipping trunks in which François and Louis had arrived. The same cases would soon serve as the men's coffins when they were unceremoniously buried at sea.

***

Three hours later in the Roach Motel's administrative office, Michelle clicked send on the email to her boss and immediately dialed him on the secure phone. Her team lead answered on the second ring. "Hey, Michael, how are you?"

"Everything's fine here in Virginia, Eden. I'm just starting to read the detail you sent on the interrogations. I'll discuss this with Wilson this afternoon. By the way, he filled me in yesterday on our misfortune with Louis. You were appropriately evasive in writing it, but today's email seems to say that you got everything we were hoping for. Maybe that's the lucky break we've been needing. We'll get to work making good use of this new intelligence. Did you dispose of the bodies yet?"

"Yeah, already done. We got four crew members from the maintenance shop to help us wheel the bodies in the cases outside. Dan told them the cases were full of classified hard drives and old crypto equipment we needed to dispose of. The sailors simply pushed both off the back of the monstrously large elevator they use to lift aircraft up to the flight deck. Plop plop. Right into the Mediterranean Sea. No one will ever find them. Anyone missing our two friends yet?"

"Unfortunately, yes. Pascal Leclerc, the third broker, has been texting and calling these guys nonstop. I guess that was to be expected, but it started a couple of days earlier than I'd hoped it would. Wilson has NSA tapping his home phone, cell and computers, both at his condo and his office. Alex and I are headed back to Nice tomorrow to take care of him, and then it sounds like we have a briefcase full of cash to send to

Sargon. I'll get DS&T to come up with a Coach briefcase for us and have Logistics expedite it to my hotel in Nice."

Michelle smiled. "With a tracking device inside, I'm sure. Right?"

"You've learned to play the game very well, haven't you? But first, I have another mission for you."

"Oh, what's that?"

"With Pascal going bat-shit crazy this week trying to contact François and Louis, he's also been phoning and texting Dario Turchi in Malta. Dario introduced Carl Sapienti to François, and I'm afraid this situation now has the potential to come down on Carl's head. I can't let that happen. I was hoping this wouldn't be necessary, but now I need you to go to Malta and take Dario off the playing field. I'm giving you the green light on Dario Turchi. Your equipment is still in the safe house there, and I had Logistics send along another couple of your favorite bags of tricks."

Michelle sighed. "Okay. I'll meet you and Alex in Nice after I'm done in Valletta."

"Good," Michael said. "One more thing." He told her about the bombing at the Westin Bonaventure Hotel in Los Angeles, and she informed him that the news had already made it to the ship. Michael added, "Wilson's not certain it's Sargon's doing, but what has *not* made it into the news, yet, is that the FBI recovered DNA from one of the stolen vans left at the crime scene. The man it belongs to comes from Turkey. I know that's certainly not conclusive, but it *does* fit the pattern we're seeing."

"Damn," Michelle said softly. "Whenever we get one step closer, it looks like Sargon's people take two more steps out of our reach. Well... I'll see you guys in France in a couple of days."

"I'm looking forward to it, Michelle, but first... it's time for Eden to go hunting. Good luck."

Chapter 33

Two days later, Eden unpacked her disguise kit onto the bathroom vanity in the Valletta, Malta, safe house and took inventory. She ran her fingers through the hair of the complex silicone-rubber headpiece, tapped the tip of one of her newly trimmed and unpainted fingernails on a bottle of disguise-specific adhesive and then ran her hand along the length of a large roll of cloth in the center of the briefcase-sized kit.

She looked at herself in the mirror and critiqued her hair. After her earlier shower, she had twisted it tightly onto itself and pinned it securely, so it sat flat on her head. *Not my preferred style, but no one's going to even see it today. It'll do.*

She untucked the end of the white bath towel wrapped around her and let it drop to the floor. She stood on the cool blue-tile floor dressed only in white underpants decorated with a tiny pink bow on the front of its thin elastic waistband. She looked at herself in the mirror and fixated for a moment on the tan lines she acquired on her previous stay in Valletta. That week now seemed like a lazy vacation of surveillances and orientation to the ins and outs of Valletta. This trip, however, had a specific business purpose and a tight timeline — to kill Dario Turchi that afternoon.

She looked again at the array of disguise components and theatrical makeup spread out on the vanity before her. Some of the CIA's most effective disguises can be applied in as little as thirty seconds by an officer in need of a quick escape from a pursuing surveillance team. Others are sophisticated enough to change the wearer's apparent race or gender but require a professional disguise artist to apply them layer by layer over the course of several hours to enable the wearer to pass scrutiny by a police officer or immigration inspector at close quarters. The one Eden chose for that day's walk through the streets of Valletta fell somewhere in between. Her months of training and years of experience applying and wearing disguises helped her hone the tradecraft skills she knew she had to use perfectly — if she wanted to live to see the sunset.

Eden removed the roll of tan cloth from her disguise kit and looked at her nearly naked form in the mirror. She ran her left hand over her flat stomach until her fingers touched the scars on the right side of her abdomen. Her mind wandered briefly back to the fateful mission in Syria on which she lost two teammates and gained a jagged reminder — in the shape of an upside-down number four — of the personal cost of the work she does for the CIA.

She sighed, unrolled the cloth in her hands and wrapped it snuggly around her chest. She rolled it around herself three times, compressing her breasts enough to hide her feminine form, but not so tightly as to be excessively uncomfortable for the hours she needed to wear it. She looked at herself in the mirror again and decided it was time to make the big leap. *Now for the "fun" part.*

She lifted the disguise's headpiece over her pinned-down hair, seated the flaps of surprisingly lifelike wrinkled silicone "skin" properly onto her forehead, neck and cheeks and applied small amounts of adhesive to the edges. While it set, she applied two thin lines of adhesive to the back of a fake mustache and pressed it into place. The large, black moustache felt out of place on the underside of her nose.

Satisfied with her new look, she returned to her bedroom in the unnaturally quiet house. There, Eden put on a man's light-brown suit, dark burgundy tie and black dress shoes. Inserts in the shoes added several inches to Eden's stature, but not as much as the high heels she wore when her boyfriend, Steven Krauss, took her out for a Saturday night back home.

She looped a black leather belt into her trousers and fumbled with the buckle. *Ugh,* she thought, and pulled the belt all the way out in one smooth motion. *Men's belts go on the other way.* Eden reversed the belt and secured it firmly. After looking around the room for anything she might have missed, she pocketed a billfold and house key.

She made one last check of her handiwork in the bathroom mirror, and thought, *Damn, girl, you make one ugly middle-aged man!*

Satisfied that even her boyfriend wouldn't recognize her disguised as a Maltese businessman, she smiled and picked up the morning edition of the *International Herald Tribune* from the top of her dresser and unrolled it. She checked the contents thoroughly and concealed them back inside the rolled-up newspaper. She clicked her tongue and said, "Special edition, indeed."

***

An hour later, Eden stood inside one of Valletta's red phone booths on St. Ursula Street, pretending to speak on the payphone. With cell phones being the most common means of communication, no one challenged her monopolizing the colorful booth far more commonly associated with London than Malta. Although Malta had gained its independence from Britain a half-century earlier, the iconic red booths stand as cultural throwbacks to the island's days as a Crown Colony.

Eden shifted her newspaper and its special contents from one hand to the other and checked her watch. Dario Turchi would have to show up soon if he wanted to make his noon lunch reservation at Luciano's Restaurant. Eden had gotten the intelligence update on Dario's plans the night before from Wilson Henry and waited halfway down the block from the banker's office for him to head out to meet his client for lunch. Dario might not intend to be late for his mid-day meal, but since Michael had green-lighted this op, Eden would make sure the banker never showed up for lunch.

She spotted Turchi leave his office building and jaywalk across the narrow roadway. The banker darted between parked cars and hopped up the curb onto the sidewalk. *Well*, she thought, *someone's thinking he's going to enjoy lunch, doesn't he? Guess again, Dario.*

The CIA officer followed Turchi from a distance along the ancient street of sun-bleached stone buildings, some almost five-centuries old. Colorful awnings jutted out above business's doorways to differentiate themselves and provide easy visual cues for shoppers. Except for the electric lights and modern signs, many of Valletta's streets have changed little over the centuries.

Eden felt confident Turchi would take the direct route down Ursula and turn right on St. John Street. Turchi did not disappoint her. He made the expected turn, and she followed her target for two blocks, closing the forty-foot-distance steadily. Turchi looked down at his cell phone as much as he looked at the sidewalk ahead of him. He stopped with a small crowd at an intersection and waited for a few cars to pass before venturing across St. Paul Street, two blocks from the restaurant.

Eden made her way through the small crowd and took a position behind Turchi, slightly to his right. She aimed the cylindrical dart gun concealed inside the rolled-up newspaper at her target and tightened her grip on the squeeze-activated trigger.

A blow to her left shoulder twisted her torso abruptly, and she instinctively clutched the newspaper. The spring-loaded dart gun fired its projectile with a barely audible click. To Eden's left, a woman in a white skirt and red high-heel shoes pushed her way through the crowd crossing the street and stampeded along the sidewalk. Pedestrians barked at her as she nudged them out of her way.

The poisoned dart from Eden's errant shot flew harmlessly past Dario Turchi and came to rest under a taxi parked across the street.

"Crap," Eden cursed under her breath, and continued across the street. She slowed her pace as she followed Turchi and considered her options. The single-shot dart gun was useless until she reloaded it, which she couldn't do in public.

Turchi strode purposefully along St. John Street and turned into Luciano's Restaurant, across from St. John's Co-Cathedral.

Eden took a seat on a park bench nearby and looked at the cathedral's sign. She squinted in the mid-day sun, and wondered, *What in the world is a co-cathedral?* She made a mental note to look that up later, but it was hardly the biggest problem facing her that afternoon. *I need to reload.*

Eden looked at the co-cathedral to her right and thought about finding a bathroom. Although not particularly religious, she decided reloading a lethal weapon inside a church would not earn her any karma points. She looked at the front door to the Italian restaurant across the street and made her decision. *When ya gotta go, ya gotta go.*

She walked to the end of the block and crossed the street at the crosswalk before heading to the restaurant. Inside, she made her way directly to the rear. As she passed tables crowded with diners—many dipping Luciano's signature Focaccia bread in imported olive oil—she spotted Dario shaking hands with a tall, thin man in a gray suit and open collar. The banker and his gangly client sat down for lunch, and Eden walked straight past them.

In the back hallway of the restaurant, Eden stopped outside the bathrooms and read the signs. She made a conscious effort to push open the door labelled *Uomini*—men. Inside, one man stood in front of one of the two urinals while another washed his hands at one of the two sinks. Self-conscious, Eden tried her best to avoid looking at the man using the urinal and walked directly into one of the two empty stalls.

She latched the door behind her, started to sit down on the toilet and then thought better of it. She wrinkled her nose at the thought and decided to stand. She turned to face the door and backed up a bit so at least her shoes would be facing the right way if anyone should glance under the stall door.

From her jacket's inside pocket, she withdrew a narrow plastic case and placed it atop the flat metal top of the toilet paper holder. She unwrapped the dart gun from the rolled-up *Tribune*, popped open the smooth metal shell, and pulled the charging lever back to reset the spring. Gingerly, she removed a dart from the plastic case and inserted it into the weapon. Satisfied with her work, she put the plastic case with its two remaining darts back into her jacket pocket and hid the dart gun inside the newspaper again.

She opened the stall door and stepped out toward the sink. With one foot still inside the stall, she stopped mid-stride.

At the sink, Eden saw a familiar man adjusting his tie in the mirror. He glanced at her disapprovingly, and asked, "Not going to flush the toilet? That's gross." Dario Turchi continued straightening his tie in the mirror, and Eden glanced back at the stall she'd just vacated.

She made a grimace at Turchi's reflection in the mirror, retreated into the stall and used her foot to depress the flush lever. She exited the stall again, stepped forward toward the pair of sinks and glanced toward the urinals. Empty. *Good.*

Turchi rinsed his hands and shook droplets of water into the air.

Eden looked in the mirror at the stall doors behind her. Both were slightly ajar. *Excellent, we're alone.*

"Aren't you going to wash your hands?" Turchi asked. He shook his head, and mumbled, "Tourists."

Damned if this guy isn't the most annoying man on the planet, Eden thought. She turned toward Turchi, looked up at him and shrugged. She didn't want to say anything knowing that her voice would not match the disguise she wore. *Well, girl, what are you waiting for?*

"Anything good in the news today?" Turchi asked. He wiped his hands dry on a paper towel and tossed it into the trashcan.

Eden couldn't help herself. She cleared her throat. "There's one interesting obituary about some shithead banker who laundered money for terrorists and died of a heart attack in the bathroom of an Italian restaurant."

Turchi's eyes narrowed as he tried to reconcile the unexpected tenor of the words coming from the mouth below the jet-black mustache of the man he expected to have a deeper voice. It took him a second to understand the reference, but he acted too slowly.

Eden squeezed her spring-loaded gun and, with a muffled click, the dart shot into Turchi's tan jacket a few inches above his brown leather belt. The surgical steel of the needle's ultra-sharp point punctured his jacket and an inch of skin and muscle with ease.

"What the fuck?" he exclaimed, and lurched at Eden. She dropped her newspaper and its contents into a sink and fended off Turchi's attempt to grab her. The banker made a second lunge at Eden, but his left knee buckled as the dart's lethal venom took effect.

Behind her, voices in the hallway grew louder. Eden stepped forward and grabbed Turchi's hand. She twisted it into a wrist lock and shoved him into the stall she'd recently vacated. He pulled and squirmed, but the fast-acting toxin coursing through his bloodstream worked faster than he could cope. With his free hand, Turchi grabbed for this chest as Eden spun him around. She pushed the banker down on the toilet seat. His limbs splayed around him as his heart sputtered in reaction to Eden's dart, then seized into an agonizing knot in the center of his chest.

Eden quickly latched the door shut behind her and stood silently watching the banker shake uncontrollably. Waves of pain and shock took turns rippling across Turchi's face. As the muscle contractions diminished, the dying man's eyes angled up and met his killer's. She watched intently as the banker's eyes transitioned from shooting daggers at her to a thousand-yard stare and then close for good. Turchi quivered one last time. His head fell to his left, hung at an unnatural angle and a line of drool descended slowly from the corner of his mouth.

Outside the stall, the bathroom door opened with a creek as its hinges complained. The voices of three men boomed into the room, speaking rapidly in Italian.

Eden stood quietly and tried to figure out the placement of the men from the sounds of their voices. As they passed her, their voices echoed from the alcove in which the urinals stood. She looked at Turchi and then at the metal wall separating the two stalls. She knew what she had to do and shuddered at the thought. *Gross!*

With the sounds of the three men in the background still taking care of their business, she knelt on the floor and slid her legs underneath the wall separating the two stalls. With a grimace, she put both palms on the bathroom floor and started to push herself backward. She stopped halfway, looked again at Turchi's body and realized there was still something she had to do.

Eden reached up to his body and pulled the dart from Turchi's stomach. She reached backward under the stall wall and placed the evidence of his murder safely next to the toilet before pushing herself the rest of the way into the adjacent stall.

Evidence! Oh crap! Eden thought with a shudder. The newspaper and the dart gun it concealed inside still sat in the bathroom sink where any of the newcomers might see it.

She stood and, as quietly as she could, closed the stall door the rest of the way. She put the poisoned dart into the toilet and flushed away the means of Dario Turchi's dispatch. She took a deep breath and stepped out of the stall as sounds of running water flooded the room from the urinals in the alcove being flushed.

Eden hurried the short distance to the sink, edging out one of the men leaving the alcove. She grabbed her newspaper, tucked it under her arm, and washed her hands thoroughly.

As she turned to leave, the bathroom door opened, and two men entered. One entered the open stall as Eden walked toward the hallway. The other pursed his lips as he looked at the closed door of the stall Turchi's corpse occupied. As she pulled the bathroom open, she heard the second man say, "I guess I'll wait."

On the sidewalk outside the restaurant, Eden shaded her eyes from the bright Maltese sunlight. She looked up and down the street and froze. To her left, two officers dressed in blue-over-blue uniforms of the Malta Police Force approached from across the street. The pair of constables on patrol strolled slowly as they chatted and walked among the lunchtime crowd.

Eden turned away from the officers and set off to her right at a comfortable pace. She didn't want to have to talk to the police, knowing her voice would not match her disguise.

Seconds later, loud voices streamed from the restaurant's open door. A man's voice behind her yelled, "Someone call for an ambulance! *Ambulanza!*"

Eden arrived at the street corner and fought the urge to look back. She wanted to know if the police were following her but did not want to draw undue attention to herself. In front of her, red traffic lights shone in both directions. She focused her attention on the two Walk/Don't Walk signals. Both held up their amber hands at her. On the spur of the moment, she decided to adjust the path of her post-mission escape route to get out of the line of sight of the restaurant—and the police. At the risk of acting out of character, she turned right and walked purposefully along the cross-street, leaving the growing commotion behind her. She continued onto the next block and melted into a crowd of tourists. She walked with them for two blocks before crossing the street and doubling back for one block to try to identify any pursuing surveillance.

Inside the men's room of Luciano's restaurant, the two Maltese police officers looked with sincere concern at the man lying motionless on the floor. He'd slipped off the toilet and sprawled onto the floor with his legs bent at unnatural angles. Having seen an arm spill out from under the closed stall door, a patron had forced the door open and alerted the Maître d'. Conveniently for his ill guest—the restaurateur hoped—the police happened upon the scene during their regular patrol.

Although the senior officer could not find a pulse on the unconscious man's wrist, he hoped for the best. He radioed his dispatcher, described the scene and requested an ambulance. The other officer urged the gathering crowd of lunch patrons to step back to give the paramedics room to enter once the ambulance arrived.

At the rear of the crowd, Behrouz Heidari looked over the heads of the shorter patrons and inhaled sharply at seeing his dining partner sprawled on the men's room floor. Dario Turchi's left hand still lay over his heart as if he'd been clutching his chest when he died. Heidari returned to his table, gathered his gray suit jacket and a slice of bread and walked quickly out the front door. Surely the police would want to question him about his now-deceased dining partner, and that was the last thing Sargon's financier wanted. The taut look of the skin on Turchi's face told him all he needed to know—Turchi was dead. So too was the husband of Heidari's cousin in Smuggler's Respite who had been Turchi's previous contact with Sargon's financial team. Heidari wondered if this was just a sad coincidence, or if something more menacing was leading to the deaths of his compatriots one by one.

Heidari strode purposefully down the block and started to cross the street. Amidst the crowd in the crosswalk, he slowed to walk and then surged forward for several blocks while he thought through his impromptu escape plan. He didn't want to go to the airport without his suitcase. That would look suspicious. He hated the thought of going back to the hotel where the police might be waiting for him but wasn't sure whether or not he had a choice.

Heidari stopped at the corner of a narrow stone-lined street until a procession of cars passed. Behind him, he heard the *WAH-woh* warble of an ambulance's siren approaching the restaurant. He turned to his left to cross the street but changed his mind. He spun around and careened into a short, mustachioed man in a light-brown suit and dark burgundy tie. "*Scusa,*" Heidari blurted out, and hurried away.

Eden regained her balance and adjusted her necktie. She turned her head and watched the tall, rail-thin man with the dark, well-trimmed beard hurry past her on his way across the intersection. "Hmmph," she grunted. *Some people!*

Chapter 34

Sargon's counselor, Rifaat, entered the office next to His Majesty's throne room, and announced, "Behrouz Heidari has arrived to see you. He's just returned from his meeting with the banker on Malta."

"Good," Sargon said, and looked up from the sheaf of papers on his desk. "Show him into the throne room in two minutes. It's time for us to arrange for the next payment to our hired hands in Turkey's security services to buy the information we need and keep the police and politicians at bay for the time being. I'll meet you both next door."

Two minutes later, Rifaat led two men into the throne room to meet Sargon. The self-proclaimed king sat perched on his golden throne and traced his index finger along one of the inlaid silver roses. Behrouz Heidari approached Sargon and greeted him formally. Sargon's bodyguard, Mert, who stood a head taller than the six-foot-two-inch Behrouz, remained in the rear of the room with Rifaat.

"Welcome, Behrouz," Sargon said. "It's time to arrange another quarterly payment for the information we need and to keep the wolves at bay. We'll also need additional cash this time for a one-time payment to further my plans in Istanbul. How goes your search for a new courier?"

"I've not found one, just as yet, Your Majesty, but do have inquiries out for a trustworthy man with the right skillset. I'm inquiring quietly, you can be sure. In the meantime, I will handle this quarter's cash delivery myself and use next quarter's payment as an opportunity to train my new courier."

"Excellent plan," Sargon said. "The additional cash I need is to pay our suppliers in Iran to smuggle high-tech explosives for us. They, in turn, will pay their Russian suppliers. Once you make the regular payment this week, bring an additional quarter-million euros back here to me. Since you're still working without a courier and you yourself are familiar with Iran, you can make that payment for us, as well."

"Of course," the chief of Sargon's treasury said. "I will call my contacts in France today and have the money made available immediately. I will pick it up from the bank in Lichtenstein and make the deliveries in Istanbul myself. I should be back here in four or, more likely, five days."

"Very good," Sargon said. "The same SUV with the hidden compartment that your courier uses—*ahem*, used to use—will be waiting for you in Liechtenstein."

Behrouz Heidari bid farewell to Sargon, and the sultan wished him luck.

Behrouz turned and looked at Sargon's imposing bodyguard in the back of the room. Mert remained motionless in front of the door, blocking most of it from sight. The gargantuan man's muscular build blocked all but the corners of the door from Behrouz's view. Standing next to him, Sargon's short counselor, Rifaat, looked diminutive beside the giant. Juxtaposed, the pair appeared to Behrouz as almost comically opposite, but their combination of brains and brawn served their sultan well.

Behrouz started toward the exit and gave the expressionless bodyguard a curt wave. The large man scratched at his unkept beard and gave the slightest of nods to Behrouz as he stepped aside.

Behrouz walked out the rear door of the throne room and down the long, central corridor of the sultan's mansion. He made his way out the back of the house he knew well and lowered himself onto a lounge chair against the low stone wall separating the patio from the expansive rear lawn.

In the distance, a roaming guard—a man Behrouz had known since childhood—adjusted the sling of the AK-47 rifle on his shoulder as he walked his rounds fifty yards away. The guard inspected the boathouse on the shore of Lake Van and then strode along the waterline.

The financial brain of Sargon's organization pulled his cell phone from his jacket pocket and thumbed through its contact list. His call went straight through to François Arsenault's voicemail. He didn't leave a message. Instead, he hung up and looked at his watch. He thought, *Is it lunchtime in Nice? What time is it in France, anyway?*

He scrolled to the next name in his list, tapped it with his index finger, and Pascal Leclerc answered on the second ring. Behrouz told the commodities broker how much money he needed and ignored the Frenchman's complaining about his boss who'd left him to do all the work in the office while François and Louis lounged about on a chartered yacht trying to bag a prospective client—and bed a couple of prostitutes.

Behrouz shook his head in disgust and hung up on Pascal mid-sentence. How can these heathens survive their own incompetence, much less thrive as well as this man does? As soon as His Majesty's rise to power is complete, things across Europe will change for the better.

He scrolled through his cell phone for the next number to call and reserved a one-way flight on Turkish Airlines to Zurich, Switzerland — the closest that Turkey's national airline could get him to Lichtenstein without drawing the unwanted attention of chartering a private jet.

Even flying in economy, the trip there would be luxurious compared to the grinding ride all the way back to Turkey in one of Sargon's specially modified SUVs. *It's better than the alternative,* he thought. *I'd hate for the police to catch me carrying that much money on a commercial flight.*

***

Wilson Henry's Boston accent came through Michael's cell phone clearly. The clarity of voice calls through the team's encrypted app — even when the Internet packets had to fly a third of the way around the world — always impressed the intelligence analyst. "They'*uh* on the move, Mike! Our phone intercepts just overheard Pascal Leclerc gettin' the money-transfer ord*uh* from Sargon's man. I don't know the gentleman's name — on the call he just said, 'It's me' like Pascal would recognize his voice immediately. The good news is that now we have *his* cell phone number, the name of the bank, the safe deposit box number Pascal's supposed to put the money into and the specific amount, in euros. NSA's intercept of Pascal's subsequent phone call to the bank in Lichtenstein gave us all we need to know about the date of the withdrawal and the instructions for the bank to load the cash into Pascal's safe deposit box the day after tomorrow. Time for you to get on the road."

"Finally, some good news, Wilson," Michael said energetically. "That's just the break I've been hoping for."

"*Yah*, sure is," Wilson agreed. "One other thing you should be aware of... Whoever this guy is, he complained to Pascal that he hasn't been able to get ahold of François Arsenault. Not surprising, though...."

"No, Wilson, not surprising at all since François went for a swim in the deep end of the Med the other day. I imagine Pascal's going to be getting more than worried, not having heard from either François or Louis since they boarded the yacht. We'll have to take care of that loose end before we head to Lichtenstein. By the way, what's the status of the briefcase I asked for? Now that the clock is ticking, I need it ASAP."

"It's been on its way for a couple *ahh* days. I'm surprised Logistics hasn't gotten it to you already. I got it back from DS&T three days ago and handed it to Logistics personally. The Logs team assured me they'd expedite it to you. They made a point of telling me *three* times they're going to bill your charge code extra for the rush job, but—"

"Yeah, okay. *Hmmm.* Please ask them again what's taking so long. I need it or we can't intercept the money. Well, we *could*, but then we couldn't track it all the way back to Sargon or wherever it's going, so it'd be a waste of time. I don't want to have to try to surveil the courier all that way visually. That'd be a nightmare."

"Don't worry, Mike. I'll make the call as soon as we hang up. I'm sorry it's taking so long. That's unusual for Logistics."

"Remind them how important it is, Wilson."

Michael hung up and looked at Eden as she stared out the hotel room's window at the French beachscape below.

Without looking back at her boss, she asked, "What's up? Trouble in paradise?"

Michael tossed his cell phone onto the bed. "Kind of. We can't go into the bank in Lichtenstein without the modified briefcase I ordered up, so we're stuck in a holding pattern on that front. But, since we have all the information we need from the three commodities brokers, I want us to take care of Pascal Leclerc now, before something else goes wrong."

Chapter 35

It took Zeki Aga a full day to drive the length of Turkey from Lake Van in the country's east to his team's warehouse outside Istanbul. The next morning, he strode into the warehouse, removed his sunglasses and waited for his eyes to adjust to the dimly lit room. The transition from the bright morning outside to the cloistered, dank interior of the warehouse took a few seconds to get used to. Bayram entered behind him, clapped the taller man on the shoulder and pointed to the racks of chairs against the far wall.

Zeki followed a few paces behind the logistics specialist. As they walked, he surveyed the wide-open expanse of the large building in an industrial suburb thirty miles west of Istanbul. The soldier wrinkled his nose. "Is that odor what I think it is?"

Bayram threw a glance to his companion walking behind him and confirmed Zeki's fear. "Yes, it's urine. This used to be an auction house for goats and sheep. We've kept the cargo doors and windows open as much as we can, but...."

Zeki rubbed his nose and agreed. "Yeah, there's a limit to how well that'll work. Nothing's going to get rid of that smell, is it?" He stopped in front of the racks of folding metal chairs lined up against the warehouse wall, and softly said, "Maybe we'll bring in some fans and incense lamps for when we set up our assembly line."

"Couldn't hurt," Bayram agreed, and pointed to the rows of folded chairs. "These are the fifteen hundred metal chairs for the majority of the audience at the US Embassy's so-called cultural festival in two weeks."

"No wonder you needed such a large building," Zeki said, looking up and down the length of the quarter-filled warehouse. "That's a lot of chairs."

"And these," Bayram added, "are just for the common people attending the fiftieth anniversary of the Turkish-American Arts Assembly. We've not yet received the high-backed chairs you need — the ones for the embassy's distinguished guests."

"The *distinguished* guests," Zeki said with a grin, "will make very distinguished corpses when my team and I are done with them." He paused, then looked at Bayram. "Just to be sure... Your contact who's providing the chairs and tables for the event didn't have any trouble getting the contract, did he?"

"No, no problem," Bayram assured him. "He bid for the contract at just over half his usual rate and had no trouble winning the business."

"And he has no idea what's going to happen?"

"No! Of course not. This will mean the end of his business. He has no clue or he would never have agreed to do it—at least not for what I'm paying him. I just told him I'd make it up to him through a rich deal I was getting on my trucking contract for this event because I have an in with the embassy. He doesn't suspect a thing."

"Good," Zeki said. "Early on the day of the event, one of my men will pay him a visit at home. I'm sure he was a good businessman, and he will die a martyr to our cause. You and I, however, will continue as the vanguard of the army of Sargon the Third, may his reign last a thousand years."

"His Majesty will be pleased with what you and I accomplish here. Very pleased."

"Yes, Bayram, he will," Zeki agreed. "He will indeed be *ecstatic* with five hundred dead, sacrilegious, American diplomats and Turkish traitors."

***

As her boss spoke from behind her, Michelle listened attentively while looking out the hotel window at the serene beach scene below the French hotel. Across the street from the hotel, the calm turquoise surface of the Mediterranean Sea glowed as the sun rose over France. The brightly colored surface of the *Côte d'Azur* extended in small ripples from the rocky beach out to two hundred feet, at which point the water turned into a dark forest green as the depth of the sea increased sharply.

Michelle pulled the hotel room's curtains closed, and announced, "It's a beautiful day out there. I'm going to miss Nice once we get rid of Pascal, but, well... that's the job, right? So, let's get it out of the way." She looked at her partner. "It's a beautiful morning for a motorcycle ride."

"You ain't kidding," Alex replied. "So, the good weather is lucky for you, since you missed yesterday's dry run. It wasn't *dry* at all.

Rained the whole damned night before and then again all yesterday afternoon, too. I got soaked through and through riding around town on the bike. As great a bike as it is, I would have preferred a car, you know?"

"Eden," Michael said, interrupting, "here's the plan for today. Pascal Leclerc is the last of the money launderers who can make any connection back to Carl Sapienti. Once we deal with Pascal, Carl will be in the clear—no one remaining will know about his involvement in setting up François and Louis for their vanishing act."

Michael spread a map across the foot of his bed and pointed to the route he and Alex had worked up while Michelle was in Valletta killing Dario Turchi. "When Pascal leaves his condo, he drives his Audi west. I'll follow him away from his condo and then along the freeway. He's been very consistent, so I can stay back and not be noticed. Once he enters Nice, he exits the N7 freeway and heads south on Boulevard Gambetta. That's where you two will be waiting on the motorcycle to pick up the eye. We'll do this just like we've practiced this maneuver back home—Alex drives, and you place the explosive on the driver's car door. Any questions?"

Eden traced her finger on the map. "And where's the parking garage for afterward?"

Michael tapped the map on an intersection six blocks from the commodities trader's office. "Right here. Two of the garage's exits provide unobstructed access to the N7 freeway on-ramp. Easy in, easy out. You'll abandon the motorcycle, do a quick costume change and...." He held up keys sporting a BMW logo. "Then it's a forty-minute drive for you two to the safe house across the border in Ventimiglia, Italy. You already know what to do once you're there. I'll meet you two when you arrive in Lucerne, Switzerland, tomorrow evening. Once we're all there, we'll finalize our plans for what we need to do at the bank in Liechtenstein. Any questions?"

"Nope. Works for me," Eden said, and tapped Alex on the shoulder. "You just need to watch out for puddles so I don't get splashed and drop the explosive charge."

Alex nodded. He knew what was good for him. Keeping himself on Eden's good side was at the top of his list. "I'll do the driving, and you just hold on tightly."

Michael smiled. "Okay, then, guys. Happy hunting."

***

Two hours later, the radio call from Michael set the wrong tone for the morning. "Something's wrong," he grumbled through the team's encrypted radio.

Eden rubbed a gloved hand across the back of her neck. Into her voice-activated mic, she said, "What's going on at the condo? Is Pascal not leaving?"

"Oh, we just got on the N7 heading your way, all right, but it's *not* the same car. Pascal had a driver pick him up, and now he's sitting in the back of a chauffeured black Audi A8L, instead of driving his own silver Audi A5 Coupe. Besides the dark-skinned driver, there's a Caucasian male riding shotgun. The windows are lightly tinted, but I clearly saw Pascal enter the vehicle."

"Why the change?" Alex asked, concern tinging his voice.

"No idea," Michael responded, "but it *can't* be good for us. I'm dying to take a look inside the car, but I don't want to get too close since we don't have any other surveillance vehicles with us today. I definitely don't want to spook them. I don't know if these two new guys are professionals, but let's assume for now that they are. Either way, I don't want to take the chance they'll spot me. At least they're headed straight for Pascal's office and aren't running a Surveillance Detection Route."

"You're right to stay back," Eden replied. "Let's stick to the plan. Just call out their progress as you go, and Alex and I will pick the black A8L up when it gets here. Same way we practiced — just a different car. Let's stick with the plan."

Michael double-clicked the radio to confirm he received the message. Over the next twenty minutes, he reported the Audi A8L's position as it progressed along the N7 freeway. As it slowed to exit, he radioed his team. "Okay, guys. They're on the off-ramp. Over to you two. Good luck."

Alex thumbed the black BMW S1000RR's electronic starter, and the motorcycle's engine hummed to life smoothly. He centered the weight of the bike beneath him, adjusted for Eden's hundred-twenty-five pounds on the seat behind him and flicked the kickstand back with the heel of his boot. Eden reached her left arm around her partner's waist and gripped him firmly.

As the Audi passed in front of them on Boulevard Gambetta, Eden tapped Alex between the shoulder blades. "That's them," she said as she secured her right arm around her partner's middle and pressed herself tightly into his back.

Alex slowly maneuvered the motorcycle out of its parking spot on a side street and leaned the bike to the right to turn onto the main drag. Twice he had to swerve to pass two of the three cars separating them from the Audi. On the next block, he jockeyed through traffic to make it across a pedestrian walkway before a large group of uniformed schoolchildren threatened to block traffic long enough for the target to get away.

Alex twisted the motorcycle's right handle to accelerate between the two lanes of cars and approached the Audi on its passenger's side. In seconds, he and Eden rode abreast of the Audi's trunk.

Eden gripped Alex's waist tightly with her right hand, holding his leather jacket firmly in her clenched fist. With her left hand, she reached into her own jacket and put her hand around the hockey-puck-sized explosive mated to a circular magnet. In practice runs back home, she found it worked best for her to back-hand the puck onto the target car's door. That way, the magnet seated it onto the door nearest the subject. Once she attached it to the door, her mark then had no way to escape the path of the shaped charge's blast that would soon end his life.

As Alex accelerated the motorcycle for their final approach, the Audi fell behind them as it slowed to avoid hitting the car in front of it.

"Holy crap!" Eden exclaimed. The voice-activated microphone strapped to her throat transmitted the urgency in her voice to the whole team. "Did you get a look at the Audi's windows?"

"No," Alex replied. "I'm trying to avoid getting us killed by these idiotic French drivers. What about the windows?"

"They're an inch thick. This is *not* good."

Michael radioed from behind them. "I'm off the freeway and doubling back your way. What's that about the windows?"

"I figured out why Pascal changed cars," Eden said, in a huff. "This Audi is armored up. *Way* up. From the look of the windows, it's at least B6- or maybe a B7-level armor. There's no *way* this firecracker in my hand is going to do more than scratch the paint on that three-ton armored beast. We need a bigger bomb and a better plan."

Alex slowed the bike and centered it in the right-hand lane. The Audi pulled forward and drifted back as the traffic ebbed and flowed. "Eden," he said as he slowed the motorcycle and adjusted his balance, "ya gotta tell me what to do. Do I stay with the target or not? Are we going to try, anyway?"

"Eden," Michael asked, "what do you think? You're the only one who can get a clear view of the car, so it's *your* call. You're the shooter."

Through the tinted helmet visor, Eden looked closely at the armored Audi to her left. For reassurance and to focus her thinking, she squeezed the short explosive cylinder in her hand. As hard as she squeezed, the custom-formed black plastic pushed back just as firmly.

Crap, she thought.

The man riding shotgun in the Audi's front passenger seat stared at her through the car's reinforced window. Fully concealed beneath her helmet and black leather riding outfit, she had no worries that he might identify her. She peered intently first at him and then at Pascal Leclerc in the luxury sedan's plush back seat.

Eden feared that if she placed the explosive disc on the door next to Pascal and it didn't kill him, he'd go to ground, and they'd have a hell of a time finding him again. And if or when they did, they'd probably also have a platoon of police to deal with. No, that would make things far too complicated.

"Abort, abort, *abort,*" she ordered. She released the disc inside her jacket and zipped the pocket. She reached her left arm around Alex, pulled herself flat against his back and turned her head away from the Audi.

Alex gave his partner a moment to secure her grip, then leaned into the turn and guided the BMW onto the cross street to their right. He twisted the motorcycle's throttle and accelerated east—away from his target. He already knew how the after-action 'hot wash' of the day's events would be summed up during the coming debrief with their boss: complete mission failure.

Chapter 36

A half hour later, the team regrouped in Michael's hotel room. Michael unscrewed the metal cap from a green bottle of Perrier and gestured for Alex and Eden to help themselves. The covert action team lead lowered himself into a chair at the small, round table near the window and grimaced at the sting of their failed attempt on Pascal Leclerc's life that morning.

He looked at Eden who was handing a bottle of water to Alex. "How thick was the armor, do you think?'

"I got a close look at the passenger-side glass. I'm sure it was an inch thick, maybe more. That's got to be a B6- or B7-rated car on the European armor scale. The explosive we brought for this job was barely large enough to scratch the paint on that beast. It would have easily done the job on any normal car, but on that one...."

"Yeah," Michael agreed, and pushed a lock of his white hair up over his head. "You made the right call. Now I need time to think about what our options are. Any ideas?"

Alex asked, "So, what windows of vulnerability does he have? When the armored car picked him up at home, could you see from the street that it was Pascal getting into the armored car?"

"No," Michael said, "the driver pulled the car into the garage of Pascal's condo. They picked him up inside, so he was out of my sightline. Fortunately, the windows weren't heavily tinted, so I saw them on the way out. I don't think we'd be able to get a clear angle for a rifle shot into the garage."

"Okay, well," Alex said, and rubbed his cheek, "he's got to be exposed at some point in the garage, like when he's walking from the elevator to the car. But even if it were a three-on-three firefight in there between us and a couple of guards, they'd have the advantage of being able to hide behind — or inside — an armored tank. I don't like those odds, and it's also too exposed to civilians heading to work at rush hour." He paused for a moment. "I suppose we could do a covert entry into his condo one afternoon and wait for him to return home after work."

"Been there, done that," Eden said softly. "Unfortunately, we don't know if the guards do a sweep of his place before they let him enter, and we'd have no place to hide in the hallway to be able to surround them. A stairwell *might* work for that, but I hate the word 'might.'"

"Me too," her boss agreed. "Not enough intel on the interior of the building. I can't approve that."

"So," Eden offered, "that leaves us looking at him in his office. Or maybe when he steps out to go eat lunch. Or we FedEx a bomb right to his desk."

Michael looked at her sideways.

"Just kidding," Eden said, and grinned. "Of *course*, I wouldn't do that, Michael. You know full-well I'd send it via DHL instead."

Michael shook his head and snickered.

Alex chewed his bottom lip and shrugged. "From the surveillances Mike and I did while you were interrogating his friends aboard the aircraft carrier, we know Pascal's got a window office on the fifth floor. It's not François' corner office, although I hear that one *has* suddenly become available." Alex smirked. "So... maybe a rifle shot from the roof of a nearby office building?"

Michael thought about it and shook his head. "I don't like the brazen approach here, but we are up against the clock. Pascal's heading to Lichtenstein tomorrow. Let's keep thinking here, guys. I doubt Pascal would accept an invitation to the yacht now, so that's out. And without knowing more about his condo building, I wouldn't want to try breaking in tonight to make it look like a suicide."

"No, not this time," Eden agreed. "That was one long-ass week in Santiago last year, wasn't it? But I do have to say that the *plateada con quinoa* was fantastic. And, guys, you know, there actually *is* a silver lining for us here on this mission."

"Oh yeah?" Alex asked. "And what might that be?"

Eden walked to the window and pulled back the curtains. Sunlight streamed in, and she squinted at the bright morning rays. She shielded her eyes and turned to Alex. "At least Pascal's still going outside."

Michael looked intently. "True. Go on...."

Eden added, "What I mean is that he hasn't fled town to go hold up somewhere high in the Alps or something like that. He's still going to his office every day and also still doing business with Sargon's people, right? Wilson told us that Pascal got the call from Turkey and then *immediately* called the bank in Lichtenstein. For him, it's money-laundering business-as-usual. Now we know Pascal's headed to

Lichtenstein. We have to go there, anyway, so maybe we get him there instead of in France?"

Michael looked at her and thought for a few moments. He scratched the side of his face and froze at the sound of a knock at the door.

Eden lunged for her backpack. She unzipped a compartment and drew a Sig Sauer pistol with a three-inch suppressor from its sewn-in holster. Her boss held up his right hand and pointed to the bathroom door, adjacent to the hotel room's entrance. She slipped past him silently, stepped into the bathroom and waited.

From across the room, Michael asked loudly, "Who is it?"

A man's voice spoke with an unconvincing French accent. "FedEx, sir. You have a rush delivery from Coach."

Michael exhaled and pointed at Eden for her to get ready. He made a show of laying his left hand flat against his trousers, then opened the hotel room's door with his right hand.

Eden watched her boss closely. If he signaled by either making a fist with the hand on his pants or used their pre-selected danger word, she would not hesitate to shoot the man outside.

Michael pulled the hotel room door open and greeted the brown-haired man in the purple-and-black shirt.

The driver handed him a white box with the FedEx logo positioned prominently on the back and smiled. Michael accepted the box and thanked the deliveryman.

The undercover CIA officer posing as a FedEx driver nodded. "I hope the rush delivery service was to your satisfaction, sir. Enjoy your briefcase." Without waiting for a reply, he turned and walked away.

After her boss closed the door, Eden relaxed and smiled. She returned her firearm to her backpack and looked on as Michael opened the box. From inside, he slid a large black leather Coach attaché onto the bed.

Eden looked on keenly as her boss inspected the modified briefcase inside and out. "When Logistics says they provide delivery service with a smile, I really thought it was, you know, just a cliché. I guess they really mean it." She watched her boss and waited as long as she thought required for politeness, then eagerly asked, "Are you going to open it? I want to see what all the fuss was about."

Her team lead turned the bag over several times and tugged up on the handle. Satisfied, he held it out to her. "You know, this has to be the most expensive briefcase I've ever held. What with the DS&T tracking device concealed inside and the extortionate surcharge Logistics is charging me for the rush delivery, I mean."

Eden turned the bag over several times and looked it over thoroughly from every angle. She traced her finger over each of the sewn leather seams and inspected each for any difference, no matter how subtle, trying to see where CIA's Directorate of Science and Technology's experts opened it, inserted their electronic beacon and carefully resewed it. After two minutes, she gave up. "Well, if I had an X-ray machine, maybe then I could find it, but I can't feel where they hid it or see where they cut anything open." She handed it to Alex. "They're good."

"The best," Michael agreed. "Okay, this takes a load off my mind. Now that *this* is here," he said, "I think you're right, Eden. We should decamp from France and regroup in Lichtenstein. We need to learn the lay of the land there and prepare for the bank job. We need to finish our work there before Sargon's man arrives and make *damned* sure Pascal never gets to the bank at all. If he does, he'll see the money's missing and would either raise a stink with the bank or call Sargon's man and scuttle the planned pickup. We can't let that happen. Before we leave here, though, I need to make sure Logistics delivers to Liechtenstein what I've ordered up for that job and let you practice on some of the gear before you and I go into the bank."

Eden asked, "I have to imagine that if Pascal has an armored car here in France, he'll have one in Lichtenstein, too. Don't you think?"

Michael nodded. "Yes, and some guards, too. Well then, if Pascal Leclerc wants to hide behind a couple of inches of armor, I think this situation calls for us to either go big or go home. And I'm not ready to go home just yet."

Intrigued, Alex tilted his head to the side and looked at his boss through narrowed eyelids. "So, what do you have in mind?"

Michael grinned slyly. "We're up against the clock here. For this job, I'm going to need Wilson to make one more call to Logistics for us."

Chapter 37

The CIA team's Lufthansa flight landed in Zurich, Switzerland, shortly after dusk that evening. While Swiss banks enjoy far greater name recognition worldwide, the banks of Liechtenstein, Europe's fourth-smallest country—sandwiched between Switzerland and its eastern neighbor, Austria—remain prized tax havens. The jet set also find the Alpine country's climate—for both winter sports and lax financial oversight—idyllic for combining personal and business pursuits.

Like their Swiss competitors, Liechtenstein's banks also attract a wide range of the world's less famous but more infamous despots and strongmen who continue to find the small country's financial institutions welcoming of money transfers from financial markets of varying legitimacy. The tiny nation of less than forty-thousand people has been surprisingly successful resisting the world's major economic powers' efforts to water down its strong bank secrecy laws, much to their clients' delight. As a matter of pride, the local bankers' tradition for discrete private banking services ran the gamut from polite ignorance to willful disregard of the true sources of their clients' wealth. By design, the banks' passive-aggressive approach appeased the world's major economic powers' regulatory officers sufficiently while still ensuring the bank's services remained popular with globally mobile clientele who frequently deal in large quantities of cash.

After leaving the Zurich airport, Michael's team stopped for a leisurely dinner at an inn just off the highway. At Eden's urging, all enjoyed *Zürcher Geschnetzeltes*—thin veal strips with mushrooms in a cream sauce served with Rösti, Swiss hash browns. Afterward, Michael offered to buy a round of beers.

As the drinks arrived, Alex caught his boss checking his wristwatch again. He winked at Michael. "Got a hot date? I promise not to tell your wife. What *would* Mona think?"

Michael chuckled. "Your reputation for discretion actually *was* one of the reasons I hired you."

SCOTT SHINBERG

Alex recognized the sarcasm mixed in with the compliment but
nodded appreciatively just the same. "Just out of curiosity, does your
watch have the same kind of concealed poisoned needle in it like
Michelle's? Or, when talking about things like that, should I say *Eden*?"

"No," Michael said, "it doesn't. It's just a watch, and, if you must
know, I'm simply making sure we don't arrive *too* early tonight. You
don't even *want* to know how much Logistics is charging me for flying
in all the equipment I had Wilson order up from Germany on short
notice. They said the van with our gear will be ready at the cabin they're
renting for us no later than 11 p.m., so we can't arrive before they're
finished. On the drive there, we'll go over the timeline for dealing with
Pascal tonight and the trip to the bank tomorrow morning. It's going to
be a long couple of days, so, in the meantime, let's enjoy the flavor of
the Old World, shall we?" He raised his golden Swiss Hefeweizen beer
and clinked glasses with Alex.

After dinner, Alex drove the team's rented BMW 5-Series for the
hour-and-a-half trip into the Principality of Liechtenstein. As they
passed through the capital city of Vaduz, Michelle admired the late-
night views of seemingly random groupings of modern construction set
between stately stone chateaus and the occasional small, but well-
maintained, castle.

A few minutes before midnight, Alex turned the sedan off the main
road just outside the capital's city limits. Over the next mile, they
passed a series of driveways leading to cabins, each spaced a hundred
yards apart. The dense forest of beech and pine trees provided the
area's visitors both a getting-back-to-nature feeling and the kind of
exceptional privacy required for the CIA team's needs.

Alex turned the BMW up the extended driveway to cabin number
nine. He pulled to a stop next to a black Mercedes Sprinter van, a model
popular with delivery services for its reliability and lack of windows in
the cargo area.

Michael located the keys to both the van and the cabin inside a fake
rock that CIA's Logistics team placed at the edge of the path leading to
the cabin's front door. He showed Alex and Michelle which equipment
cases to bring in from the van first.

***

Three hours later, the trio of CIA officers gathered in the cabin's
living room. As Eden emerged from her bedroom, Alex laughed at her.

- 182 -

"What?" she asked defensively.

"I always get a chuckle seeing you in disguise. That wart on your cheek...."

Michael looked at Eden and tugged self-consciously at the end of the black wig covering his white hair.

"Speak for yourself," Eden advised her partner. "The ungainly mop on your head doesn't match your neatly trimmed beard, but, hey, *I'm* not saying anything. And what's wrong with my glued-on mole?"

"Nothing," Michael said, "don't listen to him. With that on your cheek, everyone fixates on that one feature. No one will even be able to remember what color your hair is."

"Perfect," Eden said, and grinned. "Just the look I was going for to match my black slacks." She tossed her backpack across her shoulder, pointed to the front door, and asked, "Shall we?"

Eden settled into the second-row seat of the Mercedes van for the team's late-night drive into the capital city. She pulled a notebook PC from her backpack and opened it on her lap. The screen came to life, and she double-clicked on the geolocation application the CIA's technical services team had provided.

Alex navigated the van onto the highway, and Eden read directions from the online map.

"Turn off the Landstrasse 28 highway and onto Hintergass," she advised, and continued reading the screen. "According to their website, the Park-Hotel Sonnenhof that Pascal's staying at has free parking, free Wi-Fi and the Marée restaurant has been awarded three *toques* by the *Gault Millau* guide."

Alex looked first at Michael in the passenger seat, then back at Eden. After a pause, he quietly asked, "Is a 'toque' good?"

Through a laugh, Eden replied, "I haven't got the *foggiest* idea. Sure, Michelin stars I understand. But what the hell is a 'toque?' I mean, other than the 'smoking dope' kind of thing. Anyway, the hotel's up there on the left. The computer says his cell phone is somewhere on the east side. Circle the hotel so I can get a more precise reading."

Alex shrugged and turned up the driveway lined with low-lying shrubs. He guided the van past the self-parking lot in front of the hotel and around its west side. Behind the hotel, he drove past the tennis courts and the loading dock. As he curved around the east side of the hotel, Eden told him to slow down.

"That's good," she said, "keep going." She stared intently at the glow of the computer screen for a half-minute. "Perfect. Park near a door in the back. His cell phone is about fifty feet above us. It's a three-story hotel, so he's on the top floor in the...." She clicked the mouse button twice, tapped a few keys, looked through the van's windshield and counted under her breath. Satisfied, she said, "Third suite in from the end on our side of the hallway." She closed the laptop and slid it onto the seat next to her. "I love it that people bring their cells phones everywhere nowadays. It makes them so *damned* easy to find. Much appreciated, Pascal. *Merci beaucoup.*"

As Eden shut down the computer and put it away, Michael and Alex pulled on gloves and zipped up their jackets.

Michael asked rhetorically, "Convenience is certainly a double-edged sword, isn't it?" He looked at his watch. "Okay, guys, it's three thirty-five. He'll be fast asleep. Everyone ready?"

Eden put her gloves on, pulled a floppy-brimmed hat over her blonde wig and grabbed her backpack. She looked at her teammates and grinned. "Ready or not, Pascal, here we come."

Chapter 38

Bayram signaled to the driver as the truck backed into the loading dock on the side of the Istanbul warehouse. Once parked, he unlocked its rear door and swung it open. Under the cover of darkness, his team unloaded Sargon's precious cargo as Zeki Aga's soldiers watched closely.

Zeki stood to the side, and one of his men brought the first box off the truck to him. Zeki pointed to a table at the far end of the warehouse on which he wanted the box placed. He followed behind the man carrying the all-important cardboard box while they navigated between rows of stacked high-backed chairs their local supplier delivered the previous afternoon.

Bayram joined Zeki at the table near the front of the warehouse. "So, *this* is what you've spent the last few months working on?"

"Not me personally, but my men, yes." He withdrew a folding knife clipped to the pocket of his trousers and carefully cut the tape securing the box top. From inside, he withdrew an object covered in a generous portion of bubble wrap. He sliced the cellophane tape securing the protective wrapping, peeled the protective plastic back and placed its contents in the center of the table.

"It doesn't look like much," Bayram offered, "but I'm guessing these electronics will do what's needed?"

"Have no fear, they most certainly will," Zeki confirmed. He rotated the two-inch-thick and three-inch-wide box a quarter turn, then lifted the device and inspected it closely. "Good. There's no apparent damage from the long truck ride in from Lake Van. We'll test each of them during the assembly process over the next week."

Bayram pointed to a pair of indentations on each end of the device. "Are these where the batteries go?"

Zeki Aga shook his head. "No, those are for the vials of binary explosives. The battery goes in here," he said, and pointed to the center of the device. With his thumbnail, he popped a narrow plastic cover off, exposing a single AAA battery. "It's in here on top of the remote-control receiver."

Bayram scratched his chin. "It's not going to be dangerous for my men when they deliver the chairs to the cultural event, will it? I mean, might one detonate by accident if the driver hits a pothole or if one of the men accidentally drops a chair off one of the trucks, or something?"

"No, no, don't worry," Zeki assured him. "It's perfectly stable until activated remotely. The beauty of binary explosives is that they aren't really explosives at all—until you mix the two liquids together. Sargon's contacts in Iran are buying these military-grade explosives for us on the Russian black market. Once the shipment arrives here next week, my men will insert two vials of explosive components into these two indentations in the box. We're going to remove the padding from the back of the fancy chairs and replace some of it with these electronic boxes and a dozen large ball bearings. When we're done, we'll bring in four professional upholsterers to stitch the chairs back together so no one will be able tell that anything was ever done to them. On the day of the event—and only once the chairs are already in place at the venue—I will remotely activate the electronics myself to mix the two binary components together into an active explosive."

Bayram lifted his index finger into the air. "But won't the police have everything in the area, including the chairs, searched by explosive-sniffing dogs?"

"Yes, they will, but," Zeki said, and inhaled triumphantly, "the dogs won't alert on these because the chemicals are not explosives *until* they're mixed together. Before agreeing to the purchase of these explosives, His Majesty received samples. That's how my men developed and tested the electronics over the past few months. From our testing, we know they'll work just the way we need them to. To be certain, we also borrowed a few trained dogs from one of the police units loyal to Sargon. The dogs didn't find a thing."

"That's a relief. I know how unstable some explosives can be. After all, I'm the one who drove the truck to the church attack in Paris."

"Ahh!" Zeki said, and patted Bayram on the shoulder. "Well done, my friend. I myself led the two attacks in America recently. You may have heard of them."

Bayram's eyes opened wide. "The one in Los Angeles? I certainly did! That was you? Wow! What a set of balls you have! What was the other one?"

Zeki smiled at the compliment. "A smaller attack in North Carolina on a military base, but what we do here in Istanbul will top them both. These explosives will shoot ball bearings not just through the spines and lungs of the dignitaries seated in the plush seats you're providing, but also throughout the entire venue. In an instant, they'll shred both the Crusaders and their immoral guests."

Bayram drew his cheeks back into a wide grin and vigorously shook the hand of the man leading His Majesty's army to certain victory over the infidels.

**

Michael pulled open the door to the stairwell in Pascal Leclerc's hotel and stepped into the third-floor hallway. He quickly scanned both directions. Seeing it was empty, he pushed the door further open for Alex and Eden to follow him. Without a word, he led the small procession along the hall to the third door from the end.

Eden withdrew a black rectangle the size of a brick from her backpack. A cable with a silver rectangle trailed from the electronic device, and she gently pulled it free. Deftly, she inserted the key card size probe into the door's lock and pressed the red button on the electronic equivalent of a lockpick for digital doors.

Within ten seconds, the lock on the hotel suite's door clicked. Michael pushed it open, and the team followed him inside. Without a word, they gathered in the suite's vestibule and pulled equipment from their jacket pockets and Eden's backpack.

Michael gestured first to Eden and then the open bedroom door to her left. She nodded her understanding, placed her backpack on the floor and lifted a two-foot-long tube from inside. She took up a position behind the sofa in the suite's living room and watched Alex and Michael move swiftly to the closed bedroom door at the opposite end of the suite.

Quietly, Alex counted down from three. At the appointed moment, Michael opened the door and rushed into the bedroom. Alex followed closely behind and jumped on Pascal in the bed. A startled yelp erupted from the bedroom as Michael and Alex fought to restrain him.

A grunt from the other bedroom drew Eden's attention and she aimed the shotgun-like tube toward the open doorway. A shirtless athletic man in cotton shorts appeared in the doorway with the outline of something Eden found all-too familiar in his right hand — a pistol.

As the man took a step toward Pascal's bedroom, Eden cleared her throat. Pascal's bodyguard turned toward her, but too late.

Eden pulled the trigger of her CIA-made blunderbuss. A *pop* of compressed carbon dioxide belched from the two-foot tube, and a six-ounce beanbag shot into the belly of the bodyguard ten feet away.

His breath hissed harshly as it rushed from his lungs.

Eden dropped the now-empty tube to the floor and rushed to where the bodyguard was collapsing in anguish. She twisted the Glock pistol from his hand and tucked it into her waistband behind her back.

The face of the man rolling on the floor contorted as he struggled in vain to breathe through the pain in his lower belly. His face flushed and eyes bulged. He opened his mouth wide as he fought against his spasming diaphragm. The dome-shaped muscle in the bodyguard's abdomen—which so readily fills his lungs with fresh Mediterranean air when he races bicycles along the coastal roads of Nice—refused to obey his brain's commands to inhale.

Next to him, Eden dropped to her knees and pulled a silver packet from her jacket pocket. The label on the packet read 'Product Strength 6.' She carefully removed a damp cloth from within the ziplock packet and held the CIA's version of chloroform in her gloved hand.

She rolled the man struggling to breathe onto his stomach and straddled him across his lower back. With her left hand, she grabbed a fistful of his hair and yanked harshly to lift his face off the carpet. She cupped the damp cloth over the bodyguard's mouth and held it in place firmly.

As he slowly regained his breath, he also inhaled the chemical sedative's vapors. With every breath he drew that ordinarily would have provided him the strength he needed to use to fight Eden, the CIA drug he inhaled conspired against him. In ten seconds, his muscles relaxed as he gradually lost consciousness. Once Eden was certain the guard slept soundly, she rolled off him and backed herself against the wall a few feet away.

In the suite's second bedroom, Alex straddled Pascal Leclerc in the bed, pinning the banker's arms to his side. Pascal kicked ineffectively as the former Navy SEAL kept the smaller man trapped. Kneeling next to the pair, Michael held his own damp cloth over Pascal's mouth and nose until the money launderer was groggy but not unconscious.

As Pascal's kicks waned in force, he mumbled incoherently as his head lolled from side to side. Alex eased his grip on the woozy man to avoid leaving bruises.

While Alex kept Pascal contained, Michael retuned to the hallway where Eden was relaxing next to the bodyguard and examining the sleeping man's Glock.

"Having fun, Eden?"

She ignored her boss's question, ejected the magazine and squinted to see the bullets in the top of the clip. Moonlight filtering through the suite's sheer curtains reflected dully from the brass casing and copper-cladding over the lead projectile at the top.

She looked at Michael as he rooted through her backpack. "Nine-millimeter parabellum. Full metal jacket. Probably one hundred fifteen grains, but I can't see it too clearly in this dim light." She slammed the magazine back into the pistol's frame and laid the weapon on the floor next to her. She looked over to her boss and confirmed for him what he already knew. "Yup. Having fun."

From the backpack, Michael pulled two foam earplugs and an eight-inch-long, thin metal tube with balloons on each end. As he stood, his right knee cracked audibly. "Ugh," he groaned. He shook his head at Eden. "Some days I *think* I'm too old for this shit. On other days, my body *tells* me so in no uncertain terms."

"Not a chance, boss," she replied. "You're in the prime of your life. Enjoy it."

"Yeah right," he said, and turned.

She pointed to Pascal's bedroom. "And also, I hope you enjoy your threesome with the other two men in bed over there. I'll be right here when you're done, and I want to hear *all* about it. *Every* detail, you hear?"

Michael turned toward her, smiled and shook his head slowly. He decided to play along, and asked, "Do you have any tips for me? You know, any special positions that work well for this kind of thing?"

"I don't know," Eden said. "It's been a few years. My last threesome was in Frankfurt with a pair of German prostitutes. No happy endings for anyone that night."

Michael stood still and thought. His eyebrows furrowed, almost meeting in the middle of his face. Moments later, he nodded. "Oh, right. The Fuchs mission—father and son chemical weapons dealers. It took me a minute, but now I remember the debrief. That was a rough one for you, I know."

From the bedroom, Alex's voice asked, "You comin' back or what?"

"On my way," Michael reported, and turned away from Eden.

As he approached the bed, Pascal muttered again as if trying to verbalize something important.

"What's he saying?" Michael asked.

"I think he's trying to *sing*. I have no idea what, but he must be, you know, having some kind of half-awake dream of something or other. It's weird. Let's just get this over with."

Michael sat on the bed next to Pascal's head. "Open his mouth."

Alex gently pulled Pascal's jaw down. He secured the money man's tongue with his thumb and kept his jaw extended so Michael had unobstructed access to the Frenchman's throat.

Michael held the metal tube vertically over Pascal's mouth and lowered the end with the deflated balloon inside. He fed the tube further in until a notch on the tube's side lined up with Pascal's lips. Michael squeezed the golf ball-sized rubber sphere on the tube's other end a dozen times until the balloon in Pascal's throat—lodged between tongue, tonsils and the roof of his mouth—expanded, blocking his airway.

With his airway blocked, Pascal stopped singing and he began breathing through his nose. With each inhale, a high-pitched nasally wheeze escaped the banker's nostrils.

Alex's shoulders drooped and he shook his head. "Oh, that is so *not* an improvement."

Michael rolled the pair of foam earplugs between his fingers until they compressed to half their original size. He inserted one into each of Pascal's nostrils and waited for the inevitable.

"Okay, hold him tightly," Michael instructed Alex.

Alex griped Leclerc's wrists firmly and winced at the suffocating man's first shudder.

"Hold him firmly, Alex. He's going to buck like a bronco as he tries to breathe through the obstructions."

Michael pulled the pillow up around the sides of Pascal's head and held it in place to keep the suffocating man from shaking the metal tube lodged in his throat loose.

Michael looked at Alex's position on Pascal. "Don't sit on his chest. Just keep his arms pinned to his sides. It's like riding a horse: knees tight, butt light."

Through the bedroom door, Eden's voice floated into the room. "I hear you guys in there talking about each other's *butts.*"

Alex scowled while Michael chuckled and shook his head.

Shortly, Pascal stopped moving. Five minutes later, Michael had returned all of his equipment to Eden's backpack, fluffed the pillow under Pascal's head and closed the bedroom door as he left.

In the suite's living room, Eden gestured to the sleeping bodyguard. "Can you big strong men do the heavy lifting?" She looked at her boss and reconsidered her wisecrack. "Actually, Michael, if you need me and Alex to do it, I—"

"No, no," he replied. "I've got it. You go ahead and put his pistol on the dresser in plain sight. That way he'll see it as soon as he wakes up."

"Seems odd," Alex quipped, "that we're only doing Pascal and not both of them."

"This way," his boss said as he bent down to lift the bodyguard's legs, "Pascal's death will look like he died of an extreme instance of sleep apnea. The way we did it, the coroner won't find the usual signs of strangulation. The bodyguard will know the truth, but there's no way in *hell* he'd want to report that he got overwhelmed and failed at his job. If he did that, who would hire him in the future? No, he'll know it's much better for him to just report the death but not the late-night intrusion."

Michael and Alex returned the sleeping bodyguard to his bed, pulled the blanket over him and backed out of the room. Eden left the Glock on the dresser and closed the bedroom door behind her.

In the suite's living room, she returned her gear to her backpack and zipped it closed.

Michael checked his watch. "Time on target, less than fifteen minutes. Pretty good, all in all." He looked at Eden. "You ready for the bank job later today?"

"Sure," Eden said, scoffing at Michael's plan for later in the day. "I'm sure I'll *love* playing your secretary. It's my life's ambition."

"Now, now," Michael said, "don't be like that. You know perfectly well that you're *key* to my whole plan at the bank."

"Oh, that's very *punny*," Eden said, and hefted the backpack across her right shoulder.

Chapter 39

Zeki Aga walked through the warehouse and stopped periodically to inspect the deconstruction of the high-backed chairs. His soldiers worked in pairs at ten rectangular tables carefully removing the leather backs from the chairs destined to seat—and kill—the American Embassy's invited guests.

He stopped at one table and watched as one of his men held a cardboard pattern over the stuffing he'd removed from the back of one chair. From the center of the yellow foam padding, the two men extracted a two-inch-deep and three-inch-wide section and discarded it. From above and below the rectangular cutout, they scooped a dozen inch-deep holes and duct taped steel ball bearings into each.

Zeki smiled at their progress and complimented his soldiers.

"Thank you, sir," one responded, and wiped sweat from his forehead.

"Don't forget," Zeki advised them, "drink plenty of water. I don't want you to get dehydrated. We have a lot of work to do this week and next as we prepare for the big event."

Zeki Aga continued on through the warehouse, walking from table to table. Halfway through his rounds, he stopped and made spot corrections to two men scooping too much padding where they would insert ball bearings.

Once satisfied with their modified technique, he went outside and walked the perimeter of the warehouse. In the parking lot, he stopped as Bayram approached him whistling and spinning his key ring around his index finger.

Bayram asked Zeki, "How's it going inside?"

"We're on schedule. Where are you off to?"

Bayram dangled the keys from his finger. "Liechtenstein again."

"That's a long drive," Zeki said.

"There *and* back, yeah. It takes a couple of days round-trip, and we can't stop on the way back. Not with the cargo aboard."

"What's in Liechtenstein? I know it's in Europe, but to be honest, don't think I could even find it on the map."

"Yeah," Bayram said, and chuckled. "It's tiny and takes all of two seconds to drive through before you end up in Switzerland, but the banks are flush with His Majesty's money. And unlike Swiss banks nowadays, *these* banks don't ask where the money came from or where it's going. After all, someone has to pay off corrupt government officials, and the bankers want their piece of the action. But that's not my job. I just secure the money in my SUV's hidden compartment and tag-team with one of my guys as we drive Sargon's courier home through the night."

"Safe travels, Bayram," Zeki said, and waved farewell.

***

After only four hours of shut-eye, Michelle spent ten minutes more than usual in front of the mirror applying makeup around her eyes to get rid of the evidence of her less-than-restful night's sleep. At breakfast, she drank a second cup of strong coffee, then drove Michael to the bank in Vaduz.

With the morning sun at his back, Michael's tall figure cast a long shadow over the ornate wooden door at the top of the three marble steps in front of him. He stepped up to the hand-carved oak door and read the brass plaque on it: Liechtenstein Trust Bank. In one hand, he held the black Coach attaché case delivered to him by CIA'a Logistics team in France. With the index finger of his free hand, he firmly pressed the white intercom button to the left of the door.

Almost immediately, a woman's voice came through the plastic speaker grille. In German, she asked, "*Kann ich Ihnen helfen?*"

Michael answered in Spanish. "*¿Perdóneme señora, pero habla español?*"

"*Nein, mein Herr.* English, perhaps?"

"Yes," Michael answered. "That would be wonderful. I'm here to access my safe deposit box."

"Of course," the disembodied woman's voice said. "Please come in." Moments later, the lock on the door buzzed. Michael pulled the heavy door open and held it for Michelle.

As she stepped forward, the large purse slung over her shoulder bumped against her skirt. She clutched the bag firmly to her side and carefully stepped over the threshold into the bank's lobby. Her high heels clacked as she crossed the gray-and-black marble floor. Michelle eyed the colorful bouquet of red-and-white flowers sitting in a wide vase on a small rectangular table in the lobby's center. To its left, a woman at a small desk quickly typed something into her computer. A few feet behind her, a closed door blended unobtrusively into the wall's brown wood paneling.

Some bank, Michelle thought. *No tellers, no guards and no ropes to keep the riffraff in line. Clearly, we're not in Kansas anymore.*

Michelle slowed her pace to allow her boss to approach the desk first. She followed behind him and rested her purse on one of two chairs facing the receptionist's desk.

Michael addressed the seated woman. "Good morning. I'm here to—"

Before he could finish, the door behind the receptionist swung open and a short man with hair as gray as his three-piece suit entered. "Good morning, sir," he said to Michael. "I'm Dietrich Landau. I understand you're here to access a box? Is that what I can help you with today?"

"Yes," the CIA officer replied. "That's right."

"Of course, sir. Which box?"

As Michael recited the twelve-digit number from memory, the seated woman typed it into her computer. Landau looked over her shoulder and read the computer's report.

"Ah, yes, that's one of our bearer boxes." He gestured to the small numeric pad next to the computer on the desktop. "Please identify yourself by entering your personal access code into the pad."

Michael typed in the access code François Arsenault gave Dan Green aboard the aircraft carrier the previous week.

"I also need to access my other box." Michael gave Landau the number for the second box and rocked back on his heels.

The banker typed the second number into the computer. Seconds later, he looked up and smiled. "Very good, sir. Please enter the second PIN number as well."

Once he verified the PIN, he looked at Michael. "Would you please follow me?" Landau looked at Michelle, swept an open hand toward the chair on which Michelle leaned her purse. "Madame, you're welcome to wait here for the duration. Louisa would be happy to offer you tea or mineral water, if you'd like."

"Actually," Michael announced, "my assistant will be coming in with me."

"That would be unusual," Landau said. "The privacy rooms we have for viewing your box's contents are somewhat small. I fear fitting two boxes on their carts *plus* two people inside would not work very well. I'm sure she would be more comfortable here in the lobby."

Subtly, Michael stood up straight, extending to his full height of just over six feet. He looked down at the banker eight inches shorter than he, and said, "That is kind of you, *Herr* Landau, but I require her assistance with a few things inside my boxes. I'm sure you have larger private rooms, don't you?"

"Well, yes, sir, but they're for our private banking clients. I—"

"*Herr* Landau," Michael said, "naturally, I realize that the few million euros in business we bring to the Liechtenstein Trust Bank is modest by some of your clients' standards. My associates and I have always maintained a good relationship with your firm, and I look forward to continuing that for years to come. I don't know how busy you may be with other clients this morning and I do respect your time, but I would certainly appreciate the courtesy if you were to find a way to allow us to use one of your larger rooms for a half hour this morning."

The banker reacted to Michael's implied threat immediately. "I do apologize for the inconvenience, sir, and we certainly value *all* of our customers. If you would please give me a just moment, I'll check with my staff in the back to see if one of our few such rooms may indeed be available. Please, sir... just a moment."

Dietrich Landau disappeared through the side door, which quietly *whooshed* shut behind him.

From her seat, Louisa the receptionist asked, "Would either of you care for something to drink? We have several types of water, both sparkling and flat."

Michael declined the offer while Michelle asked for a Perrier.

As Louisa rose, the door beside her opened and Landau emerged smiling.

He said, "If you would both follow me, please. We are indeed able to accommodate your special request this morning. It turns out it is quite a busy day for us, but I don't expect rush hour to happen until later this afternoon. This way."

As they walked around her desk, Louisa made a point to tell Michelle that the private suites were fully stocked with refreshments, but if she needed assistance, she should push the attendant call button by the door. Michelle thanked her and followed Michael.

Landau led the CIA officers through the side door and into a wide hallway lined with staff offices and conference rooms. Decorative horizontal striations gave the wooden walls a distinctive and modern look. At the end of the hallway, Landau swiped his employee badge hanging from the side of his belt to open a set of glass double doors. Once through the doors, he led his pair of clients into a room labeled, "Private Viewing Suite 3."

Michael placed his leather briefcase on the small rectangular conference table in the center of the room and turned to face Landau.

The banker stood in the doorway. "Please make yourselves comfortable while I have your safe deposit boxes wheeled in. It should only take a few minutes for the guards to bring them up front the vault." He pointed to the sideboard. "As Louisa mentioned, you'll find a full complement of refreshments here that suit the many diverse tastes of our private banking clients. And, sir, if you find that your banking needs grow appreciably over time, I hope you will think well of Liechtenstein Trust Bank. If you wish, while we wait for your boxes to be delivered, I'd be happy to discuss our robust slate of financial services that our 'mobile and global' clients—as we like to call them—find indispensable for both their business and personal needs."

"I do appreciate the offer, *Herr* Landau," Michael said. "Perhaps on my next visit I'll have more time to discuss the particulars with you."

"Of course, sir," Landau replied with a forced smile. "It would be my pleasure. In the meantime, if you need assistance at any time— anything at all—simply press the button located on the call box next to the door." He pointed to a small black button next to the light switch and left the room.

Michelle placed her purse on the table next to Michael's attaché and sunk into one of the six leather chairs around the conference table. "Oh. My. God," she said with a groan. "I thought he'd never leave."

Michael took a seat across the table from her and raked his fingers through his white hair, pushing a wayward lock back into place. He shook his head slowly. "You and me both."

"I wonder just how 'mobile' and 'global' one has to be to become one of his private clients."

"You know what they say," Michael replied. "If you have to ask...."

Michelle grunted, and softly agreed, "True." She twisted in her seat and looked at the small refrigerator built into the cabinet along the wall. "Well, if I can't have immense wealth, then at least I can have a free bottle of Perrier." She rose to fetch a bottle. "Want something?"

Michael declined her offer.

They made small talk for five minutes, comparing brands of European water. After running out of idle chitchat, they sat for another ten minutes mostly in silence during which Michelle used her index finger to spin the water bottle cap on the tabletop.

A knock at the door startled her, and the bottle cap skittered out from under her finger and onto the floor.

"Finally," Michael said under his breath.

Landau opened the door and stepped gingerly into the room. He looked straight at Michael and wrung his hands. "I am *so* sorry, sir, but there's a problem."

Chapter 40

A shiver ran down Michelle's spine. *A problem?* she thought. *Oh shit. I wonder if we can even get down the hall and through the double doors without this guy's employee keycard.*

Michael looked at the banker, and calmly asked, "What sort of problem, *Herr* Landau?"

"We received your firm's instructions for the cash transfer from your deposit account to your safe deposit box in the vault. The instructions came in yesterday."

Michael's face tightened as he asked, "Yes. One of my junior associates, *Monsieur* Pascal Leclerc phoned it in. I was sitting with him when he made the call. What's the problem, then?"

"Well, sir," Landau said, and shuffled his feet, "as I mentioned earlier, we've been extremely busy this week and we execute fund transfers in the order received. There were quite a few in the queue before yours, I'm afraid."

"*And*?" Michael asked. "Your bank hasn't run out of money, has it?"

Landau's face lit up. "Oh, *no*, sir. No, of course not. We just need more time to fill your order for the transfer to be made in cash—in euros, as you requested. Quite a few of our private bank clients from Dubai and Riyadh are coming into town for the biennial cricket tournament this week. It's not a popular sport for locals, but certain foreign attendees apparently find it easier to wager on their national teams here than they can back home. I like to think the amenities we offer in our small but hospitable country—along with the pleasing climate of the Alps—are preferable to the hot and dry environments some of our clients experience in their home countries. So, I hope you can understand that it will just take us another twenty minutes or so for the staff in the vault to complete your cash-transfer request. I put in an order to expedite it because you've already been *so* very patient, sir. I hope you can enjoy the privacy of this suite and some refreshments while you wait."

Michelle slowly exhaled and relaxed back into her padded leather seat. *Well, if that's all it is....*

Her team lead scratched the left side of his neck. "Thank you for your help in getting the order expedited, *Herr* Landau. I do appreciate it."

"Of course, sir," the banker said, and backed out of the room.

The solid wood door *whooshed* closed firmly behind him, and the lock engaged with a metallic *click*.

"*Cricket?*" Michelle asked, rhetorically. "Fucking *cricket* is what's standing between us and stopping the next Usama bin Laden? Gimme a break," she grumbled, and traced a circle on the carpet with the toe of her taupe high-heeled shoe.

Michael grinned. "When you have too much money, you have to spend it on something. Or use it for the thrill of a high-stakes wager, I suppose. I haven't got the foggiest idea how one bets on cricket, but I'm sure its fans have all that figured out."

"I guess so," Michelle agreed, and sat quietly for a few minutes. "Doesn't this whole thing seem backwards to you? We're breaking into secure boxes in a high-security bank not to steal money, but to ensure that the terrorists we're trying to stop can successfully make their withdrawal this afternoon or tomorrow or whenever they get here."

Michael grinned and nodded. "True, but like the famous man once said, 'Follow the money.' That's what we're here to do." After a moment, he pointed to the small refrigerator in the cabinet behind Michelle. "Do they have any more water in there?"

Michelle spun her chair around to fetch a bottle of flat spring water. Then she helped herself to a second Perrier.

A dozen minutes later, a knock at the door lifted Michelle's sprits.

The door *whooshed* open smoothly on its well-oiled hinges, and Landau held it open for two guards in matching burgundy-and-white uniforms. Into the room, each guard wheeled a metal cart on top of which sat a large steel safe-deposit box. The custom-made boxes—two-feet square in front and just over three feet deep—fit snugly into their carts purpose made for transporting them from the bank's vault in the basement to the private rooms wealthy clients used to transact business away from the prying eyes of regulators, tax collectors and divorce attorneys.

Landau withdrew a cylindrical brass key from his jacket pocket and inserted it into the top of the hinge on the left side of each steel box. He unlocked the portable vaults' hinges and smiled at his clients. "Please, sir, take your time. You can use either your combination to open the digital locks or your physical keys. When you're done, just close the boxes, rotate the handles and press zero on the keypads at least eight times to clear its memory. Do you have any questions for me before I leave you to your business?"

Michael shook his head and thanked Landau.

"Very well, then," the banker said, and followed the two guards out of the room. Before closing the door, he turned to the pair of undercover CIA officers. "As always, if you need any assistance, just press the button beside the light switch."

"We will, thank you," Michael said, and watched the door close.

"*Finally*," Michelle muttered. She slid Michael's briefcase toward her and unzipped it. From inside, she pulled out a four-inch-wide zippered case and a soft white cloth. She laid the cloth on the table and opened the case of lockpicks and tools on top of it. She pulled a thin pamphlet and a penlight from the case and clicked the flashlight on.

She scooted her chair over to the first strong box on the cart and examined the lock's cylinder. She read the make and model, then flipped pages in the pamphlet from her kit.

She ran her finger down the page and then over to the description of the lock. To Michael, she read the line in the pamphlet, "Six-pin biaxial cam lock with rotating pins." She selected a hook pick from the kit on the table and centered herself in front of the safe deposit box. "Rotating pins," she repeated softly to herself. "Okay, then. Lift and rotate."

"You can do it," Michael said. "Just go pin by pin at your own pace."

"Yeah, yeah. These high-security locks are no fun." She inserted an L-shaped metal tension wrench into the top of the keyway and applied light pressure. She stared intently at the lock, inserted her hook pick and asked her boss, "Did you know that some people back home do this kind of thing for *fun*? They call it 'locksport.' If you believe what the guys in DS&T say, it's becoming a pretty popular hobby. People will meet up at conventions or libraries on weekends to teach each other how to pick locks. Some even create their own custom locks for fun as challenges for others." She prodded the first pin with her lockpick, then moved on to the second.

"Hmmm," Michael said. "I guess there's no telling what some people call *fun*, is there?"

"No," Michelle said, and grunted. "Some people like lockpicking, and some people like cricket. Clearly there are too many people out there who simply have no taste and no social lives." She maneuvered the lockpick back and forth in the keyway and frowned. "This second pin is being obstinate." With just the tips of her fingers, she applied a light touch to her lockpick. "*Ahh*, there."

After a moment, she cursed and pulled the lockpick and tension wrench out of the keyway. "*Ughhh*, I hit a false gate on the second pin." She flexed her fingers and reinserted her tools into the key slot.

"The trick," Michael said, "is to hold the tension wrench with a very light touch. Feather-light, so you can feel the difference between the pin's small movement if you hit a false gate or the larger movement when you get it aligned correctly with the internal tension bar. Hold the pick itself loosely and jiggle it."

Michelle continued working on the lock. "I'm not usually the *jiggly* kind of girl."

Michael quickly added, "What I meant was—"

"I *know*. I know," Michelle said, and sneered at her boss. "I'm just yanking your chain, but if you want, I might be able to set you up with Cynthia from the yacht. I bet you'd like *her* jiggles." She looked at her boss of more than a decade and gave him a wink.

Michael smiled. "I was there and saw it all, but I don't think she likes you very much after you spiked her champagne."

"*Hey* now," Michelle said, and continued working on the lock. "In all fairness, it was *Alex* who spiked the drinks. Not me."

"True," Michael said, "but don't you think she'd consider that to be a distinction without a difference?"

"Yeah," she agreed, as the lock clicked open and the tension wrench sprung clockwise, "you're probably right." She twisted the lock cylinder a half-turn to the right, cranked the steel box's handle to the open position, and sat back. "Ta *dah*!"

"Excellent. You're wonderful. I think that may be a new world record."

"I'll take the 'wonderful' part, but don't push it. I'm sure any one of DS&T's lock experts would have had that sucker open in under twenty seconds." She stood up and moved back so Michael could sit in front of the box.

"Don't sell yourself short," he said, and pulled a pair of gloves out of his briefcase while Michelle got to work on the second box. "You're far better at lockpicking than I am. I'm too out of practice. If it had been up to me, I think I would have had to beat the combination to the digital lock out of François in the Roach Motel."

Michelle sat in the chair Michael had previously occupied and picked the lock on the second lock box. She pulled the door of the empty box open and sat back. "If I'd known then that we could have just dialed in the right combinations to open these boxes, I would have simply asked him. By the end, he was in a very talkative mood. It never came up in conversation, so, well... here we are."

Michael peered into the safe deposit box in front of him and pulled out a half-dozen stacks of euros wrapped in paper Liechtenstein Trust Bank bands. He transferred the money from the box to the briefcase, turned the attaché on its side and put it into the second metal box. "I think that's it. Do you have all of your gear?"

"Yup," Michelle confirmed. "Hook pick, tension wrench and flashlight." She put the kit and cloth into her purse and zipped it shut.

Michael swung the doors of both safe deposit boxes closed, turned the handles to relock them and stood up. "Okay. As soon as the courier gets here and takes the attaché with the money, we'll track him all the way home with the beacon sewn inside. I've set it so that once he turns the case upright it'll activate the beacon—"

Michelle finished his thought, saying, "Then it's game on, courier, and goodnight Sargon."

Chapter 41

"They're moving," Alex Ramirez reported from the back seat of the team's rented BMW. He traced his finger on the screen of the laptop and read out a street name.

"Release the hounds," Michael said from the front passenger seat.

Michelle started the ignition and put the 5-Series sedan in gear. She drove slowly out of the cabin's driveway, looked to her right and, with a smirk, asked her boss, "Are we there yet?"

Michael groaned. "Are you going to be *that* kid on this trip? Because this car has a large trunk, and you would *not* be the first woman I've stuffed into one during my career."

"*Oooh*!" Alex exclaimed. "I definitely want to hear *that* story!"

"Well, Alex, I *will* say that it was a clear night under the stars somewhere outside Rabat, Morocco. Maybe someday I'll tell you the rest."

"Can't wait," the former SEAL said, and patted the back of his boss's seat gently.

Michelle steered the BMW onto the main road into the city, careful to obey all traffic laws. The last thing she wanted to have happen today was to get stopped by the police and lose their trail on the briefcase's concealed tracker. Even though the team carried little in the way of incriminating equipment, she didn't want to take unnecessary chances.

Once per minute, Alex advised Michelle of the briefcase's location as the beacon let out its electromagnetic ping. He kept his eyes glued to the computer screen and told his teammate, "Looks like they're six miles north of us, driving on highway A13."

Michelle settled into the comfortable leather driver's seat for the long drive and followed the directions her partner called out from the back.

A few minutes later, Alex cleared his throat. "*Oops*. They turned east. Must have gotten off the highway back there."

"Damn," Michelle muttered.

"Don't worry," Michael replied calmly. "Assuming they're heading to Turkey, this is a marathon, not a sprint. Let's get ready for a long day or two on the road."

"Yup, I'm with you," Michelle agreed. At the next exit, she turned the car around, retraced her path and followed the beacon east.

Michael expanded the map on the BMW's built-in GPS navigation system. "Hmm. For whatever reason, this says the fastest route to Turkey is through Austria, into Germany, then back into Austria and down into Slovenia. And by 'fast,' I mean, it's over twenty-seven hours to Turkey from here, not counting the occasional border crossing, customs inspections and pit stops. Definitely a marathon, folks, so let's get comfortable." He sat back and adjusted his seat for the long drive ahead.

A half-hour later, Alex announced, "We passed it. The beacon's behind us, now."

"Excellent," Michael said. From the backpack next to his knee, he withdrew a pad and pen. As they passed or were passed by cars and trucks on the highway, he jotted down the license plate numbers of each. Each minute, after Alex called out the position of the beacon, he crossed off each plate number of a vehicle that was on the wrong side of them and could not be the one transporting the attaché case containing Sargon's cash.

Once Michael narrowed the list to two cars and one SUV, he said to Michelle, "That's good enough for now. Fall back about a mile, and let's give it an hour or so. Eventually, they'll pull off the road to eat or get gas. We'll have to do both, as well."

He returned his pad to his backpack and pulled out three granola bars. He offered one to Alex and Michelle and ate his slowly.

Two hours later, the beacon showed the courier had left the highway. Michelle followed Alex's directions to take the next off-ramp. At the bottom, she saw two gas stations across the street from each other. She drove through the intersection and pulled into the station adjacent to the highway's on-ramp, positioning the BMW to resume their pursuit once Sargon's courier headed back onto the highway. She pulled to a stop at a gas pump and got out to fill up. Alex went to the men's room, and Michael ambled around the gas station stretching his legs and stealing looks at license plates.

Michelle finished filling the car and, when Alex returned, took the opportunity to use the ladies' room. On her way out, she purchased a half-dozen bottles of water, a six pack of energy drinks, three sandwiches and a handful of Toblerone chocolate bars.

When she returned to the car, Michael looked at her plastic bag of comfort food. "Have a sweet tooth much?"

Michelle sneered at her team lead, put her bag on the floorboard behind her seat and slipped back behind the BMW's leather-wrapped steering wheel.

Michael told her that while she was inside, both cars possibly carrying the courier got back onto the highway ahead of them, but the SUV on his list was still parked at the diesel pump at the gas station across the street. From his backpack, he withdrew a plastic bag of provisions he purchased at the gas station's shoppette and unwrapped a Nestlé bar. He handed one to Alex and offered one to Michelle.

She glared at her boss. "And you have the *gall* to accuse *me* of having a sweet tooth?"

Michael shrugged. "I never claimed I didn't, but at least I'm willing to share. I didn't see you make any such offer."

"I bought enough for everyone," she exclaimed. She looked around outside the car to see if anyone had heard her outburst, then lowered her voice, and more calmly said, "I'm not keeping it all for myself. I got sandwiches and water for all of us. The cold water will keep the sandwiches fresh for a few hours. I'm *always* thinking of you guys. I'm never selfish."

"Although," Alex said, and waved a finger in the air, "she *does* hog the bed when we travel and pose as a couple."

"Yeah, well," Michelle harrumphed, "at least I don't snore."

"That's true," Alex confirmed. "She doesn't. Lucky me." He watched the laptop computer's screen for a few seconds until the next ping showed up. "The briefcase hasn't moved." He looked across the street at the gas station. "Must be in the SUV."

"Good," Michael replied, "now we know which vehicle the courier is in. That's a big step forward. I do, though, wish we knew what the rabbit himself looks like. We'll have to make some kind of move later to get a look at him. Anyway, we'll follow the SUV back to Turkey and see where it goes. I figure he *has* to go to eastern Turkey where Sargon's base of popular support seems to be centered. I've already asked Wilson to have Logistics send a full load of our equipment to Turkey. There's no telling what we'll need, so I asked for everything except the kitchen sink." He returned the pen and pad to his backpack and removed his shoes, readying himself for the day-long drive ahead of them.

The team watched for ten minutes until the courier's SUV pulled out of the gas station's parking lot. Michael told Michelle to wait three more minutes before following so they'd stay out of the rabbit's line of sight. Then they'd follow from a distance using the beacon for the next few hours.

While waiting for the three-minute window to pass, Michelle studied the watch on her left wrist. She rotated its bezel slowly, listening attentively to each click as she spun it in a complete rotation around the watch's face. With a red-painted fingernail, she thumbed the crown sticking out of the side of the watch. On a mechanical watch, twisting the crown would wind the watch, but concealed underneath the crown of Eden's watch sat the poisoned needle she'd carried in the field for the past decade. While she preferred to keep it close at hand, she hoped with all her heart she never found herself in a situation so dire that she needed to end her own life with the help of CIA's merciful lethal agent. The scientists from DS&T who issued it to her said it would be quick and painless. She hoped to never find out.

After the second hand on her watched passed twelve for the third time, Michelle pushed the BMW's start button and the car's powerful engine purred to life. She pulled away from the gas station and took a quick right turn. The powerful engine accelerated the car smoothly up the highway on-ramp.

Four hours later, Alex's computer showed that the courier's SUV exited the highway. "They got off at the next exit, just across the border in Slovenia. That's good for me. I need to make a pit stop and walk around, anyway. This car's comfortable and all, but after six hours on the road...."

"Yeah, I agree," Michael said, and rubbed his right knee. "Next time, I need to rent a 7-Series for the extra legroom."

"Works for me," Michelle said. "We're getting low on gas, and I think it's Alex's turn to drive now."

At the next exit, Michelle signaled, changed lanes and pulled onto the exit ramp. The bang of a small explosion reverberated throughout the interior of the car and sent the car veering to the right. Michelle struggled to control the shuddering BMW as it did its best to ignore her commands to stay on the paved road and not careen into the guard rail.

"What the *hell*?" Michelle asked rhetorically, and fought the steering wheel with all her might.

Chapter 42

Michelle stomped on the brakes and aimed the BMW down the center of the A2 freeway's exit ramp. Her shoulder belt dug deeply into her upper chest, and the steering wheel reverberated violently in her hands. The wheel twisted in Michelle's hand and pulled hard to the right as the luxury sedan rumbled to the bottom of the ramp. Michelle let out a long, guttural grunt as she practically stood on the brake pedal and strained to swerve the car away from the guard rail. She clenched her jaw and pushed her foot down so hard she lifted a few inches out of her seat.

The car shuddered to a stop on a wide dirt patch a few yards past the exit ramp's shoulder. The BMW's momentum rocked it back and forth a few times before its suspension brought it to a final halt. Michelle let out a groan and shook her hands to soothe the muscles in her wrists and fingers.

In the back seat, Alex slapped the laptop closed. "What do you think? Flat tire?"

"Probably," Michael said, and pushed a lock of his white hair up over the top of his head. "Let's see what we're dealing with."

The trio of CIA officers stepped out of the car and grouped on the passenger's side, safely away from rubberneckers passing them at the bottom of the off-ramp.

Michelle inspected the remains of the front tire. "Damn! That tire's not just flat—it's *shredded*."

Alex snickered. "You don't do anything halfway, do you? You done flattened that one, and good."

Michael let out a long breath. "Well, let's not just stand here. Let's see what kind of spare they put in these things nowadays."

The team spent an hour removing the ruined tire from the BMW and replacing it with a doughnut spare. Once they'd finished and loaded their luggage back into the trunk, Alex got into the driver's seat and drove a half-mile to the nearest gas station.

While Michelle and Alex used the restrooms, Michael filled the gas tank and inquired inside the station about getting a replacement tire.

Back in the car, he told the others that the local gas stations wouldn't have a replacement on hand. The attendant had told him he'd have better luck at the BMW dealership in Ljubljana, Slovenia's capital, an hour to the east.

Michelle did a few Google Maps searches on the laptop, and reported, "Well... assuming we get there before dark, and they do have a tire, I'm sure a sizable tip would ensure we get it installed tonight. But that's going to cost us another couple of hours. As a practical matter, we have no way of catching up to the SUV now."

"Yeah," Michael agreed. "We'd have to break a few land-speed records to do that and hope there aren't any cops on the road between us and them. Not likely. Okay, Michelle, look up flights leaving tonight from Ljubljana to anywhere in Turkey. Start with the capital, Ankara, and go down the list from there."

Michelle tapped the laptop's keys and read from the screen. "Turkish Airways has a flight tonight that leaves at 7:55 p.m. and arrives in Ankara at 3:15 a.m. There's an almost three-hour layover in Istanbul, though."

"Istanbul...." Michael repeated softly. "That might be even better for us. It's between here and Ankara. Ever since we left Liechtenstein, I've been *assuming* the courier's heading to Turkey. Since the SUV's been driving in that direction all day, I'd say it's still a good guess." He took the PC from Michelle and studied the flight's itinerary. "If we get off in Istanbul, we should beat the courier there by about ten hours. Okay, that'll work, assuming *that's* where they're headed after all." Satisfied with the calculated gamble, he said to Alex, "Okay, new plan. Drive to the airport. We can return the car to the Alamo rental office there."

Alex pulled the car back onto the highway. "You know, Mike, if you think we're heading into a gunfight in a couple of days to take out Sargon and his goons, then using words like 'Alamo' might not be the best thing for us, you know?"

Michael shrugged. "Depends whether you're the ones fighting the battle from inside the walls or from outside, doesn't it?"

Chapter 43

After their late-night landing in Istanbul, the CIA team caught a few hours' sleep at the airport's Yotel hotel.

The next morning, they rented two BMW 7-Series sedans at the airport. Alex took one car for himself while Michael drove Michelle in the other. The team waited in the parking lot of a busy gas station just outside the airport while Michelle tracked the briefcase's beacon on the computer.

"Any change?" Alex asked. "Where are they now?"

"Nope," Michelle answered. "No change."

Her boss peeked at the laptop's screen. "They're still on the highway headed our way. I'd say they're two hours west of Istanbul. We just have to wait."

"I hate waiting," Michelle grumbled.

Michael thumbed at his cell phone out of boredom. "The two-hour stop they made in Edirne, just inside the Turkish border, had me worried. Hopefully, they just pulled off the highway for a long pit stop and to stretch their legs. Wilson Henry sent me the full record of their overnight trip earlier. They didn't make any other significant stops. Just for gas and grub, I suspect."

"Let's hope so," Michelle said. "But we can't just sit in our cars here for much longer. Someone's going to get suspicious. There's an outlet mall just up the street. At least we could walk around in there."

Alex sneered. "You feel the need to do some shopping while on surveillance, eh?"

"Actually," Michelle retorted, "having a couple of extra hats, scarves, jackets and the like to change your appearance on surveillances is gold. And besides, it gets us out of our cars for an hour or so."

"Okay," her boss said, "that *does* sound like a productive use of our time. Let's go. Alex, we'll meet you there."

***

Three hours later, Michelle steered her BMW into the left-most lane behind a minivan on the Otoyol 3 motorway. Four car-lengths ahead of her, the SUV with Sargon's money concealed somewhere inside signaled and changed into the highway's center lane.

In the passenger seat of the car he shared with Michelle, Michael held his cell phone at stomach-level, out of sight of other drivers. He said, "Alex, Michelle and I will continue to follow them, but you be prepared to take the eye if they exit the freeway."

"Check," Alex replied.

The SUV continued straight for three more miles along the O-3. In downtown Istanbul, the highway ended and blended into a major city thoroughfare, Adnan Menderes Boulevard. A mile further on, traffic slowed where streets converged in a roundabout.

Michelle steered the BMW around the traffic circle and watched the SUV exit onto a perpendicular street. "Shit," she muttered under her breath.

From the passenger seat, her team lead said to his cell phone, "Alex, can you follow the SUV? We're stuck in traffic."

"Got 'em," he replied. "I'm in the right-hand lane. I'll take the eye."

"Roger," Michael said as Michelle continued halfway around the circle and headed back onto Adnan Menderes Boulevard in the direction they came from.

She signaled for a lane change and cut off a delivery van when she veered into the right-hand lane. The truck driver honked, and she accelerated to avoid a collision. She glanced in the BMW's right-side mirror and threw a look over her shoulder as she cut off two small cars.

Michael called out their position to Alex. "Okay, we're on a parallel street a few blocks west of you. With this traffic, it may take us three or four minutes to get to your position. What's the SUV doing?"

"They're flying straight and level on Akdeniz Caddesi, or however that's pronounced, and they're—No... wait one," he said, and the line went silent.

Michelle drove through three intersections, thankful for both the lack of traffic lights in Istanbul and the powerful engine of her 7-Series BMW.

"They stopped," Alex reported. "They pulled up in front of a restaurant. It's the Ziya Sark something or other. I couldn't get the name. I had to drive past. From where you are, take a right turn on the Fevz—the Fevzipas... Oh hell, I don't know. Some shit like that street. It's a major road, so make a right turn. I'm passing a monstrous mosque on my left. Can't miss it."

Michelle turned right at the intersection with Fevzipasa Cadesi and maneuvered carefully through traffic. The prominent white domes of the Faith Mosque loomed above the rooftops two blocks away. "Got it," she reported to her partner.

Michael clarified, "We turned on the right street and see the mosque. You're right. Couldn't miss it. Where are they now?"

"Still double parked in front of the restaurant. I pulled over to the curb a half-block up. They're—Wait. Someone's getting out of the car. A man. Tall guy. Real thin."

Michael gestured for Michelle to pull over to the curb. "Drop me off at the next corner. I'll walk from there. Alex, can you join me for lunch?"

"As long as you're buying, I can be talked into it."

"Good. Meet me in front of the restaurant. Michelle, set up a static surveillance post somewhere you can keep an eye on the front of the restaurant. If the tall guy goes out the back, I'll follow him, but we need eyes in front."

"Will do," she replied, and pulled the car to a stop at the curb.

Michael got out, and Michelle waited until he crossed the side street before she pulled back into traffic. Without Michael's cell phone connection to Alex, she was left in the dark about what they were seeing. She navigated a wide rectangle around the mosque, and fifteen minutes later shifted the BMW into park on a side street kitty-corner to the Ziya Sark restaurant. Half a block behind her, the Malta Firini bakery displayed sheets of pink-and-green pastries in its front window. Across the street, a shop's sign showed a cone with soft-serve ice cream spiraled on top—a sign which clearly communicated in any language the universal conclusion: it's going to be a good day.

Michelle turned the BMW's ignition off, and said to the steering wheel, "Well, I guess I'm off my diet today."

Twenty minutes later, Michelle dabbed the stained napkin on her lips and held the half-eaten ice cream cone in front of her so it wouldn't drip onto her pants. She shifted to her left on the public bench as a middle-aged woman wearing a headscarf and toting a shopping bag sat down to her right.

Michelle struggled to lick the bitten-through side of the cone to catch the melting vanilla ice cream leaking through. She eventually gave up the struggle and tossed the remnants of the cone into the trashcan behind the bench. She licked her fingers and dried them on her one remaining napkin as her cell phone vibrated in her jacket pocket. She fetched the phone and read the text from Alex.

Payoff made. He got something small in return. Couldn't tell what.
Michelle responded: *How's lunch?*
Good. Lamb. You?
Delicious, she wrote, and shook her head. *Vanilla.*

Michelle laid her phone down in her lap and set her purse on top of it as the woman seated next to her showed an unhealthy interest in what she was typing. The woman said something in Turkish Michelle couldn't understand, so she just smiled in return.

The woman repeated what she said, pointed at the ornate mosque in the expansive plaza across the street and tugged at her own headscarf.

Michelle nodded and pulled a light-brown scarf she'd purchased at the outlet mall that morning from her purse. She wrapped it loosely over her hair and smiled at the woman who nodded her pleasure at Michelle's compliance.

Michelle looked down at her phone again, and thought, *I doubt that any other woman in any other part of Istanbul would care at all. But I guess in front of that particular mosque wearing a scarf means a lot to her. Oh well. When in Rome....*

Her cell phone vibrated as another encrypted message from Alex appeared in the team's chat app: *He's leaving. Set up for the takeaway. I'll take Mike with me. We're going to follow the guy who received the payoff. You follow the tall guy and the SUV.*

She acknowledged the message and glanced across the street at the restaurant. The SUV they'd followed from Liechtenstein sat at the intersection awaiting an opening to turn right onto the main avenue and pick up its VIP passenger.

Michelle hurried back to her car and turned the corner as the SUV pulled into traffic. She followed from four car-lengths back. After a few turns, the SUV got back on the highway and settled into the left lane for its drive through Istanbul.

Michelle's cell phone rang with the ringtone of their encrypted communications app. Her boss's name scrolled across the top. She tapped the green button. "How are things going on your end?"

"Good. We're making our way through city traffic following some fat guy that the money mule met for lunch. What about you?"

"This is weird," she said, and shifted in her seat. "The SUV got back onto the O-3 motorway, and I expected they'd cross one of the bridges over the Bosporus Straight—you know, to head out to eastern Turkey where you-know-who is probably based."

"But?" Michael asked.

"But they're headed back *east*. We passed the east-bound turn off to the O-1 motorway a few minutes ago, so they're not headed home—at least not right away. I mean, we've all just been *assuming* they're from the eastern part of the country, right? So, I don't know. I'll follow them for as long as I can. Single-car surveillances suck, right? They never work out too well over a long period of time."

"Yeah, you're right," Michael said, and paused. "We'll join you as soon as we can, but I really want to see where the ugly guy goes. It looked like Sargon's courier handed him an envelope which I'm assuming was full of cash. Then the fat guy gave him something small in return. It fit inside his hand completely, so... I don't know what it was. Too small for us to see."

"Okay, well, get here as soon as you can. I should be fine as long as they stay on the highways, but once they get off, I'm going to be pretty exposed."

***

Ninety minutes later, Alex parked his car next to Michelle's BMW behind an abandoned building situated next to a set of railroad tracks rusty from lack of use. He and Michael got out and joined their teammate at the building's corner from where she watched the vehicles parked in front of a warehouse across the tracks.

"Nice of you guys to come to my party," she said with a sarcastic tone in her voice.

Alex ignored her quip. "Whatcha got going on here?"

Michelle pulled back from the corner and leaned against the brick wall. "The SUV pulled up to the warehouse about twenty minutes ago. Three guys got out. One was the tall, thin man I saw outside the restaurant in Istanbul. He and another guy from the SUV both went into the warehouse. The third guy—the driver—is smoking and joking with the guards patrolling around outside. Nothing else to tell. What happened to you in Istanbul?"

"We had good luck," Michael informed her. "We followed fatso to a high-security office complex downtown. There were no signs on the buildings, but they looked to me exactly like the kind of offices that belong to a security service. I don't know if it's their domestic service or the MIT, Turkey's National Intelligence Organization. I sent Wilson Henry the GPS coordinates. He can look it up for us later—it's a rather academic point and not the focus of our mission. I've always assumed Sargon has moles or true believers inside the security apparatus here. Or maybe he's just paying them off. Either way, let's see what's going on here at the warehouse and follow the beacon in the briefcase to our elusive target, wherever he's hiding."

***

Inside the warehouse, Behrouz Heidari examined the disassembled chairs lying on the rectangular tables spread throughout the building's expanse. He walked from one to another, all the while under the watchful eye of Zeki Aga's guards. In his hand, he held a fat manilla envelope tightly.

After examining a few tables, Behrouz's driver and companion on the long drive across half of Europe, Bayram, motioned him toward a round table surrounded by four folding metal chairs. The men sat and chatted.

A few minutes later, Zeki Aga emerged from the warehouse's office. From across the room, he cried, "*Selam*, Bayram! So, this is the man you drove all the way to Liechtenstein to bring to us?" He shook Bayram's hand and turned to the newcomer. He extended his hand to Behrouz and greeted him formally. "*Merhaba*! Welcome to Istanbul."

Behrouz shook hands with Zeki and sat down next to Sargon's soldier. Sargon's financial chief smiled at Zeki. "His Majesty was very complimentary about your two attacks in America. Rifaat showed me the details. You carried them both off *very* well."

"Yes, thank you. We were completely successful. I'm glad the sultan was pleased. Now, we have the Americans chasing their tails on their home front, so they won't be able to pay as much attention to us here. We will solidify our base of support in Turkey and, with this next attack, drive the Crusaders out of our homeland. Have you brought what I need to do that?"

"Yes, I have it," Behrouz acknowledged, and tapped the envelope in front of him. "And I also brought some additional funds for you to use for this mission, if you need. I'm glad the money I provided to you in America helped you succeed there. As always, use His Majesty's funds respectfully." He placed the envelope in front of Zeki and sat back.

"Thank you for this," he said, and picked up the envelope from the table. "Between my soldiers, Bayram's logistics and your funding, it is all coming together perfectly. Excellent work, both of you!"

Zeki Aga thumbed through the contents of the envelope and let them spill onto the table. Two dozen five-hundred-euro bills splayed onto the tabletop followed by laminated security IDs bearing the pictures of two of his soldiers. Moments later, a blue plastic USB drive landed on the wooden tabletop with a *tink*. He picked it up and popped the cap off. "What's this?"

"I had lunch today with one of our contacts in the Turkish National Police. For a modest payment, I got diagrams of the layout of the event venue showing which side entrance you need to deliver the chairs through. Have your drivers show those IDs to the guards, and they'll be waved through. Using that entrance will bypass the primary security screening checkpoint."

"Good," Zeki replied. "The dogs won't find anything wrong with the chairs, but you never know what some alert guard might notice that we didn't think of or hide well enough. With these passes, we'll have no problems getting through. Well done, Behrouz. Well done."

Behrouz stood up and stretched his tall frame. He looked at Bayram. "All right, let's get the rest of this drive over with, shall we? It feels like we've been on the road for a week. No matter how many times we make the same trip, each time I just want to get home."

Bayram stood and agreed. "One quick stop for gas, and we'll be on our way."

***

"Moving, guys," Alex announced. He backed away from his perch from which he watched the front of the warehouse. "Three men are gathering outside the SUV. It's definitely the scrawny guy we saw at lunch. He's tall and hard to miss."

Michelle peeked around the corner. "I swear that guy looks familiar, but for the life of me, I can't place him."

Alex shook his head. "I've never seen him before one of the pitstops we all made on the drive from Liechtenstein. Did you see him before yesterday?"

"I don't know," she said slowly, and walked toward her BMW. "I just have one of those feelings about him, you know?"

Michael grunted as he rose from the large rock on which he'd been sitting. "Let's get a move on. Alex, I'll ride shotgun with you and work the laptop to follow the beacon. Michelle, you had the eye coming here, so you trail us about a quarter mile back. I'll call or text you periodically with updates to let you know when we need to switch out the eye or for one of us to stop for gas."

Michelle nodded. "Works for me."

"I hope you have a strong bladder," Michael said. "It's a long drive to the other side of the country." He peeked around the corner and watched as Behrouz and Bayram stood outside their SUV stretching before they began their long drive home. Michael took a picture of them, put his cell phone into his pocket and joined Alex in his car.

Alex pressed the ignition's start button, and the powerful engine roared to life with a low-pitched *thrum*. "Kinda far away for a good happy snap, aren't they?"

"True," his team lead replied, "but when we get home, I'll include the photo and the warehouse's GPS coordinates in my report to the director. If he wants to, he can task Ankara Station to check it out. Sargon must be doing *something* here, but that's not our mission. Let's follow the beacon and cut the head off this snake."

Chapter 44

Six hundred miles later, Michael phoned Eden.

"What's up?" she asked.

"I'm going to have Alex drop me off in Erzincan up ahead. That's where I told Logistics to deliver our equipment. I need you to come up here and take the eye, but don't get too close to the SUV. Alex will end up about thirty minutes behind you, and I'll have to go slower since I'll be driving the van Logs delivered our combat gear in."

"That's fine," Eden replied, "but can you also watch the PC for reports from the beacon or do you want to hand it off to me?"

"I can handle it. I'll call you when they get off the highway for a pit stop. If it looks like they're getting off for good and moving through city streets or to wherever Sargon lives, I'll pull off the road and give you directions in real time."

"Sounds good," Eden said, and yawned. "I can't wait for this to be over."

***

The cross-country drive caused Behrouz Heidari's knees to protest most of the final three hours. At one of the gas stations they stopped at, he walked around the building a half-dozen times and purchased four packets of ibuprofen.

Late that evening when they arrived at Sargon's estate on the shore of Lake Van, Behrouz entered Sargon's throne room and greeted his sultan formally. Behrouz lifted the leather attaché case, and announced, "As you commanded, Your Majesty. I made the payments today, delivered the IDs and thumb drive to Zeki at the warehouse and brought you two-hundred-fifty-thousand euros in cash."

"Ah," Sargon's counselor, Rifaat, said, "this is a pleasant ending to a very long day. You got the cash here just in time, Behrouz. Excellent. We need to make payment this weekend for the binary explosives His Majesty's subjects in Iran are set to acquire from the Russians. The schedule is getting tight for them to make the transaction, smuggle the materials across the border and deliver everything to the Istanbul warehouse."

"Well done, as always, Behrouz," Sargon added, and rose from his gold-plated throne. "Rifaat is right—it *has* been a long day, but a good one for all of us. A *very* good day indeed. The payments you made in the capital have already borne fruit. The security IDs and event schematics Zeki needs to carry out my plans are the second-to-last piece we need for this puzzle. Now, as Rifaat said, we just need to pay for the explosives." Sargon covered his mouth and yawned, then clapped Behrouz on the shoulder. "These long days really take it out of you. Well, we are on the cusp of a monumental victory here in Turkey, and *you* are one of the most valued members of my inner circle. I couldn't do this without your intricate knowledge of the world of international finance. But I'm tired, now, so, let's continue this discussion tomorrow. Get some rest—you and I are going to have some more long days this week finishing the preparations and making final payments. But, for now, go ahead and lock the cash in my office safe, and let's call it a night."

"Yes, Your Majesty. I bid you a good night, then." He turned to Sargon's counselor. "And to you, too, Rifaat. Good night."

Behrouz walked through the side door and into Sargon's private office. Without looking to his right, he said, "Good evening, Mert. How are you tonight?"

Seated in his usual chair near the door to the hallway, Sargon's bodyguard gave a nasally snort. Never more than a few steps away from his sultan—even sleeping in adjacent bedrooms—the muscular man completely obscured the chair straining to hold his considerable weight.

Behrouz stepped in front of the smaller of the two safes in the room and dialed the combination. He emptied the euros from the attaché case and stacked them onto the safe's top shelf. After double-checking that the leather briefcase was empty, he secured the safe and laid the attaché on top.

Behrouz turned to the quiet giant and put his hands on his hips. "One of these days, Mert, I'm going to get you to say hello to me."

Mert grunted as he stood up. He took three steps toward Behrouz, looked down from his six-foot-ten-inch height, and asked, "What's that supposed to mean, Behrouz? I talk to your skinny ass all the time. After all, you married my sister."

Behrouz looked up at his brother-in-law and grinned. "Yes, but there you go again. You didn't even say hello. See what I mean? Who taught you manners?"

"The same woman who taught my sister to cook."

"Yes," Behrouz said, "and your sister's a wonderful chef."

Mert grunted again. "She's a *terrible* cook. That's why you're so scrawny." He pushed Behrouz's shoulder playfully and returned to his chair. "Tell her I said hi," he said, and smoothed his scraggly beard. "And just between us, if you wanted to marry a good cook, you should have come around more before my oldest sister got married. Now, *she* can cook!"

"I will tell her," Behrouz said. "That you said 'hello,' I mean. *Not* what you said about her cooking." He walked to the hallway door next to Mert's chair, patted the big man on the shoulder and bade him a good night.

Chapter 45

Six hours later, Michael parked his van next to Alex's car. He stepped into the cool late-evening air and stretched his sore back. "Oh, man...," he complained to the starry sky, and walked to where Alex and Eden were talking beside the trunk of her BMW.

"Long day," he said to his team. He twisted his torso in both directions and his back cracked.

"Terrorist or not," Eden said, "I'm ready to kill Sargon just for having forced me to drive halfway across the continent."

"And," Alex added, "don't forget that one of his guys shot you in the foot last month."

"Boot!" she emphasized. "It barely nicked the bottom of my heel. That *doesn't* count. I've been shot before, for real. I know the difference, believe you me."

"Well, good," Michael said. "I see that a few long weeks on this case haven't put anyone on edge or in a bad mood, have they?"

"I'm *fi-ine*, Michael," Eden replied. "And now for the topic at hand: did you drive by the walled compound?"

"Yes," he said. "The beacon's emanating from the northernmost of the two houses. So, we have a choice, and I'm willing to put it to a vote. Do you two feel up to making the assault tonight, or do you want to find an out-of-the-way hotel for the night and come back tomorrow evening?"

"That depends," Alex said. "Did Logs include energy drinks in the van with the combat gear?"

"Um-hum," Michael replied. "There are five left. I had to, you know, sample the goods about two hours ago to make sure it's safe for you both." He grinned and leaned against the trunk of Eden's car.

"Give me two," she said, "and you can count me in for tonight." She looked at the hands of her wristwatch which showed the time as just before midnight. "Let's get this over with. I just want to go home."

"You're my sniper tonight," Michael said, "so I can't have your hands shaking. You only get *one* drink."

"More for me," Alex said.

Michelle gently slapped the back of her hand against his chest and walked toward the van to get her equipment.

Chapter 46

Three hours later, through the plastic pigtail fitted snugly into her left ear, Eden heard her team lead's voice with digital clarity over the team's tactical radio.

"Alex and I are ready at the fence," Michael advised over the encrypted link. "Do you see the guards?"

Eden shifted, trying to get more comfortable. Her body armor bunched underneath her while she lay angled on the roof of a neighboring mansion's boathouse a quarter mile south of Sargon's fenced compound.

"Yes," she replied softly. She slowly slewed her rifle to the left, looked from Sargon's guest house to the main house, and reported, "Two of the three guards are still smoking at the boathouse. The third guy just left them and is now walking toward the gap between the two houses. He'll soon be out of my field of view."

She looked up from the night-vision scope atop her TrackingPoint rifle and squinted into the darkness. Without the digital light amplification, she would never have been able to see Sargon's guards in the moonless night. She glanced at her wristwatch and read the position of its phosphorescent hands. *3:02 a.m.*, she thought. *Right on schedule.*

"Moving," Alex advised over the radio.

A few seconds later, Eden watched through her rifle's scope as the former Navy SEAL levered himself over the stone wall surrounding Sargon's compound and sprinted toward the front of the guest house. She watched as he maneuvered in the near-total darkness past the front door and dropped to the ground next to the shrubbery adjacent to the house.

Alex propped himself up on his elbows and aimed his Heckler & Koch MP5SD 9mm submachine gun toward where he expected the wandering guard to appear. Instead of the more common barrel-and-suppressor combination, the MP5SDs that the three operators from CIA's Special Activities Center carried that night had a suppressor/barrel combination to reduce both the weight and length of the rifle. While some consider the MP5SD an outdated weapon, Alex preferred it for close quarters battle for its reliability, compactness and ruggedness.

With his face covered by night-vision goggles and tiger-stripe camouflage paint, Alex lay prone, nearly invisible against the side of Sargon's guest house. "Set," he whispered into his microphone.

Eden answered the question her partner didn't have to ask. "No change on the other two guards. You're still black," she said, confirming for Alex that his entrance onto the battlefield had gone unnoticed by the enemy. In her scope, she placed the red aiming dot over the head of one of the two guards in her field of vision and depressed the trigger of the thirty-thousand-dollar rifle halfway. She released the trigger and the red dot remained locked on its target. The electronics inside the space-age night-vision scope took over the process of tracking the target. It maintained the rifle's aimpoint centered perfectly on the guard's head, even as he moved about.

Later, once Eden pulled the trigger again, the scope would calculate the windage, elevation and even account for the rotation of the Earth to calculate the precise trajectory for the .338 Lapua Magnum bullet loaded in its chamber. With no other effort required by the shooter, the rifle automatically fires the round at the ideal instant with an inhuman accuracy of a half-inch at a thousand yards. The shooter's pulling the trigger of a TrackingPoint rifle is more a request than a definitive command to fire. The rifle's high-tech scope makes the final decision of exactly when to shoot. As long as it maintained a lock on her target, Eden couldn't miss.

It's almost like cheating, she thought. *Exactly how I like it. Unfair to the extreme.*

From his position outside the fence, their team lead could only listen to the progress of his pair of operators. "Okay, Alex," he said. "You're on."

With his right thumb, Alex Ramirez caressed the "safety/fire selector" lever of his silenced weapon, confirming it was set to three-round-burst mode.

Eden double-clicked her radio to acknowledge the meaning of Michael's message: Game on!

With only crickets in the distance making noise that night, Alex heard the guard's footsteps before he saw the man with the AK-47 rifle slung across his back.

The guard took a final drag on his Yenidje tobacco cigarette and let the smoke out slowly. He raised his hand and flicked the remains of his favorite Turkish tobacco toward the circular driveway in front of Sargon's house. The glowing butt fell short of the pea gravel driveway and the guard grunted softly. He walked to where his poorly aimed missile landed and ground it out with the toe of his boot.

On the back of the guard's neck, the green dot of Alex's infrared aimpoint danced slowly. Invisible to the naked eye, the dot from the laser mounted under the barrel of his H&K rifle shone brightly in his NVGs.

The guard finished extinguishing the remains of his smoke and took a step forward.

Alex squeezed the trigger, and three bullets spat out of his MP5SD nearly silently. Two rounds impacted the back of the guard's head. The third flew off into the distance. The guard's body dropped to the grass and rolled onto its side.

Alex low-crawled alongside Sargon's guest house and took up a firing position where he could see the two remaining guards, now resuming their patrols.

"Okay, Eden," Alex reported. "You're on."

Click-click, she responded.

From her elevated perch, Eden watched as the guards walked in opposite directions away from the boathouse. Now that they'd finished smoking and joking, one of the pair ambled lazily toward Sargon's house while the other patrolled along the shoreline.

She waited thirty seconds for the distance between the guards to increase. When the guard approaching the main house got within a dozen yards of the stone patio behind the mansion, Eden pulled the trigger. The TrackingPoint rifle sat motionless in her hands. Slowly, she shifted the crosshairs over the electronic scope's red dot tracking the guard's skull, and the rifle jerked back in her hands.

The suppressed round flew over five hundred yards and entered the guard's skull just above his right ear. He dropped to the grass behind Sargon's house, and his body rolled to a stop.

Eden shifted her rifle and acquired the other guard in seconds. She repeated the process and within twenty seconds had killed both guards. "Done," she reported to her teammates.

"Moving," Michael advised. "Alex, get to the front door of the guest house. I'll meet you there in a minute."

Eden removed her finger from the trigger and angled the rifle to her right. She watched her boss labor over the stone wall and drop into Sargon's compound. He stood up, adjusted his ballistic vest, secured his grip on his MP5SD and bent down to rub his left knee. *Not as spry as you used to be, boss, but you've still got it.*

Eden hurried to disassemble her rifle and return its parts to the padded carrying case. She stowed her equipment in her backpack and lowered herself from the roof of the boathouse. She ran to the wall surrounding Sargon's compound and tossed her equipment over. With a strong grip on the top of the wall, she flung her left boot onto it and rolled over the top. She dropped to the ground, swung her MP5SD around to her front and searched the green glow of her NVGs for any sign of a guard she might have missed. With no one in sight, she left her TrackingPoint rifle and backpack against the wall inside the compound and sprinted across the lawn toward the rear of the main house.

Twenty yards from the single-story mansion's rear door, she dropped to the ground and aimed her MP5SD at the house. As she protected her teammates' backsides from any additional guards, she tracked their progress of "cleaning house." Through her earpiece, she followed along as Michael and Alex coordinated their search of the guest house from room to room.

"Two tangos down," Michael reported.

Eden replied, "Backyard is clear. Come on out, guys. The weather's beautiful. We can play croquet and then take Sargon's speedboat for a spin around the lake."

She couldn't tell which of the two replied to her comment with the usual *click-click*, but she felt confident that Alex was grinning as Michael shook his head.

Eden shifted her position and repeatedly scanned from the rear of the guest house to Sargon's stone patio and back again. With a soft creak, the guest house's rear door swung open.

Alex exited first and turned to his right. Michael followed closely behind and swung to his left. Seeing no threats, they jogged to Eden's side and knelt in the grass.

"Any resistance inside?" she asked.

Alex shook his head while scanning the houses and shoreline for more guards.

Michael reported, "Just two people sleeping in their beds. One older woman and one teenage girl. We cleaned house." He looked from Eden to Alex and back again. "Are you both ready? It's time to run the ball into the end zone."

Eden scanned the backyard for threats. Not seeing any, she rose, kept her rifle leveled toward the main house and led the group to the rear door. Michael and Alex took up defensive positions while Eden silently picked the locks on the door's deadbolt and handle.

She twisted the handle and looked at her partner. Alex nodded as Eden took a step back and pulled the door's handle firmly.

As the door swung open, an ear-piercing electronic screech cut sharply through the still night.

Chapter 47

Eden threw the door wide open and stepped aside to let her boss and Alex storm inside.

The two CIA operators bolted forward and took up firing positions watching the mansion's long, central hallway.

Eden searched the rear door for the source of the high-pitched sound. A cheap plastic alarm — the kind travelers often place on hotel room doors — hung from the handle, blaring a shrill, warbling squeal. She aimed her rifle at the alarm, fingered the trigger and froze. Quickly, she thrust her hand forward and pressed the large circular button on the front of the device. It turned off mid-wail.

Her ears rang as they readjusted to the silence. She pulled the alarm from the door, exhaled audibly and rejoined her teammates.

Michael stood in the small room next to women's clothing hung to dry on a rack over the sink. He looked at the small device in Eden's hand. "Is that what I think it is?"

Eden held the alarm by its metal handle and let it dangle from her index finger. She shook her head in disgust. "Yup. Really pisses me off. We can defeat the ten-thousand-dollar alarms like no one's business, but we get caught short by the twenty-buck piece of shit anyone can buy online. Go figure."

"Well," Alex said, from a doorway across the hallway from Michael, "that ups the ante for tonight. At least it's not the kind of alarm connected to a central monitoring station, so Sargon won't have backup or the police coming." He looked down the central corridor, and added, "I *hope*. But now they know we're coming. So, okay, team. Tonight's drill is a room-by-room search followed by close quarters battle with an unknown number of terrorists." He grinned wryly at Eden across the hallway. "What could possibly go wrong?"

Michael gave his team orders via hand signals. Alex moved first, leading them past a large pantry and into the kitchen. They swept the room methodically, searching behind the central island and moving through the unoccupied space quickly.

From Michael's right, a soft *crunch* filtered through the still night air. He signaled with two fingers for Alex to maneuver toward the mansion's front door. Then he signaled for Eden to advance down the main hall and cover them as they investigated.

She crossed behind Michael, navigated her way down the hallway, which her night-vision goggles tinged green, and took up a firing position along a cross-hall leading to the front door. She watched as Michael and Alex advanced toward the entrance and disappeared from view.

She chewed her bottom lip as she knelt and remained silent. She pressed herself against the wall of the main corridor that ran most of the length of the large house and waited. The seconds passed slowly. At any moment, she expected to hear either the soft sounds of an MP5SD firing or the thudding of a body dropping to the hardwood floor.

The soft rustling from the corridor behind her caught her attention. She twisted, pivoting on her left knee, and scanned the long hallway. Nothing moved in her field of view. She glanced again toward the empty cross-hallway down which her teammates had disappeared less than a minute earlier.

Eden looked along the long main corridor just as the figure of a man darted across the hallway sixty feet in front of her. She peered into the green glow of the house and rose slowly. She treaded along the hallway in a textbook tactical advance, taking half-steps and never crossing her right foot in front of her left. Step by step, she advanced silently along the hallway.

Twenty feet in front of her, the man darted across her field of view again into another cross-hall. His robe fluttered in the air behind him as he disappeared around the corner. Out of her field of vision, the man's bare feet padded on the hallway's hardwood floor, echoing slightly in the still night.

Eden continued her advance at a deliberate pace, passing the closed door to Sargon's throne room on her left. At the cross hall, she stopped, peeked to her left into the room from which the robed man had emerged and saw the office was empty. Satisfied, she peered around the corner to her right and down the hallway.

The hallway opened into a living room across which four chairs and a pair of divans were arrayed. Facing away from her, the robed figure knelt behind a high-backed chair and looked toward the front door. Jutting from the man's hand, Eden saw the familiar outline of a large-frame semi-automatic pistol waiting for its chance to fire at her teammates.

Cautiously, Eden traced her rifle's green laser aimpoint across the room. She brought it up to the right ear of the robed man where it bobbed across the side of his head. She stabilized the rifle by holding it in a push-pull grip. With her left hand under the rifle's barrel, she pulled back on the weapon's frame anchoring the stock solidly into her right shoulder. Simultaneously, she pushed the rifle's handgrip forward with her right hand, and the dot of the aiming laser steadied on the man's ear.

With a practiced motion, she centered the pad of her index finger on the curved black plastic of the H&K MP5SD's trigger and tightened her grip. In less than a tenth of a second, the suppressed rifle spat three rounds into the side of Sargon's head. Green mist sprayed from the self-appointed monarch's skull, and he dropped to the floor against the chair on which he had been leaning.

Eden looked at the dead man and raised her hand to activate the microphone she wore across her throat to report the action to her teammates. *One tango down*, she thought.

A low growl rose from behind Eden, assaulting her ears a heartbeat before two muscular arms encircled her. The unseen assailant seized her around her midsection, yanking the CIA operator up and backward. Her attacker grunted in her ear and heaved, constricting her stomach like a band of iron. Her legs flailed in midair, finding nothing solid to stand on or kick. Her breath wheezed hoarsely from her lungs as the unrelenting grip tightened. Her mouth dangled open, drooling spittle down her bottom lip and off her chin.

She watched the world recede through her NVGs. The thick, hairy arms of the mountain of a man attacking from behind her pulled her roughly through a doorway. Eden kicked wildly, aiming her heels at whatever they might find. She hoped to connect with the knees of her attacker, but her thrashing legs found only the door in front of her. The heavy wooden door to Sargon's throne room slammed shut.

The enveloping arms squeezed harder, knocking her H&K rifle from her hands. The metal-and-plastic MP5SD landed softly on the throne room's carpeted floor and receded into the distance as the arms pulled her backward, further into the room.

The beast of a man holding Eden arched his back lifting her higher, then slammed her to the ground. She landed on the outside of her right leg and tumbled to the side. Her knee exploded in pain. She tried to scream away the explosion of agony, only to find her lungs empty. The impact with the ground sent her NVGs tumbling from her head. Its nylon strap scraped across her forehead adding a searing friction burn to the white-hot pounding in her knee.

Eden labored awkwardly to her hands and knees, struggling to inhale against the searing pain in her abdomen. In front of her, the dim light spilling in from beneath the closed door illuminated the outlines of two chairs against the far wall and an ornate floor rug. As she knelt on the carpet fighting to breathe, the steel crown of her wristwatch dug painfully into her left wrist. She succeeded in taking half a breath before Sargon's bodyguard grabbed her again.

Mert's beefy hands seized Eden, encircling her entire neck. His thumbs pressed painfully into the base of her skull while his fingers squeezed her throat. Eden shifted her bodyweight to launch a kick behind her, but her attacker pulled her off balance. She again tried to inhale, but choked in only a wisp of air.

Behind her, Mert uttered a low-pitched growl and shook her like a rag doll. He angrily spat out a phrase in Turkish she could not understand and squeezed her throat harder. Eden's eyeballs bulged painfully in their sockets.

His fingers dug into the sides of her windpipe like vice grips. Blood pounded in her ears as her heart struggled to force-feed life-sustaining oxygen to her brain. Eden launched her right elbow behind her, blindly lashing out at anything she could find. It landed dully on what felt like a mattress. She cocked her elbow and struck again. Her arm felt like rubber and her weakening blows had no effect on the colossal man choking the life out of her.

Across the room, the light leaching in from under the hallway door dimmed. Eden's vision narrowed, and she lost sight of the chairs near the door. She fixated on the light beneath the door as it faded. She watched it recede into the distance as if looking at it through binoculars held backward. She tried to cough, but no air could pass the hands around her throat.

Eden reached weakly for her neck and pulled at the first thing she could find. Her fingers slipped from the sweaty hands squeezing the remaining life from her and dropped away harmlessly. She wrapped the fingers of her left hand around the man's fingers and tried to peel them away from her neck one by one, but to no avail.

She slowly slapped her right hand at the hands around her neck, floundering to grasp anything she could use to pull the hands suffocating her away from around her throat. A stinging pain shot through her right ring finger as it caught the metal bezel of the watch on her left wrist.

Eden's motions slowed as she lost the strength to resist. The blood pounding in her ears had ebbed to a slow thumping as her body, starved for oxygen, lost the ability to fight off her attacker.

She flailed in vain at the hands clamped around her throat, again finding only her wristwatch—but nothing of the man she could grab and twist and use to free herself.

A voice from deep within her brain yelled at her in Michael's fading West Texas drawl: *Time to trust your training!*

Train...? She couldn't complete Michael's thought, until it completed itself. In her own voice, she heard it clearly: *The watch!*

Darkness washed over almost the entire throne room. The diminishing light seeping in under the door became an almost imperceptible flicker, illuminating only the edge of the carpet closest to the exit.

Eden lifted her right hand to her throat and traced it across the hands suffocating her until she found her own left hand. She settled her index finger and thumb over the crown of her wristwatch and twisted it counterclockwise. Her nearly numb fingers struggled inside her gloves to grasp the false crown. After two turns, she pulled it from the body of the watch. Attached to the end of the crown sat an inch-long pin. For over a decade, she had carried one version or another of the poisoned needle intended for a CIA officer facing imminent capture and torture but had never seriously considered using it before. *There's a first time for everything*, she thought. *And perhaps a last.*

Eden watched helplessly as the fleeting light from under the faraway door closed in on itself and faded to a pinpoint.

She felt for the beefy hand of the man strangling her. Her hand numb and brain starved of oxygen couldn't tell the difference between her attacker's hand and her own. With the last of her strength, she pushed the pin into the skin beneath her finger.

Her fading thought was of her true love. *I'm sorry, Steven. I'm so sorry!*

For an instant, the light under the door across the room flashed brightly. Then, the room faded to black.

Chapter 48

Michael looked up at the sound of a door slamming somewhere farther in Sargon's house. He signaled to Alex whose head spun as he hurriedly scanned for the source of the sound. The pair maneuvered through the dining room and past the two-story foyer in the house's main entrance.

Michael crossed the hallway and stopped short behind a sofa.

After Alex cleared his side of the room, he aimed his rifle to where his boss pointed.

The body sprawled on the floor—missing a quarter of its skull—meant only one thing to the CIA officers: Eden was here. The pistol lying next to Sargon's remains laid still—unfired, certainly, or everyone in the single-story house would have heard its sharp report.

She's here somewhere, Michael thought. *We'll come back to identify the remains and take DNA samples later.*

The former Army Green Beret motioned for Alex to follow him and led the former Navy SEAL past Sargon's body. They both searched the walls for the shadows of guards or any of the house's other occupants. Finding none, the men cleared the adjacent living room in seconds, maneuvered through it and turned again into the house's long, central hallway. Ten feet to their right, faint tapping came from behind a pair of closed double doors.

Michael gave hand signals to Alex: When we go through the door, you hook left. I'll go right.

Alex nodded and tested the doorknob. It was unlocked.

He looked at Michael who nodded he was ready. Alex twisted the knob, pushed the door open and spun inside to the left making a buttonhook entry. Alex traced his rifle across the room, from the wall next to him, across two empty chairs in the bedroom's sitting area and onto the solitary figure in the king-sized bed against the far wall.

Michael entered the room and stepped two paces to his right into the corner. He spun to face the bedroom and followed Alex's laser to where the green aimpoint danced on the bed against the far wall. He stepped forward cautiously, aiming his rifle at the sobbing woman half-covered with a blanket.

The woman shook uncontrollably. She hugged a large pillow—green in the CIA officers' NVGs—and sobbed quietly. Her shaking knocked the headboard behind her into the wall repeatedly as she quivered in fright.

Michael placed the aimpoint of his H&K over the pillow and pulled the trigger. Feathers flew from down stuffing as the woman shuddered twice and dropped forward onto the bed.

"Bathroom," Michael said. "Moving."

"Check," Alex replied.

Michael led the way to the *en suite* bathroom and peered through the open door. With Alex at his back, he stepped in and quickly cleared the empty shower. He gestured to Alex to move to the side of the vanity. Michael opened two doors in turn but found only toiletries and linens.

Frustrated, he hurried back to the bed and yanked the blanket onto the floor. The body of Sargon's late wife lay hugging her pillow. Blood-stained feathers danced in the air and slowly settled onto the satin sheets.

Michael keyed his throat-mounted microphone and radioed his team. "Eden, report," he ordered his protégé.

He paused for an answer. When none came, he repeated his radio call. Once again, the plastic pigtail in his ear remained silent.

Michael grabbed the pillow from the dead woman's arms and threw it across the room. He grunted in frustration. "Where the fuck's Eden?"

"We bypassed one hallway," Alex replied. "Let's head back and go door-to-door again. But watch out for more guards. If that old guy in the room next to the front door was Sargon, maybe he kept his guards outside, and we're in the clear. But let's not assume that. On me, boss."

"Check," Michael replied.

Alex led the two-man formation out of the master bedroom and back down the large house's main corridor.

Ten feet down the hallway they passed the detour they'd taken earlier. Just beyond that, the door to an empty bedroom sat wide open. The ruffled sheets atop the bed offered proof that its occupant had fled the room in a hurry.

Michael signaled to Alex: Someone else is in the house. Stay alert.

Alex nodded his understanding.

Farther down the hall, they came to a closed door on their right. Michael signaled that he'd open the door and Alex should buttonhook to the left again while he went right.

When they were set, Michael twisted the handle and pushed the door to Sargon's office open. Alex spun into the room, and Michael followed immediately behind.

In three seconds, they'd cleared the empty office. Michael glowered at the two safes on a sturdy shelf next to the ornate desk and kicked the large chair closest to the door.

He pointed to the interior door and motioned for Alex to open it. When they were set, Alex pulled the door open, and Michael surged inside.

On the floor, Michelle lay against the mountainous outline of Mert's unmoving form, himself leaning against Sargon's golden throne. Michelle's head tilted awkwardly to her right and her jaw hung open against her shoulder.

"No!" Michael screamed. "*Eden!*"

Chapter 49

Michael aimed at Mert's face and squeezed the trigger of his MP5SD. The suppressed rifle kicked three times in his hands. Blood splattered from the back of the bodyguard's skull across the silver roses adorning the late terrorist king's golden throne.

On the floor, Eden's body lay cradled in Mert's arms as the giant's corpse reclined against Sargon's throne. The gargantuan man's shattered head rested at an unnatural angle on the plush seat cushion onto which it oozed blood.

Michael rushed forward and knelt over Eden's unmoving form. He shook her shoulder vigorously. Eden's face—green-tinted in his NVGs—remained motionless.

"Lights!" Michael ordered to Alex, and removed his goggles.

"On it," the former sailor replied. Moments later, Alex flipped the wall switch and bright lights aimed at the throne illuminated the scene.

"*Eden....*" Michael murmured softly, and stroked the side of her face. "Oh... Eden."

Alex approached from behind and knelt next to his boss and teammate. "Was she shot?" he asked, and reached for the first-aid kit on his belt. "I don't see any blood."

Michael looked at him quizzically.

Alex laid his rifle to the side and ran his hands along Eden's black tactical uniform, feeling for the wet telltale sign of blood.

He jumped backward as a cough shot from Eden's mouth.

She convulsed and her chest heaved as she sucked for air and grabbed her throat.

"Eden!" Michael screamed, and clutched a hand over his heart.

She coughed again, clawed at her throat and rolled onto her side. As she caught sight of Mert, she scampered across the room backward until she hit the wall.

"Is he...?" she croaked, and coughed violently. She dropped her head into her hands and fought for breath through her severely bruised throat.

SCOTT SHINBERG

"Yes," Michael answered with relief echoing in his voice. "They're all dead. Did you kill the man in the living room, or whatever that was?"

Eden nodded, and tried to speak. "*Yehhh* ahh...." She kneaded her neck to fight the pain. "He...." A stinging in her throat stopped her, and she abandoned her attempts to speak. She pointed first to Mert and then to her throat.

"He choked you?" Michael asked. "Got it. Don't talk. Let's get you out of here." He stood up, looked at the dead bodyguard and then back at Eden. "So, if he was choking you," he asked, "why did he stop? I shot him, but...." He looked back and forth from Mert to Eden, and asked again, "How...?"

Eden tapped her wristwatch and pointed at Mert.

Michael's eyes grew wide, and he drew his lips back into a wide smile. "You *poisoned* him?"

Eden bobbed her head slightly in response. Gently, she pressed the sides of her throat as if trying to mold her trachea back into its proper shape. Softly, she corrected her boss. "*Venom.*"

Michael knelt next to Mert's large form and looked intently at the dead man. He searched up and down the bodyguard's beefy forearms and found what he was looking for. Gingerly, Michael pulled the pin from Mert's forearm and held it carefully between his thumb and index finger. He held his hand out to Eden. "Give me your watch."

Alex helped her remove it and handed it to their team lead.

Michael carefully reinserted the lethal dagger into the watch's case and screwed the false crown back in tightly. He looked at Eden and smiled. "*That*," he said, "was quick thinking, young lady. We can't leave evidence like this here, and DS&T will have to reapply the agent to the pin when we get home. I'm sure they'll want to hear from you first-hand about how you used it and how long it took to work."

He put the watch in his pocket and helped her to her feet.

"You should give it back to her," Alex said. "Maybe she'll want to wear it for good luck. And I'm sure it still tells time just fine."

"I already know what time it is," Michael said. "It's time to go home."

Chapter 50

The sunrise greeted Behrouz Heidari as he finished his morning *Fajr* prayers. The lanky man sped through the rest of his morning routine, knowing Sargon expected him right after breakfast. After a week of intercontinental travels, he took the time to wash his scraggly beard thoroughly and trimmed a few of its harder-to-tame ends so he'd be a more presentable sight to his king.

Heidari drove his aging Nissan twenty miles to Sargon's compound, arriving a few minutes earlier than anticipated. He used a remote control to open the gate and parked on the circular pea gravel driveway in front of the main house.

As he stepped out of the car, a sight across the driveway caught his eye. The body of one of Sargon's night guards—a man Behrouz had known since childhood—lay in the grass. The gaping head wound turned Heidari's stomach and told him all he needed to know about how the man died.

He hurried to the front door and gasped when he saw it ajar. He hesitated at the fear of what—or who—might be waiting inside, then pushed it open slowly. The polished wood door swung smoothly on its well-oiled hinges. He stepped inside tentatively and listened for any sound of an ongoing struggle. With no other vehicles in sight, he didn't expect he'd walked into the middle of an attack but wanted to make sure. Heidari's value to Sargon revolved around financial matters. Behrouz knew he would be of no use in a gunfight.

Hearing nothing, he advanced cautiously into the house. He stepped slowly across the foyer and peeked into the adjacent reception room. A bare foot stuck out from behind one of the sofas. Heidari shuffled forward, and his heart dropped when he saw the head wound on the corpse. He knelt next to the body and his heart fell. "*No!* Sargon... My king...."

Behrouz hung his head low and fought to stand. He looked around for other signs of intruders—or bodies—and walked into the main hallway. He first looked toward the kitchen and then toward the bedrooms at the other end of the house. In the distance, the double doors of Sargon's bedroom suite sat wide open. Heidari walked slowly to the threshold and looked across the room at the bloody figure of Sargon's wife laying alone in bed. Her lifeless eyes stared unmoving at him from across the void.

Behrouz backed out of the room and, out of respect, closed the French doors behind him. A dozen feet down the hall, he looked into Mert's bedroom. Seeing only the unkept bed, he dared to announce his presence, and called, "Mert?"

No response came.

Behrouz continued down the hall to the closed door of Sargon's private office. He knocked gently on the door. "Mert? It's Behrouz."

He waited a few seconds for an answer that never came, then pushed the door open. Through the inner door connecting to the throne room, Behrouz saw what he expected, but at the same time feared. Mert's body laid propped up against Sargon's throne. His hairy legs stuck out from beneath his nightshirt and the large man's head dangled at an angle.

"*Mert!*" Behrouz yelled at his brother-in-law. The bloodstains on the golden throne behind Mert revealed his fate clearly. "No...."

Behrouz rushed into the throne room and knelt by the large man's side. He gripped the bodyguard's hand and flinched at the cold flesh.

He dropped Mert's hand and stumbled backward toward the door. He collapsed into one of the two chairs against the wall and wiped his nose as it began to run.

His mind clouded over with memories of the years he and Mert spent together with their families. His heart swelled as he recalled the pride he felt participating in Sargon's coronation three years earlier in this very room, and then ached when he realized those days had come to a sudden and bloody end. Behrouz lost track of time as he sat and mourned.

Suddenly, to Mert's mortal remains at the other end of the room, he blurted out, "If they found *you*, they might find me too!" He spun his head to look around the room, shot to his feet and whirled around twice. He asked the walls, "What am I supposed to do now?" He looked at Mert and answered his own question. "Home. Yes, that's it. Home to my wife."

Behrouz reached for the door handle and stopped abruptly. He looked back at Mert. "No, I can't go home... I can't do that." He shook his head, and concluded, "Whoever they are, if they know about *you*, they'll know about your sister... I can't go home now. I can never go home again...."

He dropped his hand from the doorhandle and paced the room. After a few laps, he stopped short and stared into Sargon's office. Through the open door, he glimpsed the side of one of Sargon's safes in the adjacent room. Behrouz approached the safes hesitantly and glanced to his right. The chair Mert so often occupied next to the hallway door sat empty and forbidding. Heidari's eyes watered and he shook his head to clear them.

He opened the safe with the tan attaché still perched on top and stuffed bundles of euros into the case. He zipped the top of the black leather Coach bag closed, and thought to himself, *I know where I'll be safe. I know where I have to live now.*

Heidari returned to his Nissan and opened the rear door. He pulled the rear bench seat up and hid the attaché case inside the compartment built by Sargon's mechanics. He pushed the seat back into place, and it locked into place with a pleasing *click.*

He drove east for three hours, not daring to stop until he passed through Customs at the Iranian border just before lunchtime. The rest of the drive to Smugglers Respite took another three hours. His aging Nissan complained the entire way about being driven over horribly maintained roads.

He parked outside the small house he knew so well and knocked on the front door.

The widow's daughter opened it and cocked her head to the side. She smiled at the surprise visitor who had always treated her family well. "*Salam*, Mr. Heidari. I didn't know you were coming back so soon."

"My plans changed suddenly. Is your mother —"

"Behrouz!" cried a woman's voice from inside the small house. The widow hurried to the door and shooed her daughter away. She ran her fingers through the hair over her left ear and straightened wrinkles out of her dress. "I wasn't expecting you. Are you able to stay long this time?" She looked around outside the house. "Did you not bring a suitcase?"

Behrouz smiled at her and tapped the attaché case in his hand. "I have all that you and I will ever need right here."

The widow smiled up at her tall lover and pulled the door open.

***

Michelle Reagan wiggled her toes into the cushions at the end of her sofa in the condo she shared with her boyfriend. Gently, she sucked on an ice cube and let the cold water soothe the fading pain in her throat. The cell phone on the coffee table in front of the couch rang, and she peeked at the Caller ID.

She recognized the name immediately and tapped the green circle on her team's encrypted voice app to answer. "Hello, Michael," she said in a raspy voice. "How's it going?"

"I'm fine. Just wanted to see if a couple of days off have got you feeling any better."

"Thanks for checking up on me. I'm fine."

"You *always* say that," he replied, "even when you're not. What did the doctor say?"

"Said not to talk."

"He doesn't know you very well," her boss replied. "Does he?"

"No, *she* doesn't," Michelle said, and cleared her throat. "Obviously not. I almost punched her though."

"*Really*? The Company's doctor?"

"No. Once I got home, I went to my local doc to get a prescription for something stronger than Tylenol. She must have asked me two dozen times if Steven was the one who choked me. She wouldn't take 'no' for an answer. She even wanted to report him to the police for domestic violence. I finally talked her down off *that* ledge, but it hurt my throat. One more word out of her about Steven, and *she* would have the one needing painkillers. You know I'm mostly joking, but still... So, I've been sucking on ice cubes all week. That helps."

"Well, I'm glad to hear you're on the mend. I won't keep you long."

"Mmm," Michelle replied.

The front door to her condo opened and the alarm beeped three times. Dr. Steven Krauss walked into the living room carrying a grocery bag, and Michelle pointed to the cell phone in her hand. He nodded and walked to the kitchen.

"It turns out," Michael continued, "that the briefcase we bugged made its way back to the same smuggler's village in Iran where you liberated the cell phones and laptops that started all this."

"That's nice," Michelle said curtly. "Don't care."

Michael snickered. "No? Don't you want to go back into Iran and finish what you started?"

"Um," Michelle replied, "*Crackle, crackle.* Michael—*crackle*—I think we have a bad—*crackle*—connection here."

Laughter filtered through the phone, and Michelle smiled.

"No," her boss said, "don't worry. For us, this case is closed. Mission accomplished. I told Wilson Henry to send the intelligence we collected along the way to the analysts in Persia House and let them do what they want with it."

"Good," Michelle said. "Sargon must have been up to something at that warehouse outside Istanbul. The analysts can have everything we found, as far as I'm concerned. As for me, Steven just got home from the grocery store, so now I'm going to send him out to buy me wonton soup for dinner from the Chinese restaurant across the street."

"Good," Michael said, "you do that. And take another two weeks off to recuperate. You've earned it. Once you're healthy and back to work, there's something that's been brewing in Jordan, but it's been on-again, off-again for months. It can wait until you're fully recovered." He wished her a speedy recovery and hung up.

Steven Krauss came into the living room, and Michelle recoiled her legs to make room for him next to her on the sofa. Once he sat down, she stretched her legs out across his lap and reached for another ice cube.

Steve stroked her shin. "How're you doing?"

"Ehh," she said.

"I bought you some more popsicles and put them in the freezer. Both cherry and lemon-lime, just like you asked."

"*Mmmmm,*" she replied, and stroked his arm. "You're so good to me."

After dinner, they watched two reruns on TV, and Michelle took one of the painkillers the doctor had prescribed.

In their bedroom later, she pulled back their blue bedspread and got under the covers. She laid her hand on Steven's chest and closed her eyes, feeling peaceful and safe. Within minutes, her breathing evened out as she floated off to sleep.

Steven gave her shoulder a light squeeze. He leaned his head down a few inches, kissed the hair on the top of her head and smiled.

ABOUT THE AUTHOR

Scott Shinberg has served in leadership positions across the US Government and industry for over twenty-five years. He has worked in and with the US Air Force, the Department of Homeland Security, the Federal Bureau of Investigation, and most "Three-Letter Agencies." While in government service, he served as an Air Force Intelligence Operations Officer and a Special Agent with the FBI. He lives in Virginia with his wife and sons.

Website: www.ScottShinberg.com
Facebook: @ScottShinbergAuthor
Twitter: @Author_Scott

WHAT'S NEXT?

Don't miss the next thrilling installment of this series, which is perfect for fans of Tom Clancy, Robert Ludlum, Dean Koontz, Brad Meltzer, and Len Deighton.

A SHOT IN THE DARK
Michelle Reagan – Book 5
(Releases Spring or Summer of 2022)

To remain up to date for plans and schedules related to this book, and to all works by Scott Shinberg, please subscribe to his newsletter at:
www.ScottShinberg.com

MORE FROM SCOTT SHINBERG

Is *Confessions of Eden* drawn from today's headlines, or are the headlines drawn from what little is visible of Eden's footprints?

CONFESSIONS OF EDEN
Michelle Reagan – Book 1

Michelle Reagan—code name Eden—is the CIA Special Activities Division's newest covert action operator, an assassin, who struggles between wanting to succeed in her new profession for herself and her charismatic boss, and the moral quandaries of what she must do to innocent people who are simply in the wrong place at the wrong time. Although she faces seemingly intractable decisions as she executes her missions across the globe, the adversary most difficult to overcome may very well be her own conscience.

Through it all, only one man has ever called her an 'assassin' to her face. Someday, if she has her way, she'll marry him—if she lives that long.

WINNER: Pinnacle Book Achievement Award - Best Spy Thriller
WINNER: Literary Titan Book Awards - Gold Medal

"This novel is purpose-driven; it is written for those who enjoy action, but the strength of the characters is one of the irresistible elements of this well-crafted thriller. ... Fast-paced and filled with action, it is one of those books you feel compelled to read nonstop."
~ Christian Sia, Readers' Favorite Book Reviews (5 STARS)

"For fans of crime and espionage, *Confessions of Eden* comes across as a tour de force in entertainment."
~ Romuald Dzemo, Readers' Favorite Book Reviews (5 STARS)

MORE FROM EVOLVED PUBLISHING

We offer great books across multiple genres, featuring high-quality editing (which we believe is second-to-none) and fantastic covers.

As a hybrid small press, your support as loyal readers is so important to us, and we have strived, with tireless dedication and sheer determination, to deliver on the promise of our motto:
QUALITY IS PRIORITY #1!

Please check out all of our great books,
which you can find at this link:
www.EvolvedPub.com/Catalog/

Thank you!

9 781622 536634